THE PRINCE OF VAL-FEYRIDGE

by

Helen C. Johannes

The Prince of Val-Feyridge

COPYRIGHT © 2009 by Helen C. Johannes

Cover Art by *Rae Monet*

The Wild Rose Press
PO Box 708
Adams Basin, NY 14410-0706
Visit us at www.thewildrosepress.com

Publishing History
First Faery Rose Edition, 2010
Print ISBN 1-60154-676-9

Published in the United States of America

Aerid could not recall how she came to be in the Great Hall, or how water and bandages materialized on trestle tables there. Naed sat slumped against the wall while Yormoc tugged off his tunic and armor. Blood painted Naed's arm, but she could see the wound was only a finger in length.

"Get me up, fool, or 'tis your hide I'll line my chair with!" Her master Dranoel sat up, took in the guards at the door, and his ashen face paled further.

Yormoc examined the cloth he had been holding to his gashed jaw. "They haven't killed us yet. 'Tis like they don't mean to."

Dranoel visibly fought for control. "Mayhap the bastard Prince has some honor, then."

"Some honor!" Aerid sputtered. Did no one but she understand what they faced? "Belike they'll be keeping us for their sport, killing us one by one to feed their savage appetites. These be Tolemaks we speak of, and what be they if not barbarians and their master a Prince of savages!"

Dranoel blanched at her words. Yormoc froze. Even Naed's head came up. But not a man of them stared at her.

Cold dread filled Aerid. She whirled.

In the doorway stood a scarlet-cloaked figure so tall his ebony hair brushed the cross-beam, so lean Aerid sensed nothing but bone and muscle and will, a will so strong it emanated from the deep-set, stone-gray eyes. High cheekbones gave his face a noble, arrogant look. The curve of his lips mocked her. The scar cutting across the left side of his face from behind the eyebrow to the corner of the chin mocked nothing.

"Pray, go on." The Prince of Val-Feyridge planted his boot on a bench and rested a hand on the upraised knee. "Or have you lost your nerve?"

Awards for
THE PRINCE OF VAL-FEYRIDGE

Winner
> ~Colorado Romance Writers' Heart of the
>   Rockies Contest, FFPT (Fantasy, Futuristic,
>   Paranormal, and Time Travel) category
> ~Gold Coast Chapter's First Impressions
>   Contest
> ~Lowcountry Romance Writers' Jasmine
> Contest

Finals
> ~Wisconsin Romance Writers' Fab Five Contest
> ~Outreach International Romance Writers'
>   Award of Excellence Contest
> ~RWA New England Chapter's First Kiss
>   Contest
> ~The Silicon Valley's Gotcha Contest
> ~The Red River RWA's Ticket to Write Contest

Dedication

To my critique partners, Julia and Melanie,
who read this book when it began
and encouraged me to continue to work on it;
and to my husband,
who has believed in me from the start.

List of Places and Characters

D'nalee
D'nalee: the middle land, a low and marshy place
Lord Dranoel: master of Druemarwin
Naed: Free Swordsman and Dranoel's nephew
Aerid: young healer of Adanak birth
Dlaniger: Dranoel's absent son
Yormoc: Free Swordsman
Elthred and Gert: kitchen maids
Ekwul: Dranoel's personal servant
Wullauf: steward
Old Gam: healer who trained Aerid

Places in D'nalee
Druemarwin: fortress in southern D'nalee
Tumin: Naed's home in the north
Kassi: fortress near Druemarwin
Myrinnen Marsh: near Druemarwin
Ort: town in northern D'nalee

Tolemak
Tolemak: the western land, rugged and mountainous
Prince Arn: current Prince of Val-Feyridge
Erodasi of Roines: Prince Arn's betrothed
Yinnad: deceased former prince

Members of Prince Arn's army
Krenin: Arn's Second
Gorm: Master of Horse
Borth: Master of Wagons
Illien: Master of Archers
Nemmon: Master of Footmen
Yarl: First Horseman
Banir: tracker from Albon
Grodar and Morys: soldiers from Albon
Lord Tylus: in charge of defending Val-Feyridge

Raell: Tylus's daughter

Lord Rolnar of Roines: leader of eastern Tolemak lords opposing Prince Arn

Lords allied with Rolnar of Roines

Edad of Koth

Lede

Belac

Vad of Vral

Ladnar of Ormo

Nor

Places in Tolemak

Val-Feyridge: fortress of a long line of Tolemak princes, west of the Arbez River

Albon: rustic fortress belonging to Arn's late father

Adanak

Adanak: the eastern land, fertile and rolling with mountains in the north

Gaelwynn: Master of the Guard

Leumas and Avika: soldiers of the Western Sector

Foderor: master of the Golden Horse Inn

Mairim: Foderor's young wife

Sevig: a Lancer

Estra: a palace maid

Sima: head of the city masters

Places in Adanak

Herset: market town near the western border

Eidvondin: grain trading town

Otlesend: grain trading town

Alaris: north of Vinvinnysee

Vinvinnysee: walled city in central Adanak, center of commerce, defended by Lancers

Panting, Aerid yanked her cloak from yet another blackberry briar. Her fingertips still glowed green, and she paused for a precious moment to rub at the evenroot stain. If only she had worn gloves while pulling the tubers, she could have stripped off the gloves and hidden their glow in her pouch when she heard those men. But the evening seemed so mild, and it had been so long since she had encountered anyone in the forest after sunset, much less the rampaging Tolemak horde the local ale-drinkers daily predicted would descend upon the land of D'nalee from the west.

Aerid spat on her nails and scrubbed again. Whatever those in their cups thought, she should have been better prepared to conceal herself. Outside the walls of Druemarwin fortress, not every D'nalian looked kindly on those of Adanak blood, not even those Adanaks who had lived among them for years. Touching the birthstone fastened at her throat, she thanked the Three Sisters again for showing her the sow-bear's den under the oak.

Her fingertips still showed faintly green. Gulping a breath, Aerid hid her hands under her cloak and listened for sounds of pursuit. Nothing came to her but the chirp of crickets and the blood thrumming in her ears.

She set off again, telling herself if those men were not close upon her heels now, they would be hard put to find her. Only old Gam knew Myrinnen Marsh better than she. Years of gathering evenroot in the hour of deepest twilight, when Gam said it was most potent, of filling her healer's pouch with foxtail and moonlily, alderrose and sweetwort, had made the pathways of the forest as familiar to Aerid as the halls of Druemarwin.

Perhaps the two men in the clearing had not seen her after all. Had they not withdrawn without a word into the far trees? Yet before going, the rider had circled the oak twice, slowly, as though suspecting she huddled under the tangle of roots. She had glimpsed his cloaked silhouette against the cloud-patched sky, and the vision imprinted itself on her mind. Like Death itself, he seemed—faceless, silent, and dark as moon shadow—the sweep of his unseen, probing gaze making her skin crawl. And tall too, impossibly tall, taller than any man who dwelt within the walls and lands of the fortress Druemarwin. As prentice to old Gam—indeed, as healer in the old woman's stead these last two winters—Aerid had encountered them all.

The other man wore the livery of Druemarwin, a yellow cloth visible even in the dark, especially when he had nearly fallen into her hiding place. Several of his build were among the servants, but neither the cook's prentice, the smith's son, nor the steward's new assistant would likely have the master's leave to be outside the walls at this hour. And if he did not...

Aerid quickened her pace, following a deer trail that intersected the main road. The sooner she crossed Druemarwin's bridge, the sooner her heart would cease ramming her throat. And the sooner she could tell the master what she had seen.

****

Arn, Prince of Val-Feyridge, handed his stallion's reins to one of the soldiers pressing about him. Firelight sharpened their features, giving their expectant faces a ghoulish look. He strode past them, seeing in the trees the flicker of hundreds more campfires, knowing his men stirred around each as word of his return spread.

Arn fought his own rising excitement. Weeks of travel, months of preparation, years of planning, a lifetime of dreams—nothing could be certain until all was in place, every last detail. Already he had mobilized a third of Tolemak. Another third paid him lip service, remaining carefully neutral between Val-Feyridge, seat of an unbroken line of Tolemak Princes, and Roines, seat of the ambitious Lord Rolnar. Arn frowned. So much depended on keeping Rolnar and his cohorts completely unaware.

And so little depended on visions, however certain Arn was he had seen someone—or some thing—glowing

2

green and kneeling as if in worship at the roots of that enormous oak. The glimpse of a face bearing the other-worldly look of the Tree Folk—high cheekbones, pointed chin, and slanted cat's eyes—and a body as slim and supple as a young willow had imprinted itself on Arn's mind. Those cat's eyes had looked at him, and her gaze, even at that distance, mesmerized. He had felt himself drawn toward the edge of the thicket, tempted to step out of its protective blackness, to show himself...

He scowled. Tree Folk were legends, nothing more than fireside tales. Indeed, he barely believed in the Three Sisters themselves. His friend Krenin would have spat between his fingers and offered the Sisters a hair of his head, but Arn placed no trust in charms. From childhood, he had been gifted with a single-minded focus his allies envied and his enemies dreaded. That this...illusion plagued him only signified his concern that nothing, however unusual, upset his plans. He would personally see nothing did.

The officers had already assembled outside the command tent. At the center stood his Second, the broad-shouldered Krenin, fists on hips, a hint of gray flecking the temples of his flowing brown hair. Eight years Arn's senior and his one-time mentor, only Krenin dared voice every man's question: "Well? Do we move tomorrow as planned?"

Arn tugged off his gloves and tucked them into his belt. "Is the army in place?"

Krenin grinned, a flash of teeth in the firelight. "Piece by piece, the whole army's crossed the Arbez River under the very noses of Rolnar and his lackeys and, 'tis sure, they've not smelled a thing!"

Arn allowed himself a small, tight smile. "Well, then, 'tis time we declared ourselves."

As one, the men fell back, forming a ring about Arn and the fire, the action signaling other camps to form similar circles. Arn's blood sang as he surveyed the faces, turned gold and orange, in the flickering light. From earliest childhood, held aloft in his grandfather's arms, he had yearned to be one with these warriors, to participate in their ceremony. He had come to the Sacred Circle earlier than most, a mere 12-year-old with the smoke-

and-blood smell of his family's massacre fresh in his nostrils, the stain of his first man-kill soaked into his boots. Rolnar's Roinesmen had destroyed his home and thought they had drowned him, but the gangly orphan with a scavenged sword and cast-off shield had fought his way into the Sacred Circle. Now, as he had so many times in recent years, Arn stood at its center. Yet his heart still thumped as hard in his chest as it had the first time he beheld the men of Tolemak thus assembled.

Dipping his right forefinger in one of the clay pots Krenin held, Arn drew a streak of Tolemak blue across each cheekbone and down his nose. With the fingertips of his left hand, he touched the Val-Feyridge red in the second pot and laid three dots over his left brow and temple.

Krenin withdrew with the paint, and the men pressed closer, silent, expectant.

Arn unsheathed his dagger and turned a slow, full circle, showing the naked blade to every man. Halting, he gathered his shoulder-length hair at the nape of his neck and, holding the thick, black mass taut away from his head, sliced off the excess.

A roar erupted from the men.

Arn stilled their cry with outstretched arms. He turned full circle and, with hair and dagger suspended high over the fire, proclaimed the ancient Tolemak words of war:

"By Fire and by Wind,
the Sons of Rock and Earth make pledge,
by this, the very hairs of our heads,
that as we fight so may we die,
Heroes and worthy of the name of Tolemak!"

Opening his fingers, he let his shorn hair fall into the flames.

Another roar erupted. Men surged forward, daggers in hand, tossing handfuls of hair of every shade into the flames, where each strand turned instantly gold and vanished.

Arn's nostrils tingled with the familiar scents of singed hair and paint while his blood hummed with their meaning. What a man might offer the Three Sisters was a bargain made of superstition, vanity, even fear. This ancient ceremony took men and made them into an army.

And this army was destined to reunite a kingdom. By summer's end, the Crown of Tolem, stolen by Prince Adan so long ago all but the wise had lost count of the years, would finally rest where it should—on the head of the last king's lineal heir. Arn drew his fingers into a fist. Bastard or no, the blood was his, and not even Rolnar of Roines dared dispute that.

****

Aerid slipped through a honeybush and ran headlong onto the rutted track that passed for a main road in southern D'nalee. Her momentum carried her directly into the path of three riders.

The lead horse shied. Aerid flung up her arms while curses, shouts and milling hooves assailed her. With a gasp, she spun and bolted for the hedge.

Laughter and a booming, "What, girl? Are you yet about your collecting?" stopped her as her master, Lord Dranoel, rode alongside. "By the Sisters, the Tree Folk will steal you away if you persist in tempting them. Look, girl, how you startled poor Yormoc straight off his horse." He indicated a man slapping dust from his tunic and leggings. Aerid could not see his face, but she sensed the flash of Yormoc's look. He snatched his mount's reins from the third man, who smothered a chuckle.

Beside her, the Master of Druemarwin heaved off his helm and shook out hair so threaded with silver, even darkness could not conceal the streaks. "Well, 'tis time to cease, for I am home now and hungry. Ekwul the lazy is doubtless asleep with my wine. We shall roust him, and he shall fill my cup till the flask is dry, for I have need of it tonight." He tossed the helm to Yormoc, who caught it with a grunt. "Naed," he told the third man, "take her upon your horse."

Aerid started. Only lords, swordsmen, and important folk rode. "Good master, I can—"

"Silence!" A solidly built man, Dranoel's thick neck spread into broad, bull-like shoulders. "Ride when you may, girl, and cross me not tonight. Later, perhaps, you may ply me with one of your brews, but for now I desire peace. Peace from prating tongues, liars, and bumbling fools!" Signaling Yormoc to follow, he heeled his horse and

5

galloped toward Druemarwin's stone hulk.

Aerid watched his form grow small against the torch-lit gate. In the years since Dranoel had taken an abandoned girl-child of foreign blood into his household and placed her in the care of the healer Gam and the servant Ekwul, Aerid had learned much about her master's moods, when to speak and when to hold her tongue. Tonight, she could not tell him what she had seen.

"Aerid?" Lean yet sturdily built, his tanned face lightly freckled and eyes a green-brown D'nalians called hazel, Naed smiled down at her. The young swordsman had removed his helm, and his hair, which the sun turned more red than brown, hung in loose strands about his face despite the proper D'nalian queue meant to confine it. "Will you ride?"

Aerid flushed. She had entirely forgotten his presence. Avoiding Naed's gaze, lest he realize she had slighted him, she focused on the cleft in his chin and nodded.

With one easy motion, he gripped her waist and lifted her into the saddle, setting her sideways upon it. Once or twice, Aerid had ridden the ass Gam kept now the old woman no longer walked her rounds, but this war steed of Naed's towered above the road. She dug her fingers into thick shearling covering a high-pommeled and high-backed saddle frame.

Gathering the reins, Naed swung up behind the saddleback, leaving the space between their bodies D'nalian propriety demanded. Those rules, Aerid knew, did not apply to foreigners, but the young Free Sword who had ridden south from Tumin the previous spring extended his courtesies to everyone.

"The hour is late." Naed nudged his mount into a walk.

"I did mistake the time."

"As did Lord Kassi." He spoke so dryly, she turned. "He begs more time to deliver the promised grain. Mud, he protests, has delayed his wagons. The master bore the news poorly."

Hardly a surprise, Aerid thought. Until Druemarwin's winter-depleted provisions were restocked, the fortress was vulnerable. While the sporadic war between her Adanak countrymen and their pale-skinned Tolemak enemies rarely ranged far from the disputed borderlands north of D'nalee, no one rested easy during periods of apparent quiet. Every day "peace" reigned was but one day closer to the next blood-letting.

Thrice in her memory, the blood feud between her people on the east and the Tolemak on the west had erupted. Each time, fighting overran D'nalee, sending refugees pouring south as far as Druemarwin. The first time, Aerid's kin had been among them, though she could scarce remember them. Instead, her memory locked on thick, choking smoke, panicked shouts, a headlong rush through a burning town and a forest full of frantic souls. Even now, at the mere thought, the smell of blood reeked in her nostrils, and her stomach turned in on itself. Did her master's angry words mean yet another war brewed? The men in the wood, did they...?

The horse skirted the cluster of stone and thatch huts bordering Druemarwin's moat and approached the drawbridge. Aerid glanced at the man behind her who, the local ale-drinkers said, had come like a boon from the Sisters. True, Naed had arrived in good time, scant weeks after Dlaniger renounced his father and rode away, and the skills Naed brought were adequate replacement, especially when Dlaniger had spent more time away from Druemarwin than guarding it. And, truth be told, Naed treated her with far more respect than Dlaniger ever had.

"Seek me ere you go to bed," she said. "I would be speaking with you."

****

Naed leaned against a stone pillar at the foot of the Great Hall steps and yawned. Rabbit stew had warmed his night-chilled body, making him long for his bed, but he would wait a little longer because Aerid was coming.

If he closed his eyes and breathed deeply, he could even now discern the fragrance identifying her in his mind, the scent of tiny purple bellflowers he once watched her gather in the glade by the brook. It was not often he found himself in such close proximity to Aerid as he had this eve. By the Sisters, when she turned in the saddle, her shoulder had almost brushed his chest. Through plate, mail and tunic, he fancied he had sensed her warmth.

If only he had not made a fool of himself with Yormoc afterward. Naed pressed fingers over his eyes, trying to blot out the memory, but it only played with greater clarity...

The older Free Sword had greeted him in the stable yard with a leer and a wink. "You took your sweet time in following. Did you lay your hand to some hot brown flesh, or did the wench refuse you? 'Twere me, I'd be yet in the wood, and it wouldn't be my horse she'd be astride."

Usually, Naed endured in silence, hoping Yormoc would tire of the game, but the man seized every opportunity to enlarge upon his favorite theme.

"You waste your courtesies on one of her blood. A foundling and a bastard, and Adanak besides! Take her in the hay and teach the wench her place. 'Tis time someone put her on her—"

Naed could not remember acting. He only knew his fists somehow twisted themselves into Yormoc's tunic, and the startled man flailed for balance. Yormoc's breathless, "I-I meant no offense," should have settled the matter, but the fool had to continue. "Though you live among the guard, 'tis common knowledge you are the master's nephew and—"

"Not by blood!" Naed had not meant to speak of his mother as sister to Dranoel's late wife. Nor had he meant to manhandle his fellow Free Sword, but he had done both and in front of stable-boys. Within minutes everyone below stairs would know of the altercation. He only hoped they had not heard the topic. If Aerid should discover—

He had flung Yormoc away and warned, "Speak of this to no one!"

But Yormoc, like a Tumin rat-hound on the scent, only spread his hands. "Blood or bond, as nephew you may take what you fancy. Why should that baggage be excluded just because the master is blind to her bloodline?"

Even now, at the memory, Naed made fists. In truth, he understood how Yormoc, with his years of blade-bearing and loyalty to the errant Dlaniger, might resent losing command to a youth like himself, and an outsider, too. But what right had the man to consider Aerid as something less than—than the kitchen maids? Had he not left Yormoc with Elthred on his lap and Gert draped over his shoulder? No doubt Yormoc and Elthred—and perhaps Gert, too—had by now moved to the hayloft.

Naed shook off a shudder. Elthred had more than once laid hands on him in the kitchen, but he had thrust her away. Her garlic breath and dog-in-heat scent gagged him. It was all he could do to keep his disgust to himself as she—and Gert, too—pawed his companions under the table. Yet Yormoc would have him consider Aerid less than these two merely because of her coppery skin and prominent cheekbones.

Naed snorted. Less than them, never! She was too gentle, too kind, too innocent...

Footsteps echoing off rough-hewn stone walls brought him out of his reverie. Recognizing the light tread, he smiled and stepped out of the shadows.

Aerid jerked to a halt, her indrawn breath a hiss. Even in the flickering torchlight, her face within its frame of thick, dark hair showed paler than he had ever seen it.

Naed's smile faltered. "You start like a mouse out of her hole. What's to fear?"

"Men." Seizing his sleeve, she steered him toward a recessed doorway. "Two men—"

"Men! Aerid, tell me, has any man dared—!"

She smiled, and her eyes gleamed like liquid in the shadows. "Be assured, no man has done me any ill deed."

Naed flushed to the roots of his hair. By the Sisters and their Four Winds, he should have better restraint than to make a fool of himself twice in one night. "I, uh, men, you say?"

"Two. I did think them poachers at first, but..."

The tale she poured out sent a renewed rush through his veins. Tumin had been besieged twice in his youth, and he had lost kin to both Adanak and Tolemak invaders. The last conflict, he had paced the watch, having not yet earned his sword. This time, however...

Aerid must have seen his expression alter, for she gripped his arm. "Naed, no! Do not be thinking of war."

He gazed down at her, noting how her eyes glimmered, as frank and blue as the summer sky. "Why, Aerid, 'tis but how I earn my keep. And, truly, I am paid

9

more in war." The logic of this seemed inescapable, but her eyes grew wider, as if with shock. He shifted his stance. "'Tis not that I wish for war, but should it come to pass—"

"You will do as all men do," she said, turning away. "Kill to make the peace."

Her reproach stung, but no more than his mother's along the selfsame line. He wished women could understand why a man took up arms, but perhaps it was better if they did not. After all, women had not the strength to cope with the demands honor, duty, and loyalty made upon men. And because women did not, it was a man's duty to allay their fears.

"I shall discover which man of Druemarwin has been in the wood this eve, and if there is aught to fear, I shall tell the master. Let his wrath be upon me if he dislikes the intrusion."

Aerid's smile spread like the coming of the sun.

Naed's whole body warmed. When he regained his logic and Aerid was gone, his mind formed two thoughts. First, why had he not kissed her? They were alone, and it would have taken a mere step and a stoop of his head, but he foolishly had stood like a stag dazzled by hunters' torches. The second thought depressed him further; 'twas no likelihood he would soon prove his mettle in war, for Myrinnen Marsh could swallow an invading army whole, and a southern traverse of D'nalee would add weeks, even a month, to a march into Adanak. Only a fool or a madman would choose such a route.

****

Aerid rose as usual in the predawn gray and, unlike most of the D'nalians she lived among, splashed water on her face and washed with a bit of tallow soap. Over her shift, she pulled on a loose fitting blouse and homespun skirt. She had barely laced the leather vest gathering her blouse from bodice to waist when three blasts of a horn ripped the air. She froze, remembering what the sound signified. Grabbing her pouch, she forced shaking legs to carry her to the outer wall.

CHAPTER TWO

Aerid emerged from the tower stairs into a glare of sunrise. Nearby, Dranoel growled, "Leave that be, fool!" and shook off his manservant's attempt to fasten his chest armor. Sallow-faced in the golden light, he stepped to Naed's side at the wall and stared over it. Keeping her back to the tower wall, lest she interfere with the men lining the parapet, Aerid followed their line of sight.

Druemarwin and its clutch of stone huts sat in a clearing. Or it had yester eve. Now the green bristled with hundreds of armed men, archers dressed in so dusky a brown they melded with the long morning shadows, horsemen bearing shields so polished each seared the eye like a flare of torchlight, and every man's face ghoulishly painted.

"Tolemak," Naed said, his brows a dark slash. "And with shorn hair."

Hunching beside an archer's slot, Yormoc peered through the narrow opening. "The banner, 'tis of Val-Feyridge."

"The bastard Prince, here?" Dranoel sputtered. "Why?"

"He is Tolemak. Is that not reason enough for him to make war?" As he spoke, Naed's gaze locked on Aerid. She stared into hazel eyes so fierce she could have sworn they were not his except they looked out above familiar cheekbones. "But he would not be here had not the steward taken in a spy. Yester eve, Aerid saw Wullauf's new man meet a stranger in the wood, and no one has seen the new man since."

Dranoel opened his mouth, but movement below seized everyone's attention.

A rider detached from the mass. He carried upright a spear fitted with a white cloth, and his ebony steed pranced under tight rein. A cloak fell in blood-red folds over the horse's haunches and skimmed saddle and boots

11

polished to a sheen only the finest leather could achieve. A hammered shield of remarkable workmanship hung from his saddle horn, but the splendid helm that should have matched it was nowhere Aerid could see. Instead, he hid his face within the folds of his hood. Something about his silhouette, however...

Aerid's limbs trembled and she clung to the parapet rail. It was he, the bastard Prince himself, he who had shed enough Adanak blood to fill cauldrons, pits, ponds! And yester eve she had come within body's length of touching the pale-skinned demon! *Sisters!* She wrapped fingers around the birthstone at her throat; how had she chanced to escape?

"Stop there and speak!" Dranoel bellowed at the figure below. "What do you seek here?"

The rider drew rein near the moat's edge, and the hooded head tilted up a fraction. "Why, that should be obvious, my lord. I require your fortress."

Dranoel's eyes bulged in his broad face. "You—you impudent, impertinent pretender to a title! If you would have Druemarwin, you must fight for it!"

"I should be sorely disappointed if that were not so, my lord. As you see, I came prepared." With the spear he gestured to the army filling the clearing. "But hear me awhile, Dranoel." The Prince flicked the scarlet cloak from his left shoulder, the casual gesture revealing a polished chainlink belt from which hung a broadsword housed in a dark leather scabbard.

"Your provisions are scant—three weeks of food, perhaps—while I can afford to be patient. My army may sit here feeding off your land—and Lord Kassi's wagons— quite contentedly, and at no risk to ourselves, until you weaken. Then, 'tis sure, either you will surrender or these painted warriors will satisfy their blood lust." He dipped the spear.

A roar erupted from the assembled host, a wild frenzied howl that hit Aerid full in the throat, squeezing off her breath. Around her, men on the battlements paled. Naed's shoulders stiffened and his lips compressed to a white line. The servant Ekwul, holding his master's helm, closed his eyes. Dranoel swayed as though the cry gusted against him while his fingers clung like claws to the masonry.

The Prince raised the spear, and the sound ceased, silence almost as deafening as the cry—and more chilling. Aerid knew little of battle and leadership, but she understood the Prince's will alone controlled the fate of everyone within Druemarwin's walls. Raw savagery could be unleashed with a gesture, and just as easily contained.

An archer, too young to sprout a beard, turned from the wall and vomited. An older archer laid a hand on his shoulder, but his own face, even in the gold of morning, had gone white. All along the ramparts, men shifted their stances.

Below, Prince Arn rested the spear butt on his stirrup. "Because I am in a sporting mood, my lord, 'tis inclined I am to offer you another choice. Ten of your best men against ten of mine. The side to which the last man standing belongs, gains possession of the fortress. Offers of surrender will, of course, be honored by both victor and vanquished." The hooded head cocked sideways. "Do you prefer this choice, my lord? Or, with your son gone, do you lack the men?"

Dranoel paled. His men cast each other sidelong glances. Aerid shivered despite the sun. What more did this demon know about their defenses?

"Druemarwin lacks nothing! That I promise you!"

Aerid's gaze shot to Naed, who stood atop the wall, sword drawn and shield flashing in the sun. The position exposed him to the man below and to any archer on the green. Panicked, she stared at the man on horseback, willing the spear not to dip, certain if she had guessed Naed's vulnerability, the Prince must now be considering a suitable response. For heartbeats, Naed's words hung in the air while the man on the rampart and the man on the moat's edge assessed each other.

"Hear, hear!" Yormoc cried, vaulting onto the rampart at Naed's side. Behind him, a shout of acclamation erupted from Druemarwin's defenders.

Scant steps away, Aerid saw her master's chest swell at the sound. He leaned over the wall and addressed the Prince in a strong, clear voice. "Draw your men off to the tree line, and we shall come forth in an hour. At the least sign of treachery, my men shall destroy the fortress rather than hand it over."

The Prince wheeled his horse. "A fair bargain. Enjoy your last hour as Master of Druemarwin." With the merest nod to Naed atop the rampart, the Prince loosed his reins and galloped toward his lines, the spear's white flag snapping.

Dranoel pushed away from the wall. The bold look had vanished, leaving his face set in rigid lines. Noticing Aerid, he gestured toward her healer's pouch. "I fear you'll soon have need of that, girl."

To Naed, who with Yormoc had descended to his side, he said, "Choose eight men and meet me before the gate."

Aerid, Naed, and Yormoc exchanged glances. Naed spoke, "M'lord, you do not—"

"Silence! Though I have fathered a son older than you, I am hardly feeble. 'Tis my honor and my property. 'Tis only right I should defend it. If you lack the stomach to stand by me, then I shall stand alone!"

"That shall never be," Naed vowed, but Dranoel had already plunged into the tower stairwell and only his footfalls clattered out of it. Ekwul, bearing Dranoel's helm and shield, paused at the doorway. With a look of resignation, he followed his master.

Naed glowered after them. "He'll die on that word *honor*."

"So will we," Yormoc said, "on his honor."

Naed swung on him. "Will you refuse to fight?"

"And forego my gold? 'Twill be a pretty purse to those who win. See your blade rings true, lad, and we may make our fortunes indeed. Shall I help you choose men to join us?"

"Aye, do so." When Yormoc was gone, Naed heaved a sigh. He had sheathed his sword and his shield hung from his back, but his shoulders seemed burdened with a weight too heavy for his years.

Aerid touched his sleeve. "'Twas brave—"

He grimaced. "And foolish." He noticed her hand, considered it, and clasped it suddenly between both of his. "Pray, Aerid. Please." Then, as if he had trespassed some boundary, he flushed and fled down the tower steps.

****

Prince Arn glanced at the distant rampart,

visualizing again the man who had stood there. Red-colored hair, unusual even for a D'nalian, and easy enough to locate in a 20-man mêlée. Average height. Young. Was that his excuse for bravado? Arn hoped not. Youthful bravado died far too easily. Arn was in the mood for something more spirited. He unclasped his cloak and handed it to Krenin, only now noticing his Second was speaking.

"—to let me fight. This fog-bound rockpile is hardly worth the risk."

"Risk!" Arn laughed. "These are civilized D'nalians. Lord Dranoel thinks too much of honor to fight unfairly."

Krenin tugged on Arn's chest plate, checking the fit for the third time. "Perhaps he does, but what of that son-of-a-whore on the wall? 'Tis sure he'd think your death a coup."

Arn swung into the saddle before his Second could meddle further with his shoulder straps. "Indeed, I hope he tries."

"What—no!" Krenin seized Darkstar's bridle. "You'll go straight for him, won't you?"

Arn tested the draw of his sword. Satisfied, he glanced at his best friend and one-time mentor. Despite twenty-odd years of blade-bearing, Krenin's face was free of obvious scars and his teeth intact, circumstances which, Arn had observed, made most women deem Krenin "handsome." That effect was somewhat marred by a perpetual frown grooving furrows across his forehead.

Arn grinned, knowing he was about to add another groove. "No, I'll let him find me. 'Twill be more interesting."

"I should've left your scrawny carcass in that river years ago! If I'd known how my innards would burn every time I watched you tempt the Sisters, 'tis sure I'd have left you for the river rats, but no, I had to have my own Second, didn't I? 'Twas only my luck you turned out to be bloody royal." Krenin glowered up at him. "And a damned stubborn bastard to boot."

Arn chuckled. "You've taught me well."

"Aye, but not to be a fool. The Sisters can be fickle."

Arn grasped the shield Krenin passed to him and fitted it to his arm. "Rest easy, old friend. I'll not die today. 'Tis too much yet to be done. Even the Sisters know that."

He reined Darkstar away before Krenin could insist he "at least" wear a helm. Once Arn's combat skills had surpassed his teacher's, Arn simply stopped listening. No metalworker could make a helm without restricting vision, hearing, or mobility, and Arn refused to give the smallest edge to his opponents. Savoring the breeze ruffling his hair, he led nine hand-picked men toward the defenders of Druemarwin.

At fifty yards, Arn scanned his opponents and found a red-colored queue dangling from the second helm left of Dranoel. A frisson of anticipation stirred his blood, but he nonetheless set himself opposite Dranoel. *First things first.* Drawing his sword, Arn shouted the charge.

Horse hurtled at horse. Pounding hooves churned the sod into a spray of spring green. With a thunderous crash, sword smashed into shield and shield rang against sword. Most men counted on muscle and momentum to remain astride, but skill and timing could even the odds for a smaller or slighter man. Swiveling in his saddle, Arn threw up his shield at an angle, deflecting Dranoel's blow. Bringing his own sword down from the side, he pushed.

The Lord of Druemarwin's horse floundered, pitching its rider to the ground. Apparently unhurt, Dranoel rolled over and retrieved his sword and shield.

Reining in Darkstar, Arn assessed the field. Three riders were unhorsed, and their opponents dismounted to engage on foot. Six other pairs remained astride, clashing their swords and wheeling their mounts.

Satisfied, he threw his leg over the saddle and leaped to the ground. With a flick of his hand, he unbuckled his scabbard and dropped it. "Well, Dranoel, defend your honor. I've come to teach you respect."

"Druemarwin is mine!" Dranoel shouted and bore in swinging.

They locked swords at once, determined faces close, muscles straining. Dranoel, a husky bull of a man, employed superior weight in a ferocious display of strength and raw power. He gained ground.

Arn let him come. There was a dance to swordplay, and he had learned it by heart. *Give. Give. Give. TAKE!*

Arn kicked the Lord of Druemarwin's leg out from under his bulk. A sword swing divested him of his weapon, and Arn's boot, planted on his left arm, pressed his shield into the turf. Arn lowered the point of his blade to Dranoel's throat. "Surrender!"

Dranoel spat grass from his mouth. "To you? I'd rather die!"

Arn applied more weight to the shield arm. Another push would pop the shoulder joint from its socket—an effective disarmament, bloodless yet extremely painful.

"Once more, my lord, do you surrender?"

Dranoel panted, his face drawn and white, but he only sputtered, "Son-of-a-whore!"

Arn pushed. To Dranoel's credit, he emitted only a strangled scream before his eyes rolled up into his head.

"Fool," Arn muttered, wheeling away. He hoped the mêlée was not already decided. He had barely broken a sweat. To his relief, he saw two men still engaged. Dangling from the helm of one was a queue of red hair. Arn smiled.

****

Naed felled his second opponent with a blow to the head. The first had gone down, horse and all, in the initial charge. This second Tolemak had taken down Yormoc almost as quickly. Naed jerked off the man's helm, saw a trickle of blood under the ear, and knew the Tolemak would not stir for at least an hour. Shoving sweat-soaked hair under the rim of his helm, Naed straightened and scanned the field.

The sight of Dranoel's limp form hit him like a body blow. His master—his uncle—down?

"He's not dead."

Naed spun. A dozen feet away, a man leaned on his sword, a tall man with shorn black hair that stirred in the breeze.

"His blood wasn't worth my blade," the Prince was saying. "Yours might be. Unless those bold words were no more than hot breath."

Fury surged through Naed's veins. His master and uncle was fallen, and the man who had dealt the blow was within reach. With a yell, Naed charged.

Prince Arn side-stepped. Naed's sword skittered off

the Prince's shield, and he stumbled. On reflex, he threw up his own shield. The Prince's sword smashed into it, the force shuddering through Naed's forearm. He pushed into the blow, struck quickly, and whirled away.

Two paces apart, the men circled. Naed swallowed. Sweat trickled past his ears. The Prince's move was a clever trick, but he should have anticipated it. Instead, he had rushed in, thinking of Dranoel rather than the skills upon which his life—and the future of Druemarwin—depended. Flexing his fingers on his sword, he decided to wait for the Prince's next move.

Over the embossed rim of a shield, granite-gray eyes assessed Naed. "You're quick. 'Tis a pity you're so green."

Naed found himself driven backward under a flurry of blows. He barely countered one before the next rained on his shield. His sword hand burned, his shield arm ached, and sweat ran into his eyes. He stumbled, recovered, and swung. The chink of chainmail and a grunt told him he had scored.

"Hah!" he shouted, driving forward.

"Luck." The Prince spun, bringing his blade down.

Tolemak steel sliced into Naed's upper arm, into the unprotected spot below chainmail sleeve and above forearm guard. His own blade, screeching edge-to-edge against the Prince's, stopped it from finding bone. Swords locked and faces close, the two men stared at each other.

"Better." The Prince grinned, a flash of bared teeth. "But I've drawn first blood."

Naed's wound burned. More than sweat made a trail to his elbow. His muscles shook as he strained against the taller man. The Prince had the advantage of leverage, but... Flexing his legs, he gave ground, then surged upward.

The Prince's sword flew through the air.

"Surrender!" Naed cried.

Flinging hair out of his face, the Prince laughed. "What, when I still have my shield?"

Naed hesitated. 'Twas hardly a fair fight, but if the fate of Druemarwin rested on pursuing this attack, so be it. He swung once, twice, then bore in for the finish. Too late he saw his mistake. Instead of backing up, the Prince charged. Naed's sword sliced air. He glimpsed feral eyes

18

before shields collided, his head snapped sideways, and the ground rammed into his back.

"Krenin will no doubt tell me I should've killed you."

Naed forced open an eye and saw a blade poised above his throat. The figure holding it seemed to have three heads.

"However, with your master incapacitated, someone will have to order Druemarwin's gates opened." The blade lifted and the Prince backed a step. "Well?"

Naed rolled to an elbow. His head buzzed and his body ached as if it had been trampled, but his heart stubbornly insisted on beating. He closed his eyes, wishing the Prince's blade had spilled his lifeblood. Then there would be no need to face the people whose hope he had lost. For a moment, he considered defying the Prince, but duty and honor required he act otherwise.

"As you wish," he said thickly and rose.

****

Aerid could not recall how she came to be in the Great Hall, or how water and bandages materialized on trestle tables there. Since Naed had arisen from the field, she had functioned as one in a daze, aware only her nightmares had come true. She and the inhabitants of Druemarwin were in the hands of Tolemaks.

Servants brought Dranoel in on a litter and, mercifully, he remained unconscious while she realigned his shoulder and bound his arm to his side. A whiff of pungent bearberry oil revived him enough to sip a pain-numbing brew of powdered shepherd's bane dissolved in wine.

She left him in Ekwul's hands and addressed the others. Ministering to broken bones, head injuries, and blade wounds so occupied her mind she could not—would not—think what the next hour might bring, life or death or—worse yet—such brutality she and those about her would plead for death. Had she not already seen what Tolemaks did to captured towns?

Swallowing against the rock in her throat, she glanced at Naed. Eyes downcast, he slumped against the wall while Yormoc tugged off his tunic and armor. Blood painted his arm, but she could see the wound was only a finger in length.

"Get me up, fool, or 'tis your hide I'll line my chair with!"

Over her shoulder, Aerid saw Dranoel struggle upright. Ekwul sent her a resigned look and maneuvered his master onto a bench. Dranoel took in the guards at the door, and his ashen face paled further. He shot a glance at Naed, who did not appear to notice.

Yormoc examined the cloth he had been holding to his gashed jaw. "They haven't killed us yet. 'Tis like they don't mean to."

Dranoel visibly fought for control. "Mayhap the bastard Prince has some honor, then."

"Some honor!" Aerid sputtered. Did no one but she understand what they faced? She flung a blood-soaked rag into the bowl Gert held for her and stood. "Belike they'll be keeping us for their sport, killing us one by one to feed their savage appetites. These be Tolemaks we speak of, and what be they if not barbarians and their master a Prince of savages!"

Dranoel blanched at her words. Yormoc froze. Even Naed's head came up. But not a man of them stared at her.

Cold dread filled Aerid. She whirled.

In the doorway stood a scarlet-cloaked figure so tall his ebony hair brushed the cross-beam, so lean Aerid sensed nothing but bone and muscle and will, a will so strong it emanated from the deep-set, stone-gray eyes. High cheekbones gave his face a noble, arrogant look. The curve of his lips mocked her. The scar cutting across the left side of his face from behind the eyebrow to the corner of the chin mocked nothing.

CHAPTER THREE

"Pray, go on." The Prince of Val-Feyridge planted his boot on a bench and rested a hand on the upraised knee. "Or have you lost your nerve?"

Aerid did not know what she felt more strongly—anger, indignation, embarrassment or panic. Before she could decide, one of the Prince's men sauntered to her side.

The Tolemak grasped her hair and fingered the curls. "'Tis clear to me now why D'nalians are so easy to defeat. Their men wear their hair like women. 'Tis only to be expected they fight like women too." He laughed. "All words and no substance."

Out of the corner of her eye, Aerid saw Naed rise along the wall, fists clenched. Knowing their lives depended on avoiding provocation, she eased her hair from the Tolemak's hand. If she were careful, the man would not notice and, once out of contact with her, move on.

His response was to catch her arm in a bruising hold. "What's your hurry, wench? Can't wait to warm my bed?" He dragged her against his chest, his breath hot on her face, his horse-and-paint smell choking her nostrils.

Aerid's memory seized on the odor, flashing before her a town aflame, moans, shrieks, pounding hooves and savage, painted, pale-skinned faces. This white face, this body loomed too close, too big, too...hated! From her childhood rushed the only words she knew for his kind. "*Mortraeder!*" she hissed. "Demon's spawn!"

She reared back to knee him but was knocked aside before she could connect and his fingers were ripped from her arm. When she stumbled to a halt, Naed's hand was clamped about her wrist and the Tolemak's dagger had drawn a thin trickle of blood from Naed's throat.

"Hold!" The Prince's command echoed from the vaulted rafters.

The Tolemak's eyes narrowed. He eased the point of his dagger back a fraction.

Naed, face a rigid mask, maintained the nose-to-nose glare.

Aerid's wrist throbbed where his fingers dug into it.

"Didn't I say you should have killed him?" The Tolemak traced an invisible line across Naed's throat. "'Tis not too late to reconsider."

Tugging at each finger and thumb, the Prince carefully removed his gloves and folded them over his knee. While the tension in the air ripped at Aerid's nerves, he seemed oblivious, as if Naed's life—indeed, all their lives—concerned him no more than the dried mud he flicked from his boot. "'Twill be no killing," he said at last. "And no taking spoils." He tucked his gloves into his belt. "Lord Dranoel, your standard will remain flying, and you may keep your chambers and certain of your servants. We intend to remain here no more than a few days—just long enough to resupply."

Dranoel found voice. "Then why take Druemarwin? Why not—?"

"Negotiate? You? With a man of my kind?" The Prince laughed, but no humor showed in his eyes. "My needs require possession of this stronghold. A contingent of my men will form the guard, dressed in your livery, of course. To all outside eyes, Druemarwin will remain unchanged. No word of this day's events will pass anyone's lips. Do I make my intentions clear?"

Dranoel blinked. "Your intentions, aye, but you have been seen by too many—"

"And every one of them is trapped within these walls." The Prince perched on the table's edge and dangled a long leg.

While her body seethed with fear, Aerid's mind fixed on the single moving object in the Great Hall, the Prince's swinging leg. Her absurdly detached mind observed his boots, noting, while as finely made as they appeared from a distance, they were nonetheless creased with hard use. His tunic and breeches, while woven with skill and cut precisely to fit, were free of ornament save a rampant black panther, no bigger than a fist, embroidered on the chest. Even his sword belt, which had gleamed so in the sun, showed nicks and dents in the intricate metalwork. Except for the scarlet cloak, which seemed barely worn, his garb bespoke a man who cared for use and service and hardly at all for appearance. In truth, Aerid had seen Free Swordsmen more ostentatiously dressed.

Choosing a winter apple from a nearby reed basket, the Prince polished the fruit on his tunic sleeve. "At this moment, my men are separating families, selecting one member to keep as hostage. The village folk will go about their business, keeping their tongues firmly in their heads, and your soldiers will serve me. Included is, of course, your own nephew." He inclined his head toward Naed.

"Demon's Blood!" The Tolemak lowered his dagger and assessed Naed, who had neither moved nor altered his fierce expression. "So, we're to make the son-of-a-whore one of our own. All the better. 'Twill be my pleasure to put him to the test."

"Your spy," Naed bit out, shifting his glare to the Prince, "was more than thorough."

Prince Arn inclined his head again. "But perhaps not alone." His gaze settled on Aerid, scrutinizing her face, her form as though memorizing her features or worse, placing a memory.

Sisters Three! He had seen her yester eve! Aerid swallowed, but no other part of her body seemed to function, so chilling was the look he fixed on her.

"Choose yourself another woman, Krenin. 'Tis doubtful you'd want Dranoel's Adanak pet curled up to your back."

The one called Krenin looked thunderstruck, but the Prince maintained his focus on Aerid. *"Mortraeder.* An Adanak word for something like 'white-skinned demon', aye?"

He stood and again Aerid felt as overwhelmed by his height as she had yester eve. At arm's length, his red-and-blue-painted face terrified her more than last night's cloaked silhouette. This was no figment of legend and nightmare, but the demon made flesh, and he stood so close she could smell the blood he had shed—Naed's and others—not yet dried on his weapons. 'Twas something else, too, in the man-scent that enveloped her...something

23

that did not repel but made her nostrils flare to take it in. Something that set her body vibrating deep inside where panic did not go, but heat did.

Awash in unfamiliar sensations, she backed a step to collect herself, but the Prince followed, his longer stride bringing the wall of his presence closer. His unrelenting gaze told her even if a bench did not stand at her back or Naed's grip anchor her to the chamber, she could not hope to escape his power and his reach. She ought to lower her head, submit. 'Twas what he expected. But her chin rose instead, and Aerid returned his glare, hating him for the way those two granite-chipped eyes had read every note of her panic and confusion.

His expression hardened. "What do you do by the oak, witch, gather poisons?"

"Evenroot," she said, shocked she could find voice, much less dare to use it. "'Tis a stimulant."

"So you make men dance before they die, do you? Show me your hands."

Aerid glanced at Naed, who reluctantly uncoiled his fingers.

Prince Arn did not touch her, nor deign to bend, but the line of his scar silvered against the pale Tolemak skin.

She opened her mouth to tell him evenroot did not glow in the day and, in any case, she had since washed, but Dranoel's voice cut across hers.

"Prince, I beg of you. Druemarwin has no other healer."

"No other active one, you mean."

Dranoel blinked. Sweat beaded on his forehead. "Gam, aye, well, so infirm she—"

"Enough." Disdain showed in the Prince's expression, but Aerid sensed offering her even that much of his notice rankled. "Since you've obvious need of this creature's skills, keep the witch—for now." Turning with a swirl of scarlet, he swept out of the Great Hall.

Krenin looked down his nose at Naed. "D'nalian and an Adanak lover. 'Twill be my special pleasure to see to your training, boy." Sheathing his dagger, he pushed bodily past Naed. He paused beside Aerid and shot her a venomous glare before striding after the Prince.

Aerid's heart thudded in her throat. Where had she

found the nerve, the lunacy, to think what she had thought and to let the Prince see it? Her muscles strained like too tight springs with the trip-lever jammed. She wanted to bolt, to scream, to faint, but her mind had no control over legs gone aquiver. They failed, and she thumped down onto a bench.

"Stay away from them." Naed hunkered down before her. His arm oozed blood and the nick on his throat showed a raised red welt.

"Your wound, 'twill need stitching." She stretched a trembling hand toward his arm. On her wrist, his fingerprints showed dusky against the copper skin. A dull flush rose on his cheeks, but he held her gaze. "Heed me, Aerid. Never be alone—ever—while they stay here."

Nodding, she fumbled for the table's edge. "Sit. I shall mend your wound." She did not trust herself to see if he complied. She only knew she had to move, to serve, to do something before the fragile limits of her control snapped. 'Twas not the time to consider what had passed between her and the Prince. Mayhap, for her sake, 'twould be best not to look at all, but thank the Sisters 'twas over.

****

Arn leaned against Druemarwin's stone rampart and surveyed the inner courtyard. The occupation was proceeding according to plan. What justified this niggling sense of...unease?

He pressed fingers to his ribs and assessed the bruise forming there. Chainmail deterred blade wounds yet did nothing to cushion the blow. Still, he would have forgotten the injury were it not further proof of his spy's reliability. Dranoel's nephew did indeed have a strong arm.

Picking at a pebble in the mortar, he decided his unease had more to do with a glowing green figure and its resident incarnation. It had taken him but moments to place the face with the high cheekbones and slanted eyes, a startlingly vivid blue. The chin was not quite so pointed as he remembered and the hair not black but dark, like polished cherrywood. An image of those softly curling strands imposed itself on his memory, and of their own accord, his fingers opened as if to cup their silken warmth. Her scent still teased his nostrils, an exotic mix of herbs, ointments, and woman... Arn scowled. 'Twas no wonder Krenin had gone straight for her.

Fisting his hand against the image, Arn turned from the courtyard and filled his vision with Druemarwin's green. Dranoel had not properly patrolled the perimeter. Arn would ensure his men were far more thorough. Everything depended on being thorough. Absolutely nothing depended on Krenin's penchant for anything in skirts.

Arn's scowl deepened. An Adanak, and this deep into D'nalee. A mere woman, but who better to stalk a man known to prefer company in bed? Arn laced long fingers together and contemplated his thumbs. Tip to tip, they pushed against each other like swordsmen in combat. Like Krenin's good sense versus his lust.

At least Arn's enemies had learned not to throw women at him. "Colder than the Arbez River in First Month." Even Krenin said as much of him. Why not, Arn thought, when a cool head, open eyes, and a disciplined body could bring an orphan from bastard to prince? He had women when he chose, and before he needed, because need made a man foolish.

His father had been foolish, loving a landsman's daughter on his holding at Albon and getting her with child. Visiting her in secret, paying her family to say nothing, believing his older brother Prince Yinnad would never know he, alone, had sired a son.

And heir.

Arn understood why that would drive a man like his uncle to murder. After three wives Prince Yinnad had sired but one child, a daughter. But Yinnad had underestimated Arn's father, who, besides passing on the unmistakable traits of the Tolem line—tall angular build, thick black hair, and stone gray eyes—had given his heir a parchment claiming parentage.

Over Arn's heart the cylinder containing his father's legacy and his grandfather's gift shifted a fraction against his skin. He rarely looked back on his past, but the sensation, and the golden, late afternoon haze painting long, soft shadows across the green made him feel as though he were 12 again and sitting on the stone bench by the family quarters on his grandfather's holding, listening to the old man speak...

"Take heed, lad. The mistakes of the past become the mistakes of the future—"

"—if not learned from. Aye, Grandfather, I know." Reed-thin and tall as a yearling colt then, Arn remembered wriggling his toes inside his grandfather's cast-off boots. They already fit him, and he had years yet to grow.

"Do you, now?" The old man laid his whittling knife in the lap of his tunic. "'Tis what all men say...till the time comes for each to make his choice." The setting sun burnished his hands, face, hair, even the weathered buildings behind him, turning everything in the mud-and-stone compound to gold.

Arn loved this time of day, when the shadows grew long and the sun glowed on the fattening heads of grain in his grandfather's fields outside their compound's timber wall. Through the open gate and between the dark shapes of cattle, goats, and herdsmen returning from pasture, he could see the fields stretch far away to black-topped trees beyond. "My choice would be to stay here, now. Forever."

The old man smiled a slow, sad smile, but his eyes shone. "Aye, lad, I understand, but hear me awhile." Straightening shoulders that ought to belong to a younger man than the line-scored face indicated, he said, "Do you remember me telling you of the Last King and how he had everything a king could ever want?"

Arn nodded. The story was a favorite of his grandfather's and Arn knew it by heart. "Great power, great wealth, a peaceful land, and three fine sons."

"Why was he the Last King, then?"

"He thought he could rule his life as he ruled his kingdom."

"What did he forget?"

"Death. And jealousy. Death when he died without naming an heir, and jealousy when the youngest son, Prince Adan, stole the Crown from the eldest, Prince Tolem, and the middle son, Prince D'nal, refused to take sides."

The old man nodded. "Thus breaking the Kingdom."

"What, are you telling him that story yet again?" Arn's mother ruffled her son's hair, then bent to kiss her

27

father's cheek. She had come up from the garden, and she smelled of fresh-turned earth from the root vegetables in her basket. Her hair gleamed copper in the sunlight...

Arn closed his eyes. He had not thought of her in years. 'Twas a pity his child self had flushed, wishing his mother would realize he was no longer a little boy. Indeed, his chin already topped her head when she hugged him, something she did far too often for a 12-year-old...

"No," the old man had said, catching her hand. "'Tis his story I'm telling. The lad is old enough to know."

"Old enough to know what?" Arn knew his long-absent father had not wed his mother, making him a "bastard" to those who whispered behind his grandfather's back. Their sons dared to throw the word in Arn's face until his body grew into his anger and he learned to make them suffer for saying it. He looked like his father, too—so his mother said—all limbs and ungainly height with wild black hair, stone-gray eyes, and a face too angular to ever be handsome.

His mother's mouth tightened. She tugged her hand free. "He knows about his father."

"Aye, the man...but not the destiny."

"'Tis safe we've been all these years, without the knowing. Let the past stay buried."

"Would that it could, child, but we're not alone in the knowing. 'Tis but a matter of time before someone with clear eyes sees what he is becoming and counts back the years."

Her face crumpled, and she blinked tears from her lashes. "Tell him, then, if you must." Turning, she ran up the steps into the hall.

Sighing, the old man pulled from his tunic a narrow wooden cylinder dangling from a leather thong. The necklace was one Arn's baby teeth had chewed when his grandfather had carried him about his landsman's holding. Now the old man removed the thong from his neck and fastened it around Arn's. "I've carried this since you were born, lad, but 'tis yours." He tapped the cylinder. "Inside is a letter your father wrote claiming you as his heir."

"My father was a soldier—"

"Your father was heir to the Crown of Tolem, second only to his brother, Prince Yinnad."

"Prince Yinnad...this Prince of Val-Feyridge?"

"Aye, your uncle, and the man who sent Rolnar of Roines to murder your father..."

On the wall of Druemarwin, deep in D'nalee, Arn's fingers dug into his tunic. The cylinder resting against his chest represented all he possessed of the father he had never known, a letter and a bloodline. It was all that remained, too, of the family he had loved, a battered piece of wood and a burning desire to avenge their blood. Just days later, Rolnar and his Roinesmen, on orders from Yinnad, swept down on the compound and slaughtered everyone—men, women, and children—then torched the buildings. Arn shuddered, remembering his mother's death shriek as flames raced through the thatch and timber...

He had been in the fields with his grandfather. At the screams, Arn hurtled forward, grabbing a rake for a weapon, but his grandfather seized his tunic and spun him around. "Run, lad! Run for the river and don't look back!" Ripping the rake from Arn's hands, he shoved Arn toward the trees and the river beyond.

"But, Grandfather—"

"They've come sooner than I expected, but they'll not get what they've come for. Not as long as you heed me and run!" With another shove that knocked Arn to one knee, he hefted the rake like a spear and turned to face the billowing smoke. "As you love me, lad, do as you're told. I'll hold them off. Now, go!"

Arn stumbled to his feet as riders emerged from the smoke and set torches to the ripe grain. They looked up as the flames caught. One shouted and pointed. The swords they raised gleamed wet and red, and blood spotted their horses' legs.

Horrified, Arn backed a step and fell into a furrow. Scrambling up, he forced legs gone wobbly to break into a run. He heard the rumble of hooves, the crack of wood on steel, the squeal of a horse in pain. Falling again, Arn pushed himself up with smoke curling around his arms. Flames raced toward him, devouring the dry grain. Behind, he heard his grandfather's shout cut short. He looked once, saw riders milling around a heap in the furrow, then fled.

The riders caught up to him in the trees, but Arn dodged between trunks. Blinded by tears, throat burning with bile, Arn's mind fixed on one thought—they had murdered his family! Fury rose up within him and he seized his knife. Turning suddenly, he slashed at the nearest onrushing rider, taking down the horse. He leaped on the fallen man, stabbing him in the throat and grabbing his sword. Like a madman, Arn fought the others, suffering wounds for his lack of skill and being driven to the riverbank. When, bleeding and overcome by smoke, he tumbled with two of his attackers into the water, the Roinesmen tried to hold him under, but the swift current tore his body from their grasp.

By all rights, Arn knew he should have drowned—he could not swim—and Demon knew he had nothing left to live for, but somehow he ended up on shore half a league downstream and was pulled from the water by an itinerant Free Sword. That former Free Sword, now some 15 years older, stepped up to Druemarwin's wall at Arn's side and leaned on it.

"The Sisters smiled on us today," Krenin said.

At the sound of his Second's voice, an image of flashing blue eyes and a woman's up-thrust chin leaped into Arn's mind. He should have welcomed relief from his memories, but the image pinpointed the unforeseen problem niggling at him. Dranoel's witch-woman was too thin, too dark, too Adanak for his own taste, but her fire and the challenge of bedding an enemy might tempt others.

"Keep the men away from that Adanak witch," he said. "Her healer's oath may not prevent her from poisoning them."

"Why not kill the whore, then? 'Twould be simpler."

"Dranoel's nephew went for you when you touched her. We can use whatever is between them to keep him beholden."

Krenin snorted. "If he thinks of anything but shoving his cock between her legs, 'tis sure he's a fool, and you're twice the fool not to have killed him."

Arn sighed. Krenin's view of life, like most Tolemaks,

reduced men's motives to lust and power, both of which could be managed by a good killing. While the Tolemak view made their people formidable warriors, it limited their outlook. Arn knew he had not risen from presumed-dead bastard to feared Prince by limiting his own. "He's young, good with a sword, and blood-kin to Dranoel. We can make use of his blade. Meanwhile, fear for his nephew's life should keep the uncle in line."

While Krenin grumbled assent, the pebble Arn's fingers had been picking at broke free of the mortar. Arn watched it fall into the moat below. Allowing the witch her freedom was a risk, but it might be prudent to wait to dispose of her until the army had left the fortress. Let Dranoel's nephew think her safe. After all, how would he learn otherwise? Arn smiled. Would that every problem resolved itself so neatly.

****

The fortress of Val-Feyridge in Tolmak loomed like a predatory bird, the mist so shrouding its massive rocky base it seemed to have taken wing in the moonlight. Dlaniger, son of Dranoel, closed the window flap of the goat herder's cottage he sheltered in, shutting out both the image and the chill air raising gooseflesh on his naked skin. In dimness made fragrant by smoldering honey-bush logs, he turned to the fire-pit occupying the center of the tiny structure and bent to a low table. Palming a leather pouch that lay on the tabletop, he assessed by weight the value of gold coins within. A liberal sum for a pleasant night's work.

He thought it unfortunate his father refused to see how readily gold found its way into the hands of one who offered specialized skills. Oh, the old man knew well enough the ways of the world despite the Sisters-forsaken marshland he called a holding. But that pathetic honor he held fast to came constantly between them.

Dlaniger considered the pouch. Any intelligent man would choose gold in the hand over some outmoded philosophy. Surprisingly few intelligent men did. Fortunately, that left him in exclusive and extremely well-paid company. Already he had means to buy holdings twice as vast as Druemarwin's, and far more pleasantly situated. But—he smiled—when one did not limit oneself with archaic notions of honor, a little gold could be made to go much, much farther.

Reaching for a pack hanging from a wall peg, he slid the pouch deep into it and then fastened the outer straps. A hand brushed his foot and stroked up his bare calf. Dlaniger turned and smiled down at the naked woman luxuriating on a bed of thick cragsheep skins underlain by fresh straw and scented with alderrose petals.

The soon-to-be "Princess" Erodasi's face showed not a whit of her famed Tolem blood-line. Her hair, attractively strewn across the sheepskin, was the color of cream, and her eyes, when not so sensuously darkened, reminded him of blue lake ice. She was neither tall nor angular, her body being appropriately curved and padded. It was, Dlaniger thought, a complete mystery why her betrothed would insist on taking her into his house only to leave her untouched.

Oh, he understood why the Prince wanted her within his grasp. That her father coveted Arn's title was common knowledge. Had not Rolnar married the former Prince's daughter and produced the only other living blood heir to the Tolem line? Once Yinnad was dead at Arn's hand, the apparently "repentant" Rolnar had proposed a marriage alliance as an alternative to continued war. In truth, faced with such a father-in-law and a dowry as coveted as the Tolem Stone, Dlaniger would have done exactly as Prince Arn had done. But he also would have immediately wed her, or at least got her with child.

She had risen on an elbow and her breasts rubbed his shin while her teeth teased his knee with little bites. "Sweet," Dlaniger murmured, catching her hand where it roamed upward on his thigh, "know you what you do to me?"

She bit.

At his sputtered curse, Erodasi sprawled back on the bed. Watching him with hooded eyes, she locked her hands behind her head, the action drawing his attention to the perfect globes of her breasts. "Again. Love me again."

Dlaniger's knee smarted, but remaining irritated in the face of her obvious charms was both difficult and, considering his motives, unwise. "Sweet, you are

32

insatiable."

"You know," she said as he dropped to her side and fastened his mouth to a ripe nipple, "you're not the first to touch me."

He stilled, parted his lips, and looked up.

Erodasi laughed deep in her throat. "Don't look at me like that. 'Tis only 'touch' I said, nothing more. As well you should know." She giggled. "Well, 'tis sure one or two did a bit more, but only so far as I wanted."

Pushing him on his back, she straddled his hips and smiled cat-like at his body's response. "Why, even Krenin, the mighty Prince's Second, goes hard like this practically every time he sees me. I fell on him once—slippery tower stairs—and he had his hand up my skirts before he knew what he was about. 'Twas a seven-night before he'd look me in the face again. He's like a dog to the Prince, you know. He's hoping I won't tell, but it still makes him sweat to see me."

Dlaniger fit his hands to the indentation of her waist. She was a luscious thing. How sweet she paid his expenses for what he had already been paid to do. Well, perhaps his instructions were not so precise as to deflower the Prince's betrothed, but he had been given a liberal hand to act as he saw fit and forming this relationship fit neatly into his plans. In fact, he could hardly have asked for more.

Her fingertips made tiny circling motions over his nipples. Dlaniger sucked in a breath. "And your betrothed, sweet, does he not show his desire for you too?"

"That icicle? I wouldn't know. I can scarce look at him as it is. He has a scar here." She drew a line down her left cheek. "'Tis hideous, all white and knotted. Even without it, 'tis sure his face would fright demons." Erodasi shook off a shudder and, flinging her hair back, ran her hands through it.

Her breasts tempted Dlaniger, and he rocked up, catching her with a strong arm behind her back and taking into his mouth the nipple he had wanted before.

She squealed and fisted her hand in his queue. "'Tis a pity you're not Adanak. Not that I'd let one of them touch me, but 'twould be near the death of my father if you were. Still, I wish he could see me now, his coveted brood

33

mare, with a D'nalian."

"I should rather think," he said, rolling her onto her back, "seeing us thus would be more a concern of your betrothed. Does he not return soon?"

Erodasi shrugged. "Those close-mouthed people of his tell me nothing. I did hear, though, something about the Crown of Tolem."

Dlaniger stilled, but he covered the hesitation by pretending to reposition his elbows on either side of her body. "Indeed. What a foolish notion. Would he seek it, do you think?"

She wrapped sleek legs around his torso. "I'm bored with talking about him. And you said you'd show me something new tonight. I'm not nearly tired, and 'tis sure you're ready." She rotated her hips. "Don't tell me you're not."

He sighed, but only half-heartedly. The little minx was right about his need. He wished his body were not so blunt in its responses, but at least he could control his need, denying it if circumstances required. This was not one of those circumstances. Tomorrow would be soon enough to investigate her Crown of Tolem reference.

****

Sunlight sliced through a barred window, thrusting horizontal shafts of blinding white into a chamber high in the tower keep. The first shaft flung into relief the chamber's only furnishing, a crenulated pedestal of polished granite. The second shaft illumined the cushion resting upon the pedestal, a cushion the color of blood. The third fell full upon the crown reposing there, a circlet of ancient gold, wrought in intricate whorls and pointed with elaborately filigreed daggers.

In the tower vault, high in the citadel overlooking the hilltop city of Vinvinnysee in Adanak, the Crownkeeper reverently regarded the Crown of Tolem. Pity, he thought, as he did every time he beheld the Crown thus illuminated, that those for whom he guarded this treasure had all but forgotten its existence. Too many generations had come and gone since the Breaking of the Kingdom for any to remember the union that once was. Or the peace that had marked it.

These self-appointed merchant Masters of

34

Vinvinnysee knew only the storyteller's fable, how every stone had been ripped out of the Crown by the Three Sisters and given to their Four Winds to scatter, and the gold ground to powder and blown away like dust. This complete destruction was to punish the Royal Brothers who had betrayed each other, and the People, and broken the Kingdom. Never again would the People be whole. A pretty fable, he thought, but one that had long enough served the needs of those who preferred a lie: the Kingdom was dead and its relic destroyed. In truth, only the three Princely stones were missing, their vandalized settings leaving the tri-cornered Kingdom Stone pointing at nothing but broken prongs. Still, the Crownkeeper had never believed the stones were lost. Just as he and his predecessors had always believed this day would come.

He entered the pool of sunlight and gold-fire, gnarled fingers smoothing open a tiny, tightly rolled note he had carried up 136 steps. He had read the message twice, but he wanted to read it once more in the presence of the Crown. Extending a long forefinger, he delicately brushed a dust mote from the Kingdom Stone. When, as if in response, the faceted sapphire refracted blue fire onto the parchment in his palm, his eyes welled.

"One is coming. One who believes by his blood he is worthy to claim you." With a slight bow, he laid the note before the Crown, placing it like an offering on the burgundy cushion. "Let us see if, by his blood, he is."

CHAPTER FOUR

"'Tis sure they mean Aerid harm. I can see it in their eyes, the sons-of-whores." Naed leaned elbows on knees and stared into the fire burning in his uncle's chamber grate. His hands itched for something to do, but throttling Tolemaks—though immediately satisfying—would resolve naught. A prudent man would make ready his gear for the army's morning departure, but he had already polished sword and shield until both gleamed and packed all that needed packing.

"Aye." Dranoel swirled the wine in his cup. He sat sunken in his deerskin-lined chair, feet so close to the fire an occasional spark threatened his hose. "But what's to do? There'll be no hiding her. Not with that bloody spy about. Damn that Wullauf's eyes!"

Naed made fists. His wound pulled, but it was clean and healing. "I'll not go then. I'll not fight for the bastard Prince."

Dranoel slammed his cup down on the chair arm. "'Tis sure you shall! I'll not break a bargain, unholy though it be. 'Tis my word that's been given, and yours too!"

"To a Tolemak, Uncle!"

"Aye, and were it to the Demon himself, 'twould be no less binding." Dranoel levered up in his chair and seized a fistful of Naed's tunic. "Honor, lad, 'tis a man's soul! Sully it and you'll be no true D'nalian."

Naed broke eye contact first. Dranoel was right, but it made him feel no less sullen. He shrugged out of his uncle's grip and hunched toward the fire again. "Then she'll die."

His uncle sank into his chair and pulled the deerskin over his injured shoulder. His face had grayed and he looked every one of his 52 years. Naed swallowed against a rising tide of shame.

"What's to do, then?" Dranoel repeated.

A log popped, sending out a spray of sparks. Naed wished he could read them as ancient seers were said to do. "Would that we could smuggle her out the gates."

"Aye." Dranoel sighed. "'Tis the way they'd least expect."

An idea exploded in Naed's brain with the suddenness of a popping log. Sitting bolt upright, he swiveled toward his uncle. "As you say, they'd least expect an Adanak woman to walk out the gates, but 'twould be perfectly natural to see a D'nalian lad do so, especially tomorrow when all the army's afoot and 'twill be much coming and going."

Dranoel stared, but his expression lightened. "After she crosses the bridge, then what?"

"We'll be days crossing Myrinnen Marsh. 'Twill be cover enough to slip her away—if not by day, then by night."

"Where will she go?"

Naed hesitated. "I—we'll send her to Tumin. To my mother. With a letter."

Dranoel ran a hand through silver-threaded hair. "'Tis a gamble. Sure death for the both of you should they discover her."

"A shepherd's hut would be safer for her than staying with the sons-of-whores the Prince leaves behind tomorrow!" Naed flushed at his vehemence, but his uncle seemed not to notice.

"Aye, put it to her. The Sisters know she's as much to me as kin. Despite her blood." Dranoel heaved a sigh and stared at his feet. "'Twill be strange to have the girl gone."

"Better gone and alive than here and dead."

"Aye." Reaching out a hand, Dranoel cuffed Naed's elbow. "And keep yourself so, lad. Sisters be thanked you came into your blade when you did. And blessings on your mother for thinking to send you to me."

Flushing, Naed looked at his hands. "She sent you no great prize. Did we not lose? Dlaniger would have served you better."

Although he had met Dlaniger but once when he was six and Dlaniger a tall and sturdy thirteen, Naed had heard enough from Druemarwin's guard to know the golden-haired cousin he remembered as a conceited bully had exceptional skill with weaponry and traveled widely. 'Twas common knowledge there had been a falling out between Dranoel and his son, but not even Aerid seemed privy to the details. Naed suspected Ekwul, if the man ever chose to use the tongue he had been born with, could tell all, but D'nalian propriety insisted on respect for others' privacy.

Naed slanted a glance at Dranoel. His uncle had not spoken for so long, Naed thought he had fallen asleep. He rose from the bench, thinking to summon Ekwul, when he noticed a glint of eyes under his uncle's heavy brows.

"With more skill, perhaps," Dranoel said, staring fixedly ahead, "but with no greater honor." His shoulders sagged, as though the words cost him a great effort.

"Uncle," Naed said, kneeling beside his chair, "are you—?"

Dranoel's fingers curled around Naed's forearm. His gaze roamed Naed's face in the dimming light and he smiled a sad, sickly smile that alarmed Naed more than any grimace of pain, so unused was he to seeing Dranoel smile.

"You have your mother's coloring. When I look at you, 'tis her I see. She was well when last you heard, was she not?"

"Aye. She's not a sickly woman." Naed searched Dranoel's face for signs of dementia. "Does your shoulder pain you? Mayhap I should fetch—"

"Here, lad." Dranoel's grip kept Naed anchored while the hand of his injured arm opened. On the palm lay a leather cylinder the length and thickness of a finger and attached to a leather cord. "Take this and keep it safe. 'Tis my will."

"Your will? But—but I am more like to die. Go I not with the Tolemak army tomorrow? Does not their Second, Krenin, want my blood? Uncle, I—"

"Silence! Am I yet your master and are you yet pledged to do my will?"

Naed dropped his gaze. The chastisement smarted, but at least his uncle sounded more like his usual bear-like self. "Aye, on my life."

"Then keep this close by you and open it only when you hear I am dead."

Naed took the cylinder and fastened the cord around his neck. In less than a twelvemonth, he had learned there was no arguing with his uncle. "I shall return, Uncle, while you yet live. You have my word upon it."

Dranoel's grip loosened. He sank back into his chair and closed his eyes. "So you shall, lad, Sisters willing."

****

Aerid slipped behind a door and, for the fourth time since dawn, discreetly adjusted her breast-binding. Sisters, she had to breathe! Or did her heart slam against her throat because she was about to enter a courtyard swarming with hard-eyed men whose hands seemed ever on their knives? Men who hated her blood and would not hesitate to shed it? Men who, if they discovered the deception, would gladly slay Naed for his part in it?

Touching the birthstone fastened at her throat, she gave thanks once more for being small-breasted. The oversized tunic Naed had given her reached to her knees, covering most of her nut-brown breeches and hanging on her slender frame like a man's tunic hangs on his son. With her hair cut to mid-back length and fastened into a proper D'nalian queue, and a hood deep enough to shield most of her face, no one should guess she were anything other than a boy.

Just to be sure, she had boiled down redroot. While it cooled, she crumbled into a pouch a mix of herbs Gam had imparted to her in strictest confidence. Depending on the dosage and the timing in a woman's cycle, the mix could either prevent conception, stop persistent bleeding, or stop a woman's monthly bleed entirely. She took the first dose. After sneaking Elthred's coveted looking glass from under the girl's straw mattress, she sat by the fire and carefully stained the side of her face, part of her lips, and half her throat with the redroot paste. When she was done, Aerid could hardly bear to look at herself, so artfully had she captured the look of a hideous purple mark she had once seen on a stillborn infant.

Aerid pulled the hood close about her face. She felt once more of her pack, assuring she had both the herbal mix and enough redroot paste to renew the stain should it fade before she reached Tumin. At the thought of Tumin, her heart thumped. Naed had given her directions, and she bore her master's letter safe under her breast-binding, but she had no clear memory of how the road lay away to the north even though she must have passed Tumin as a child. Druemarwin and its marshy forest she knew intimately, but to go so far into the unknown. And alone...

Or die.

Aerid swallowed. Truly, Naed had made it clear she had no other choice.

She sighted him halfway round the courtyard as he adjusted straps on a pack horse's load. He looked wan in the early light, and she guessed his frown signified worry. She must not let him down. After all, he would have to endure months with these pale savages while she, Sisters willing, would be away and free in days. Touching her birthstone once more, she willed him a blessing and stepped into the courtyard directly into Krenin's path.

"Watch where you're going, you D'nalian donkey!" he bellowed, shoving her.

She staggered into a cart wheel and dropped her pack.

Soldiers loading the cart laughed.

Aerid's face burned, but she kept her head lowered. 'Twould do no good to call attention to herself. She picked up her belongings and slung her pack over her shoulder. As she turned, something snatched at her hood. Panicked, Aerid spun.

The soldiers laughed again. "Something bite you, donkey-boy?" said one.

Sweat trickled between her breasts. Seeing a break in the crowd, she sidled toward it, praying they would tire of their game, but Krenin himself closed the gap.

Hands on hips, he drawled, "What's the matter, ass? Wearing blinders? I'll fix that."

Aerid saw the intention in his eyes before his hand moved, but her recoil was too slow. In an instant, he had bared her head and every man around her stood dead still, staring.

"Demon's Blood!" Krenin made a warding-off gesture and spat between his fingers.

"Sisters save us!" someone said. Others rubbed or kissed charms. All backed away.

Aerid stood frozen, like a rabbit bayed by hounds. To

40

her left the throng shifted as if it might part. Her muscles bunched to bolt through the opening, but Naed pushed his way in.

Even though every freckle showed red on his blanched face, he crossed the cleared space and pulled the hood over Aerid's head. "Leave the boy alone. 'Tis not his fault he's marred."

Krenin recovered voice first. "We drown the freaks at birth. Leave it to you lowlanders to pity such...*things.* 'Tis but one more reason you D'nalians roll over and play dead for us."

Inches from Naed, Aerid saw the cords of his neck stand out. *Please, no!* She dared not say the words, so she willed them over and over while the air in the courtyard pressed in on her, thick with sweat and fear.

Turning slightly to face Krenin, Naed said, "You understand little of D'nalian honor."

"Honor? In a Free Sword? I know your kind of bend-with-the-wind lowland tripe! You think—"

"What's the matter here?"

Aerid's skin crawled. She recognized the quiet yet commanding voice. Around her belligerent heads lowered. Naed's whole body stiffened. Krenin swung around.

Prince Arn, astride at the fringe of the crowd, seemed to tower over the entire courtyard. 'Twas not his clothing, Aerid noted, for unlike the scarlet cloak he had worn days earlier, a plain brown cloak covered his shoulders. Nor was it the face paint, for that was gone too. Instead, the morning light threw into relief the harsh planes of his face, making the scar on his clean-shaven cheek stand out like a white cord.

Krenin sputtered, "This lowlander is trying to bring a *freak* among us!"

The Prince rode forward, and the soldiers parted before him. He drew rein at the edge of the circle and addressed Naed, "Why?"

"The boy has some skill with herbs."

"And?"

"Will you deny us the right to tend to our own? 'Tis sure your healers will not sully their hands with our blood, yet you expect us to fight for you."

Aerid wanted to grab Naed's tunic, to shake him into

41

realizing their lives depended on being submissive, not defiant. Around her, soldiers elbowed each other. Even Krenin smiled. The Prince could hardly ignore such an outburst.

Prince Arn stroked his chin with a gloved hand. "True enough."

The men looked stunned.

Krenin spun, grabbing the stallion's bridle. "'Tis hideous, a purple monst—!"

"Indeed." The Prince raised his hand, and two gloved fingers traversed the scar on his cheek.

Krenin reddened. He released the horse and backed away from the Prince, who returned his gaze to Naed. "'Tis my experience D'nalians prefer to avoid conflict. You seem to be found often at the center of it. Beware how frequently you test my patience."

Naed bowed his head. "Aye, m'lord."

The Prince turned his horse and rode slowly away. Krenin, with a furious glare at Naed, followed. The soldiers, stealing furtive glances, bent to their tasks. Some kissed charms before drifting away.

Naed gripped Aerid's arm and steered her to his horses. Knees like jelly, she stumbled after him while her thoughts cleared enough to realize no one had seen through her disguise. And Naed—*Sisters be praised!*—had escaped the Prince's fury, although she sensed Krenin more than ever wanted his blood. What left her still shaken was the Prince, if she had read his action right, had actually defended her.

Turning, she located the tall silhouette framed in Druemarwin's open gate. In the morning light, his hair gleamed black and his shield flared like the sun. He had not precisely defended *her*, Aerid told herself as he vanished through the portal, but a D'nalian boy with a disfigured face. Still, it was the last thing she would have expected of such a savage.

Did the demon actually have a heart?

He killed her people. He was planning to kill her, was he not? And this army was destined to invade her homeland. Even demons had moments of weakness. Stiffening her knees, she focused on Naed and the tasks he set her to. She would be out of the demon's hands in a day or two, and 'twould not be a day too soon.

****

The Tolemaks divided the men of Druemarwin into small groups. Archers marched with footmen, laborers with the supplies, and Free Swords with the horsemen. "According to skills," Yormoc remarked as he and Naed rode side-by-side.

"So it would seem," Naed said, but since early morning he had noticed how five or six Tolemaks at a time rode along either side of the small group of Free Swordsmen. The horsemen never lingered, but acted as if they had been sent to communicate with those ahead or behind the D'nalians. Their watchful glances told Naed they were not messengers but guards. The Druemarwin contingent had been divided to prevent a wholesale break for freedom.

Naed's spirits sank. Unless their captors relaxed, it would be impossible for Aerid to slip away. By all that was holy, how could he manage to keep his promise to Dranoel to see her safely free? He bit his lip and glanced back at Aerid bouncing along atop the pack horse. She had no saddle, only a perch astride bundles. He could not see her face, but the droop of her hood suggested the sun had made her drowsy. He hoped she dozed. Come nightfall, he would try to sneak her out of camp before the army settled into its traveling routine. The sooner she got away, the better, before their guardians catalogued every D'nalian face.

But the camp-setting confusion Naed counted on never erupted. In predawn cold he huddled in his blankets by a dead fire-pit and realized his mistake. Only the D'nalians were new to the march. The Tolemaks had traversed part of Tolemak and half of D'nalee. They were battle-seasoned, wary, and vigilant. Not even a mouse could pass undetected through their lines.

He glanced at the snoring Yormoc, then at the small mound that was Aerid. He had made her sleep among the packs, telling Yormoc they would be fools to trust Tolemaks near unguarded goods. Yormoc agreed, but Naed would have parted with all his belongings to ensure Aerid's safety. Keeping her surrounded by bundles kept her separated from everyone, including Yormoc, who had the nose of a Tumin rat hound and knew everyone within Druemarwin's walls. Yet he seemed to accept Naed's explanation the disfigured boy had been living in the forest with old Gam.

Nonetheless, only Yormoc among the D'nalians had spoken to him since the incident in the courtyard. Naed wished his people were more tolerant but Aerid's appearance had shocked even him. Everyone would give her a wide berth now, but the whole army would notice if the "freak" disappeared. He wondered how long the stain would last. By the Sisters, he hoped it would not fade before he found a weak spot in the Tolemak line.

Unclenching his jaw, he stretched out on the ground between Aerid and Yormoc to catch a few hours of sleep. Tomorrow he would tell her the situation if he could get a moment alone with her. Their self-appointed traveling companion seemed to think sharing a servant who was a "freak" was preferable to having no servant at all.

Nearby, Yormoc let out a snort worthy of a horse. Pulling up his hood, Naed turned his back on Yormoc and went to sleep.

****

The army marched hard and fast. Nightly, Aerid tumbled into her blankets, exhausted and aching all over. Had Naed told her to escape at midnight—or any hour of darkness—she could not have stayed awake long enough to pull on her boots. After a week, she regained energy and toughened her body, yet each day they traveled put her farther from Tumin. Huddling into her cloak, she wondered how much longer before she could make a break.

This day, Naed and Yormoc, with hoods up and shoulders hunched against rain that had begun before dawn, sat their horses ahead of her while the army reorganized to cross a river. They had waited so long in the open, water dripped from Aerid's hood every time the gray mare shifted beneath her. She pulled a piece of drycake out of her sleeve, cracked off a section, and put it in her mouth. Sucking on what was left of her breakfast took her mind off the chill seeping into her tunic.

A stone's throw away, Krenin rode his horse once more into a river neither wide nor fast but churning yellow-green. For the better part of an hour, while the army bunched up behind, Aerid watched the Prince's Second search the rain-swollen water for a ford. Finally, his horse trudged across chest-deep and lurched onto the far bank. Men cheered. Krenin fastened the rope he had been towing to a stout tree. A group of horsemen brought across more ropes. As soon as the ropes were pulled taut, squadrons of archers waded into the river. Clinging to the ropes while sinking to their armpits, the men crossed. More horsemen followed.

Knowing their turn would come soon, Aerid slipped off the mare to tighten the pack's straps, but a strange hissing, like a thousand angry snakes, arrested her hand. Turning, she saw arrows pour like rain onto the men in the river. Horses squealed, bucking, falling, dragging their riders into roiling water. Screaming men grasped at saddles, at ropes, at the arrows spinning them sideways into a yellow-green current that swallowed them whole. Disembodied hands, fingers grabbing at nothing, rushed down the river and vanished.

"Back! Back into the trees!" Naed shouted. Grabbing Aerid's tunic, he plucked her off the ground and flung her across the packs. Before she could right herself, he lashed the gray mare into a gallop. Aerid clawed at the horse's mane, the packs, anything to keep herself astride. Men, horses, grass, stumps flew past; rain-soaked leaves slapped her cheeks.

Naed dragged the mare to a halt amid over-reaching willows. "Are you hurt?"

Aerid levered into a sitting position and gulped in air. Her face stung, and her cloak hung askew on her shoulders, but she shook her head.

A squadron of archers rushed toward the riverbank. A troop of horsemen followed, their harness jangling. Naed's warhorse shook its head and danced after them, but he hauled the animal back. Every freckle stood out across his nose. He darted a glance toward the river, then over his shoulder as his horse champed the bit.

He was weighing a chance for her escape, but the moment she realized it, his face stiffened. He shrugged out of his cloak and tossed it to her. "Stay here."

"Wait! Why do we not go?"

"'Tis not safe." He pulled on his helm. "And 'tis my duty to fight."

"Fight? But they be Tolemak!"

"Aye! And 'tis to them I'm sworn! Or have you forgotten?"

Shame stung Aerid's cheeks more than the whiplashing branches. She, of all people, should have remembered how Naed—indeed, any D'nalian—valued honor.

"Wait for me here. Understand?" When she nodded, he hoisted his shield, laid his heels to his horse, and was gone.

Aerid inhaled to calm her still-pounding pulse. Despite her disappointment, she understood why now was not the time to make her break. The enemy could have them surrounded.

The enemy.

A shudder rippled along Aerid's spine. The flush drained from her cheeks. *Her own people were the enemy!* Any of those arrows could have as easily killed her, or Naed, as any Tolemak. How could the archers know the difference? A second shudder started deep in her belly and rattled her to the core. *What in the name of the Sisters had she gotten herself into*?

A shout of "Healer!" snapped her attention to the willow wood, the rain, the moaning of wounded men. Automatically, she unfastened her healer's pouch, slung it over her shoulder, and...hesitated. These men were her true enemies, were they not?

Another shout for help, more insistent.

By the Sisters, she could not think. Not now, not with the sound of so much pleading. Sliding off the gray mare, she headed toward the shouting.

****

The men Aerid treated seemed to notice nothing about her except, according to one whose lacerated back she stitched together, "You D'nalians, at least, keep your needles sharp." He was gap-toothed and scraggle-bearded, yet his skin where the sun never touched it was whiter than Naed's. All the Tolemaks were pale as milk under their tunics and breeches. *Mortraeder, Demon's spawn,* her people called them, as if they were creatures that crawled out from under rocks. A fitting name, she thought, relieved this Tolemak, at least, would do no crawling until his wound mended.

The man's companion handed him a flask, and he took a pull of it. After a moment's hesitation, he wiped the neck and offered it to her.

Aerid blinked at the gesture. It was far more notice than she had received from the D'nalians she marched with, to whom she supposedly belonged.

"Have a swallow, boy," he growled. "'Twill put hair on that bony chest."

"Aye, and make that face all the redder," said his companion.

She glanced up at the remark, but saw no malice in the man's grin.

"Can't get redder. 'Tis purple already," said the first. He waggled the flask. "Go on."

The last thing Aerid wanted was to share a flask with Tolemaks, but their offer, of acceptance as much as ale, caught her off guard. Refusing would insult them. Accepting might make her time among them, and Naed's too, more bearable.

Leaning forward, she took the flask, raised it to her lips and pretended to drink. When she lowered it, she wiped the neck and splashed some of the contents on the man's wound.

He wheezed and his eyes bulged.

"'Tis as good outside as in." She handed the flask back.

His companion guffawed. "Give the lowland brat credit. 'Tis as fine a piece of stitching as any I've seen."

The wounded man glowered at her, but he grunted out, "Thanks," and took another pull of the flask while she bandaged his injury.

They were only Tolemaks and she had done no more than was necessary, but Aerid could not suppress an odd sense of satisfaction while she rose to offer her help elsewhere.

A voice she instantly recognized commanded, "You there, give me a hand."

Aerid turned with dry mouth, hoping the Prince had not addressed her, but straight for her he came,

47

supporting a limping Krenin.

The Prince's tunic was bloodstained, mud-spattered, and soaked. On his cheek, the scar gleamed silver. Gray muck streaked Krenin's pinched face, and more plastered his back and side. The Prince eased him to the ground beside a tree. "Have you any skill with bones, boy? His horse fell on him."

Aerid ducked her head before those eyes she remembered as piercing could delve into hers. The rain made her tunic stick to her skin, and she desperately wished she had not thrown her cloak back from her shoulders. If it should shift, the outline of her breast binding might show over her ribs. Perhaps if she knelt quickly beside her patient, the Prince would not notice who or what she was. But she had not counted on Krenin.

"Demon's Blood!" He recoiled into the tree trunk, swore, and grabbed the charm at his throat. "Keep your hands off me, you—you monster!"

Aerid's face burned, but she kept her head down and drew her cloak around her body. Part of her wanted to stand up and stalk away. After all, there was no open wound, no blood, no obvious deformity of the leg. His injuries could wait. "If 'tis your own you'd be wanting, sir—"

A hand on her shoulder arrested her intent to rise. Long fingers curled into her bones with just enough pressure to make their presence known. "How many have you tended today, boy?"

Aerid resisted the impulse to shrug off the hand. The gesture would be useless. Those fingers, whose heat was penetrating her sodden cloak and tunic, would tighten like steel if she moved. "Ten...mayhap a dozen, m'lord."

"The bastard's lying," Krenin said through gritted teeth. "Not a man of ours would let that freak touch him."

The hand's pressure remained constant, communicating to Aerid she should focus on the voice that came again from above. "You were brought to tend your own. Why are you willing to tend mine?"

Aerid's stomach fisted against her throat. *Why indeed*? Had she not asked herself the selfsame question? "Healer's oath, m'lord," she choked out, "but I'll not be doing it again—"

"Aye, but you will."

Aerid gaped. She surged to her feet, and the Prince's hand, which remained on her shoulder, had not resisted. She slanted a glance upward and risked a look at his face. "Why?"

The long mouth curled into a grin. "Healer's oath."

He squeezed her shoulder and strode away before Aerid recovered her senses. Her skin still burned with the imprint of his hand, and the heat was spreading, running down her arm and toward her chest, warming her almost as much as the shock of his smile. He was the white-skinned, black-haired, scar-faced epitome of the race she feared. How could he smile at her as if they were somehow allies? *By the Sisters, she hated him!*

Did she?

Aye, indeed! That was no friendly smile. He knew her oath trapped her into doing what benefited him and his army. She shuddered, shaking off the residue of his touch. The demon had no heart. She was a fool if she even for a moment thought he had.

She looked down at Krenin who sat slack-jawed and staring after the Prince. "Wait but a moment, sir, and 'tis sure I'll be finding one of your own to tend to you."

His gaze jerked upward, caught her face, and flinched. But before she could step away, he seized the hem of her tunic. "Do something, damn you! My knee feels like it's in a vise. But don't expect me to look at you! You're uglier than the Demon's Nine Whores combined."

Aerid stood with fists balled. She had never understood what provoked one man to kill another, but she could see it clearly now, could taste it in the gall burning the back of her throat. It would be so easy, her healer's knife across a vein, a double measure of powdered shepherd's bane, and the world would be free of one of her people's murderers. How many had he killed? The knife he drew to rip at his breeches was bloodstained. One of her own had surely died today.

But so had many of his own, including the man whose hands Aerid had folded over his chest, whose companions had sworn at least one among them would deliver his longbow to his eldest son. Her mind whirled with images of the dead and wounded, now Adanak, now

Tolemak, now neither, now both. Dead men had wives, children, parents, brothers, sisters. To kill one meant to plunge the knife of grief into other hearts. Aerid closed her eyes. To kill the Prince's Second would save many more lives—and many more hearts—but to kill him would go against everything she had sworn to do and be as a healer.

She unclenched her hands and sank to her knees beside the injured man. His whole being repulsed her, but the thought of breaking her oath repelled her even more. Schooling her features into a blank, she said, "Tell me where it pains you."

****

Prince Arn stood with fists on hips at the edge of the willow break that served as healing tent. He surveyed the sky, river, and bank beyond, noting the rain had ended, finally. The attack itself had been brief—several volleys—but long enough to kill at least two dozen in the river alone, unless some who were swept downstream found their way back. He had sent a search party but held out little hope.

The Val-Feyridge archers returned fire immediately, and he had sent two groups of horsemen across, one northward and one to the south, to cut off the enemy's escape, but he held out little hope there too. The attack was too well-planned to leave an escape route to chance.

He watched his men move the column of supply carts one-by-one from the tree line to the river's edge to float them across. With a contingent of soldiers riding pursuit, another providing defense, and a third searching for survivors, the cart transfer was undermanned. A slow business under the best of conditions, Arn estimated this crossing could take till nightfall, as long as no other carts followed the one that had mired a wheel in the muck. Weary, soaked men surrounded it and pushed, but it made no progress.

The men stopped pushing at his approach. They watched him wade into ankle-deep mud and grip the stuck wheel's spokes. "On the count of three." He braced his feet. "One!"

The soldiers looked at each other.

"Two!"

50

The men hustled into position.

"Three!"

The cart rocked. It strained, rolled back, strained again harder until, with the *thwock!* of a pulled cork, the wheel popped free. The cart master maneuvered his team to the water's edge.

Arn wiped muddy hands on his tunic. "Good work. Carry on."

The men standing beside him exchanged grins. "Aye, m'lord," said one.

"'Twill be a pleasure," said another.

"Heave to, lads," said a third. "Here comes another." The men grabbed hold of the cart and shoved it to the water's edge with a shout so loud other soldiers turned and looked at them.

Stepping aside, Arn let them work. Experience had taught him most who assembled armies, including his soon-to-be father-in-law Rolnar, led their men without ever dirtying their boots. Arn pitied his enemies' ignorance. Wallowing in mud with the lowest soldier gave a man a healthy respect for his army's heart. And it benefited morale, too, especially when the men knew their commander had worked his way up from origins as lowly as theirs.

"Healer!"

A horse burdened with two riders slid to a halt near the willow break. First to reach the horse, Arn took the wounded man from the rider's arms.

"Stomach," the rider panted. Hooking a leg over the horse's neck, he leaped down and pressed a wad of blood-soaked cloth to the wounded man's midsection.

Two healers rushed in, one to gather the man in his arms, the other to take hold of the cloth. Together, they hurried under the trees. The horseman wiped bloody hands on the wet grass. From the back of his helm dangled a reddish D'nalian queue.

Arn swept an assessing glance over the whole man, noting bloodstains, caked mud, and branch scratches. Clearly, Dranoel's nephew had not shirked his duty.

Naed straightened and reached into his saddlebag. "First Horseman Yarl bade me bring you these, m'lord."

Arn scanned his face, finding it composed, even

51

blank, except for the eyes. No man with an ounce of courage could keep the thrill of battle from shining in them. The youth's eyes fairly blazed, one more confirmation his life had been worth sparing. With the ghost of a smile, Arn took two halves of a broken arrow from the D'nalian's hand. Separating the pieces, he examined first the arrowhead, then, as his mouth compressed, ran his fingers along the fledging. Vinvinnysee, without a doubt. He had seen enough of them during the Northern Wars.

The army was weeks from Vinvinnysee, days from the Adanak border. How in the name of the Demon had Gaelwynn known to intercept him here, this far south and this deep in D'nalee? Arn had deliberately chosen the least likely path, had concealed his intentions by splitting his army into sections, had given no one but his commanders precise instructions. Even his bride-to-be, that pampered, self-absorbed sharer of his ancient bloodline, knew nothing but he would be away from Val-Feyridge for an unspecified time. And that to keep her traitorous father in the dark. Rolnar, if he guessed anything was afoot, would have the Demon's own time learning what.

That was, if everything had worked according to plan.

Arn's fingers tightened on the arrow shaft. A well-placed spy, a message fastened to the leg of a Vinvinnysee-bred homing bird, and...an ambush. But who? And where? Among his men now? Or someone they had passed along the way? Racking his memory for clues, he ran his palm back and forth across the arrow's feathers until the tingling made him stop, look at his hand, and remember a pair of slender, green-glowing hands.

The Adanak witch.

Arn's scar twitched. Krenin was right; he should never have let Dranoel keep the girl, even for a few days. The only good Adanak was a dead Adanak; had he not learned that in his first battle when the Adanak he had shown mercy to rewarded him by slicing his cheek? He had been stupid, thinking with his heart, not his head, and he had not made the same mistake since.

Until Druemarwin.

With a shift of his thumbs, he snapped both arrow shafts. "Tell Yarl I want prisoners. Ones that can talk."

"Aye, m'lord."

While the D'nalian swung into the saddle, Arn dropped the arrow pieces and ground them into the mud under his boot. He would dispatch a messenger to Nemmon and see if the other half of his army had been attacked too. They followed a more likely northern route, but if attacks had been coordinated, it would mean the spy lay somewhat nearer to home. If not, well, the Adanak witch should have been silenced days ago, but he would send a man to Druemarwin to be sure his orders had been carried out. In the meantime, he would send a bird of his own home to Val-Feyridge and inform Tylus of the ambush. Tylus could be trusted to ferret out any turncoat.

For the present, Arn decided to abandon any pretense of surprise. As long as the enemy knew of his approach, he might as well step up the army's pace. By Seventh Month, the Crown of Tolem should be firmly in his grasp. If not, Vinvinnysee would have the Demon to pay.

Whistling up Darkstar, Arn fitted his foot to the stallion's stirrup. Acting as the Demon's own enforcer was a role he would relish.

CHAPTER FIVE

Aerid noticed the army no longer skirted gray-green marshland or traveled a track beaten through wildflower fields or bordered by birch, brush, or shrub. Now, cart wheels clattered over stone-studded paths through small, hummocked meadows. Willows and birches mingled with firs and spruce. Mists that shrouded them till mid-morning vanished now with the sun.

Two days before, the army had crossed another river. A stone's throw wide and waist deep, the river seemed no different than the half dozen others they had crossed since the ambush. This time soldiers who unslung their shields before crossing did not return them to their saddle horns. Nor did archers loosen their quiver belts for comfort in marching. Naed's constant frown deepened into a scowl, and he ordered her to ride close upon his horse's tail. Aerid did not need Tolemak murmurs to tell her they had crossed into Adanak.

Her homeland.

Aerid sat up straighter. Soon she would be among her own people who would accept her as one of their own. Among those who preferred gold-brown skin to ghostly white. If only she could find a way to join them.

She rode at Naed's stirrup, studying his profile as he flicked a black-winged fly from his hand. Small lines had made themselves at home in his face, appearing as the branch scratches healed. She knew he slept little, prowling the camp at odd hours to search for a weakness among the sentries, but every morning his gloom deepened. Yet he still insisted she go to Tumin. Aerid always nodded, but while she carried Dranoel's letter under her breast-binding and Naed vowed his mother would take her in, she knew each day's travel put Tumin another day away and her kinfolk much closer.

She had precious little to base a search on, only her birthstone, a milky green, translucent stone the size of a man's thumb tip, flattened on top and smoothed round, and vague memories of her parents. One of the clearest was of her mother, cheeks flushed with fever, insisting the stone was a rare Sisters' teardrop. She told a tale of how, when the world was young, the Demon held the Three Sisters prisoner on the highest mountain, and they wept green-water tears until the Four Winds gathered the Storm Warriors and rescued them. Aerid must trust, her mother said, smoothing tangles from her five-year-old daughter's hair, when the time came she too would be rescued, for the Demon could only delay, not destroy love. "The stone, 'tis your destiny, little one," she had said. "Proof, if ever you'll be needing it, of the power of love." Aerid wrapped fingers around the stone at her throat and sighed. Her father must have needed such proof more than she, else he would not have died as they told her he did, running headlong into a Tolemak charge, armed only with a pruning hook. He had killed two, they said, before the raiders swept through their caravan and set wagons ablaze. She had fled into the trees with the other women and returned to find nothing left of her life but ashes and memories.

The memories always caused her heartache, but she could not dwell on pain now. Having a rare birthstone meant she must have been born near its legendary source, Three Sisters Mountain. It followed some of her kin still lived in the highlands there. Much as she loved old Gam, and much as she owed Dranoel and her dear friend Naed, living among D'nalians had not been easy. Far better to live among her own kind. If only she knew the lay of the land and how near to her goal the army might take her.

She cleared her throat. "The Tolemak do speak of Vinvinnysee. What be this place?"

He glanced at her through eyes slitted against the sun. "'Tis a great city, fortified with many walls, said to house ten thousand folk, if travelers' tales be true. They say, too, it's stood unbreached since long before Prince Adan stole the Crown of Tolem and broke the Kingdom."

Their horses had picked a path slightly apart from the main body, and the untrodden grass brushed their stirrups. Naed reached down and pulled several heads of sweetgrass. "Tumin merchants traded with Vinvinnysee ere the city's Masters broke their word and sent their Lancers to shed our blood in the Northern Wars." Instead of putting the blossoms in his mouth and chewing out the nectar, he crushed them and flung them away.

The scent of succulent, fully ripened sweetgrass made her mouth water. "Lancers?" she said, picking several blossoms.

"Cowards who fight with long lances or spears. They hide behind head-to-toe armor only the most precisely placed arrow can pierce. A man with a mere sword dreads meeting one."

Aerid watched him rip and shred more purple heads. "You've lost kin to them, then."

"Second eldest brother, two cousins."

The purple grass suddenly smelled over-ripe, sickeningly sweet. She opened her fingers, letting the blossoms drop between them. "'Tis clear to me now why you do ride with the Tolemak against my people. You have much reason to hate them."

Naed snorted. "'Tis no love lost among my kin for either Adanak word weavers or Tolemak warmongers. Both insult us and ignore our borders. Mayhap, I ride today alongside the very Tolemaks who killed my uncle and wounded my father in the siege of Tumin." He wiped his hands on his leggings. "My people follow the ancient way of Prince D'nal. When Adan stole the Crown, D'nal refused to choose between his elder and his younger brothers. The people of D'nalee have chosen to maintain his neutrality, but, if truth be told—" His face turned dull red as he examined sweet-grass stains on his palm. "—most say Adan was a thief and a liar, and his folk have followed him. The Tolemak, for all their bloody ways, have at least some honor. They mean what they say, and they fight as we do, face-to-face."

Aerid could scarcely believe her ears, scarcely believe Naed, who had defended her countless times at Druemarwin and was even risking his life for her, could have uttered such slurs against her people, could even— *Sisters forbid!*—believe them, but his careful avoidance of her eyes confirmed the unthinkable. Her fingers tightened on the gray mare's reins, digging short nails into her palms. "I see. The difference between my people and others does seem to lie in how close to one's hands a man spatters his opponent's blood."

Naed stifled a groan. "'Tis not possible for you to understand. You are a woman and—"

"Understand what? Honor?"

"Aye! And courage! And skill!"

"My people possess none of these?"

He rolled his eyes. "I knew you'd take ill of my words. But, Aerid, 'tis true you know little of your own kind. How could you, living so long at Druemarwin?"

Naed had a point, but she refused to either unbend her ramrod spine or unfix her straight-ahead stare. "Perhaps, since 'tis certain I must go forward into Adanak, 'tis like I'll soon be learning enough to judge for myself."

Her remark brought fresh color to Naed's cheeks. His horse danced sideways, then, at his sudden lash of reins, bolted.

Aerid opened her mouth, but he had already galloped out of range of her apology. The remark was cruel, even if true. Yet it was not Naed's fault she had stayed so long with the army. He had tried his best, taken enormous risks on her behalf, and kept her safe this far. But if what he said about D'nalian beliefs was true throughout the land, 'twas all the more reason to forget going to Tumin and to instead try finding her kin.

****

Naed slowed his horse. Tolemaks scowled at him for raising dust, but he returned glare for glare. They detested him. He cared not a Bedian pig's whisker what they thought. His D'nalian comrades avoided him. The intolerant cowards were not worth their weight in paving stone. Krenin wanted his blood. Naed slapped dust from his leggings. *Let the bastard eat that!*

And the Prince? Naed slouched in his saddle. The Prince had spoken to him but once since Druemarwin. Still, he had relived his memory of the conversation, the Prince's expression, over and over until he had nearly convinced himself those assessing gray eyes had, momentarily at least, glinted with something like satisfaction. Or was it approval? Naed knew he should not care what a Tolemak thought, but this Tolemak had bested him. And given his life back.

But at what price?

Naed slumped lower into his saddle. Aerid hated him now. He had told only the truth about her people and his, but he should have known better than to speak of that. Everything he had done involving her burned like a candle at both ends. He slashed at a cloud of gnats floating about his head. Why had he not taken a chance at the river and run with her? He could have taken her to Tumin himself. He could have asked his mother to accept her as his...as his...

He ground the heels of his hands into his eyes. What was the good of imagining choices when he had none? Better to face the truth—he could no more alter the Will of the Sisters than he could the dictates of D'nalian honor. Both bound him to the Prince, bound Aerid to a boy's identity, and bound all of them on the road to Vinvinnysee. He could do nothing but let his horse's plodding gait take him onward.

****

The army made camp on the west bank of a clear, twisting river. Long after sunset, Aerid carried water skins to the bank. Kneeling in tall, reedy grass, she cupped her hand and lifted the liquid to her mouth. Errant drops ran like bits of ice into the neck of her tunic, making her gasp. She wiped her skin, and the water beading on her hand sparkled in the light of a half moon.

The urge to wash, to untie her hair and let swift, pure water swirl through its length overcame her with such power she lowered her head before sense ruled. Suspended between shore and surface, she stared at her shadow on the water.

The possibility of finding her kin thrilled her. The thought of striking out on her own left her disquieted. She had grown accustomed to life as a boy, speaking in grunts, keeping her head down like the runt in a wolf pack, living with men who swore, spat, belched, scratched, gamed and joked without the least thought a woman walked among them.

The Tolemak whose back she had stitched—Grodar, he said his name was—and his companion Morys, nodded a greeting whenever they saw her. Two days ago, Grodar

58

showed her how well his wound was mending by playfully punching her in the shoulder. She had dropped her armload of firewood, and Morys laughed, but both helped her pick up the sticks. Yester eve, while bedding the horses, she had seen them stroll past her fire-pit and surreptitiously drop something next to it. When she walked over to investigate, she found a freshly killed rabbit.

It had run between the horses' feet, she told Naed and Yormoc later, and the gray mare had stepped on it.

"I'd not make charms of this rabbit's feet." Yormoc tore into a roasted thigh.

Naed regarded Aerid over the meat spitted on his knife. She sensed he did not believe her, but with Yormoc present, he would not dispute it. Since the quarrel, he had closed himself off from her, speaking so little he had become a stranger.

She sat on her heels and stared into the water. Her mind swirled, as confused as the eddies. After what had happened in Druemarwin's courtyard, she would never have expected Tolemaks to "adopt" a D'nalian, much less a disfigured one. Yet, if Grodar and Morys knew who and what she really was, 'twould be no such "gifts" at her fire-pit. They raped and murdered her people. 'Twould do her well to remember that, no matter how nice they might—

A splash?

Aerid shrank down in the tall grass, fingers curling around the hilt of her healer's knife. Her gaze swept the far shore, searching the ink pooled under an unbroken line of trees.

Nothing.

She scanned right and left as far as she could see without moving her head.

No one.

Yet the sound again, like water disturbed. She stared at the glittering surface, at something dark that glided slowly toward the near shore and grew steadily, as if rising out of the river.

Aerid's blood roared in her ears. She wanted to rock to her feet and run, but her knees locked and everything beneath seemed boneless, numb. Helpless, she stared as the figure paused and the faint moon silvered it.

A head, two limbs, and a torso took shape. The head shook, spraying water from thick hair. The limbs lifted, hands slicked the hair from a face all angles and planes. The torso tapered lean and long from a chest and shoulders corded with muscle to narrow hips, long, powerful thighs, and sculpted calves. The man, for the moonlight left no doubt in Aerid's mind about his masculinity, climbed onto the bank not twenty paces away and bent to a pile of clothing.

A flush crept up Aerid's throat. Her heart pounded. Though she had drunk her fill moments ago, her indrawn breath sucked her mouth dry. *The Prince! Sisters Three, she had been gawking at the Prince himself!*

He pivoted at her gasp. Aerid heard the scrape of drawn steel, saw the glint of his longsword blade.

"Who's there?" he hissed.

By the Sisters, he would kill her if she did not identify herself! Squeaking out, "P-pardon, m'lord, but I—uh—'tis water I've come for," Aerid lunged forward, groping in the grass for the water skins. Her fingers closed on one and plunged it into the river with such force she nearly fell in after it. Her reward was a breath-sucking backsplash of frigid water on her face, arms, and chest.

A hand fisted in her tunic dragged her back and sat her upright, gasping, on shore. A voice, surprisingly gentle, said, "If you fancied a swim, boy, 'twould be best to undress first."

Undress! Aerid flushed to the roots of her hair. A scant moment ago she had been staring at the very naked Prince of Val-Feyridge. Now he hunkered down so close, she could smell the water-fresh man-scent of him, feel his body heat radiating into her very pores. She peeked through waterlogged lashes and saw, to her relief, he had pulled on his breeches. Scooting back a few inches, she swiped at her face with her sleeve.

He was still too near, face in shadow as eyes but a glimmer scrutinized her. "You're the D'nalian boy."

'Twas not a question, but she felt compelled to nod, as if her confirmation might deflect the penetrating gaze that trapped her between an icy river and a wall of lithe-limbed manhood. For all the lean spareness his height emphasized, this close she could see what his tunic concealed: shoulders and chest as broad as the bull-like Dranoel's, and a body corrugated with the kind of muscle that made a man powerful yet lightning-quick.

Dry-mouthed, Aerid realized she was staring again. Ducking her flushed face, she shuffled to her knees and fumbled in the grass for another of the water skins.

Their hands collided on the skin's neck.

Aerid jerked back as though snake-bitten. The Prince's shadowed eyes drilled into her, and she realized she had made a mistake. Aerid tried to cover for it by seizing another water skin and plunging it into the river, but even as he leaned over beside her and dipped the first skin into the water, she knew his gaze remained upon her, watching her every move.

"Your master shouldn't have sent you out here alone."

With fingers all thumbs, she stoppered the skin and tied it tight. "To my way of thinking, m'lord, there be two of us here."

He swiveled, and Aerid slapped a hand to her mouth. *Sisters, could she not keep her tongue firmly in her mouth?* Just because he had startled her, coming up out of the water like that—*naked!*—she still ought to be able to keep her wits about her. As a healer, she had seen many a naked man, treated all manner of bodily ailments. This one, for all his nearness, should be no different, except this body needed no treatment.

He straightened, rising head and shoulders above her. "Are you as outspoken as your master, or is this but a momentary lapse in character?"

Clutching the water skin to her chest, Aerid cringed, unable to nod or speak.

"'Tis uncommon enough to find a warrior's heart in a lowlander." He levered to his feet, bringing a naked broadsword up from the grass with him. "'Twould be rarer still to find it in one such as you."

She sat on her heels, gaping at the impossible height of him and the unexpected hint of amusement in his voice, until she realized he expected an answer. Face aflame, she scooped up the water skin he had filled and, under the weight of both full pouches, struggled to her feet. "'Twas not to fight that I did come, m'lord. 'Twas but to heal what you and others break."

"Ah, I see, a true son of D'nal." The Prince plucked a scabbard from the grass and slid his blade into it. "You believe a man should fight only to defend what is his."

Aerid's senses screamed at her to admit nothing, to avoid his eyes, to return to camp, but his smug tone drew her response before she could shut her mouth. "'Tis only right."

"Indeed." He buckled the sword belt and, slinging belt and scabbard over one bare shoulder, regarded her with hands on hips. "Then tell me, boy, why is it your people find themselves the ones always being trodden on?"

'Twas not too late to escape. All she had to do was sidle away from the riverbank and mumble noncommittally—if she could ignore the derision in the Prince's stance. Her chin ratcheted up a notch. "Because, m'lord, men be naught but fools and savages."

He looked her up and down the way she had seen the Druemarwin men, from the least kitchen boy to Dranoel himself, take the measure of an opponent. "I'll grant you there are fools enough in the world. They align themselves with some ideal, group, or person, and when that proves false, have neither the wit nor the will to break away. But as to savages..." He bent and tugged on a boot. "Scratch any man, no matter how fine and cultured his surface, and 'tis sure you'll find a savage beneath. My people are simply less deceptive about our underpinnings."

Aerid fumed. His look made her respond exactly as she had seen the scrutinized opponent respond—with narrowed eyes and closed fists—but the Prince seemed oblivious to her irritation, bending instead to pull on his other boot. "And that does justify taking what you would possess by force?"

He had the gall to smile while scooping his tunic from the grass. "Would it suit your D'nalian sensibilities if I took it the way the Adanak do, by guile? 'Tis the same in the end, my gain and another's loss. You D'nalians are fond of discoursing about honor. Tell me, is it more honorable to give a man a chance to fight, or to sneak behind his back and steal him blind?"

The way the Adanak do. Aerid's tongue itched to refute the implied slur, but her better judgment reminded her he believed her to be D'nalian. Taking a moment to adjust the water skins, she tried to frame a careful, D'nalian response.

Crack!

The Prince dropped into a crouch, spinning, sword a silver blur in his hand.

Petrified, Aerid stared at an enormous, gleaming, mounted giant exploding from the brush and pointing directly at her the most monstrously long spear she had ever seen. The water skins slid unheeded from her arms.

"Down!"

The Prince slammed into Aerid, his arm a clamp dragging her to the ground, his weight crushing her body prone in the grass, his hand shoving her face into damp, pebbled earth. Bits of stone stabbed at her cheeks and chin. There was a roar of hoofbeats, earth shaking under her body, a spasmodic tightening of his grip, and then silence.

He rolled away, hauled her upright with him, his face ghastly in the moonlight. "Lancers! Warn the camp!"

Thirty yards away, the armored horseman wheeled his mount. The spear swung around, a slow, graceful, bird-of-prey circling that held Aerid mesmerized.

"Go!" The Prince shoved her toward the trees. "Run!"

Aerid staggered backward, fell. Under her hands, the ground trembled. The odor of raw-turned earth and broken grass bit at her nostrils. Scrambling up on shaking limbs, she launched herself at the trees and the camp beyond. She heard the thunder of hooves, the crack of steel on wood, the rend of cloth. Stumbling, she retched but dared not vomit or look back. The Lancer would be after her next, riding her down, driving that spear, that awful, grotesque thing from a nightmare, into her back.

Screaming, "Lancers! The Lancers are coming!" she plunged headlong through bordering trees and burst into camp.

Tolemak soldiers erupted from tents and bedding. They scattered from fire-pits and carts, seized swords, shields, bows, logs, pots, anything they could lay hands upon as armored, mounted men crashed through bushes

63

and leveled deadly lances. One Lancer flung a torch onto a lean-to as he swept past it. Dry firs hissed and snapped, flames roaring up and rushing toward the next shelter, the sudden heat searing Aerid's face. She veered away, away from tethered horses that reared and squealed, from half a dozen men who leaped at a Lancer and dragged him from his horse, from arrows whizzing everywhere and splintering on trees. She dodged between wagons, panting, throat a raw line of pain, searching for her campsite, for safety, for Naed.

Stumbling into the open, she saw him some 20 yards away, charging from between tents to hack with his sword at a Lancer's spear. The Lancer's horse hurtled past, clipping Naed and careening his body to the ground. With a little whimper, Aerid lurched forward to help him, but he sprang up at once. With his forearm a bloody smear, he raised his sword and roared.

The primal sound stopped Aerid short. She backed a step, shaken by the savagery profiled on a face she thought she knew.

Across the open space, Naed roared again. Sword gripped in both hands, he charged another Lancer. The Lancer veered, angled his spear at Naed's torso, and heeled his horse. Naed raised his sword, but the lance caught him in the side, folding his body toward the spear. With a savage thrust, the rider plunged the lance into the ground and galloped past it.

Aerid staggered, knees weak, mouth open. She thought she was screaming, but she could not tell over the rushing blood in her ears and the thundering of her heart. She stumbled in the direction of Naed's body and the lance impaling him to the ground. She would pull it out, she would stop the blood, she would—

Hoofbeats pounding closer brought her head around, slowly, like motion in a dream. Horse and shining, armored rider, gauntleted hand reaching out, galloped toward the lance he had left quivering above his victim. With a blood-curdling laugh, he wrenched it free of Naed's body and spurred straight at her.

Aerid bolted. Her panicked brain told her she could reach the trees, could outrun a horse. She knew she could not when pain exploded through her body. Suddenly, through streaks of colored light, she flew toward a black pit that opened wide and sucked her into it.

CHAPTER SIX

Consciousness returned with soft light, voices, a gradual increase of sensation allowing movement of fingers, toes. Something cool seeped into the hair at the back of her neck.

Voices. Again.

"The bastards scattered Yarl's horses from here to the Four Winds! They'd have torched the supply wagons if Gorm's men hadn't driven them off! How many were there, a hundred?"

"Only twenty. Illien counted the tracks."

A shadow crossed Aerid's face. She frowned and opened heavy-lidded eyes. The Prince stood in profile a few feet away, head brushing a tent ceiling, hands clasped at his back, hair a disordered shock of black. The hem of his tunic was ripped, a hole at his hip exposing grass-stained breeches. Something about that hole stirred her memory, but before her mind dredged up details, the Prince moved, and she found herself looking across a table at his Second, Krenin. In the yellow lamplight, Krenin's eyes were like a hawk's, low-browed and intent on the Prince.

"Twenty! Why those tin-headed stew pots! They made the Demon's own mess of the camp. And 'tis sure we well enough let them! That tripe from Druemarwin ran like women. I told you we should have butchered the lot."

She wished Krenin would not talk so loudly. Every syllable jarred her brain.

"'Tis of no account. What matters is this: we were surprised—twice—by what appear to be small, hand-picked forces whose intent is to hit us and run." Unclasping his hands, the Prince picked up from the table a narrow piece of wood about a man's forearm long.

Through eyes still hazed, Aerid saw one end was jagged, as though broken. The end the Prince rubbed a fingertip over was sharpened to a point and looked

66

stained, but she could not imagine why it should be.

"Terrorize and demoralize. Do you recognize the tactics?"

"Bloody bastards! Turning our tricks back at us! They've made fools of us!"

Aerid winced. She wanted to cover her ears, but her arms felt weighted with lead. She managed instead to turn her face toward the tent's ceiling. Overhead, it slanted steeply down, forming a sleeping place of a raised, wood-frame bed covered with skins on which she lay. Puzzled, she wondered how she had come to be in what was clearly the Prince's own tent when the last thing she remembered was—

"'Twill be my personal pleasure to skewer our captive on his own bloody stick!"

She wished Krenin would leave. The Prince at least spoke softly and calmly.

"I want the Lancer alive. For a little longer."

"He'll not talk. Those tinheads never do."

"Nonetheless, strip him and march him throughout the camp. I want our men to see what hides behind such armor and weaponry."

They caught one. Good, Aerid's fogged mind celebrated. *At least one Lancer would not be going about terrifying people and—*

"Aye, good. Show the men there's naught to fear."

"Strip the dead and hang the bodies in trees. Make sure seeing them will make Gaelwynn think twice before sending his pride-and-joy Lancers at us again."

"Oh, aye. I'll prick them with their own knife. 'Twill be my pleasure to teach the word weavers to try Tolemak tactics against masters of the trick!"

Something in Krenin's voice made Aerid's stomach clench. A wave of nausea swept over her, but she bit her lip against it.

"But first, dispatch messages to Nemmon and Tylus, telling them what's happened here. Set Gorm to tally the casualties, put his men on the sentry line, and send the men about my tent to help Yarl. Aye, you know I've no need of guards when the whole camp is alerted. 'Tis more important we catch our horses." Krenin grumbled something Aerid could not decipher before the Prince spoke again. "And wake me the moment the messenger from Druemarwin arrives."

A stronger nauseous wave followed the first. Aerid wished Krenin would leave. For reasons she could not quite remember, she dared not move while he stayed.

"You're sure there's a spy, then?"

"With every one of my bones. Gaelwynn knows more than he should about our whereabouts. By the Demon, I'd give anything to lay hands on Gaelwynn's informant."

"Dranoel's nephew, 'tis sure. Say the word and I'll gut the bastard for you myself."

"In good time, if and when 'tis true."

There was the crunch of departing footsteps, but another lurch of Aerid's stomach cut short her relief. When the spasm passed, she turned and saw the Prince standing alone at the table, apparently studying parchments strewn about the base of an oil lamp. He plucked at one roll, moved another, then leaned heavily on one arm and rubbed his free hand across his brow. In the lamplight, his face had gone as gray as his eyes and his cheeks looked sunken, the flesh stretched tight across the prominent bones.

Another round of queasiness seized Aerid. Drawing up her legs, she hugged her stomach.

When she opened her eyes, Prince Arn was settling himself on a stool at her bedside. He smiled, a faint creasing of stubbled cheeks rather than a pull of lips. Fine lines crinkled the corners of his eyes, but his color was sallow for someone so white-skinned. Before her healer's mind could wrap itself around the incongruity, his image blurred and wobbled.

"So, the D'nalian warrior's returned at last," he said over the buzzing in her ears. "'Twas such a pleasant rest you were having, I suppose, that you—steady, now."

How he managed to produce a bucket, raise her up and bend her over it was more than Aerid's aching head could assimilate. She only knew as she sat back and wiped her mouth, that she had vomited in front of the Prince of Val-Feyridge and he, as calmly as if it happened every day, was setting the bucket aside and handing her his own pewter mug filled with water.

"Y-your pardon, m'lord." He was altogether too close,

sitting at her right shoulder and near enough for his breath to stir the air between them. Wrapping hands around the mug, Aerid fixed her gaze on the neutral territory of the tent wall and tried to think. There had been a raid. She remembered running, yelling, from...somewhere. Her head still ached and she was not sure why. "How—how did I come to be here, m'lord?" she said between sips.

"I found you just outside. 'Tis like you were struck soon after you raised the alarm."

A vision of cruel eyes seen through metal slits sent a chill crawling up Aerid's spine. *The lance!* Heart thudding, she mentally checked her body, discreetly flexing limbs, muscles. Everything felt intact and functional, except for a dull ache across her entire upper right shoulder, but the discomfort was minor compared to that radiating from the back of her head. And that was minor compared to what she would have suffered had she not somehow escaped the lance. Something else had struck her, the horse, perhaps, but—*Sisters be thanked!*—she had not been trampled. She let out a breath she did not realize she had been holding, then abruptly sucked it in again.

Inches away, she sensed the Prince's scrutiny, saw in her peripheral vision how he leaned forward with elbows on knees and hands clasped, watching her with those penetrating eyes that missed nothing. "You've not had the sense knocked out of you before, have you? 'Tis one thing to tend injuries, quite another to suffer them. But fear not, this muddle-headedness will pass."

Aerid clung to the mug she had sipped dry, holding it as if she could divine from the bowl a critical piece missing from her memory, a piece that might tell her how to interpret the peculiar wash of sensations his gentle voice and too-close presence inspired in her body. There was fear, most definitely. He was her enemy, and she must not forget that, ever. She had every right to be wary of him, to watch him with the coiled tension of a rabbit watching a hawk. Yet there was this strange heat that swept too readily to her cheeks when he was near, this heightened sensitivity of the tiny hairs on her body to his every word, movement, gesture that had no connection to terror or wariness. Preoccupied with the contradiction, she offered no resistance when the Prince removed the mug from her grip and set it aside.

"Now," he said, reaching for the neck of her tunic and pulling loose the lacings, "let's see if you've a reason to be favoring that right arm. Or is it the shoulder?"

One hand was at her nape, long fingers probing businesslike down her spine, the other had pushed the tunic off her shoulder before Aerid's sluggish brain could fix on one panicked thought: *Sisters Three, here was the Demon himself skating fingers over her naked skin!*

"*Mortraeder!*" she erupted, shoving him with both hands square in the chest. "Take your hands from me!"

Prince Arn rocked back and might have fallen from his stool but for the hand still wound in her tunic. The homespun ripped a few inches. Aerid seized his fingers, meaning to twist the fabric from his grip, to sink her teeth into his wrist. She had angled her head over his arm when she realized he had gone stock still. An icicle of panic arrowed through her belly. She shot a glance upward and saw blank astonishment mirrored in his eyes.

"What the Demon—?"

He stared at her chest. Gulping, she saw her breast-binding partially exposed and, worse, an edge of Dranoel's letter protruding from the hollow at the center. "No, 'tis mine!" she cried, but her fingers grabbed at air.

"This bears the seal of Lord Dranoel." Eyes narrowed to slits, Prince Arn looked to her from the letter he held between thumb and fingertips. "And 'tis addressed to the Lord of Tumin."

"'Tis mine...to deliver."

"We've long since passed the way to Tumin."

The cool deadliness of his tone made her throat close. Gone so completely was the solicitous expression of moments ago she wondered if she had dreamed it. Instead, he loomed above her, beard shadow and black brows throwing his features into stark, terrifying relief.

"From the very first, I've wondered about you. 'Twas only the face, I thought, that mark and living in that Sisters-forsaken marsh made you strange, even for a D'nalian. But now I think 'tis naught I can *see* that's left me puzzled." Gaze pinning her to the bed, the Prince raised the letter to his nose. "'Tis what I can *smell*."

Aerid flushed from head to toe. The letter had spent weeks between her breasts, and now the Demon himself was breathing in her pure scent!

"'Tis not evenroot alone, though there's always that about you. And redroot, too, but why? 'Tis hardly a healer's herb." He inhaled again. "'Tis more for color—" Over the letter, his eyes darkened. Their wide-open stare fixed on the stained side of her face.

Aerid's mouth went dry. Something coiling in the pit of her stomach prompted her to snatch the frayed edges of her tunic and snap them together under her chin.

His nostrils flared in a face gone to granite. Only his mouth worked, hissing out, "Sisters be damned if you—" before he flung the letter aside.

Aerid shrieked at his lunge, crossing her arms over her chest, fearing he meant to rip apart her breast-binding. Instead, his hand went straight to the V of her breeches and closed on her most private place. She recoiled as if lightning-struck.

The Prince sprang away from her, toppling the stool, his expression a rapid sequence of disbelief, astonishment, and fury. "You!" he choked. "You Adanak *witch!* All this time...right in front of me...right in front of my whole damned army!"

Both hands snared Aerid's tunic. Like so much clothing, he hauled her off the bed and held her, dangling, inches from his face. Up close, the scar was a pinched blue line in a murderous face. "You bloody spy! Were you all in it? Dranoel's nephew and the lot?"

She shook her head and pried at his fingers, unable to speak or even breathe.

"How did you signal your countrymen, you shape-changing witch?" He shook her, rattling her teeth. "By the Demon, I'll make you tell me how!"

Blackness flitted at the edge of Aerid's vision. Her head throbbed. She had to get away, to break his grip before, before—

Her feet touched ground. Instinctively, she pushed off and found a foothold on his knee. Gripping his wrists for leverage, she pulled her other leg up and kicked.

They dropped into a heap on the packed earth floor.

Aerid broke away, rammed her shoulder into a tent pole, and sat panting until her surroundings stopped their crazy tilting. "*Not*," she bit out as soon as she had breath, "a spy!"

The Prince rolled into a crouch, left arm hugged to his abdomen, eyes glazed with fury. Pain, too? Aerid took in the dilated pupils, watching as he reached for the table's edge and slowly pulled himself up. She had not kicked him that hard, had she? 'Twas a trick to draw on her sympathy. Had he not already used her oath against her at the river crossing? Brandishing her healer's knife, she rose, using the tent pole for support while her head rang with dull thunder.

"You expect me to believe that?" Upright now, shoulders still hunched, he rasped, "After this?"

Part of Aerid's brain told her to push away from the pole and run. Hobbled as he was, he could not possibly stop her. Not without the guards he had sent away. And she had her knife, too. Another part of her brain heard the derision in his tone. She had deceived his army, true, but she never intended any harm, any treachery. She was *not* a spy! Snatching Dranoel's letter from the ground, she thrust it at him. "Read the letter! 'Twas intended I go to Tumin. Within a week I should have been gone from your—your infernal, bloody army!"

"A week has long since passed." Not even glancing at the object in her outstretched hand, he backed a step along the edge of the table. "What happened? Naed change his mind? Or did he panic?" Between strands of wild-flung hair his eyes gleamed, flat and dark, like a snake's eyes.

A frisson of danger feathered along Aerid's spine. She tightened her grip on the knife and countered his move. "We did not spy! Naed did mean only to save me from your orders! Do not deny you did mean to have me killed!"

"I should have killed you when I first saw you. Stupid of me not to. Look how much trouble I could have saved."

His words so stunned Aerid, it took her precious seconds to realize he had backed nearly far enough to put the table between them. "Stop! Do not move! Or I shall have to, to—"

"Kill me? Isn't that contrary to your healer's oath? Or

does it allow you to close your eyes to the men who die as a result of your spying?"

"I did not spy!" Aerid cried, slamming the letter so hard on the table, the oil lamp teetered. She gasped. One drop of burning oil would ignite the parchments and send the tent up in flames. Without thinking, she reached to steady the lamp.

The Prince lunged. He seized her wrist, jerking her knife hand forward, slamming her bruised shoulder into his chest. His other hand snagged her free hand, forcing it across her body, holding her clamped at the waist while he battered the knife hand against his knee.

The first blow loosened her fingers. Biting back a whimper, Aerid willed her fingers to tighten, but they seemed to have forgotten how. Instead, the purpled digits opened while she stared at them, and the knife hilt slid through them, her last chance for freedom, for safety, for life itself, dropping uselessly to the ground.

No! She could not let him kill her, could not let her life end here, now, at the hands of this *mortraeder!*

With a feral snarl, Aerid exploded in the Prince's arms, bucking, twisting, snapping teeth at anything within reach until, suddenly, she tore free. She bolted for the tent flap, but the hand still manacled to her left wrist yanked her arm nearly out of its socket. With a yelp of pain, she recoiled face-first into the solid bone of his shoulder. She caught a glimpse of bared teeth, a twisted mouth, then she was floundering in air.

Her legs took only seconds to recover their balance, but the sticky wetness streaked across her palm sent everything else careening out of control. Scant feet away, the Prince stood with a white-knuckled grip on the table's edge and eyes squeezed shut. His left arm hung slack by his side, a dark stain spreading across his tunic over the shoulder between the bladebone and the spine. Aerid looked from his shoulder to her bloody hand. By the Sisters, had she somehow stabbed him? Her knees trembled.

"I, 'twas not my intent to hurt—"

He choked out a laugh but did not look at her. "That puny knife of yours didn't cut me. 'Twas your countryman." He laughed again, a short, bitter sound.

"Demon take me for a fool, but if I'd guessed who you were, 'tis sure I'd have left you for that lance."

The river. The lance. The Prince pushing her down, flinching as the rider swept past. Aerid's blood ran hot, searing her with the knowledge he had been hurt saving her life. He had thought her D'nalian then, but that scarcely altered the balance. Tolemaks cared for none but their own kind. Princes, of all folk, would not—should not—be expected to trouble themselves over the life of a mere boy. A prince should protect himself first. Yet this one had not.

Swaying, she closed her eyes. Whatever he thought she was, he had nonetheless saved her. She had to get out. Run away. Take that life and live it elsewhere while she had the chance.

Opening her eyes, she saw the bloodstain on his tunic had widened. A red drip line bloomed over his hip. Her practiced eye told her this was no little cut, but a gash requiring stitching, especially now she had jarred the clotting loose. Maybe even widened the gash. Aerid's stomach knotted. Her oath required her to do no harm, and here she had both caused and worsened a wound. She took a tentative step toward him.

His gaze skewered her. "What are you, a complete and utter fool? Run! And take your D'nalian lover with you! By the Demon, if I get my hands on you again—"

"'Tis *dead* he be! And how? Fighting a Lancer all by himself, for *you!*"

The words hung in the air before the full import of what had spewed from her mouth crashed over Aerid. *Naed? Dead?* She staggered, clammy with shock, while her mind's eye showed her over and over again the spear driving into Naed's torso. "Sisters damn you! All of you!" Jamming a fist to her mouth, she spun and ran blindly out of the tent.

****

Arn stared at the swinging tent flap and the darkness beyond. Then he bent slowly and deliberately, righted the stool, and sank onto it. With his good hand, he gripped his right knee until it ceased trembling. He would have to send men after the Adanak witch, but not now, not until he could face them with the show of strength they expected from their leader, their Prince. By the Demon, he had suffered worse wounds and barely broken stride except to have the wound wrapped. Sometimes he had gone without even that, feeling no pain until Krenin or Illien or Nemmon had seen the blood. More than once it had taken all three of them to contain him long enough to have his injury tended. Why should this...*scratch* be any different?

'Twas the witch's doing.

He rubbed his abdomen. Her kick had taken him by surprise, and he cursed himself. How could he have been so blind as to not see a *woman* right in front of his face? No wonder he had been so drawn to the "boy." Arn forced out a laugh. All this time his instincts had told him true, but he had convinced himself 'twas only the boy's disfigurement, nothing else, that made him take an interest in the D'nalian. That the witch had made him wonder, even for a moment, about his own inclinations was proof enough of her power.

Bending, Arn retrieved his mug from the ground near his bed. A few drops of blood had collected at the foot of his stool, and when he straightened, his vision swam for an instant. A little water would clear his head. He set the mug on the table and saw next to it a folded piece of parchment. The paper curved up from the tabletop, retaining the shape of the place where it had been concealed these many weeks. *The shape of the place...*

Arn sat immobile as his mind absorbed the full import of where the letter had so recently resided. Even now, her scent lingered in his nostrils. And his fingers— he stared at them as though they belonged to a stranger— his fingers tingled with the memory of her skin, its color in this light like copper and...cream. Her hair, especially at the nape, as silky and warm against his palm as he had imagined weeks ago...

With a snarl, he slapped his hand down on the parchment, flattening it. By the Demon, he would *break* this spell! 'Twas only because he was wounded and tired that she affected him at all. With rest and mending, he would be free of her power.

Relaxing his hand, Arn's fingers drifted across the letter's seal, surprised to find it smooth and unbroken.

The witch was obviously a spy. The messenger from Druemarwin would confirm what his own eyes and ears had told him. He had no need to see what Dranoel had written. It would be lies anyway, or written under duress. With Naed dead, and the witch exposed, the letter could be nothing of significance.

Unless it might somehow point to other spies.

He had read the salutation when he heard the tent flap rustle. "Fetch a healer," he said without looking at the figure that came in from the dark, "and then find Master of Archers Illien."

A battered leather bag with many pouches thumped onto the table, inches from the letter. "What in the name of the—!" Arn sputtered, turning.

A pair of slanted cat's eyes, brilliant blue but red-rimmed and swollen, pinned him to his stool with a glare of pure defiance. "'Tis your healer I be, m'lord, for once and no more, for 'tis my fault you be injured, and 'tis my duty to make you well."

CHAPTER SEVEN

Aerid shook like a dry leaf in the breeze. From her belly to her limbs, every muscle trembled. 'Twas partly shock, a reaction to her injury and the impact of Naed's death, but 'twas also fear, for this man she stood before—foolishly and idiotically exposing herself to—could rise from his stool and kill her. In *his* mind, the Prince had every right to. And she had absolutely no reason to return to him and place her life in jeopardy.

No reason except the most important, not returning would be contrary to her oath, to everything she was and stood for. She had caused his injury and worsened it. If she did not treat it, she could not call herself a healer. Even if it meant her life, she had to do her duty.

The Prince stared, his face even sallower. Aerid noted the worsening drip line and the dark spot near his foot. He seemed stunned into immobility by her reappearance, so she used the opportunity to act as her training had taught her. Finding a basin, she filled it with water and set it on the parchments littering the table. She tossed in a pinch of ground willow bark and another of powdered gumstone, the first to clean the wound, the second to speed clotting. She added a cloth, stirred everything, and reached for his tunic neck to unlace it.

He seized her wrist before her fingers could make contact. "What kind of *fool* are you?"

She closed her eyes against the violence emanating from him. She ought to be terrified, but she felt suddenly, simply numb. At least she had chosen her fate, and she had chosen with integrity. Drawing a long breath, Aerid let it sigh out through parted lips.

When she opened her eyes, the Prince had swiveled on the stool and entrapped her between his knees. Their bodies were mere handspans apart and, with him seated, she actually looked *down* at his face. The sensation was heady, and she indulged it, gazing upon a wide forehead with beads of moisture visible between strands of disordered hair, black brows pinched together with, what? Rage? Or pain? Thick eyelashes framed pewter gray eyes glittering with a hint of fever. Taut lips. And pallid cheeks shadowed with stubble except where the scar ran like a silvery seam down the left side. She raised her free hand toward his forehead, intent on testing the temperature of his skin.

"Don't!" He reared away as though from a deadly snake.

This was too much. If she were to lose her life for returning to treat him, then treat him she would! She gave her imprisoned wrist a shake. "Who be the fool now? 'Tis sure I be, m'lord, for I've come to render *you* aid, and of my own choice. But you fight me like a wild beast that knows no better. There be fresh blood on the floor, and 'tis not mine. Would you faint for loss of it?"

The Prince glowered, all black brows and narrowed eyes. She feared she had spoken too sharply until she realized the gaze peering at her from under fierce brows had become assessing. He tilted his head toward the bowl. "How do I know what you've put in there, *witch*?"

She rolled her eyes; he had watched her mix it, after all. With her free hand she shoved the basin toward him. "Smell it! You've a nose for herbs, or so it seemed before!" Aerid flushed at the memory of how he inhaled her scent on Dranoel's letter, but she refused to break eye contact. When he leaned toward the basin and sniffed, she added, "And while you be about it, m'lord, you could be freeing my hand, for I've need of both to tend you."

He straightened away from the basin. The same assessing gaze traveled down her body, halting at her chest before flicking back to her face. "Put your knife on the table."

She grasped her sheath, found it empty, and remembered how the Prince battered her healer's knife out of her hand. Her wrist still ached. "'Tis where it fell." With a jerk of her chin, she indicated where the knife lay alongside his boot.

Again, he perused her with half-lidded eyes. "Pick it up and put it on the table."

That lingering, unreadable look left Aerid feeling

mutinous. She bent as far as his grip allowed, then stretched out her free arm to gather in the knife. Straightening, she slapped the blade down beside the basin, making the water in the bowl jump.

His gaze flicked once more to her chest as he released her. "And while *you* be about it, witch, lace your tunic."

Horrified, Aerid realized her tunic hung off one shoulder while the tear at the neck exposed part of her breast binding. With clumsy fingers, she pulled the tunic edges together and fastened the lacing. The rip would need mending, but for now she was at least decently covered.

Decent.

By the Sisters, she had been *decent*, as her breasts had been fully covered! Besides, 'twas *his* fault her tunic was ripped. *She* had no need to be embarrassed or discomfited. *Sisters Three!* Even if she were in the habit of showing herself to men like any common wench, the last man she would display for would be a Tolemak! Shooting him a glare, she reached for the neck of his tunic. "'Twill need to come off, m'lord."

"Tunic only. Not the necklace," he said, releasing a breath that, to her knowing ear, revealed how much moving his upper body pained him. While the Prince reached down his good hand and helped her raise the tattered longshirt over his head, her indignation evaporated. She tried not to touch him unnecessarily, but it was next to impossible, standing as she was between his thighs. His forehead bumped her collarbone, feathering his hair along her throat. 'Twas only an instant's contact, but her mouth went dry. His male scent, musky with his exertions, and the sweet odor of fresh blood filled her nostrils. Aerid tried to convince herself the heat washing over her was caused by the oil lamp confined in the tent space, but her senses knew full well it radiated from his body.

At the river, she had seen his form in the moonlit dark, smelled him wet and clean. Now she saw the dark hair that dusted his breastbone and descended in a narrow trail down the center of his rib cage. His abdomen was lean and hard and corrugated with more muscle than she had seen on most of the men she treated, even those who fancied themselves warriors. In the lamplight, his skin was not as white as she expected, despite the contrast between it and the worn leather thong dangling from his neck. A golden tint suggested he had gone shirtless in the sun. The same golden tint highlighted silvery scars of varying widths and lengths that revealed themselves on upper arms, lower arms, shoulders, chest, ribs, neck, even close beside the narrow wooden cylinder dangling over his heart.

Noticing her preoccupation, he said, "'Tis why I know my herbs."

Aerid looked up from under her lashes and noted, while he watched her closely, his face had grown more haggard. "'Tis a wonder you be still alive, m'lord," she said, easing out from the cage made by his thighs.

The Prince snorted while she filled his mug from a water skin and set it beside his good hand. "Most of those who cut me aren't so fortunate."

Out of the range of his body heat, she shuddered, but she told herself 'twas only because of the threat his words implied. Sucking in a deep breath, she opened her bag and laid out everything she needed to clean, stitch, salve, and bandage his wound. Last of all, she set before him a small pouch. "'Tis shepherds' bane," she said, risking a glance at his face. "For the pain."

Ignoring the pouch, he picked up the mug and sniffed it. "I prefer to keep my wits about me." Apparently satisfied she had added nothing to the water, he drank.

Indignation rushed through Aerid even though her mind told her the Prince had every reason to be suspicious. She was, after all, the enemy. Nonetheless, she retorted, "Then if you flinch, m'lord, do not blame me if the stitching be not straight."

"Fair enough." He pushed his empty mug toward her.

Compressing her lips, she poured more water into it. Then she walked around behind the stool, moved the lamp to throw light on his back and set to work.

It was an uncomplicated wound, long but not as deep as she had feared, and essentially clean. If he did not dislodge the stitching she carefully laid down, the wound would knit together nicely, leaving no more than another long, thin scar. While she worked, she wondered when he would react to the constant pricking and pulling. Each stick, she had been told often enough by men with clenched teeth, stung worse than a hornet, and the threading burned like dripping wax. Most men took a pinch of shepherd's bane or filled their stomachs with whatever liquor was at hand to endure the discomfort. The Prince sat entirely still, his breathing measured, as slow and steady as if he were trying to make the work easier for her. Aerid would have been convinced if she had not glimpsed his white-knuckled grip on the mug.

When she finished, he inhaled deeply and drank the mug dry.

She picked up a jar of unguent and gently spread it over the ladder of stitches. While she worked, her gaze drifted over the Prince's back, noting scar after scar. His skin was warm under her fingers and textured with fine, light hairs that conformed to the contours of muscle and bone, except where a scar interrupted, laying down a taut, smooth, pearlescent cord.

So many wounds. So much pain.

The thought surprised her. How could she feel sympathy for a man who caused so much death? Had he not implied, for each wound he had killed the man who hurt him? Killed that man and others? Too many others to count, if his reputation told true. With trembling hands, Aerid laid on a bandage. *And now?* she wondered as she ripped his discarded tunic into strips. She knew full well what would happen. As soon as she finished, he would kill *her!*

A whimper escaped her. She tried to cover it with a cough. Head bent to her work, she fastened the bandage by winding the cloth strips over his shoulder and around his ribs. She had planned to tie them off at his back—anything to avoid the Prince's eyes—but she ran out of cloth over his left ribs. Her fingers shook badly, but she managed to tie a passable knot.

"'Tis done," she murmured, eyes downcast, arms at her sides.

Silence.

For several beats the Prince neither moved nor spoke while Aerid's heart jabbed at her throat. Then, slowly, she sensed a coiling tension before he turned toward her and again entrapped her between his thighs. By then his hand, moving so subtly she had not noticed, had encircled her throat just above her birthstone. She trembled at the menace in the fingertips lightly touching her nape and the thumb ever so gently pressing against the pulse under her jaw.

"'Tis such a small, slender neck you have," he murmured while his thumb traced slow circles over her racing pulse.

Sensation rioted through Aerid. Prickly fear warred with something languid that unfurled deep in her abdomen, clenching and releasing. He looked at her with hooded, unreadable eyes, and her blood turned molten. She closed her eyes as a wave of heat swept up her body. *Sisters Three!* What a fool she had been! He was Tolemak. He would not simply *kill* her. She knew what his kind did to women.

"Look at me, witch!" His breath beat at her face while he tipped her head up.

"No!"

"Oh, aye, you will."

She felt him surge to his feet, felt herself hauled forward by fingertips snarled in the hair at her nape. Hips and thighs collided as her hands flailed for purchase, finding nothing to wind themselves in but the bandage she had fastened across his ribs. Against her stomach, hot and hardening, pressed all that made him a man. Aerid clenched her eyelids against the terror knifing through her. She was going to die and he was going to make her plead for it!

Panicked, she burst out, "If there be any mercy in you, m'lord, kill me now and quickly! 'Twas only to honor my healer's oath that I did what I have done!"

The Prince stilled. Only the ribs under his bandage stirred, expanding and contracting against her knuckles. "Quickly, aye," he murmured, "'twould be quick and easy, if I *could!*"

The last was choked out with such vehemence Aerid risked a look at his face.

His features, contorted with fury, glared down at her. "Killing you would be easy, but not—" His mouth worked, then spat out, "*honorable.* Not after I let you—"

He froze, pupils dilated, and looked between their bodies where, she realized with sudden and acute heat, no space existed. Recoiling as if scalded, the Prince yanked her hands out of the cloth binding his chest. "By the Demon, witch, how *do* you work your spells?"

Aerid stumbled backward. "'Tis a healer I be, m'lord. There be no magic in what I do."

"Oh, aye, none whatsoever. Only enough to make me, *me,* let a spy tend my wound." He spun away from the table, upsetting the stool, and plowed his hand through his hair. "Now, what the Demon do I *do* with you?" He cast about, looking like a man who had just tasted bitterfruit, before stalking across the tent to throw open a trunk at the foot of the bed. "Help me put this on."

While he strode toward her, she fumbled with the tunic he had flung at her head. He still looked furious, but somewhat more rational. Nonetheless, he had changed moods so rapidly over the last few—was it only moments?—she regarded him warily. "I—I do not understand, m'lord."

"No? I thought 'twas your plan to trick me into accepting your help. 'Tis sure you've succeeded!" He spat out an oath as crude as any goatherd's. "I have to find a way to get you out of my camp. The least you can do is make yourself useful and help me put this damned tunic on!" He yanked it out of her hands and began threading his left arm into the sleeve.

She was not going to die. The Prince, for whatever reason, was going to let her go unharmed. Seeing him struggle to fit his head into the neck hole while using only one arm, shamed her into motion.

His gaze flashed over her, hot and fierce, but when she had pulled the tunic gently over his bandage and down his body, he spun away. Snatching up her healer's knife, he hurled the blade into her open bag. "Pack your things while I get my cloak."

****

Arn fumed. Of course, the witch had no mount. Whatever beast the D'nalian had given her must have bolted with the lot during the raid. He should count himself lucky Darkstar had not been lost, too. At least she was perched astride his saddle rather than walking beside him where he could smell that damned scent of hers. By the Demon, he still could not figure what made her scent unique, but now at least he knew who and what it belonged to.

The moon had set and, though the sky sparkled, he could make out only silhouettes of the trees lining both banks of the river they followed. The swift water lapped at rocks, its gurgle covering the sound of Darkstar's hooves, and the noise of enemies, should any be about.

Arn's skin prickled, but he sensed no particular danger. If his guess was correct, the Lancers had retreated across the river. They would regroup somewhere farther east to celebrate, assess their losses, and send a message to Vinvinnysee. Anger at having his army surprised coursed through him, but he tamped it down. He had another, more immediate concern.

His boot slid off a stone, sending a jolt through his shoulder. Arn sucked in a breath. 'Twas bad enough she had to help him into his tunic, but what still grated was she had seen him fumbling with the buckle on his sword belt. Without a word, she had come and, with downcast eyes, offered her help. And he—*Damn the witch's power!*—had let her fasten it. What was worse, his body had tightened at her touch. By the Demon, it was tightening even now, at the thought.

He bit off another, cruder oath. Years of subjugating his desires, years of iron-willed self-discipline—for what? Just so the merest scent, touch, even look of this...*woman* could turn his will to weakness? With her stained face, dark coloring, and prominent cheekbones, she was hardly what his people considered beautiful. Average height, as skinny as a boy, except for a pair of rounded buttocks that had wedged neatly against his groin when they had struggled over that knife, and her breasts, if unbound, were probably so small they would barely fill his palms.

His body ached at the vision, and Arn bit off another oath. He was no better than Krenin if he let lust lead him. Besides, he was betrothed, and Erodasi of Roines had buttocks and breasts round enough and large enough to satisfy any man. Did not every man in Tolemak look at her with longing, wishing he could be Prince Arn of Val-Feyridge and have the right to possess such a beauty? 'Tis sure they did. He had no reason to look elsewhere for satisfaction when he had everything he needed—and a bloodline besides—in the woman waiting for him.

Arn gave himself a mental shake. By the Demon, what had he been thinking when he let a *spy* tend his wound? The sour reality was the witch had obeyed him and warned the camp of the Lancers' attack. 'Twas not much of a warning, but it made the difference between his men being totally overrun versus organizing enough resistance to capture and kill a few of the enemy. Nonetheless, if his thinking when she reappeared in his tent was as sharp then as it was now, he would have realized Gaelwynn of Vinvinnysee was shrewd enough to risk a small loss in order to establish a spy's credibility. And the fact she had been injured by her own people? If his wits had not been so dull, he would have remembered spies took risks. He took them himself. Sometimes the Sisters smiled. Sometimes not.

Still, she had taken an enormous risk by coming back. That move completely blindsided him. If he had not been so stunned, Arn was sure he never would have allowed her to touch his wound, much less treat it. There were moments where he could not quite recall what happened, what was said, but he was certain of one point: however much the witch might deny her power, when she looked up at him with those bottomless blue pools that passed for eyes and offered—No!—insisted he accept her aid, the Obligation of Tolem and its long, sacred history could have been dust for all his mind retained of it. She must have known, but how could a woman know what Tolemak men never spoke of openly but passed with private dignity from father to son, warrior to pupil, that once she surrendered herself and rendered him aid, he was obliged to protect her?

The river widened, opening into what an earlier reconnaissance told him was a sandbar. The ford was too narrow for his army, and the water rushed along hip-deep, but a man could cross safely enough. Arn halted Darkstar and dropped the reins. The stallion lowered its head and nibbled marsh grass. The witch remained frozen in the saddle, both arms hugging her pouch.

Arn scowled. Now he knew her for what she was, he

wondered how he had ever believed she was a boy. He ground his teeth. He wanted to believe she had entrapped him with some spell. Blaming her would ease the chagrin gnawing him raw. But he had never been superstitious, and he suspected, despite all the logic he could apply to the night's events, he had somehow *allowed* himself to be fooled. And that made everything worse.

"Can you swim?" he barked at her.

"Swim, m'lord?" There was no mistaking the squeak in her voice.

He squeezed his eyes shut. *Of course not. Why would anyone living in the middle of marshland need to swim?* He reminded himself most people did not force themselves to learn just because someone had once tried to drown them.

Sucking in a breath, Arn assessed his options. She was small and slight. Water to his hips would threaten her chest. One misstep on the narrow sandbar and he would have to pull her out of a freezing current. He could send her over on Darkstar, but he would have to trust her to send the stallion back. No, there was only one solution, and he did not like it. Picking up the reins, he snarled, "Move your legs in front of the stirrups. I'm coming up."

****

Aerid had only a moment to lever herself forward before the Prince slid into the saddle, reached around her and, with a pull of his forearm, planted her on his lap. She gasped as the shearling pommel divided her legs, forcing her thighs atop his and her buttocks into intimate contact with what solidly defined him as a man. Mortified, she tried to bolt out of the obscene embrace, but his arm clamped her like iron and he had already urged the horse into the water.

She clenched her fingers into his sleeve, holding herself stiff, fighting each shuddering step, each slip of a hoof that insinuated her body further into the cradle of his hips. Not enough layers of homespun and wool separated her vulnerable private parts from the violating pressure of his. *Sisters Three*, if he had chosen to assault her earlier, he could not have caused her this much consternation! Flushing from head to toe, she squirmed in his grasp.

"Sit still! Or 'tis sure you'll drown us both."

The horse chose that moment to flounder, or Aerid would have retorted. Instead, she sucked in breath as icy water sloshed up to her knees. The Prince swore. She could not make out the words, but each one rumbled along the back of her skull where he had wedged her head against his throat. The horse righted itself, found the sandbar and lurched to higher ground.

Aerid's arms trembled with holding her body rigid. Despite the predawn chill, heat suffused her body. Feverish and dizzy, she did not immediately notice the horse gain the far bank and halt. The Prince dropped the reins, and the horse lowered its head to browse.

Behind her shoulder, where his breastbone lodged against her blade bone, his heart pounded out heavy, solid thumps, echoing the staccato rhythm of hers. She tried to swallow, but her mouth had gone dry. Along her ribcage, his fingers flexed. The thumb spread outward, finding the telltale swell where no binding could completely compress her breast. Aerid's abdomen clenched. She held her breath while his thumb traveled slowly upward. Through tunic and layers of binding, her skin tingled with every tiny movement. She found herself arching imperceptibly toward his hand while her head leaned into his throat.

The Prince stiffened so violently, Aerid thought he had torn a stitch. She twisted to look at his face, but his arm clamped her like iron again, only tighter. "M'lord, be you—?"

"Get down." His voice was hoarse, and a tremor shook his arm, but he levered her toward his right hip. "Lift your leg up over the horse's neck and slide down."

Aerid did as she was told, but her legs were so wobbly, she staggered against his stirrup before she found her balance. "M'lord, 'tis sorry I be—"

"Don't make us both sorry, *witch*. Go far away, and don't ever show yourself to me again. Should I see you, 'tis sure I'll have no reason to stay my sword. Understand?"

Heat swept her face. "Oh, aye, I understand well enough, m'lord." She was an embarrassment to him. Someone he ought to kill but, for some reason, could not. Someone he ought to rape but could not, although his body was willing. She had seen enough of Elthred's admirers in Druemarwin's kitchen and stable to know when a man was aroused.

Well, he had embarrassed her, too. Her face burned when she recalled how her body had responded to his—a Tolemak's!—touch. And *this* Tolemak insisted on insulting her. "I be neither witch nor spy, m'lord, but a healer. No more and no less. Think what you will, but 'tis the truth."

The horse shifted under the Prince. Aerid sensed the force of his gaze even though she could not make out his eyes. Raising her chin, she showed him she meant every word.

"You were green and glowing when first I saw you."

"'Twas the evenroot. Did I not tell you so when first we met? Or be it the honor of rank to forget such things?"

"Mind your place!" The horse shook its head and stamped.

Even though she was playing with fire, Aerid thrilled at the knowledge her words had scored. "Be that all, m'lord, or have you aught else to say against me?"

"You vanished—without any means of doing so—from the clearing." His unseen gaze dared her to respond, to explain what, to him, clearly seemed impossible.

"'Twas a bear's den under the oak. You could not have known about that, m'lord, your spy being too new to the forest."

The stallion danced in a tight circle. "Indeed. Then 'tis a pity you're not truly a witch. 'Twould be easier for you to vanish if you were. Take heed, woman—"

"Aerid."

"What?" The word was bitten out, as if he could not believe she dared interrupt him.

"Aerid," she repeated, though her nerves quivered at her audacity. "'Tis my name."

The horse backed two steps and fought the bit. The Prince wheeled it around again. "Well then, *Aerid*, take heed. Go far away and quickly for, by the Demon, I owe you nothing." That said, he urged the horse toward the river and splashed across.

He was gone in heartbeats, a black shadow dissolving into the black shadows of trees, but still she stared after him. *Sisters Three!* What had possessed her to insist he know her name? Her reward had been the insolent way he spat it back at her, as if his mouth could not bear to form an Adanak word. Just as well. Enough of Tolemaks and their arrogance! She turned away from the river and surveyed the trees.

Now she was alone. And cold, for she had not found her cloak when she had run blindly back to where she, Naed and Yormoc had camped. The place was a shambles, and she had been lucky to find her pouch. Aerid choked back a sob at the thought of Naed, dead in a foreign land, far from those who loved him. She wished she could put a stone on his grave or bear the news to Dranoel, but she had put herself in enough danger this night.

The river flowed north. She would follow it till daybreak, then seek the cover of the wood. All she possessed were a few small coins, the clothes on her back, and the tools of her trade, but 'twould suffice. She had redroot enough to maintain her disguise, and if she could find a cottage or village, 'twould be easy to tend villagers' ailments in return for food and, possibly, a cloak. She touched the birthstone at her throat. The Sisters would guide her. They always had.

****

"Where have you been?" Krenin demanded when Arn entered the tent.

Arn pulled off his cloak and flung it on the bed. "Getting my shoulder stitched." That was true enough. Krenin did not need to know by whom. "I need a drink."

"So do I." Picking up Arn's mug and another from the opened trunk, Krenin reached for the wine flask inside. "The messenger from Druemarwin just rode in and he says—"

"—the witch disappeared the day the army marched and no one knows how she did it."

"Demon's Blood! How did you know?"

Arn took the mug Krenin was in danger of spilling and drained it. "Fill it again." Sitting on the stool, Arn realized the witch must have righted it or Krenin would have noticed. She had emptied the basin, too. And all while he had been struggling with his sword belt, damn her!

Krenin looked askance as Arn emptied the mug a

second time. "Stitches hurting?"

"No more than usual." Arn scowled at the empty mug. Krenin knew his drinking habits. Already Arn could sense the questions forming in his best friend's mind. Well, he had questions of his own. "I've heard Dranoel's nephew was killed tonight. Find out if 'tis true."

"That lowland bastard? Aye, I'll have a look. 'Twould save us the trouble if those tinpots slaughtered the lot. Bloody bunch of women they are." Krenin paused before the tent flap, and the furrows above his brows creased. "Take some rest," he said in a gentler voice. "You look like Demon fodder. Or worse."

Arn closed his eyes. He could let Krenin see his weariness. Krenin could be trusted. Arn had to remember that. Especially now, when he had something to hide from the man who knew him best. "Aye," he said, waving Krenin out. "I'll do my best."

Under his fist lay Dranoel's letter. His fingers itched to crumple and burn it, as if doing so would somehow exorcise her presence from his senses and his memory, but he had not yet read it. Perhaps he should, in case there was something there he needed to know. He could always burn it afterward. Pressing the parchment open against the table, he leaned forward and read.

PART II: ADANAK
CHAPTER EIGHT

Eyes bleary from the smoke hanging in a flat, thin cloud over the ravaged camp, Naed watched sunrise shimmer through the trees. He sat on a stump and rested his arm on Yormoc's shoulder while his countryman changed the dressing over his ribs.

"You bleed still." Yormoc tossed the soiled cloth into the remnants of their fire. "The lance took too much skin."

"Better skin than bone." Naed glanced at the bandage smoldering in the ash. "'Tis not half so much as before." He fingered scabs forming on his elbow and allowed himself a huge yawn—bitten off when his ribs smarted in protest.

"Aye," Yormoc said, nodding. "Two or three, broken."

"Bruised. 'Tis the cut that pulls."

"Think what you will." Yormoc secured the bandage with strips of cloth wrapped around Naed's torso. "'Twould be better if our healer tended you. 'Tis a miracle what the lad can do."

Naed wondered how many wounded there were since Aerid had not yet returned. The thought she had been out of camp fetching water when the Lancers struck had comforted him all through the long night. Now, though...

He spotted Krenin approaching, a frown denting the Tolemak's brow. "Here comes the Prince's Second."

"Aye, and about to soil himself by speaking to worms such as us." Yormoc winked.

Naed chuckled, but it made his side burn. He pressed his hand to the bandage.

Krenin halted a body's length away and planted his fists on his hips. "So, you're not dead after all. Pity. I would've danced on your grave."

Naed rose, conscious that—even though he stood shirtless before this sneering Tolemak—he still wore his sword. "Why do you hate me so?"

"Hate you?" Krenin snorted. "You're too low to hate. So you broke a Lancer's weapon, what of it? The Sisters are as fickle as their Four Winds. Don't count on their continued favor."

"I rely on naught but my sword."

"What kind is that? Lowland forged? Tempered with swamp water and tested on mist?"

Tolemak soldiers hunching around a nearby fire laughed.

Naed resisted the urge to retort. They outnumbered him and 'twould be as pointless as insulting swine. Instead, though the Tolemak had at least an inch and two score pounds on him, Naed looked him square in the eyes. His wound pulled, but he would not wince before these barbarians. "Now that you know I am alive, what is it you want of me?"

"I? Naught but to see you lowland tripe dead. 'Tis the Prince who wants you. Now."

****

Naed halted just inside the command tent. Having to appear before the Prince in his bloody tunic was demoralizing enough without compounding trouble by stumbling over something in the dimness. "You sent for me, m'lord?" he said while his eyes adjusted.

"So, you're not dead." The Prince threw down a quill and stood. "'Twould be better if you were."

Naed flushed. His tunic chafed where the blood had dried on it, his side ached, his eyes burned, and every muscle in his body protested a general lack of sleep. "I am heartily sorry, m'lord, if my continued life distresses you, but whoever reported—"

"'Tis kind of you to acknowledge your inconvenience. Your attitude is most helpful. Please, do sit down."

The hair on Naed's arms prickled. He could see now, and the man opposite was clean-shaven, freshly dressed, and clearly not in the mood for D'nalian insolence. Naed could dismiss Krenin's animosity as endemic, but how had he offended the Prince? He had been dazed after being lanced. Had he said or done something then? Bending carefully, he perched on a stool. Something in the tent did not smell right, but he could not discern the oddity amid the scents of lamp oil, sweat, musk, and the sweet blood lingering on his own tunic.

The Prince thrust a folded piece of parchment in his face. "Is this the seal of your uncle?"

The wax had been broken across, but the imprint of Druemarwin's crest was clear. "Aye," he said, wondering what the letter had to do with his summons. "You know that it is."

"Oh, indeed I do." The Prince tapped the folded letter against his palm.

Naed's skin crawled. If the Prince's unblinking stare and methodical tap were not menacing enough, there was something familiar about that letter. His mind dredged up the sound of a quill scratching, the smell of hot wax, an image of his uncle, arm in a sling, laboriously affixing his signature—

Surging to his feet, Naed grabbed for his sword. Prince Arn's dagger at his throat stopped him in mid-motion. He froze, acutely aware of the blade lying across his jugular, of his own half-drawn sword, of his fist on the hilt a handspan—a mere *handspan*—below the Prince's elbow. A jerk of his forearm could—might—knock the dagger away.

"'Tis but a flick of the wrist for me," the Prince warned. "And my blade is sharp."

The pulse under Naed's jaw throbbed against the dagger. Sweat beaded on his forehead and, under the bandage, a damp warmth told him his side bled again, but he refused to yield. If Aerid had been harmed, what did his life matter? "Where is she? What have you done—?"

"To her? Not a thing. Her countrymen knocked her about, but then they didn't have the privilege of knowing what you and I know, did they?" Prince Arn leaned closer, increasing the dagger pressure with a small adjustment of his wrist. Inches away, his eyes were unblinking and hawk-bright. "How many others knew about her? Two? Three? The whole D'nalian cohort?"

Dots of color flitted at the edge of Naed's vision. If he fainted, he would slice his own throat, but that hardly seemed important. Aerid was important. "Where is she?"

"A half day's walk from here by now, I should hope. And far safer than you unless you sheathe your weapon and sit."

Every muscle in Naed's body shook with the need to explode, to fight, but the portion of his mind not yet dazed told him he had no chance. What good would he be to Aerid if he died? She was free, was she not? The Prince had said as much. Nothing in those predatory eyes suggested the man was lying.

Unclenching his fist, Naed let his sword slide into its scabbard. He eased away from the dagger and lowered himself to the stool. Heart still thundering, he folded his arms and fixed what he hoped was a sullen expression on his face. "You gave orders to seize her after we left Druemarwin. Why would you let her go now?"

Prince Arn sheathed his dagger. "I'll ask the questions. And this time you'll swear on that D'nalian honor you hold so dear that you'll answer me truthfully and completely."

"I do not lie."

"We both know that's not the same thing. Swear."

Naed flung back a glare, salve to his dignity, but spoke what discretion told him was the only possible reply. "I so swear."

The Prince gestured to the letter discarded on the ground. "Explain, then, why you and your uncle conspired to circumvent my orders and conceal an Adanak—and a woman, at that—within my army, knowing full well I intend to attack the Adanak. To even the dullest eye, 'tis sure that seems like aiding and abetting a spy."

"Aerid is no spy! We intended to send her to Tumin, to safety in my mother's household, but 'twas impossible to get her out of camp."

"Impossible? Or was it that you couldn't bear to part with your lover?"

"What—no!" Naed flushed to the roots of his hair. How could the Prince—or anyone, for that matter—think that he...that she...that they... "Aerid is but a maid!"

"Indeed. 'Tis a great deal to risk for any woman. Incomprehensible to think you dared so much for one of no blood, and an Adanak besides—however talented a healer—without there being something between you. Don't tell me that you, a lord's nephew, hoped to *wed* a creature so far beneath you."

Although he opened his mouth, Naed could not deny

the truth. Aerid's innocence and exotic beauty had charmed him the moment he rode through Druemarwin's gate and saw her drawing water, but he hesitated to declare himself in part because of her alien heritage and low position. He was only the nephew, after all. He had to toe a careful line before he could—

"By the Demon, you *are* a fool—a naive, romantic fool. Someone should have taken you to a brothel when you came of age. Then you wouldn't find yourself so completely at the mercy of a fluttering eyelash."

Naed flinched as though slapped. He was a fool, indeed, for not declaring himself to Aerid, but Sisters be damned if he would let this Tolemak look down his long nose at all he held holy. "I am D'nalian. We do not rut about like deer in season!"

Prince Arn guffawed. "Perhaps you don't, but don't make claims for your countrymen."

Naed stood. "'Twas *your* countrymen I meant to impugn." After a deliberate pause, he added, "M'lord."

If the atmosphere in the tent had seemed tense before, now Naed felt it seethe, like a heavy day about to break into violent storm. He held himself unmoving, body in flex, poised to channel into action the energy churning in his blood. 'Twas the moment he had been taught to hate, the moment a proper D'nalian should at all costs avoid and certainly never initiate unless his honor was at stake. Even then there should be none of this excitement, this singing in his veins. Confrontation was to be a duty, nothing more.

The Prince had not moved except for a muscle twitching along his jaw. His brows were like black wings drawn together over eyes that delved into Naed as if seeking his soul. "Why are you so determined to die?"

"Why do you care, m'lord? 'Tis treason I'm accused of. What does it matter how or when I die?"

Naed thought the man already stood at full height, but he had been mistaken. The Prince towered over him while the silence stretched like a winch rope ratcheted tighter and tighter until Naed thought the blood rushing in his ears would whine with the strain of it.

"Your perception is amiss," Prince Arn said at last. "Oh, 'tis treason I suspect, but what you stand accused of is poor judgment. You chose a woman over your duty—a pathetically common error in one so young. And so naive. Don't you agree?"

A thread of rationality warned Naed not to rise to the bait. Besides, there was some... *truth* in the Prince's words. And that truth was leaking acid into his stomach.

"I'll take your silence as agreement."

Naed's pride refused to let his gaze drop, but the burn eating at his innards told him he had lost the right—if ever he had truly had the right—to meet the Prince's eyes.

"In addition to your first error of judgment, you committed a second—you preferred loyalty to your uncle over the oath sworn to me. 'Tis understandable, I'm told, to prefer the ties of blood kin, but 'tis a mistake nonetheless, for your uncle swore allegiance to me, and you are duty-bound to honor his oath as well as your own. Or does D'nalian honor allow exceptions?"

"It...does not, m'lord." That it took a Tolemak to bring him to his senses was shame enough, but that he was capable of so completely setting aside his honor he had not even known it was compromised, mortified him. Dranoel had warned him, but he had brushed aside the wisdom of age and let his heart lead. A true D'nalian knew better than to commit such folly.

The leather cylinder his uncle had given him dangled over his breast, exposed in the haste of dressing for the Prince's summons. Naed wished Dranoel had chosen someone more worthy, since he had proven himself a colossal failure, both to his uncle and to this Prince. Well, he would return this sign of his uncle's misplaced trust upon his return to Druemarwin—if he would be allowed to return, having so thoroughly disgraced himself here. Forcing a swallow, he said, "I beg your pardon, m'lord. 'Tis as you say—true, all of it."

The Prince did not respond. Instead, he indicated the cylinder. "Is your birthstone within? Or do you not subscribe to that particular superstition?"

"I—no. 'Tis my uncle's will."

"And he entrusted you with the keeping of it?"

Unable to choke out any more words, Naed nodded.

"Then he must have thought you worthy, though—

Demon knows—'tis sure you've done naught but provoke me. Your life is mine. I trust you know that."

Naed nodded again, but something in the Prince's voice compelled him to raise his eyes.

Prince Arn regarded him with folded arms and a face as impassive as stone. "Then heed me well and do exactly as I say. Your healer is dead—so you'll say to anyone who asks. You'll communicate nothing of this to Dranoel or to any other D'nalian. Finally, you'll remove yourself at once from your fellows and report to Master of Horse Gorm. He can use someone with a good arm and no particular fear of Lancers."

The Prince was offering him another chance. Such leniency was far more than he deserved, and entirely unexpected from a Tolemak, even if the man did—astonishingly—credit him with some skill. A peculiar sensation ran up Naed's spine, causing his shoulders to straighten and his chin to rise. "At once, m'lord."

Neither the Prince's expression nor his stance altered. Naed waited.

"She saw you fall under that lance. 'Twas she who told me you were dead. Believing as she does, 'tis unlikely she'll go to Tumin or to any other D'nalian place, especially now she's among her own kind. Consider yourself blessed by the Sisters that you're free of her."

The words stunned Naed, as they were undoubtedly meant to, but he understood the Prince's message. Aerid had put him behind her. He must do the same. There was nothing more he could do for her. Perhaps when he had fulfilled his obligation—two lives' worth now, he thought with chagrin—he could seek her out. In the meantime, he must dedicate himself to serving the man who held his oath.

"With your permission, m'lord, I should like to gather my belongings and report to Master of Horse Gorm." At the Prince's nod, Naed left the tent.

****

"What was that all about?" Krenin demanded, pushing inside almost before the tent flap had stopped swinging.

What, indeed? Arn located the stool and sat upon it. He could reply he had expelled an Adanak witch and silenced her D'nalian devotee, and neither seemed to be a spy. He could add the D'nalian was infatuated with the witch, and the *girl*—he wanted to think of her as a woman, but too much of her behavior pointed to innocence even before the D'nalian confirmed it. Regardless, the...*witch* clearly had not acted as if she had lost a lover. But if he mentioned that to Krenin, he would have to explain why discovering the exact nature of their relationship was so important he had bullied the D'nalian into admitting it. Then he would be forced to consider why learning they were not lovers had tipped the scales toward sparing the D'nalian's life when logic should have pushed him to that decision sooner.

Arn scowled. He had no time for this. "I've separated Dranoel's nephew from his fellows." Spotting the letter lying beside the stool, he covered it with his boot. In the dimness, Krenin would not notice such a small, natural movement. And there was no need for Krenin to know anything about the letter or the incident involving it, especially now it was settled. "'Tis he alone who's of some value to us."

"Some value!" Krenin snorted. "About as much as—"

"He took on a Lancer, single-handedly and on foot." Catching his friend's eyes, Arn indicated the broken lance point lying on the table. "No mean feat, I assure you."

Krenin had the grace to flush even though he blustered, "'Twas luck. He hasn't anything near your skill. And he didn't score a kill."

"No, not yet." Arn noted how his blood had soaked into the wood. His wound drew, but the stitches held despite the exertion required to master Dranoel's nephew. Although it irked him to admit it, the salve the witch had smeared on the wound seemed to have a numbing effect. His shoulder ached, but not nearly as much as was usual with such injuries.

"What's to be done with the rest of that lowland baggage, then?"

Krenin's voice pulled Arn out of his reverie. "I'll leave that up to you. Use them as you see fit."

The grooves scoring Krenin's forehead almost vanished. "'Twill be my pleasure. You won't be needing me for a while, will you? Good."

When the tent flapped shut on Krenin's back, Arn eased his leg into a more comfortable position. If the Three Sisters existed, and if they answered a man's prayers, there would be nothing but dust under his boot. The Sisters could be perverse, even with devout believers—which they knew he was not—and Arn imagined their pleasure at thwarting him now as he stared at the ground.

Bending slowly, he retrieved the letter and considered what to do with it. Best to burn the thing, but what if setting it aflame released a burst of scent more potent than that even now teasing his senses? Crumpling, tramping underfoot, coating with fine clay dust—nothing tempered the smell of her embedded in it, nothing dulled the image that arrowed straight to his brain, nothing muted the desire that rushed like fire along his nerves. Arn folded the letter over and over, creasing it hard, until it fit into his clenched fist. Unlike the D'nalian, he recognized lust when he saw it. 'Twas only the strangeness of the witch that tempted him, those startlingly blue eyes and that copper-cream skin. That and not knowing if the taste of her would in any way fulfill the extravagant promises made by her scent.

He wondered if the D'nalian had tasted her.

The thought hit like a punch to the gut.

The D'nalian was too much the fool to take what was not offered. And Arn was certain it had not been offered.

Almost certain.

His nostrils flared as he sucked in air, willing his muscles to unclench, to relax. However much he preferred to think of her as a witch, she was just a woman, after all. And an Adanak. At a green fifteen he might have fallen under her spell as readily as the D'nalian, but at nearly thirty and a prince, he knew nothing about a woman ever lived up to its promise.

Women on the whole had little place in his life. They did not fight. They knew nothing of weapons, strategy, or command. They knew nothing of ideas, philosophies, or visions. Their vacuous conversation and childish demands bored him. Even his bride-to-be could not keep his attention for more than minutes. But then, he had not chosen Erodasi of Roines for that purpose.

That she was beautiful would be a boon to his bed. That she was spoiled and proud would be a further benefit. Mastering her body would give him added pleasure. But he had not selected Erodasi for those reasons either. No, he had betrothed himself to her precisely because she shared his bloodline, because she was the only other heir to the throne of Val-Feyridge and the Crown of Tolem, and because her dowry included the Tolem Stone.

With the Stone, the Crown, and the bloodline secured, there would be no more questions about legitimacy thrown in his face or, as they were now he had become so powerful, whispered behind his back. At his inhalation, the cylinder over his breast shifted on its leather cord. Arn laid his hand over the container, pressing it against the steady throb of his heart. He had a plan, and he was well on his way to achieving the goals he set for himself years ago when his family was murdered and he himself looked at death. He had survived the attempt to drown him, and by sheer willpower he had overcome a lingering fear of water. By sheer willpower he would overcome this...*lust*, too. To prove it, he would keep the letter, just in case he needed to remind either Dranoel or his nephew of their obligations.

The witch was gone, was she not? Far away by now. Perhaps the Sisters had answered his prayer after all.

****

In the goatherd's cottage within sight of the fortress Val-Feyridge, Dlaniger had received two messages, and neither pleased him. The first told him Prince Arn had reached the Adanak border and demanded to know what he intended to do about it. He set that aside. His employers had paid him a third of his fee on engagement, and the sum was substantial. He could afford to wait until the moment was right to conclude his business. It was not his fault his employers' informants were so inept they had failed to see the Prince's gambit, but their inadequacy irked him nonetheless. Better to henceforth rely entirely on his own sources.

Those sources had sent the second message, which he crumpled in his fist. This was personal and Dlaniger needed to control his fury before he could devise an appropriate response. Emotion was costly. It distracted, made a man tense, jumpy. It could get him killed. There was no room for emotion in his profession. Clever, observant, intuitive, decisive, steel-nerved—those qualities determined a man's success more than skill with weapons. Of course, he possessed superior skill in that area, too. But what had made his reputation was cool, ruthless efficiency.

Unfolding the message, he read it once more before tossing it into the fire-pit. So, Druemarwin was under Tolemak control. He took a moment's pleasure in imagining his father's consternation. How the old fool must be chafing with shame. 'Twould serve the stubborn old goat right to have to bow and scrape to superiors. And his cousin, that self-righteous brat from Tumin who thought he was grown enough to handle a sword. The skinny redhead always walked about with his chin stuck out. How it must gall Naed's all-consuming pride to be responsible for Druemarwin's fall.

Dlaniger stirred the fire, making sure every bit of the parchment had been reduced to ash. If the Sisters smiled, he would personally see his cousin learned his proper place. If the rest of his business went well, he might even consider letting the upstart live.

Dlaniger straightened and retrieved his employers' missive from the goatskin rug. The Tolemak Prince had made the business personal by capturing Druemarwin. Of course, Prince Arn had no way of knowing just whom he had offended by doing so. 'Twas likely even Dlaniger's employers had not discovered the link, certainly not if their informants were as worthless as they had thus far appeared. Dlaniger dropped the message into the fire and gave himself a moment's satisfaction by skewering it with a poker and shoving it into a flaming brand.

With the Prince on the move toward Adanak, Dlaniger had anticipated leaving the lovely Erodasi soon in order to pursue or, if possible, arrange an interception upon the Prince's return—assuming the man survived the Adanak's best efforts. Now Dlaniger reconsidered. The soon-to-be-princess Erodasi was beautiful, lush and lusty, but not very bright. She was a fool to have given up her innocence before her wedding night. Her husband would have to be either stupid or blind drunk not to notice. Everything he had learned about Prince Arn suggested the man was neither a fool nor a drinker. The Prince would wring his bride's pretty little neck.

Dlaniger watched the flames consume every trace of the second parchment. For weeks he had been thoroughly—and frequently—debauching Lord Rolnar's precious heir. He wondered if Erodasi had troubled her delightfully empty head with any thought of preventing conception. He knew he had not.

A slow smile spread across his face. 'Twould be possible here to gain more than his fee. Much, much more. Done right, revenge would be a three-course banquet, made all the sweeter for being served cold. And after that, there would be the Crown...

CHAPTER NINE

In a seven-night of traveling toward the rising sun, Aerid worked her healing art on a cow, two pigs, and an infant with fever. The cow's owner gave her bread and stuffed her with stew. The pigs' owner gave her a cloak. 'Twas worn thin in places, but she was glad of its warmth when she curled up in thickets at night. The infant's parents, a tanner with a bristling beard and his plump-cheeked wife, gave her a ride to the market town Herset where, they assured her, lay a road that would take her anywhere in Adanak, even to the great city Vinvinnysee.

Aerid touched the birthstone at her throat and sighed. Much as she desired to see the greatest city in the three lands—and the pride of Adanak—she intended to leave the main road once she found one leading northeast. The Sisters' tear she wore had been shed high in the Mountains of Morning. Somewhere along the upland road, she ought to find her kin.

She told her benefactors none of this. All of them knew her only as the strange, shy boy with the ugly face and gentle hands. After all, she had played the part for so long, 'twas nearly second nature. And only one person had seen through the disguise. She tried to banish the Prince's image from her mind but had no more success than on the countless other times his face and his form leaped unbidden into her consciousness. 'Twas only because he had let her go and she had not understood why. 'Twas the not knowing that troubled her. Not the texture of his skin, the tracery of pain her fingers had read in his scars. Nor the black hair, tousled over eyes so many changing shades of gray, eyes that looked long and looked deep. And saw too much, mayhap. He had seen enough to know...and still he had let her go—had even, at considerable risk, taken her to safety. And then he was gone. And she was alone.

Alone at night in an Adanak market town ringed by a stout wooden wall and guarded by a small troop of

Adanak soldiers, she ought to feel comforted, even secure, to be surrounded at last by her own kind. Instead, Aerid stood in the shadow of a tailor's shop and pulled her cloak tighter around her shoulders. She was not cold. The air barely stirring in the narrow street was warm and heavy with the scent of sweetgrass. All the way to town she had seen farmers swinging their scythes on patches of green. What drew her concern was the raucous singing issuing from the inn across the square from where she stood.

Her benefactors all warned her to stay away from soldiers. She had sensed fear in the farmers' hushed voices and darting eyes, but she could not understand it. The gentle folk seemed unaware of the war about to break and the soldiers they spoke of were men of their own kind. Why should they fear those assigned to protect them? Still, Aerid had no wish to tempt the Sisters. 'Twould be better if she found herself an empty stall or a pile of straw for the night. She was about to leave when a man and a woman stumbled out of the inn.

The woman's blouse was unlaced and bared one shoulder. The man groped under the cloth while she laughed and kissed him. He tripped over the hem of his long traveling cloak and staggered against her when she led him away from the lights of the inn.

Aerid leaned back into the shadows, disgusted by the sight of the local whore and her customer. The woman made her think of Elthred, and for a moment she saw Druemarwin's courtyard, the stone-rimmed well she had drawn water from every day for fourteen years, the kitchen alcove and her cozy bed of straw, her beloved master with his gray-threaded mane barely tamed into a queue. With a catch in her throat, Aerid wondered how the world went with Dranoel. She hoped he was well, and that Ekwul was dosing him properly with the medicines she had prepared in that short, rushed night before—

There had been a sound. Several sounds—thuds, a groan, the chink of coin, voices. A man and a woman, speaking low, hurried. Aerid pressed herself into the doorway, stone chips and mortar digging into her back. Two figures emerged, the woman fastening her blouse, protesting, "If he be dead—" The man—a different man— dragging her across the square and away from the inn, retorting, "He'll not be telling the soldiers then, eh?"

Thieves!

Aerid's mouth went dry. Had she just overheard a murder? The thought made her stomach heave. For weeks she had lived in the thick of battle, but men went into war knowing the consequences. Who entered an inn expecting to be murdered? She dug her fingertips into crumbling mortar and considered running to the inn. 'Twould rouse the soldiers...but she had been warned to stay away from them. A low moan cut through her quandary. Her skills were needed. Pushing away from the wall, she followed the sound.

The man lay in a heap at the entrance of a narrow passageway, his cloak tangled about him. Aerid glanced around the market square, and, seeing no one, stepped over the man's body and into the alley's mouth. The inn's torches cast only faint light this far, and to use it best, she had to turn her back to a foul-smelling black hole, but she told herself 'twas unlikely another villain lurked there. Still, the back of her neck prickled as she knelt to uncover the man's head.

He groaned when she worked her fingers between unbound hair and a twisted cloak collar to check the pulse at his throat. Satisfied his blood beat strong, she searched for signs of injury and found nothing except some blood oozing from a lump the size of a duck's egg behind his right ear. A whiff of bearberry oil would restore his senses, and then she could move him to the inn yard where he could seek further help. No need for her to personally trouble the soldiers.

Sitting back on her heels, she reached into her healer's pouch—and froze.

Had she seen what she thought she had seen? Aerid swiveled and stared at the man's neck. With the cloak's high collar raised, no one in the inn would have noticed he lacked a queue. 'Twas naught to that. Men occasionally went about with unbound hair. Forcing herself to lean over the man's shoulder, she looked once more at the wavy mass and confirmed what her hard-pounding heart already suspected—the ends were all of one length, having been deliberately shorn!

Sisters! A Tolemak!

Aerid recoiled into the alley, slamming up against a wall. The man awoke at the noise, thrashing in his cloak like a tomcat in a sack until, free, he flung himself against the opposite wall. Huddling there, knife glinting in his hand, he hissed, "Who's there? Show yourself or, by the Demon, I'll gut you where you stand!"

Even if Aerid had forgotten the face, she could never have forgotten the voice. She had heard that hate-filled, angry sneer too many times, even in her nightmares. And now her people's sworn enemy was staring straight at her.

Krenin, the Prince's Second, flashed the knife left, then right, his breath a rasp. He blinked rapidly, dashed a hand over his face, and blinked again. His gaze roved across her, up the wall, down the passageway, back toward the inn.

He could not see her.

Aerid fought the panic coiling in her legs. She was hidden in deep shadow and he had taken a blow to the head. Sight was the last sense to return. She knew that well enough; 'twas how she had last heard his hateful voice in the Prince's tent—but what was he doing here, now, in this village a seven-night's journey and a world away from where she had last seen him?

Krenin squeezed his eyes shut, opened them wide, and blinked several times. Then he shook his head like a dog with a rat.

Aerid winced. A man with his battlefield experience ought to know better, but he deserved none of her pity. She held her breath as he lurched to his hands and knees and retched into the market square. She considered moving down the alley while he was incapacitated and before his vision returned. Voices stopped her.

"Will you be looking at that? The whore's koshed him and run."

"Where'll be our share of his purse, then?"

"The whore's taken it, ale-brain. She and that partner of hers."

"They'll not be far," said a third man. "Take our lads from the inn and bring back that purse. And mind you, don't be dropping a coin, or 'tis your hide I'll be taking it out of."

"Aye, sir. And the whore and her partner? Should we be bringing them back?"

"Make 'em pay, lads, for trying to cheat the Herset Guard. After all, 'tis kind we were to let 'em work the travelers here."

Barks of laughter erupted, then the sound of one man running—toward the inn, Aerid guessed. Her skin turned clammy and bile rose in her throat as sour as that Krenin was vomiting onto the paving stones. Soldiers. *Thieves!* No wonder the farmers had warned her away.

Shadows, half a dozen or more, fell across Krenin's kneeling form. Head down, he panted, now and then wiping a shaky hand across his mouth. He seemed unaware of the men encircling him, their hands resting on sword and knife hilts.

"'Tis certain to be a horse somewhere. A fine one, to be sure, and with a good saddle."

"Have a look at his boots, sir. And that cloak."

"Strip him." The speaker planted a boot in Krenin's ribs and shoved. "Mayhap the whore overlooked something."

"Aye! This!" Krenin exploded off the ground. Sword flashing in one hand and knife in the other, he ran one man through and slashed another before his enemies could rear back and draw blades. The initial surprise spent, they were on him in a flurry of grunts and shouts.

One man crashed into the stone corner beside Aerid and crumpled almost at her feet. Panicked, she scrabbled deeper into the passage. She had to get out of there. *Now!* Before they killed her in the mêlée. Krenin was outnumbered and injured, but he was Tolemak—and her enemy. The soldiers were Adanak, her own people, but they were thieves and murderers.

A tangle of limbs and bodies flew into the passage and crash-landed in a puddle, spewing water into Aerid's face. On the bottom of the tangle, Krenin glanced at her with eyes still out of focus while his opponent forced a knife to his throat. Krenin's own knife lay just inches from his groping hand. He was going to die, and she would see it happen.

"No!" she cried, horrified. "Not this way!"

The startled soldier looked toward her.

Krenin rammed a fist into the man's temple and flung him off. Scooping up his knife, Krenin lunged at Aerid. Blade at her throat, he stared at her in the darkness like a man trying to see a phantom. "Are—are you with me?"

She could not think, could barely speak. "I—"

Apparently mistaking the sound for assent, he pulled the knife away and leaned into the wall. He looked ill, exhausted. The passageway they huddled in was barely wide enough for a broad man to walk comfortably. At least two men's bodies blocked the entrance. Outside, hands grabbed at the blockage and soldiers shouted for help and torches.

Krenin seized her tunic. "Move, boy. Find us a way out of this bloody rabbit warren."

****

Krenin was late. Arn had expected that. Sending a man of Krenin's appetites into a town that likely supported more than one whore had been a conscious decision on Arn's part. If his old friend found relief for his chronic testiness while scouting this market town and Adanak outpost, so much the better—for all concerned. But now Krenin was too long overdue.

Under other conditions, Arn might have given him more time, but already this night a half dozen Adanak soldiers had been observed riding out of town at a gallop. Concerned they might have been sent to warn others of his army's presence, Arn dispatched the men with him to intercept them. Left on his own, he did what Krenin had done, cloaked himself and rode through the still open gate, telling the lone attendant he was a benighted traveler. The obliging soldier gave him directions to the inn.

Now he stood in Darkstar's stirrups at the edge of the market square with the reins tight in his fist and his sword sliding noiselessly out of its scabbard. Eyes narrowed and muscles coiling into readiness, he surveyed the inn and surroundings, noting signs of a recent mêlée—bodies, assorted weapons and burned-out torches littering the cobbled ground. Three horses tethered to the inn's main rail. Krenin's chestnut standing in the shadows at the building's near side. The inn, door open, torches bright, but seemingly empty. Homes and shops dark, doors bolted shut. And into the silence, a sudden cacophony of shouts, clangs, and pounding feet.

Figures, Arn could not be sure how many, spilled from a street across the square. Light from hand-held torches flashed on swords and threw wild, gyrating shadows across stone walls and cobbles. At the forefront, two figures fending off three—Krenin, wielding sword and knife, partnered with a slight, hooded figure in an oversized tunic who jabbed awkwardly with a torch. Krenin struck down one attacker, grabbed the torch from his partner and elbowed him back, shouting something. The partner—who seemed no more than a youth—stumbled backward, then turned and ran toward the inn.

At the top of the square, more foot soldiers rushed around a corner. Arn spurred Darkstar toward the tethered horses. Cutting their reins and yelling, he drove the horses at the new arrivals. The spooked animals thundered past the youth, who fell down and covered his head. Arn galloped after the horses and slashed at the scattering men, taking down two before two more rushed him from either side. With a boot to the shoulder, he shoved one man under Darkstar's hooves, but the second dragged Arn out of the saddle. They fell together on the cobbles and broke apart. Arn's knife slid between the man's ribs before he could rise.

Knife and sword in hand, Arn spun. The enemy seemed momentarily routed, dispersing to the shadows at the square's perimeter. He was glad of it. The fall had reminded him his shoulder was still healing. He rotated it, satisfying himself the arm had all the power he needed, and sprinted to Krenin's side. With two strokes, Arn dispatched the pair that had forced Krenin down on one knee and knocked the sputtering torch from his hand.

Arn grabbed Krenin's arm and hauled him upright. "Do they know you're Tolemak or is this about a woman?"

"Glad to see you, too," Krenin panted, swaying. Blood ran down his temple, and more soaked his left sleeve. Painted in filth and clothes reeking, he grinned. "The damned town is a thieves' nest. But this traveler's a bloody sight better with a sword than they expected."

"Let's get out of here before they figure out why." Arn

whistled for Darkstar.

"I sent the boy for my horse." Krenin turned toward the inn, stumbled, and would have fallen had Arn not caught him.

"Easy, old friend." He could not spare time to check Krenin's wounds, but the way his friend's weight sagged against his side worried him. "I saw your horse by the inn," Arn said, half-walking, half-dragging Krenin toward it.

There was no sign of Krenin's helper in the square, but if the boy were smart, he would have kept running. The soldiers would execute him for a traitor if they caught him.

"Who's this boy? How did you meet him?"

"I've a dozen blacksmiths pounding in my head." Krenin stumbled again. "How the Demon should I know? The brat was there when they jumped me."

They were halfway to the inn when Darkstar trotted up. Grabbing the stallion's reins, Arn glanced around the square. The enemy seemed disorganized, but there was the chance an enterprising soul had gone for reinforcements. Possibly even Krenin's partner. If the boy realized his mistake, he might have decided going for help could buy back his life.

Deciding it was better to lose Krenin's horse than risk being overwhelmed, Arn was about to heave Krenin into Darkstar's saddle and climb up behind him when, from the shadows beside the inn, Krenin's chestnut appeared. It trotted toward them, hustled along by a hooded figure in an oversized tunic. More than once, the horse tossed its head against the unfamiliar hand, lifting the slight figure off the ground.

Arn kept his sword at ready, but the figure appeared unarmed, and no suspicious shapes stirred in the shadows behind the boy and horse. Slung across the youth's body under his cloak, he wore some kind of large bag or pouch. A traveler, Arn decided. Poor *and* weaponless.

"Why are you helping us?" he demanded, catching the chestnut's bridle before the horse could shake off the boy and bolt.

The boy ducked under the chestnut's neck, putting the horse's bulk between them. Head down and hood so low Arn could see none of his face, the boy handed the reins to Krenin.

"Good lad," Krenin said, reaching for the saddle. "Give me a hand up, will you?"

"No," Arn said. "Let me." With a pointed look at the boy, who backed a step, Arn ducked under the horse's neck and heaved Krenin into the saddle. He was too rough, but time was not on their side. He could sense the enemy regrouping in the shadows. In moments, they would reform into a fighting unit. And behind him, the boy—the damned, unexplained boy—was still backing away, turning as if to run. *Run where? Why?*

Arn lunged, grabbing a handful of tunic. "Don't be a fool! They'll kill you."

He read panic in the stiffened legs, in the hands yanking at the tunic, trying to pull it out of his fist, in the voice stammering, "So—so will you, m'lord."

M'lord!

By the Demon, the boy knew him! "Who the—?"

Cloth rent. The boy sprawled backward, landing on the cobbles with enough force to throw the hood from his face.

Her face.

Arn stood rooted while shock washed over him, stealing blood, breath, movement. Everything but thought—the all-pervading conviction that he should have guessed, should have recognized, should have known—was not this damned woman's face, her form, her very scent burned into his brain?

Immediately, fury rose like gall—bitter and burning—to flood all the shock-drained places. "What in the name of all that's holy—!" he roared, but he had run out of time. He heard running feet, saw terror in her eyes as she scrambled upright, heard Krenin shout, "They're coming!"

The attackers were on him in a heartbeat, but Arn fought them off in a haze. He had no idea how many there were or how he repelled them; he knew only the wind was in his face when he galloped out of the town gates with the woman before him in the saddle and Krenin riding alongside.

CHAPTER TEN

Shivers racked Aerid, coming so hard and fast she had bitten her lip bloody, but she refused to make a sound while the Prince rode with her clamped to his body. Her life depended on saying nothing until this man—the Demon Himself for all the cruel efficiency with which he had dispatched their attackers—gave her leave to speak. Trees whipped by; a bit of moonlight beamed down on a narrow track, and always the horse's mane lashed her face. She had given up breathing, gulping air whenever the horse's stride loosened the Prince's grip a fraction.

The horse slowed, and the Prince straightened in the saddle, allowing a sliver of night air to slide between their bodies. She shuddered at the shock of it, realizing the skin under her tunic was damp with the sweat soaking through his. She had ceased to feel his heartbeat as separate from hers. Both thundered in her ears, and the sweet scent of fresh blood—on his hands, his clothes, his weapons—mingled with horse lather, man-sweat, and her own fear.

He guided the stallion off the track and into a stream. Krenin followed, as did a riderless horse that had raced with them out of the village. Aerid guessed it was one of those that had charged her in the square. Instead of crossing, the Prince headed the stallion downstream, letting it pick its way through fetlock-deep water. Krenin made no comment. Aerid stole a glance in his direction, but the Prince's Second seemed still in control of his horse although he slumped over the animal's neck. Around them, water rushed and hissed over stones, the sound echoing the blood-rush in her veins.

The Prince's arm tightened, drawing her hard against the planes of his chest. Aerid sucked in breath, digging her fingers once more into his tunic sleeve. Every movement reminded her, perched sideways as she was on the saddle pommel, all that kept her out of the water and away from trampling hooves was the strength of his arm—and that arm was trembling. Not with the fear still rattling through her, for he was Tolemak and a warrior. Nor with weakness, though the wound she had stitched a scant seven-night before could yet give him cause. No, in that moment when he had recognized her—in that awful moment *after* the shock—she had seen all too clearly the fury vibrating through him now. And the knowledge that it had not abated even a whit made her flinch when he bent and his voice lashed at her ear.

"Tell me, witch, and tell me true—does Krenin know who you are?"

The question itself startled Aerid, not its harshness, for she had expected that. Twisting her head, she caught a glimpse of eyes like coals in a face dark and set.

"I mean," he said, each word measured and knife-sharp, "either who you are or who you pretend to be."

She flushed, knowing full well what he meant. "I—I think not, m'lord. 'Twas dark and—"

"Then you'll do nothing to enlighten him. Hear?"

She heard him clearly despite the water-song and hoof splashes she was sure prevented their voices from carrying to Krenin. She understood, too, what underlay his warning. He wanted no one to know that he, the exalted and invincible Prince of Val-Feyridge, had been tricked—*trapped*—into sparing the life of an Adanak—and a *woman!*—only to cover the fact he and all his army had been duped into believing—*for weeks!*—that she was a boy, and a D'nalian. Oh, he had chosen well the moment for his question, Aerid thought, a rush of indignation beating back her shivers.

"Aye, m'lord, 'tis safe with me, your *secret*."

His arm clenched so, she feared he would crush her. "I should have let them kill you!"

He had to feel how her heart fluttered like a trapped bird under his arm, but the breathlessness made her almost giddy, not frightened. Her words had power, and her tongue spat out more of them. "Why did you not? If I be to you what you believe of me, why did you not leave me to them? 'Twas surely—"

"You helped Krenin. Why?"

Why indeed? Krenin was Tolemak, her enemy. But he

had been alone, and injured, and there were so many of them, and they were thieves, not good men, and she could not stand by and watch while... Tears scorched her throat. The Prince would not understand any of that—not he, the warrior who swung his arm and lopped off heads and limbs without thought of who the bearers might be or where they might be from or who they might have waiting for them—

"'Twas—'twas not by *choice!*" Turning away, she pressed knuckles to her mouth to stop its trembling.

He made no response, only straightened away from her and turned the horse toward a grassy bank. When the animal had climbed out of the water, he opened his arm. Unprepared, Aerid slid straight down and fell into marshy grass. She gaped as he dismounted and, looking impossibly tall and featureless in the faint moonlight, stood over her. "Understand then—'tis not by *my* choice that you're here, now." Dropping the stallion's reins, he walked toward Krenin's horse, pushing aside the stray that had followed them.

Aerid stared after him until the mucky ground dampened her breeches. Shoving herself upright, she yanked her cloak around her body and jerked her healer's pouch over her hip. So, the Prince wanted her to know he had defended her and thrown her atop his horse for no more reason than he owed her for helping Krenin. *Sisters Three!* She was no soldier—*and glad of it!*—but she understood duty. And obligation, too. Far better than the high and mighty Prince of Val-Feyridge seemed to think she did. She was a healer first and foremost. Her healer's instincts had brought her to Krenin's aid. Her healer's obligation insisted she finish the task.

Plowing through the tall grass on legs still unsteady, Aerid drew up beside the Prince where he had settled his companion against a large rock. When he crouched, she had the advantage—however fleeting—of height. Lifting her chin, she said in a voice she hoped was both as level and as cold as his had been, "You did speak of duty, m'lord. 'Tis mine to heal. Will you let me be about it?"

Under his brows, his eyes glinted with moon sparks, but she could read no expression in them. "By all means."

He did not touch her when he turned, but his

swirling cloak slapped her arm. In the contact, Aerid sensed just as surely as she had while pressed against his body that same low vibration of fury, tightly reined now and tamped down, but humming nonetheless behind the mask he had put on for Krenin. Well, she could conceal herself just as well. Kneeling beside Krenin, she examined his injuries, shushing him when he tried to speak.

When Aerid had washed Krenin's wounds and bound those that bled, he revived enough to peer at her. "Demon's Blood, I think I know you. Did you—?"

"Here." She handed him his own water skin and dropped two pinches of powdered shepherd's bane on his palm. "Put this on your tongue and drink. 'Twill ease the pain."

Weeks before, Aerid had considered killing him with an overdose of the herb. Now she merely watched while he tossed the powder into his mouth and took a long drink. Weeks before, her life had been entirely different. Her enemies had seemed clear. Now the lines had become far too muddied for her comfort. In return for her one act of assistance, however unwilling, Krenin himself—the man who for her most personified Tolemak evil—had defended her—and himself, of course—against all attackers. When he thought she was on his side, he had put himself in harm's way for her—even if he had first thrust a torch into her hand and yelled at her to use it. She wondered what he would think, how he would react if he knew her true identity.

Krenin lowered the skin. Rivulets of water ran down his chin, glistening in the thin light. He made no effort to wipe away the dribbles.

Aerid stood. She could hardly expect him to wipe away his prejudices because one Adanak had helped him when so many others had gleefully joined in battering him. Thieves or no thieves, her countrymen's actions shamed her. She turned away, wondering if it was a delusion to think any other man—now Naed was dead and Dranoel far away—might behave in any measure like the Prince. He, at least, had some sense of honor. Furious as the Prince seemed, she felt safer in his presence than anywhere else at the moment.

She looked about, wondering where he had gone. His horse stood some distance away, cropping grass with Krenin's chestnut and the stray. Aerid wandered toward them. She told herself she intended only to tell the Prince she had finished tending Krenin, that he and his friend could ride away now, if he wished. Then he could be quit of her, and she of him. The thought left her with a sudden, sharp emptiness in her chest. Stroking a hand through the stallion's mane, she tried to swallow down the sensation. 'Twas foolishness, after all, naught but the result of nerves stretched too thin in a night over-full with danger and emotions and—

He was behind her.

Aerid sensed the Prince's presence as surely as she sensed the horseflesh warm under her hand and the slice of moon glimmering overhead, but neither raised the hairs on her body the way the sensation of his nearness did. Heart in her throat, she whirled.

Disturbed, the horse shook its head and moved off before grazing again.

The Prince ignored the animal, his eyes under heavy brows fixed on her. Looming against the star-drenched sky, he closed half the distance between them with a single step. "What were you doing in that town?"

Instinct told her to back away, to maintain the space between them—already too narrow—but his tone, rife with the implication she had no right to be where she was, prompted her to stand her ground. She raised her chin. "Hard by it lies a road that leads where I would go."

"Where is that, woman?"

"As this be Adanak and not your camp, m'lord, 'tis no duty I have to be telling you, nor no right of yours to be asking. I'll go where I wish, but be assured, 'twill be far from the likes of you and those who wage war upon one another! 'Twas not my intention to be finding your Second bleeding at my feet, but 'tis sure 'twas your intent to be spying on the folk living there. Will you be slaughtering them on the morrow, m'lord, or be that the plan for the day after?"

Breathless, Aerid wondered where her tongue had found the audacity to speak such words, words her heart applauded even as her mind warned her of the danger.

116

That danger emanated in palpable waves from him now, the air seething with pent-up energy the way the air in a place seethes the instant before a lightning strike.

But he said only, "Mind your place, witch!" and it was she who exploded.

"*Woman! Witch!* Call me *Adanak*, m'lord, and be done with all three! Only two be true, and well do you know it!"

There, she had struck something in him. Even in the darkness, she could see the scar on his cheek stand out silver against a whitened jaw. He stepped still closer, and the air seemed suddenly too thick for Aerid to breathe.

"Woman...Adanak..." His words sounded musing, but every fiber in Aerid's being hummed with the wire-tight tension underlying that deceptive softness. "More witch than anything...bewitching... How in Demon's name do you do it—appearing where I least expect you? How do you call men to you? Dranoel and his nephew—how did you beguile them into hiding you? And Krenin—did you work the same charm on Krenin to make him lie down at your feet? Tell me true, do you dance naked under the full moon and whore with the Master of Evil himself? Or are you one of the Demon's own depraved Nine?"

Aerid gaped. Her mouth worked. All the blood that had drained away at his insults rushed into her face like an igniting flame. She swung without thinking, aiming for the mouth that could spit such venom.

He blocked her hand and, catching hold of her wrist, jerked her forward. Aerid fell against his chest. Before she could do more than put up her free hand to brace herself, he seized her chin with a hand that trapped her entire jaw in its grip. That hand forced her head up, allowing her a glimpse of eyes as sharp and predatory as a hawk's before he swooped.

Eyes wide, Aerid was conscious of a mouth—the Prince's mouth!—locking on hers. Of lips and teeth and tongue that forced her lips apart and invaded her being. Of heat, and wetness, and beard-stubble scraping her chin. Of shock and helplessness and outrage. Of the thought that—*Sisters!*—this was what people called a kiss?

He freed her, and it felt as if he had flung her away, yet he stood no more than half an arm's length away.

Gasping, Aerid stared, unable to find voice or summon thought, if only to name the emotions roiling through her. His eyes mesmerized. She seemed incapable of aught else but staring until the Prince raised a hand and pulled the knuckles of it across his mouth.

Aerid's face flamed. So, he had forced himself upon her and then decided to wipe away her essence! As if she had asked to be assaulted in the first place! As if, prince or no prince, he had any right—!

Her left hand flew at his face, but he caught it as easily as he had the other, and yanked her just as easily against his chest. Aerid tried to close her lips against him, but his hand at her throat forced her head up and his fingers on her jaw pressed open her mouth. Then there was naught but sensation, the rasp of his beard-shadow, the rush of his breath on her cheeks and eyelashes, the thrust of his tongue into every soft, secret place of her mouth.

She was breathing.

No, *he* was breathing.

Breathing into her. For her. *With* her.

Her bones had gone liquid, and her body melted into every angle and plane of his. He drew back a fraction, made a sound—something between a growl and a moan— and ravished her mouth again. Her hood fell back, his fingers slid into her hair, the tips massaging, the palm hot against the back of her head. Her hands, somehow free, anchored themselves in his tunic. She was conscious of nothing but how the long, taut muscles of his thighs burned as if skin-to-skin against hers, how the power of his encircling arm drove her abdomen hard against all that made him a man, how the hidden places of her womanhood clenched in tingling spasms of response.

Gravel crunched. A twig snapped.

The Prince shoved her away, spinning toward the sounds so quickly, Aerid nearly fell. She swayed, dazed and breathless, while he straightened and lowered his sword. Only then did she realize Krenin was slowly picking his way along the stream bank toward them.

Half-turned away, the Prince sheathed his sword. Fisting his hands on his hips, he drew a deep breath, held it a moment, then spoke. "Go. Take the stray and leave—

now—before I forget what you've done for Krenin and remember that I owe you nothing."

Aerid heard the words, but her consciousness was too overloaded with a maelstrom of emotion to comprehend their full import. That his voice had been pitched too low for Krenin to hear over the music of the stream, she perceived first. The understanding each word had been enunciated with precision, as if to prevent any misunderstanding on her part, dawned next, followed by the realization only a slight hoarseness betrayed any trace of the emotions that must have driven his body but a moment before. When he turned and looked at her, however, his expression was as cold and remote as the moon.

Aerid's blood still hummed, her flesh still burned with the imprint of his hands, his arms. If she could but touch him now, she would know whether the heart that had thundered under her palms had been his or merely the echo of her own. The contact must have shaken him as much as it had her; she was almost certain of it. Yet he was giving her no time to consider, no time for questions as he turned away and, catching up his stallion's reins, strode to meet Krenin.

"The boy is leaving," she heard him say. "He's taking the other horse." Krenin replied, but she caught none of it. Instead, Krenin turned at his urging, and both men walked away.

Some sense of self-preservation prompted Aerid to catch the stray before it followed the other horses. When she looked again, the Prince and Krenin had mounted and crossed the stream. She willed that ramrod-straight back, that forward-focused head to turn, to look at her just once before he followed Krenin into a copse of trees, but the Prince rode steadily on and disappeared.

He had saved her.

He had left her.

Again.

But this time he had taken something from her. Aerid touched her swollen lips and beard-scraped chin. He had taken her first kiss, and the thought made tears well up in her eyes and burn the back of her throat. *Sisters Three, why did she have to lose that to a Tolemak!*

Dashing her knuckles across her eyes, she mounted. Well, at least he had given her a horse, if the gesture of handing over a stray could be called "giving." Now she could take herself far away from him and his kind—and all the turmoil they provoked. Heeling the horse into a trot, she pointed the animal away from the direction the Prince had gone and toward the northeast, toward the mountains where she would be safe.

****

Fool-ish. Fool-ish. Fool-ish. Darkstar's hooves beat the refrain into Arn's brain. His shoulder ached with it. His body—despite years of disciplined subjugation to the will of his mind—throbbed with it. *Demon's Blood!* He had spent the last seven-night wondering with every stray thought—and he had far too many of *them!*—what this woman tasted like, whether the secrets of her mouth would yield in any measure the intoxication a mere whiff of her scent did.

He had his answer now.

Arn expelled a string of oaths and wished he had an enemy at hand. The skirmish in town had barely vented his earlier fury, and this, pent up because of Krenin's presence, strained his bodily limits. Were he alone, he would be tempted to take his sword to the trees until some of this *madness* was spent.

Yet it was his own traitorous body that needed the punishing. From the moment he recognized her, he had spent every minute fighting his body's response to her. She was just a woman, *Demon-be-damned!*

But a woman who tasted like paradise, who stirred his body like no other woman ever had. A woman who drove him crazy with fury at his own inability to resist her.

He had beaten back the attackers in the square. She could have fled before they recovered, yet Arn knew from the moment he recognized her that nothing he did after that was for Krenin or his own safety, but solely because he had to have her in his arms, however much it cost him. To that end, he had manhandled her like a piece of baggage, called her names his good sense knew were not true, and when he provoked her into raising her hand against him, used her puny threat as an excuse to pull her into his embrace and take what he had wanted all along.

He closed his eyes at the memory of her shock, her outrage. He ought to be ashamed of his behavior, but when she exhaled into his mouth and her body melted like molten heat against every line of his, the sensations surpassed even those in his most vivid fantasies. A persistent heaviness in his groin reminded him he had been heartbeats away from stripping her of those ridiculous boy's clothes. Had Krenin not come upon them, he would likely have taken her there in the marsh grass. Under his breath, Arn cursed Krenin's inconvenient sense of timing.

The stallion flicked its ears at the rumble of his voice. Arn glanced over his shoulder, wondering if Krenin had heard, but his friend made no sign, riding steadily with his head down. Overhead, the sky was already pinking while the receding night thickened the forest shadows. They could not be far now from the rendezvous point Arn had set with his troop, but he knew they were well past the time. If only he had not stayed so long at the river.

He had stayed so long at the river, the functioning part of his brain inserted, because he had *not* been using his reason. If he cared to use it now, he would see Krenin's "inconvenient" timing had likely saved him from a fatal mistake. This woman was, after all, an enemy, a potential spy with access to poisons. Arn ground his teeth at the thought, but the logic of it was clear, and he had never been one to disregard logic out of hand.

Nevertheless, his gut, with its usual absolute certainty in its own judgment, insisted his brain's logic was faulty. Every encounter with this woman had led him to the truth eating at his innards and fueling his fury— she was no spy. Nor was she an enemy, except by accident of birth. She was something more dangerous—a truth-teller, a woman with a pure heart and independent mind who told him what she thought of everything he had done and called him to account for it.

Being harangued by this slip of a girl, this child-woman who responded to his assault on her body with the innocence of the untouched, yet who treated the wounded with the skill and worldliness of one twice her age was a novel experience. In his youth he had enjoyed his share of whores—Krenin had seen to that—and serving maids bedazzled by soldiers. Later, women of status warmed his bed, discreetly leaving before dawn. Not a one had told him what she thought, nor would he have listened if they had. This one, however...his mind did not know how to react to her, making him feel clumsy and stupid, while his body knew exactly what it wanted, making him at war with himself.

If he could blame his lust on witchcraft, he could redirect his fury, channel it against something outside himself. Despite the many times he had accused her of bewitching him, Arn knew in his gut 'twas nothing supernatural about her allure. He wanted her because *he* wanted. The need was overwhelming, but to act on it would be wrong, a critical mistake in a time when—

"Go ahead," Krenin's voice broke into Arn's thoughts, "tell me again what a fool I am for anything in skirts."

Blinking, Arn swiveled in his saddle. Part of his brain noted the predawn bird and tree frog chatter had ceased and the clop of the two horses' hooves seemed overloud in the ensuing silence, but the main part noticed Krenin had ridden alongside, and the looks he cast from under his brows were both sullen and penitent.

"'Tis what you're thinking, whether you say it or no," Krenin growled. "For my sake, I'd rather you say it and be damned because, for once in this string of years the Sisters have given me, I know 'tis true. Right now, I'd give anything for that iron will and cold cock of yours."

Arn choked. He coughed. He wheezed until Krenin reached over and pounded his back.

"What's the matter—swallow your tongue?"

"In—in a manner of speaking." Arn wiped his mouth, hoping the shadows hid the true source of his flush, hoping he had it under control now, that impulse to laugh like a lunatic. Krenin would not understand, and Arn could not possibly explain how—

"If that boy hadn't been there," Krenin plowed ahead, "'tis like I'd have died in that alley, and—by the Demon!— 'tis not how I want to come to my end. 'Twas a sign from the Sisters."

"'Twas a sign," Arn agreed. If his superstitious best

friend and Second had decided to overcome a weakness, Arn could not find fault with Krenin's interpretation of the night's events. After all, he had come to much the same decision about the need to overcome a weakness of his own. Sign or no sign from supernatural beings, Arn's future—indeed, the future of all the people—depended on his maintaining a clear and consistent focus on—

—on the sounds that were not there!

Arn reined in sharply, the hairs on the back of his neck prickling. He reached for his sword and shield as Krenin rode on ahead, turning in the saddle, a question on his battered face. Even as Arn's lips formed the word, "Wait!" the enemy erupted from the trees, an explosion of noise and motion. Darkstar reared. A charging horseman plowed into the stallion and Darkstar lost his balance, tilting over with a scream. Kicking free of the stirrups, Arn braced himself for the impact, but it came before he was ready.

CHAPTER ELEVEN

Naed's wound itched. His chest armor chafed his undertunic across the peeling scab with each shift of his horse's weight. He tried sitting up straighter, or to the left or right, but nothing availed. For the fourth time in as many days, he found himself missing Yormoc's company.

For weeks Naed had endured his countryman, holding his tongue when Yormoc made crude jokes or speculated about the gold that service in the Prince's army might bring them, yet now that Naed had been removed from the D'nalian cohort and assigned as an under-officer to Master of Horse Gorm, he had never felt more alone. He ate alone, bedded down alone, tended his wound alone while Tolemaks near his solitary fire snickered at his attempts to refasten his bandage.

Now, with the sun barely arisen on a day promising unseasonable heat, and sweat already stinging the raw scab, Naed knew his clumsily tied bandage had shifted to a useless bulge above his sword belt. He yearned to roll up his tunic, pull apart the laces of his armor and yank out the offending lump, but the men riding on either side were hard-eyed Tolemaks who already looked at him with derision despite the fact a half-dozen had been assigned to follow his orders.

He had as yet no chance to test their obedience since each day his unit had patrolled with a larger group. The previous night, however, Gorm had split the company, sending twenty with the Prince and Krenin. Glad not to be among the chosen, Naed had bedded down, only to be roused before dawn and told to report.

There were thirty-odd horsemen now, spread into five groups with each man visible to at least two others and riding slowly through forest and glen in the fan formation that spoke to Naed not of mere patrol but of search. Master of Horse Gorm, a burly, bearded giant who towered over even the Prince—and likely weighed twice as much, according to Yormoc—had placed himself at point, signifying a mission of significance. Naed hoped it was something more energetic than getting saddle sores and collecting dust. Even though his wound still pulled, his muscles were in serious need of exercise. Yormoc, at least, had been a decent sparring partner.

There was a stir in the line where the trees thinned. Ahead lay an area with reeds winding through it. The rising sun sent bars of tree shadow across everything it touched, including a narrow, beaten-down path bordering the meadow. To this Gorm summoned his under-officers. He pointed a huge hand to freshly churned soil and a scattering of clear hoof prints.

"Adanak," said one of the under-officers, and spat.

"No more than 10," said another, fingering his weapons.

"Within the hour," said a third.

Drawing aside his horse, a heavy-boned mountain breed as bristle-haired as himself, Gorm pointed at the farthest mark. "But not this one." He signaled two other men.

The newcomers—trackers, Naed guessed—dismounted and studied the ground. "'Twas made before the others," said one, straightening and dusting his hands on his breeches.

"Aye, but not much before," said the other. He glared at Naed, who had moved his horse close and peered at the hoof print over the man's shoulder. "'Tis Tolemak—see the hammer pattern?" He paused a beat before adding, "Sir."

The soldier was one of his assigned six, a compact man of twenty-odd years with dark eyes full of challenge. "Aye." Naed returned the man's stare. "I know the difference."

"Mount up." Gorm waved a huge fist. "We've two men missing and the enemy to find." He barked orders, sending groups fanning out alongside the trail to follow it. To Naed, he said, "Follow the stream south and cross below the main group," before riding away.

The dark-eyed Tolemak had mounted. He and his companions sat on their horses in various poses of sullen indifference while the dust raised by departed horsemen twinkled in the sunlight shafting across their bodies. Like *magic powder*, Naed thought, wishing as he stared at the men that the legends were true and he had a handful of the Tree Folk's powder. He would toss it at the men now and change...*everything*. But there was no magic in this Adanak dust, and he knew the men who stared at him did not want his leadership any more than he wanted to lead them.

He could leave. Naed doubted any of them would lift a sword to stop him if he merely rode away. Indeed, they should be glad to be rid of him, and he of them, these savages who passed for men, who painted their faces and hacked off their hair, leaving it jutting out every which way from their helms. He was not one of them, nor did he wish to be. He straightened, and his horse danced beneath him, as if sensing a change.

The men watched him, their eyes unblinking, cold. Only the dark-eyed one seemed to openly dare him, as if the man could track a heart as well as a hoof print. *Go on*, his look said, *leave. We know you D'nalians are cowards.*

Naed's fingers tightened on the reins. His horse stamped as a breeze shivered the trees. He was not a coward. He knew in his heart he feared no more than these men feared, perhaps even less. After all, he had faced down a Lancer. Did not his tunic, though mended, still bear the stain of that encounter? He had naught to prove. Naught to uphold.

Naught but his honor.

"'Tis my word that's been given, and yours too!" Dranoel's words came to him on the sigh of the wind. *"Honor, lad, 'tis a man's soul! Sully it and you'll be no true D'nalian."* Naed's jaw clenched. 'Twas the way of honor, his uncle had tried to tell him, to be a two-edged sword— expectation on one side, obligation on the other. An honorable man fulfilled his obligations, whether they were to honorable people or not.

Suddenly furious, he barked, "You heard Master Gorm. Spread out and move south."

The men hesitated. They looked at each other, then at the dark-eyed man who sat with one hand resting on his sword hilt and his gaze fixed on Naed.

Naed's fingers tensed, but he made no move toward

his weapon. He had faced down challenges to his command at Druemarwin before anyone knew he was the master's nephew. This was a test, and he would pass it—even if he had to take them all on, individually or together. "Are you not true soldiers?" he threw at them. "Or do you defy Master of Horse Gorm's orders?"

"We defy nothing that is Tolemak," said the dark-eyed man. "Sir." Nodding to the others, he touched his heels to his horse. They fell into positions without comment, like men who had long served together, and began to sweep south along the near bank.

Naed wheeled his horse. The animal's mouth frothed, and it chewed the bit. He walked the horse in another circle, seeking to settle it when he realized the quiver he sensed came from his own legs, from the sweat-drenched easing of his own tension. Leaning forward, he patted the horse's neck, soothing it as much as himself before he turned it to catch up with the others.

****

Krenin woke to a fuzzy view of legs, tree roots, and blood. *His* blood, he realized as what felt like drool slid warmly from his mouth and splashed red onto a breeches-clad thigh. *His* thigh, he surmised as his cloudy mind registered the sensation of leaning against ropes cutting across his chest. If he had hands, he could no longer feel them. He certainly could not see them with his hair like a ragged curtain around his face and his head like a full-to-bursting water skin dangling from his neck. His clearing vision registered his manhood still intact.

Well, that was something to thank the Sisters for. There was something else he should thank them for, but he could not at the moment recall it. Not now when this blissful numbness was fading and various parts of his body screamed painfully awake.

He heard voices, movements around him, but something in the men's speech warned him to stay still, to keep his head down.

"Is it certain this one tore up the square?" said a voice seeming to belong to a pair of polished boots that had planted themselves squarely beside Krenin's knees.

"Aye, sir," said another voice, one without feet. "Bloodied him we did—see?—afore the other come. 'Tis done for, that one. Horse fell on him. But this one be ours, dead to rights."

"Aye, more dead than right. Is it daft you be, you empty-headed sons-of-whores? 'Twas alive, I said, not battered deaf and dumb. 'Tis Tolemaks they be, you lice-ridden asses! Be you blind to the swords, the hair?"

A hand seized Krenin's hair, the grip all but tearing at the roots. The nerves in his scalp exploded into red-hot, tooth-rattling agony. He bit his tongue, not caring that more blood filled his mouth. He had to play dumb for as long as he could while he learned—what? He wished his brain could function, could grab a thought and hold it. He had not been alone, he remembered. He had been in Herset, that nest of thieves. A boy had rescued him. A boy and...Arn!

It came back with a choking rush—the ambush, Darkstar going over, Arn disappearing beneath the horse, the sickening scream—cut short—of a creature in agony. And then Krenin himself, overwhelmed, fighting with nothing but blind rage and fear, fear for the one person he cared for, the one he loved more as a brother than a friend, more than himself. The one whom the Sisters had always smiled on...

The voices said Arn was dead.

Krenin wanted to gag on the blood he tasted, but something made him withstand the urge. This was not how it was supposed to end, the dream, the destiny. But, by the Demon, if this was how the Sisters saw fit to treat him, he was damned if he would go willingly. He would spit in their eyes, *the bitches!*

****

Naed had ridden long enough through the sparse trees beside the streambed for the sun to bake the shield he carried slung across his back. Where sweat had trickled before, it ran on his body now, making his wound burn and itch. He wanted nothing more than to throw himself into the shallow water whispering over pebbles and rocks. He would settle for pouring a helm-full down his undertunic—anything to relieve this demonic itch.

A whistle from the dark-eyed Tolemak brought his head up. Naed rode toward him as the others gathered. Fresh hoof prints marred the opposite bank. A horse had come, stood, and turned back into the trees. The prints were clear, the hammer pattern Tolemak.

Naed looked at the men ringing him. Even though they knew the track belonged most likely to one of their missing companions, Naed understood these men would do nothing unless he ordered it. They would obey his orders, grudgingly, but only until he made a mistake. Well, he would not give them the satisfaction. Choosing to remain as silent as they, Naed gestured for two men to take the left, two the right, and one the rear. Pointing to the dark-eyed one, he indicated the Tolemak should follow the track. When the man, with a narrowing of his eyes, heeled his horse across the stream, Naed followed him while the others spread out on either side.

The forest thickened, bringing relief from the sun but so densely packing tree upon thicket Naed lost sight of all but the man ahead. The vegetation swallowed sound, too; where once Naed could locate his men by the occasional chink of hoof or snap of a branch, here he heard naught but his own animal's muffled footfalls. Something other than sweat tickled along his spine, prompting him to loose his sword and pull his shield forward, fitting it to his arm.

A crackle of branches brought him wheeling sideways, weapon in hand. Scant feet away, a horse pushed through the undergrowth and nosed his mount. The black stallion was limping, favoring a gashed hindquarter. Its saddle was askew, its coat thick with dust, its mane and tail festooned with twigs, pine needles, and leaves. Naed's mouth went dry. He knew the Prince's horse as well as any man in the army.

His companion's face had gone whiter than any Tolemak's Naed had ever seen, save a dead one. Sword drawn and eyes smoldering, the man wheeled his horse toward the brush.

"Don't be a fool!" Naed hissed, heeling his mount across the man's path. "We have no idea how many there are, nor where. And 'tis our duty to signal Master Gorm before we act."

"He's not one of yours! 'Tis different you'd be acting if he were!"

"'Twould be no difference," Naed retorted. He had lost his head over Dranoel's injury, and it had cost

Druemarwin. "'Tis sworn I am to do my duty. We'll send a man back to Gorm and continue on—together."

The Tolemak's stare knifed him, but the man made no further move to ride off alone. Instead, he caught the black stallion's reins while Naed whistled for the rest of the men. Only the one riding rear guard appeared, saying when Naed questioned him that he had heard nothing but had merely followed their tracks.

Naed knew either Tolemak could give the appropriate signal to gather in the others, but neither would offer to do so despite the danger to their own leader. The muscles in his neck corded, but he refused to play their game. Instead, he handed the Prince's horse to the other man and sent him off with the news to Gorm. If these Tolemaks were as loyal as they claimed, he expected this one would summon the others and give them the news before he left. With a fervent hope that at least four other Tolemaks would trail them through the forest, Naed signaled to the dark-eyed man to backtrack the stallion.

The trail led them between bramble thickets to where an Adanak soldier stood relieving himself into the shrubs. Naed's companion reacted first, cutting the man down before his stream ended. "Good work," Naed whispered.

"Quiet!"

Naed had overlooked the man's omission of "sir" before, but this was not such a charged moment. He was about to issue a reprimand when he noticed the cocked head and alert dark eyes. *Voices.* Dismounting, he signaled the man to follow him into the undergrowth. Licking sweat from his upper lip, he prayed to the Sisters that however many of the enemy he discovered on the other side of this thicket, he would not have to face them alone.

From his vantage point behind a screen of knife-edged pig thistle, Naed counted one man holding horses—Krenin's chestnut among them—under a willow, one sweating in the sun beside a narrow track's entry to the clearing, and one leaning against a tree at the trail's exit. Something—a body?—lay amid the tree roots near that man's feet. A fourth Adanak dragged a fifth, likely dead, companion from those trees toward a waiting horse. The remaining two stood before a prisoner bound to a substantial oak about forty feet away. One of those appeared to be an under-officer who was not pleased. The man had hauled up the semi-conscious captive's head by his hair.

A sharp indrawn breath from the Tolemak at his side told Naed the man had recognized Krenin too. As far as he could tell, there was no sign of the Prince.

"'Twere ten tracks at the stream," Naed whispered. "If these are the same, 'tis six here alive, one dead, and three where we cannot see them."

"Two dead."

Naed remembered the Adanak they had surprised. "Aye, but still eight to two."

"Three, once we free Krenin."

Naed stared at his companion. "He's barely conscious."

"He's Tolemak. He'll hold a sword."

The man could hardly have issued a more blatant challenge. Naed trembled. He was better than this. He knew how to think, unlike these savages who rode roughshod into battle. He was D'nalian, a master at keeping his temper in check. At the moment, however, doing so had sapped every ounce of his concentration, and the thoughts stampeding through his brain formed no clear plan.

Krenin was in danger from the angry officer. If Naed sent his companion for help, it could arrive too late. Yet, for two to attack at least eight—even with the element of surprise—was extremely foolish. Assuming they could even get to Krenin, Naed knew better than to count on help from a man who appeared so badly beaten. Then there was the matter of the Prince who was yet nowhere to be seen.

While his mind raced, Naed felt the soldier watching him, reading his every thought, and waiting. He guessed the Tolemak had ideas of his own, and the man's smugness made Naed's fingers itch for his throat. "Well, have you a plan?"

"'Tis you who's the officer."

"Have you no loyalty? Krenin is of your kind!"

"Aye, but you are not."

Naed's fist shot out and cracked the man across the mouth.

The Tolemak sprawled backward, snapping dry pig thistle under his body. The sound was like a thunderclap, shattering Naed's fury and bringing him instantly back to the time, the place, the danger. Flinging himself atop the outraged Tolemak, he slapped a hand to the man's mouth. Over his shoulder, he watched two of the Adanak soldiers glance about, but the officer made no sign he had heard anything.

Rocking to his knees, Naed freed his companion's mouth. Blood streaked his palm. With a grimace, Naed wiped it on a patch of moss.

The Tolemak pushed up, eyes ablaze, and touched his cut lip.

If a look could murder, Naed was sure he would be dead, but nothing the man threw at him mattered now. Not when he had shamed himself by drawing blood in anger. He could not—would not—shame himself further. "If 'tis Tolemak you say you are," he hissed, seizing the man's tunic, "then prove it! 'Tis sworn I am to fight for the Prince—your kind—and, by the Sisters, I mean to do so! Stand now and aid me, or slink away to your fellows. But never say that a D'nalian shirked his duty!"

For the span of heartbeats, the Tolemak returned Naed's glare. Then he lowered his gaze and wiped bloody fingers on his tunic hem. "I can shoot a bow," he said when Naed released his tunic. "'Twas an archer I killed. I saw his bow and quiver. 'Tis like I could take two."

"While I free Krenin." Two quickly taken and the element of surprise would reduce the odds. "Fetch it. I'll work my way round to behind the oak and wait for your shot."

The man nodded and moved off.

Naed located his sword beside his boot and picked it up, noticing his knuckles bled. He ignored another stab of shame and wormed his way into a low hedge a body's length behind the oak. Sprawled on his stomach, he could see how the ropes cut into Krenin's wrists, purpling the man's hands. Such swollen fingers would never hold a sword, no matter how fervently his companion insisted they would. Even if he freed Krenin, the man was unlikely to be of assistance. Naed could only hope the other four Tolemaks—having found the dark-eyed one and realizing the risk to Krenin—were even now spreading through the trees. If not, well, the dremel beads were cast; he could do naught to call them back.

A soft thunk. A gurgle. The man holding the horses crumpled.

Even as the soldiers spun toward the sound, even as the second arrow drove into the sweating man's thigh and he shrieked, spooking the horses, Naed leaped up and charged. His first stroke sliced Krenin's ropes, pitching the prisoner to the grass. The second took the under-officer at the shoulder, splitting mail and armor, flesh and bone. The next caught the man's companion in the helm, felling him with a ring of metal to metal that shuddered along Naed's arm. He stepped over the body, pausing long enough to seize the man's sword and toss it toward Krenin, who had raised his head from the ground.

Four down. Naed scanned the area. *Four to go.* One of those had dropped his dead companion and raced toward Naed. Eyes fixed on the man's face, Naed bounced three steps forward, then poised on the balls of his feet. When the Adanak rushed him, Naed side-stepped, driving his sword into the gap between helm and shoulder armor. Wrenching his sword from bone, Naed knew—with a surge of satisfaction—the Prince would have approved the maneuver.

A flurry of shouts brought his head up. His Tolemak companion had been rushed by two soldiers who must have come from the forest, for Naed had not seen them before. The Tolemak had abandoned the bow for the close-fighting sword and shield, but his attackers had driven him against a tree. The remaining Adanak, charging from the shady track, ran headlong through the skittish, milling horses to join his companions. One of them had already knocked the Tolemak's helm off, and blood streamed down his face while his shield shook under their combined assault.

Naed roared. The fierce, inarticulate yell that seemed ripped out from his very toes, brought all four men's heads around and scattered the horses. The Tolemak recovered first, landing a blow to the helm of one attacker, staggering him before the second swung back to the fray. The third Adanak spun to meet Naed, but Naed's momentum carried him too far forward and they collided, shield to shield. The Adanak crashed to his back. Naed flew over the top, his helm chunked into earth, and the chin strap broke. He rolled to his feet, flinging sweat-soaked hair from his face, and charged before the man could rise from his knees. With one stroke Naed disarmed him and, with a kick to the jaw, laid the man flat.

Pivoting, he saw his companion go down with a blade to the thigh. Naed leaped at the attackers, slashing and smashing and hammering sword against sword, shield, helm. One man stumbled over a tree root and fell. The other reared back to strike a mighty blow, and Naed spun to brace his shield under it, but the blow never came. Instead, a startled expression stole over the Adanak's face, and he dropped to his knees before toppling over face-first at Naed's feet.

His shield and sword still poised, Naed stared at the Tolemak knife buried hilt-deep in the man's neck. With enormous effort, like a man waking from a deep, dreaming sleep, Naed lowered his sword and raised his gaze. Four Tolemaks, swords drawn, stood amid the milling horses. They surveyed the bodies in the clearing, looked at the blood on Naed's lowered sword, then regarded each other. Without a word, two spread out to check the bodies and disarm the wounded, and two walked toward Naed. The gap-toothed man knelt to the dead Adanak, pulled out the knife, and cleaned the blade on the grass.

"We—uh—heard the shouting," said his companion, a pale fellow with pocked skin. He glanced at Naed out of the corners of his eyes, but focused his attention on guarding the Adanak who had tripped and still lay on the ground, holding his head.

"Begging your pardon, sir," said the first, rising and sheathing his knife, "but 'tis sorry we are to be late. 'Twill not be happening again."

Naed could see in their eyes a disgruntled, reluctant admission they had not lived up to their duty. He knew they were unhappy to be shown up by a mere D'nalian, but he understood they would not compromise him again.

"It matters not," he said, suddenly weary of the issue. Dragging a hand over his face, he found his fingers shook. He rested his sword tip on the ground before his muscles turned to the jangling, shivering mass they always became after such violent exercise. "Look for prisoners. And see to Krenin. I left him somewhere by the oak."

The men nodded and left, taking with them the Adanak Naed had felled.

Naed stood a moment longer, mastering his breathing, before turning to his wounded companion. The dark-eyed Tolemak sat on the ground, blood seeping between fingers pressed to his thigh. His face was moon-white under the rivulets of red streaking the left side of it.

Laying down his sword, Naed knelt. He tore strips from the hem of the dead man's tunic, then pushed aside the Tolemak's hands and bound a wad of the cloth over the wound. Tearing another strip, he wrapped it around the man's head. Dark, unblinking eyes followed his every motion. "'Twill serve till your own healers come," Naed said when he finished.

He rose, intending to fetch a water skin from one of the milling horses when Master of Horse Gorm and his men thundered into the clearing. Almost at the same moment, a frantic shout rose above the commotion: "The Prince! I've found the Prince!"

****

Krenin sat before the command tent entrance and shifted the poultice he held from his eye to the cheekbone below it. Every inch of his scalp ached and, while his hands had recovered feeling, the rope burns around his wrists would linger for weeks. The welts stood out from his tunic cuff whenever he reached for his cup, the marks a fire-red reminder to everyone that he, Krenin—the Prince's Second, for Demon's sake!—had been taken prisoner. Only the knowledge he had killed several of his attackers in the village gave him any comfort. That and the fact Arn was alive and being tended within the tent behind him.

He took another sip of wine, careful not to let the liquid burn the cuts inside his mouth. If only the D'nalian had left more than one of the bastards in the clearing for him! But, no, even the one the fog-whelped pup had not killed had his brains so addled from a blow to the helm he was easy prey. Krenin scowled, pulling the stitches above his hairline.

"Is it true," Master Archer Illien said, leaning arms atop knees, "the red-tailed D'nalian took down the whole cohort himself?"

"'Twas impressive," Gorm said, dusting wheatcake crumbs from his beard. "I'd not be believing it, but for seeing it myself."

"'Twas no more than five for the lowland bastard," Krenin snarled. "I killed one when they jumped me. Our men from Albon took four more among them. Don't be forgetting that."

"Oh, aye," Gorm said. "A sorry-faced lot they were too, those lads from Albon."

"For letting a lowlander best them?" Illien said. "'Tis more than sorry they should be."

"Aye, there's that to their account." Gorm stared into his empty cup. "But 'tis like there's more. Close-mouthed, that lot from Albon. Used to their own."

"Bunch of women," Krenin muttered. "Did you punish them?"

Gorm shrugged. "'Tis for the D'nalian to decide, him being their under-officer."

"Oh, aye, as if he'd punish them for letting him act the warrior!" Krenin tossed back another gulp of wine, this time stinging his mouth. He coughed. "If 'tis done you are with singing the praises of a marsh-spawned, son-of-a-whore sword-for-hire who the Sisters in their infinite perversity have chosen to favor, let's move on to matters at hand."

"Aye," Gorm said, grinning as he picked his teeth, "let me be the first to avenge you. Tell me, will you be wanting your Adanak bones ground to powder, or is it more to your liking to cleave away the flesh yourself?"

"Tend to your own kills, you ill-mannered Bedian bear." Ignoring the look that passed between the wiry Illien and the giant Gorm, Krenin spread out a map. "I've sent a message to Nemmon, and Yarl is tending to our camp boundaries. Gorm, take your men and secure that thieves' nest of a town. Illien, cover our position from everywhere else. We'll not be going forward till the Prince revives."

"'Tis bad, or so I've heard," Illien said, looking squarely at Krenin.

"He'll not die," Krenin retorted, "and 'twill be accounted treason for anyone to go about suggesting it!"

Gorm reached out a hand and engulfed Krenin's shoulder. "Aye, we know that, old friend, but is there aught we can say to the men?"

"Tell them to pray," Krenin choked out. Raising his cup, he sloshed the entire contents into his mouth. His cuts burned, but he ignored the fire in favor of the comforting numbness the wine would shortly bring. He poured another cup and drained that while Gorm and Illien rose and left him alone in front of Arn's tent.

****

The air had begun to cool near sunset when Naed turned his horse over to the stock-master. Bone-weary, he wished to do nothing more than ladle out a bowl of stew, eat it and sleep, but 'twould be no pot stewing at his campsite. The Tolemaks had their own cooks, just as the D'nalians had, but he had been separated from his own kind and the Tolemak horsemen made it clear he was not welcome at their fires.

He had a bit of dried meat in his saddlebag. Taking it out, he gnawed off a piece. He was almost too tired to chew, but he forced his jaws to work. Knowing the meat would make him thirsty, and remembering how he had emptied his water skin hours ago, he reluctantly diverted his steps toward the stream. While he was there, he would wash, too. Or perhaps throw himself in, clothing and all; he felt so filthy.

As he knelt by the water's edge, the last rays of sunlight showed red on his hands. Naed turned them over, knowing as he did so the redness was no trick of the light. He had wiped his hands on grass and moss, but the blood still stained them, even under the fingernails. 'Twas no sin to shed enemy blood. Indeed, 'twas only right to protect one's self and property. But a D'nalian fought only for honor and with honor. He did not take pleasure in it.

But he had—both pleasure and pride.

Not only that, he had fought without thinking, like a beast. *Like a Tolemak.*

Naed shuddered. Pulling handfuls of grass, he sat back on his heels. There was Tolemak blood on his hands too, shed on impulse for an insult he should have been man enough—D'nalian enough—to bear. Rubbing a thumb over the scab crusting on his knuckles, he forced himself to look at his hands again. Whether red, dark, or rusty brown, blood stained his hands all the same, regardless of the source. Indeed, he could not tell where Adanak left off and Tolemak began, nor would he have known his own lest it was fresh. Mayhap, he considered, under their skin all men were alike, but he immediately dismissed the notion.

He was not like these others. At least, he *should* not be. Truly, he did not *want* to be. D'nalians thought and reasoned. They trod the narrow road of virtue and honor. 'Twas hot-blooded Tolemaks who followed the path of beasts, and Adanaks who wove lying word-spells and obeyed no rules but their own. The true D'nalian walked the straight path between passion and deceit.

Clearly, he was no true D'nalian. He had strayed off the path in both directions, first lying about Aerid and then conducting himself like a savage in battle. 'Twas just as well he had left Druemarwin. Dranoel would be ashamed of him, and so would Aerid if she knew.

Aerid. She whose eyes were as bright as stars, as deep as the night sky. If he closed his eyes, he could almost catch a whiff of the tiny purple flowers whose scent would forever remind him of her. He wondered where she was now, how far away. He trusted she was safe, for his heart sensed nothing amiss when he thought of her. And he thought of her frequently, seeing her in his dreams as he had so often seen her, standing before him and looking up, smiling, her hair a dark cloud about her face. *By the Sisters, would he ever find her again?*

Though his heart felt squeezed in a vise, Naed knew he had no time, no energy to indulge the misery threatening to overwhelm him. Who knew what the next day would bring? He had to rest, to be ready for it. Plunging his hands in the stream, he threw water over his face and head till his entire upper body dripped with it. Then he filled the water skin and, shouldering his saddle, pointed himself toward his campsite.

He could not find it.

Where he thought it lay, near Tolemaks he vaguely recognized, smoldered a small fire with a pot simmering on the coals. *His* pot, he realized as he recognized his bedding neatly spread out alongside. Opposite lay another prepared bed with a saddle for the pillow. Beside the fire, perched on a log with his bandaged leg stuck out from it, sat the dark-eyed Tolemak. He had washed and no longer wore the bandage Naed had fastened around his forehead, but under the ragged fringe of his black hair, Naed could see the pucker of a newly stitched wound.

The dark eyes flashed over Naed, then returned to the fire. "There's stew," the man said, pushing a bowl toward Naed.

The saddle slid from Naed's shoulder. He caught it, lowering it to the ground and setting the full water skin beside it, but despite the time he gave himself to think, his exhausted brain remained stunned. "Who—what are you doing here?"

The man slanted another look at him. "'Tis from the river crossing that we've been without an officer. None of the horse's asses Master Gorm's given us since have lasted out a day." He picked up another bowl and ladled some stew into it. "You're different."

Naed blinked. "Aye, 'tis D'nalian I am, in case you've forgotten."

The dark eyes flashed again. "Even so, you're no horse's ass." The Tolemak moved his jaw, calling Naed's attention to a bruise purpling his chin. "To my mind, 'tis alongside you I'd rather be fighting."

—*than against you.* The unspoken words hung in the air between them.

Naed understood he was being offered an apology. He sensed, too, how much the man risked to sit in company with a D'nalian in full view of a score of his countrymen. Sinking down on his bedroll, Naed ran hands through his wet hair. He could not in good conscience refuse such an offer even if he did not understand what had prompted such an extravagant gesture. Reaching out, he picked up the bowl. "What's your name?"

"Banir, from Albon. 'Twas the Prince's home ere he proved himself heir to Tolem." With a stick, he lifted the edge of one of the wheatcakes baking on a stone and peered at it.

Naed ladled out some stew and sat cross-legged on his bedroll to eat it. His belly growled, and he realized he was ravenous, but not too ravenous to miss the pride evident in Banir's statement. "You've served with him long?"

"Aye, all of us, since the Northern Wars." Evidently satisfied the wheatcake was done, Banir slid it onto a trencher and pushed that across at Naed.

Although his stomach still growled and his mouth watered around the stew he chewed, the gesture made Naed's throat tighten. "I—do not mistake me, for 'tis grateful I am for...this—" He gestured at the fire, the food, the bedding. "But 'tis not...necessary, and you do yourself a disservice to stay—"

Banir cut him off with a rude noise. He glowered across the fire with the same challenge Naed had seen that morning. "'Twould be a disservice not to do for my officer what needs to be done. 'Tis *my* duty."

Naed understood. Without any intention on his part, he had acquired a second, a man who would care for his needs, carry out his orders, and defend him to the death. Along with that realization came another—this Tolemak, for all his brusqueness, would serve him better than any D'nalian ever had, including—and especially—Yormoc. Reaching out, Naed picked up the trencher and placed it beside his knee. "Thank you."

****

Arn woke with the sun spilling through the partially open flap of his tent. He had slept fitfully, his dreams violent, disconnected. Voices had interrupted them, voices and hands—low, harsh voices and hard, callused hands that probed and prodded until each finger's touch left him snarling. He had slipped away then, into a dark wood where a bird fluttered softly along branches that had become his body. He longed for the fragile wings to brush his cheek, to stroke his face with the airy coolness of down, but the bird had only looked at him with great, unblinking blue eyes and vanished.

Aerid.

He started at the name, wondering why it should

come to him now. He had not called her by it—leastways, not more than once, for he had no clear idea how the name tasted on his tongue.

You've tasted her.

Heat rushed up from Arn's chest, warming him to the roots of his hair. Oh, aye, he knew how she tasted. And he knew how she felt, both the supple curves that had molded themselves to his frame and the delicate tenderness of her touch as she—was it only a seven-night ago?—tended his shoulder. If he had not driven her away, she could be here now, filling the tent with the fragrances that from the first he had noted about her.

A faint scent of evenroot tickled his nostrils, sending such a jolt of response through his body that Arn sucked in breath. The sudden expansion of his chest set off spasms of pain so intense sweat popped out on his forehead and he spat curses through gritted teeth. Well, now he knew he had broken a rib or two, and the healers had drugged him. No wonder his tongue felt furred and the scent his body had mistaken for one of hers lingered in the tent.

He had endured broken ribs before, the first time when he was thirteen. Three drunken Roinesmen, unaware of his identity, had beaten him because they could not find Krenin, who had bedded a woman one of them coveted. Arn remembered the boots driven against his side as he lay on the ground. Years later, he had found the two who still lived and killed them, but they had presented such a poor match for his skills he had stood over their bodies with none of the satisfaction he had so long anticipated. Instead, he had felt a curious emptiness.

Shaking the memory from his mind, Arn shoved the bedding aside and concentrated on pushing his body upright. It was a slow, agonizing ascent, and sweat ran down his face in rivulets. He wiped it with a trembling hand. Besides heavy bandages swathing his mid-section, his hip ached and he noticed an array of bruises purpling the entire left side of his body from hip to knee. His back felt as though it had been rammed into a tree, and his head pounded as though he had cracked it open. Perhaps he had, he thought, feeling gingerly around the nape.

"What in the name of all that's sacred are you doing?"

Arn slanted a look at Krenin, who stood in the tent's entrance. Green and yellow bruises decorated his friend's face. The town, Arn remembered. "Get me my clothes," he said, swinging his legs over the edge of his cot. "And some water."

"What kind of fool are you? 'Tis no more than a day and—"

"And I hurt and I'm thirsty—satisfied?" Arn growled. "But I'll be damned if I'll stay flat on my back. You know better than anyone I heal faster upright."

Krenin glowered for a full moment, his still-swollen brows crammed together over the bridge of his nose. "You're worse than an Arbez goat!"

Arn grinned despite wooziness. "You lucky bastard. They missed your nose again."

Krenin flushed, but the color only accented the pallor of his face under the bruising. "You bloody great fool! I thought you'd died! You nearly did!"

"Aye." Arn measured the puffs of air it took to speak without aggravating his injuries. He understood Krenin's concern and knew he needed to allay it, but he damned well needed a drink of something, anything, to ease the tremble in his hands clenching the bed frame. "But I didn't, did I? So be helpful and fetch me that water before I do die—of thirst."

Krenin's flush deepened. "Bloody great fool!" Swinging to the table, he sloshed water into a cup.

"And don't be putting anything in it, either. I can smell what those heavy-handed healers used on me. What possessed you to let them pour it down my throat in the first place?"

"You were thrashing around so much, I had to let them do something." He placed the cup in Arn's fingers, but his hand hovered underneath, offering support.

Arn appreciated his friend's concern, and his hand did shake alarmingly, but he managed to drain the cup without assistance. "That's better." He inhaled carefully. "How's Darkstar?"

"Better than you." Krenin shot him another glower. "Gorm's seeing to him personally."

Arn nodded. The movement sent stabs of pain up his backbone. He warded off Krenin with a raised hand. "Get

142

me into my clothes. The men need to see me."

"They can see you tomorrow. 'Tis enough for them to know you're awake."

"No, 'tis not enough," Arn articulated carefully. "'Tis for *my* sake that they've left home and family. 'Tis for the Crown that will sit upon *my* head that they are willing to fight and die. 'Tis essential that they see *me* now." His limbs trembled, sweat ran freely down his body, and he had no clear idea how he could get to his feet, much less stand, but he had to show himself—the sooner the better. "Help me do this, old friend, and I swear I'll take my ease till morning."

"Aye, as if I'd be fool enough to believe that." But Krenin opened a trunk and pulled out tunic and breeches. "'Twill be no farther I take you than just outside this tent. Demon knows how you'll manage that. 'Twill do you no good, you know, if you faint in front of the men."

Arn closed his eyes and conserved his strength. Krenin would go on muttering because it was his way, but his friend understood. He could rely on Krenin to do whatever was necessary to protect him—and his reputation, the one they had spent long years forging together, first of him as soldier, warrior, and victorious leader of men, then as Master of Albon, Prince of Val-Feyridge, and rightful heir to Tolem. Arn had lost count of the times Krenin had slapped hasty bandages on his wounds and stood behind him while he showed himself as the invincible leader his men needed to see and his enemies needed to fear.

Idly, he wondered how Krenin had managed to get him safely back to his tent this time. "Tell me, did you fight off that last pack yourself?"

Krenin coughed. The trunk lid snapped shut as if dropped.

Arn opened his eyes as Krenin flung a tunic over his head. "Aye? No?"

"Gorm went out looking for us, if you must know." Krenin held out a sleeve for Arn to lift his arm into. "That tracker from Albon found us, him and that red-tailed sword-for-hire from Druemarwin. Gorm, whose head must be as empty as it is large, made the lowland whelp under-officer to that leaderless bunch from Albon."

143

"Let me guess," Arn said as he slid his arm into the other sleeve, "instead of being run off by those hardheads, Dranoel's nephew scored a few kills."

"Too many," Krenin muttered, drawing on the tunic laces. "The bog-born bastard left me only one!"

****

Naed polished his shield. He had beaten out two dents with a stone wrapped in cloth, but a third narrow groove remained. A fingertip examination convinced him he would have to engage a smith to remove the indentation. He tested the arm and hand straps, then leaned the shield against his saddle.

Banir sat opposite, his back propped against his saddle. He hunched over Naed's helm, concentrating on fastening to it a new piece of leather to replace the broken strap. Before Naed had awakened, the Tolemak had spirited away his filthy tunic and washed it in the stream. It and his undertunic, which Banir had divested him of immediately upon arising, dangled from a nearby branch, both slowly drying in the breeze stirring Naed's queue. Tendrils tickled his naked shoulders, and he shivered, but not from cold. The sun beat down warmly on the lance wound he had bared to it, easing the itch.

Around their camp other men moved about in various degrees of nakedness, also taking advantage of the lull in the army's advance to wash, mend, and sleep. Now the Prince was known to be up and recovering, the somber mood that had gripped the camp had lifted, and more men gave themselves over to casting dremels, making idle music, and even engaging in horseplay and wrestling contests. Naed was glad to note that Banir seemed disinclined to gamble.

From close study of his new companion these past two days, he had decided Banir was eight or nine years his senior. The sun had worn creases beside his eyes, yet the black hair standing out in uneven tufts from his head showed no hint of graying. Square and compact, slightly shorter and perhaps broader than himself, Banir was efficient, steady, and given to long silences which, after Yormoc's constant chatter, was a pleasant change. After watching the man hobble about their camp the first morning, Naed had gone into the trees, found a stout sapling, and fashioned a crutch from it. He had handed it over without words, and Banir had accepted it in like manner. It lay beside his injured leg now, ready to his hand.

Two men approached their campsite, the first a pock-marked one carrying a roll of cloth and the other wearing a gap-toothed grin. The second swaggered, throwing daring looks right and left, despite a left eye that had nearly swollen shut. Naed recognized him as the Tolemak whose knife had brought down the last Adanak. Yester eve, when Naed had returned from sentry duty, he had found the two of them hunkered around Banir's fire, talking with him in low voices. They had risen upon Naed's arrival and inclined their heads in salute. Watching their faces as they left, he had seen none of their former contempt in their sidelong glances. Nor had he seen the black eye.

"'Tis here you are then, sir," the gap-toothed man said, drawing up to the campsite with a grin. "We've brung you a change of tunic."

"'Tis only right," said his companion before Naed could object. "Banir says your other's patched and stained."

"Aye, 'tisn't proper for an officer to go about in tatters—leastways, not an officer of ours."

"Grodar and Morys," said Banir by way of introduction. He reached for the tunic the one called Morys held out, but the pock-marked man thrust it toward Naed.

"You'll be needing this straight away, sir."

"Aye, 'twouldn't be proper to go before the Prince without putting it on."

"Going before the Prince?" Alarmed, Naed stood. "What do you mean?"

Banir struggled to his feet too. "What have you heard?"

Grodar shrugged. "'Tis not what we've heard, 'tis what we've been told. Master Gorm sent word to fetch you, sir, so we set off straight away."

"Bringing the tunic, of course," Morys added. "Banir asked for it yester eve."

Naed looked at each man. Morys seemed to prefer

looking at him sideways, but there was no ill will evident in his expression. Grodar continued to grin as though the summons were nothing to be dismayed about. Only Banir looked concerned.

"'Tis best you put that on." Banir nodded at the tunic Morys still offered. When Naed fixed eyes on his face, he added, "Master Gorm questioned all of us."

A sick feeling clenched at Naed's stomach. He had known it was a risk to go on into the forest without gathering his patrol. He should never have attempted an attack on his own. Now he would have to face the consequences. "What did you tell him?"

"The truth." A flush darkened the Tolemak's cheeks. Eyes downcast, he leaned on his crutch. "Leastways, about you."

"Aye," said Morys, nodding vigorously. "'Twas about ourselves that we—ow!"

"To be sure," Grodar interjected, withdrawing his elbow from his companion's ribs and ignoring Morys's scowl, "we've said nothing ill of you, sir. Indeed, 'twas only yester night that some of Yarl's men were doubting our word as to what you did the other day. Morys and me, we took it upon ourselves to convince 'em of our honesty."

"Aye, and we did, too," Morys said, his sudden grin revealing a swollen lip Naed had not noticed before.

"You were fighting?" Naed said, astonished. "With others of your own kind?"

Grodar hooked thumbs in his sword belt. "Oh, no, sir. Not fighting—as such."

"'Twas—'twas a difference of opinion," Morys interjected.

"Aye, but they've come around."

"And 'tis necessary that we be going." Banir snatched the tunic from Morys and thrust it at Naed. "The Prince'll be waiting. Demon knows how long it's taken these two asses to be about delivering his summons."

Morys looked chastened, and Grodar lost his grin. "We came straight away."

The tunic Naed flung over his head was short but wide enough in the shoulders—and clean. He felt naked without his undertunic and chest armor, but the first was still wet and he surely did not need the second in the presence of the Prince.

CHAPTER TWELVE

When Naed entered the Prince's tent, he found it filled with every major officer in the army. Eyes fell upon him, and the hostility projected was palpable. Clearly, he had arrived in the middle of a council, but the guards outside had acted as if he were expected. He stood in the entrance, wondering how to back out gracefully, when Master of Horse Gorm beckoned him. The giant Tolemak pointed to a space between himself and where the Prince sat upon a stool. The silence that had fallen upon Naed's appearance remained until he crossed the crowded tent and stood beside Gorm's enormous shoulder.

"Now that we're all here," the Prince said, capturing the attention of the assembly, "we'll get down the business at hand—our approach to Vinvinnysee."

While the men offered various expressions of eagerness, Naed stood dumbfounded. Had the Prince really meant what his words implied—that he, a D'nalian, was specifically invited to sit in on a Tolemak council of war? He scanned the group once more, but the survey only confirmed what he had noted upon first glance—this was an assembly of senior officers; there were none so minor as himself. What could they possibly want with him?

"Borth," the Prince was saying to the gray-bearded man Naed recognized as Master of Wagons, "how many days' march to Vinvinnysee?"

Borth scratched his whiskers. "Two weeks at best, m'lord."

"Gorm, how long with horsemen alone, day and night?"

"At the very fastest, m'lord, two days and nights, but the horses would be near death."

"Two weeks with the entire army against three—I'll give four, five days with horse alone." The Prince frowned over a chart spread on his knees. He looked pale and

148

there were shadows under his eyes, but other than the unnatural thickness of his torso under his tunic, Naed could see no other sign that scarce days ago he had nearly been killed.

"Vinvinnysee must be isolated at once." Picking up a piece of charcoal, the Prince circled the icon designating the city. In a continuous motion, he drew the circle tighter until it became a large, blackened spot. "To do so, the army will divide into two parts, a smaller, first assault troop and the larger main body. This first group will be made up of the better, faster half of the horse and half of the mounted archers. They'll reach Vinvinnysee after a march of four to five days and proceed to cut off all supply and communication routes. The other half of the horse and archers will remain with me as an escort. This body should be joined by Nemmon's footmen in eight or nine days. The combined force should reach the city in about three weeks."

He paused and a flurry of discussion rippled through the tent. Naed watched as Krenin, who stood at the Prince's right, glared at him while alternately responding to comments from Borth and Yarl on his right. The Prince's Second had not spoken to him since the morning after the Lancer raid, and the last time Naed could be sure Krenin had seen him was when he had tossed a sword to the Tolemak. Their eyes had met, but Naed had been far too preoccupied with the fight to see what Krenin had done with the weapon. Plainly, whatever the Tolemak had done had not tempered his hostility. Naed could practically feel the heat of Krenin's repeated glares.

Gorm leaned down and said in a low rumble, "Those lads from Albon, were they insubordinate? 'Tis in your power to discipline them, you know."

The Master of Horse's concern astonished Naed. No wonder Banir and the others had acted so chagrined. "I understand, sir, but 'tis no need." They would not defy him again.

"All's well, then, eh?" Gorm said, studying his face. "I thought as much." Shifting on his feet, the huge man turned to talk with the officer on his left.

Watching the bristled profile, Naed sensed he had passed yet another test. At least one Tolemak in the tent

149

did not hate him. If anything, Gorm seemed to accept him as both worthy and competent. It was a heady feeling, and he was still disoriented when the Prince passed the chart into his hands and resumed speaking.

"Because isolating Vinvinnysee is of utmost importance, I'm placing Krenin in command of the assault force. Gorm will be his Second. You have no more than five days to reach the city and commence encircling it. 'Tis for you to determine how best to accomplish this goal."

While Naed rolled up the chart, the Prince's officers reacted with surprise but general agreement. Only Krenin said nothing, his expression betraying foreknowledge but not approval. He fixed his gaze once more on Naed, and the venom in his look shocked Naed. But he had no time to contemplate the reason because Gorm leaned forward and addressed the Prince.

"'Twill be a pleasure to serve you, m'lord, but 'tis one thing I'm wondering." He scratched his hairy throat. "Who is it you'll be having as your Second now that Krenin has a separate command?"

"Excellent question," the Prince said. "You'll be pleased to know that I've given the matter considerable thought. Naed, here, will do very well."

Naed lost his grip on the chart. It unrolled and bounced off the toe of his boot.

The officers burst into a volley of objections: "bog-mother's son... lowlander... red-tailed, wet-behind-the-ears whelp... fog-born..."

The insults burned Naed's ears even though he understood why officers who had fought together for years would resent an upstart they hardly knew stepping into a position any one of them might covet. If only they realized how astonished he was and how little he desired what they all clamored to deny him—and merely because he was not one of them! By the Sisters, he might have been summoned here, but he did not have to stay to be reviled!

Naed froze when hands gripped his arms, the Prince on one side, Gorm on the other. He was astonished to see amusement in the giant's expression before the big man released him. The Prince regarded Naed out of the sides of cool gray eyes, his expression unreadable, but his grip was warm and steadying.

"Why not Naed?" the Prince was saying into the silence that had fallen. "He's quick, intelligent, brave, and loyal."

The officers exchanged glances. Illien cleared his throat as if to speak for the group. "Begging your pardon, m'lord, but killing a handful of Adanak single-handedly hardly makes the lowlander loyal. Any one of us would've done the same."

"Aye," the Prince said, looking at every man in turn, "but every one of *you* is Tolemak."

In the ensuing silence, Naed heard the blood rushing in his ears, felt the heat lingering where the Prince's fingers had encircled his arm, saw the antipathy in Krenin's look—and understood it at last.

"That's enough discussion," Krenin said. His nostrils flared and he glared around the tent. "'Tis nothing important that's changed. Borth and Illien, you'll share my former command, reporting directly to Prince Arn. 'Tis only in service to the Prince himself that the D'nalian will act as Second."

"'Tis honor enough," Naed said, while the back of his mind wondered where he had found the audacity to speak, not to mention with pride.

Krenin strode toward him, and Naed wished he had put on his chest armor after all. His hands would do little to blunt a knife to the belly, and Krenin's expression suggested he might use the weapon sheathed at his waist. Instead, Krenin thrust out his hand and seized Naed's before he had a chance to flinch. The gesture had the appearance of a handshake, and Naed guessed those behind Krenin may have perceived it as such, but the delivery was that of a vow.

"Guard him with your life," the Tolemak hissed, "or, by the Demon, spilling your entrails will be too good for the likes of you!"

Naed returned the crushing grip with one of his own. "Depend upon it!"

Jerking free, Krenin said to Gorm, "Let's go," and plunged out of the tent.

"Gorm," the Prince said, "watch over him."

The giant inclined his head. "Aye, m'lord, as I would you." Turning to Naed, he held out his hand. "In three weeks, then, eh? Sisters be with you."

"And with you." The handshake heartened him, and he suspected Gorm's "interviews" had played more than a small part in his sudden change of fortune. "My thanks."

Gorm shrugged. "'Tis not a task for the faint of heart. The Prince'll be in the saddle afore another day, and, mark me, 'tis at his heels you'll be galloping afore the week is out." With a wink, he straightened, inclined his head to the Prince, and left.

The other officers looked at each other, at the Prince who sat silently watching, then at Naed. Master of Archers Illien was the first to offer Naed his hand. The others followed, one at a time, and, in the same sequence, each took his leave of the Prince and filed out.

Naed stared at the tent flap. The pressure of a dozen hands lingered on his palm and fingers, but 'twas not the sensation of friendship. They would abide him only because the Prince required it. The situation was altogether too familiar, and Naed was heartily weary of it. "M'lord—" he said, turning.

"Tolemaks are born into a certain way of thinking," the Prince said, as if reading his mind, "but we're not blinded by it. What we see tends to take precedence over what we've been told or taught. You've made them think. 'Twill not be long before they see for themselves."

"What will they see, m'lord?" He had been in this tent before and, despite the conflicting emotions of the moment, he remembered the incident too well. "Begging your pardon, but 'twas only days ago that you suspected me of treason. What has changed?"

"Everything." The gray eyes looked not at Naed but through him, and for one skin-prickling moment, he wondered if the Prince had the fabled Gift of Sight. "And yet nothing that truly matters. You're simply beginning to show others the potential I've seen in you all along. Removing you from your fellows provided you that opportunity." Leaning back carefully, Prince Arn massaged his ribs.

Naed could see how movement pained him, and how he had grown paler since the officers left. Clearly, the man was weaker than he had let on in the conference. Naed stepped forward, and the Prince smiled. "Do you accept your new position?"

"Have I a choice, m'lord?"

"Always. But that doesn't mean I'll change *my* mind."

Naed felt drawn once more into the gray eyes. Warm and friendly now, they promised something Naed had never known but did not until this instant realize he yearned for. All his life he had fought to gain respect, first at home among his brothers, then among neighbors in Tumin and among strangers in Dranoel's guard, and now among these grim Tolemaks. He had always fought to prove he was better than others believed. What the Prince's look offered was something entirely different— faith in his abilities and a chance to live up to expectations greater than he had ever dared consider for himself. The realization dizzied him and he had to grip the tent pole. "My lord, you honor me."

The Prince laughed. "Then you accept?"

Head spinning, he nodded. "What would you have me do first?"

"Tell your men to move your things into the tent next to mine. You can keep those hardheads from Albon for your own, if you wish. From what Gorm has told me, 'tis like they'll not want to be parted from you."

"Aye, m'lord. And then?"

"You're to be my eyes, ears, and limbs until I'm fit enough to do for myself. After that," he said with another flashing grin, "'twill come the truly difficult work."

"Keeping up with you. Aye, m'lord, I swear I shall."

Outside, the sun was so bright after the dimness of the tent the air about Naed seemed to glow. If 'twere not natural light, it must be the Sisters smiling down on him, for they had bestowed such blessings upon him this day. Pausing, he plucked two hairs from his head and offered them in thanksgiving to the Sisters' messenger, the Wind.

Banir and the others gathered about him, their expressions wary. "There's a hurly-burly about the camp," Banir said. "What's to do?"

"We've a new assignment, and we must live up to it." Naed eyed Grodar and Morys. "'Twill be no more fighting except against the Adanak. 'Tis the Prince himself we're in charge of, and we must do ourselves proud."

"Demon's eyebrows!" said Morys, whistling under his

breath.

"To be sure," Grodar said. He squared his shoulders. "You can count on us, sir. 'Tis an honor to serve with you."

Banir shot Grodar a glare. When the dark eyes shifted to Naed, their expression was somber. "'Tis your doing, not ours."

Understanding Banir still regretted their behavior at the clearing, Naed laid a hand on the Tolemak's shoulder. "'Twas not I alone that's given us this chance. 'Tis due as much to what you—each of you—said to Master Gorm. And for that I thank you."

The men of Albon dodged his gaze and shifted their feet.

"Well, then," Naed broke the awkward silence, "there's moving to be done. 'Tis best you were about it."

Grodar and Morys looked up, their grins restored.

Banir frowned at them, but his glare seemed less intense. "Asses," he muttered after sending them off with various orders. "Are you sure you want them?"

"Aye," Naed said, heaving a sigh. "'Tis best I have my men about me. For good or ill, they seem to be mine."

****

Arn watched from within the tent as the men from Albon surrounded Naed. Experience had taught him how a man stood when he trusted his leader and how he stood when he did not. Gorm had been right about the D'nalian. The young man had a following.

Satisfied, Arn closed his eyes. His ribs throbbed, and he cursed silently. A shadow darkening the entry drew his eyes open.

"Look at you," Krenin growled, "white as milk after nothing more than a council." Crossing the tent, he poured water into a mug and handed it to Arn. "Does your D'nalian 'pet' know yet the lengths you'll go to pretend all's well?"

"He has eyes." Arn drank, remembering Naed's expression of concern. He would have to trust the D'nalian to keep his secrets—those secrets he had no choice but to reveal. The rest—well, even Krenin, who knew him best, did not know everything.

"Demon's Blood!" Krenin stormed across the tent. "You know I don't like this!"

Inhaling carefully, Arn set the mug down. "I'll explain it once more, if you like. Gorm is the best Master of Horse in all of Tolemak, and you know my mind better than anyone. You and I designed the tactics. 'Tis you alone who can do what needs to be done to isolate Vinvinnysee."

"I understand all of that. But why in the name of the Demon did you choose the D'nalian to take my place?" Krenin waved off Arn's retort. "Even aside from what you call my 'prejudice,' you can't deny he's green. What does that beardless pup know about running an army? What, in the name of all that's holy, do you know about *him*?"

Gratified Krenin was displaying logic, Arn smiled. "Did you see him just now, outside with those men?"

"That muck from Albon's always gone their own way."

"Aye," Arn said, "*we* have."

Krenin flushed. "You know I didn't mean anything against your birthplace. 'Tis just that—well, he's won six hardheads without a brain among them—what of that?"

"Then it must be something other than their brain he's won. That gift is precisely what makes me want him with me rather than against me. He's young, aye, but that's to our advantage. He doesn't yet know what he has, what he's capable of, or how to use it. I do, and 'tis best for us if he learns while his allegiance is mine."

"If he's that dangerous, why not kill him? 'Twould be simpler."

Arn smiled, knowing how his friend's mind worked. "'Twould seem so, but remember 'twas the path my late uncle chose when he tried to deal with me. We both know how 'simple' that proved to be." Krenin grunted, and Arn knew he was listening. "Besides, when we've captured Vinvinnysee and won the Crown, we'll need an ally in D'nalee. Naed could be the one to help us reunite the Kingdom. 'Tis less likely D'nalee would fight one of its own."

Krenin stood with hands on hips and regarded him. "It all sounds so logical, the way you put it, but to my mind, 'tis still a risk. You and I, we're bonded by more than blood. He's D'nalian. How do you know you can trust him?"

"Precisely because he's D'nalian. His honor means more to him than blood."

Krenin snorted.

"He risked his blood to save you, didn't he?"

"He's a glory-seeking fool. Trust his 'honor' if you want, but, 'tis sure, I'll be keeping my eyes open wide enough for the both of us."

Arn smiled. "Give me your hand on it, then."

Krenin's frown broke. He gripped Arn's hand in both of his. "Three weeks—mark me—I'll serve you Vinvinnysee sealed tighter than a barrel pasted with pitch."

"I'll hold you to it."

With one last shake, Krenin turned and was gone.

Arn drew breath into his lungs. His ribs protested, but he welcomed the ache. Naed would serve him well, he was sure. But he was not Krenin.

PART III: VINVINNYSEE
CHAPTER THIRTEEN

The bush under which Aerid slept sheltered her from the predawn rain, but the risen sun revealed an earth still bedecked with liquid jewels. Mist rose like smoke from the hollows, and moisture clung to every blade of grass, soaking her to the knees when she saddled her horse. The dampness did not distress her, for the day promised to be hot and the sun would soon dry her clothes. Besides, her homeland was a delight to behold—gently rolling green hills, broad vistas of forest and meadow bordered by dark, winding streams and an occasional scar of broken rock.

What gnawed at her was, since leaving Herset, not one northward turning she had passed led where she wished to go. Farmers and peddlers she met assured her she would find the road before she reached Vinvinnysee, yet she was less than a day's journey from the city, and she had come upon no such crossroads in a hollow marked by a stone well under a solitary oak. Nor had she come upon soldiers, but ever alert for the clatter of hooves, she had more than once urged her horse off the road and into trees or thickets to avoid being overrun or, worse, accosted. Most groups had been small, but yester eve more than 50 had galloped westward, their shields scattering the twilight.

Shortly after noon, Aerid peeled the neck of her tunic away from her skin and wondered how much longer she could last before draining her water skin. Flies buzzed around the horse's ears, and it plodded along with its head down, evidently too hot and tired to flick them away. The land was so lush, she could not imagine how this stretch of road managed to go so far without crossing at least one stream.

Finally, the track dropped into welcome shade and, when the aspens receded, she saw below a narrow meadow broken by a northward branch in the road and

Helen C. Johannes

dominated by a massive oak. Under the oak's far-reaching branches, sat a round stone well with bucket, crank, and basin. Aerid's spirits leaped, then hung suspended.

A figure lounged in the shade and a horse cropped grass nearby. The shield dangling from the saddle bore crossed lances, an insignia she had been told belonged to the Vinvinnysee guard. *A soldier.* What should she do? Her horse had already scented water, and it chewed the bit, trying to take it between its teeth. Aerid needed refreshment herself, but she could wait if she must. Yet, if she did, more soldiers might come. He was only one; what could one do? She pushed away thoughts of the Prince. She knew very well what he could do single-handedly, but he would not be a Prince if he were not so gifted. This slouching figure in dusty boots and breeches looked no more like a prince than she. Steeling herself, she let the horse have its head.

He could have been asleep, leaning against the oak, but as she dismounted by the well, Aerid saw the man chewed on a blade of grass and watched her, one arm draped over a raised knee. She should offer a greeting, but he had not, and she did not wish to tempt the Sisters by inviting conversation. She hoped he had glimpsed her face under her hood and reacted as everyone else did, with repugnance at the stain. Stepping to the moss-covered wall, she pushed the bucket into the well and let down the crank. The metallic screech startled crows from the oak's top branches. They flew off squawking like the Demon's own messengers, and Aerid touched the birthstone at her throat to invoke the Sisters' protection. She hoped they were still inclined to smile on her, for as much as she was tempting them this day.

Aerid was sweating by the time she hauled up three buckets of water. The first two she poured into the basin for her horse. She set the last on the wall and splashed her face and neck with handfuls of the cool water before drinking from her cupped hands. She had just unfastened her water skin from the saddle to refill it when she noticed the man no longer lounged against the tree trunk. *Where was he?* In her panic, she spun, blundering into the bucket. It pitched over, throwing its contents across the rim—and onto the man who perched there.

He sprang up with an oath. Her horse shied. She grabbed the bucket—too late—and hugged it to her chest. With a huff, her horse returned to drink. The man, turning as he wrung out the hem of his tunic, chuckled. "I do want for a bath, 'tis true, but I scarce thought I smelled so foul as to warrant a dousing."

"I—forgive me—"

"'Tis naught." He grinned and, selecting a dry spot, sat again, brushing wisps of sand-brown hair from his face. Like most Adanak men she had seen, he wore his hair away from his face and formed into a single loose braid dangling down his back.

Her own hair, exposed by a fallen-back hood, fell over her shoulder in what he should recognize as a D'nalian queue—if only he would stop staring at her face! Most people, after the initial shock, had the decency to avert their eyes. Thumping the bucket on the wall in an effort to divert his gaze, she yanked her hood over her head and pulled it together under her nose, but he continued staring. Unnerved, she spun away, threw the bucket down the well, and cranked mightily. If she did not need to refill her water skin, she would mount now and ride away, so uneasy did his scrutiny make her. Over the squealing gears, she panted, "Your pardon. Give me but a moment to fill this bucket, and 'tis immediately I'll be leaving your sight."

"I should not be liking that."

His voice was at her shoulder, his hand beside hers on the crank before she could back away, bump against the well, and lunge for her horse's reins. His hand was there, too, claiming the horse's bridle. Aerid shrank back, realizing she was trapped between the horse's body, the well, and the man. Her hand went to the healer's knife sheathed at her belt. "Stay back!"

"I mean you no harm. 'Tis not my nature to be ill-using a woman."

She stared. His eyes mesmerized her. The green of pond water, they danced—not horrified at all—and they watched, looking into her the way only one other set of eyes had done. Her heart thudded. Breathless, she tore her gaze away, looking at his feet, the well, the horse she inched toward—anything to prevent those green eyes from seeing more than they already had.

"A—a what?" she sputtered. "'Tis not enough that I be Demon-cursed and shunned by all, but that you'll be heaping names upon me for your own pleasure. 'Tis a healer I be, sir, and bear no weapon. I cannot fight to defend my honor. I can only deny I be what you believe me to be." If she reached the horse, she could duck under its neck and pull it around after her, trapping the man against the well while she threw herself into the saddle.

"I mean you no harm," he repeated, his expression earnest, open, as honest as Naed's. *But Naed was dead.*

Aerid choked on the memory. Indeed, this man was of Naed's years and similar in build. Even the green in his eyes reminded her of the green flecks in Naed's.

He held out his hand, palm up, as if asking her to put her hand into it. "If 'tis from Herset you've come, 'tis understandable your being wary. 'Twas a corrupt place. Even so, 'tis no excusing what the Tolemak did there." Anger flashed in his eyes before they gentled again.

He must have recognized the markings on her saddle. No one else had commented, but she had avoided all soldiers, until now. He had mentioned the Tolemak, too. It had been nigh a seven-night since the Prince had so coldly ridden out of her life. Determined to put anything Tolemak from her mind, she had refused to consider what he—or they—might have done since. Now she could not prevent herself from asking, "What—what did they do there?"

"Burned it to the ground."

The stone wall scraped Aerid's spine when she backed into it, but the images before her eyes overwhelmed a sensation so minor. She saw flames licking through roofs, smelled pitch and scorched wood, saw the painted riders, heard the shrieks of the people around her, felt herself running with them, throat raw, heart pumping...

She was sitting on the packed earth at the base of the well when her vision cleared. The man squatted beside her, his expression full of concern. "Your face—'tis white as milk. Be there aught I may do?"

Aerid studied him. She had hidden for weeks among the Tolemak, yet a man of her own kind had seen through her disguise in scant moments. "Tell me, how did you mark me?"

He grinned. "D'nalian clothes, Adanak face, woman's throat." He pointed to his own throat, to the obvious protrusion over which grew a bit of stubble.

Aerid flushed, knowing all too well such a feature was not common among women. With a deepening flush, she realized that, in the heat of the day, she had bared more of her neck than usual. *Sisters Three*, how could she have been so stupid!

"The stain—redroot, aye? 'Twas clever to pretend to be marred."

She drew her feet under her, and when he offered his hand, she looked him over once more. His clothes were dusty but of good quality. The buckle of his sword belt shone with the gleam of regular polishing. His hand bore the calluses of a horseman and a soldier, calluses she had become only too familiar with of late. Everything about him suggested he could be trusted, if only she dared.

Even his face called to her. Truly, it was an unremarkable face, except for the eyes and a long, thin mouth that curved upward at one corner. But it bore the same rounded cheekbones as hers, the same widely spaced brows over clearly defined eyes that did not hide in pockets of flesh as did those of D'nalian faces. Nor was it angular as the Tolemak, or possessed of a long, narrow nose. It was a face of one of her own kind, and Aerid found it much to her liking. "'Tis Aerid I be," she said, accepting his hand and allowing him to pull her upright.

"Leumas of Vinvinnysee." He bowed over her hand and—to her shock—pressed his lips to the back of it.

"What—Sisters!" Aerid yanked her hand away. "It does smell of horse!"

Laughing, Leumas laid his hand over his heart. "A sweet perfume, and one—I must be confessing—I share." Eyeing how she clutched her hand to her body, he raised one eyebrow. "Do not be telling me but that's the first a man's kissed your hand."

"Even so, 'tis no concern of yours." Pushing past him, she picked up her water skin and laid it on the well rim. Those green eyes saw altogether too much and, while she no longer feared he would harm her, he stood entirely too close. 'Twould be best if she filled her water skin and continued on her way as soon as possible—alone.

Leumas outreached her and pulled the full bucket onto the wall. "The D'nalian clothes, is it wrong I would be to guess 'twas among those lowland stiffs you've served?" When she did not reply but concentrated on filling her water skin, he continued, "'Tis a pity such as they have women. For all their claims of courtesy, not a one among them knows how to treat the fairer sex." When she stoppered the skin and fastened it to her saddle, he took hold of her reins. "'Tis a blessing from the Sisters to be meeting you here, Aerid, for this day I be bound to Vinvinnysee and 'twould be my pleasure to see you safely there."

"Vinvinnysee? No." Aerid faced him. "'Tis northward I go."

The smile vanished from Leumas' face. "I wait here for a messenger from that very road. Only yester eve we in the city learned how the Tolemak—*mortraeders!*—" He spat. "—have sped toward us. They do come at us from all ways westward."

"Not the north—"

"Aye, Master of the Guard Gaelwynn does suspect as much. 'Twill not be long afore a man comes to tell me if 'tis true. Abide a while, Aerid, for 'tis not safe."

His face was as open to her as Naed's, and she could see plainly the same stubbornness that bound both of them to what each perceived as his duty. "Tell me, Leumas, if 'tis dangerous, will you be preventing me from going where I would?"

He smiled as if she were an obstinate child. "'Twould betray all I hold dear to act otherwise. But," Leumas continued before she could protest, "have you eaten? Come, partake of such fine fare as I have persuaded the baker at Eidvondin to part with. 'Tis the finest pastry in Adanak. You'll not be insulting me by refusing, now, would you?"

With a clatter of hooves, a speeding horse topped the northward road and galloped down, skidding to a halt near them. The rider slid off, falling to the grass. The horse, drenched in sweat, stood with heaving sides and lowered head.

"Avika!" Leumas cried, running to the man's side. Pausing only to grab her healer's pouch from her saddle, Aerid joined him.

The man called Avika, face pallid under thick dust, gripped Leumas' arm. "Dead. All...."

"Be still," Aerid said, reaching for a bloodstain near the man's waist. "Be this from arrow or knife?"

He gulped air, teeth white under a drooping black mustache, and waved her off. "'Tis not blood of mine." Grabbing a handful of Leumas' tunic, he levered himself to a sitting position. "Alaris. 'Tis taken. Burned. The guard—slaughtered. But for one...who did say...'tis the same all about. 'Tis a noose...they be making..."

"To strangle the city," Leumas finished, his face hard. "'Tis swiftly the *mortraeders* come. How many, Avika?"

"Hundreds. All mounted." Avika turned dark eyes on Aerid. "Water, please. For me and my horse."

"Aye, at once." By the time she had emptied the bucket into the basin and drawn another, Leumas had raised Avika and helped him to sit in the shade of the well. While the exhausted horse drank and Aerid drew another bucket for it, Leumas found a cup in Aerid's saddlebag and filled it for his comrade.

"Your horse be spent," Leumas was saying. "Take mine and ride on ahead."

"Aye, 'tis good, but follow me quick. 'Tis not safe to remain here. 'Twas still burning—Alaris—when I arrived. I did not linger other than to note 'twas eastward the *mortraeders* rode, but—" Avika coughed, sipped more water, and wiped his eyes with the back of his hand. "—not all did so. 'Twere at least a score came this way. Mayhap 'twas faster I rode than they, but 'tis more like they did not follow the road."

"Aye, we'll not be caught outside the city."

Draining the cup, Avika stood and Leumas rose with him. They clasped arms, a sign, Aerid suspected, more of genuine friendship than mere camaraderie. She had seen enough such gestures among the Tolemak to perceive the difference.

"May the Sisters give my horse wings for you," Leumas said.

"Aye, and bring you safely inside the city before

nightfall," Avika replied.

"Look for us at the Golden Horse. 'Tis a tankard you're still owing me."

Avika flashed a grin as he caught up the reins of Leumas' horse. "Aye, I'm not forgetting." He swung into the saddle. "And a tankard for your friend too, in thanks for the water." With a wave, he set heels to the horse and galloped away.

"*Mortraeders!*" Leumas muttered, snatching up his saddlebag from under the tree. Turning, he met Aerid's gaze as she stroked the exhausted horse's neck. "'Tis as I feared—all ways be blocked. You must come to Vinvinnysee. Do you yet doubt me?"

There was naught for it. She knew better than most what carnage the Tolemak had likely wreaked at—Alaris, was it? Had she not seen hacked limbs, pools of thickening blood, and bodies frozen in grotesque positions at the river crossing? After the Lancer attack? In the villages of her childhood? Had she not smelled the blood, heard the screams of the dying and wounded, stitched the gashes and tied the tourniquets to save a limb—or a life? Alone, she might make it through the stranglehold the Tolemak seemed intent on throwing around Vinvinnysee, but she—shamefully—did not want to take the risk.

"Be the city safe?"

Leumas smiled, taking her hand from the horse and flattening her palm over his heart. "Aye," he said when she looked at him with startled eyes, "more than a hundred years safe. This, I do swear to you, Aerid."

Aerid's skin prickled, but not with fear. Under his tunic lay chest armor, yet under that she could sense how Leumas' heart beat, a solid, steady throb. He looked at her in a way men did not usually look at her—save Naed, but he had been her friend, and this look was different from his—all eyes with wide, dark pools in the center. Another's look—equally intent, but hotter and more dangerous—stirred at the fringe of her memory, but she refused to acknowledge it. Still, Leumas' expression made her uneasy, and she pulled at her hand. He eased his hold, letting her withdraw her fingers slowly from under his, but his eyes remained fixed.

Swallowing, she dropped her gaze and clasped her

hands together. "'Tis naught you know of me, Leumas, that you should be so...so forward."

He smiled. "Ah, but I beg to differ. 'Tis a healer you be. And brave to come so far alone. Tender-hearted, too, or you'd not be so quick to see to Avika. And, for the last, the redroot—'twill wash—and under it, unless I miss my mark, 'tis a fine, fair face."

Aerid flushed. "'Tis best we be going, think you? 'Tis far to walk, and this horse requires walking."

"Aye," he said, still smiling as he handed her the reins of her own horse. "But remember, Aerid, when we enter the city, 'twas I who did see you first."

****

An hour before sunset, they entered a wide road on which heavily-laden mules tethered nose-to-tail followed men riding horses. Wagons loaded with wool and grain creaked and groaned from rut to rut, and pigs by the scores grunted and squealed under their herdsmen's sticks. People on foot, alone or in families, wove among the traffic, bearing their belongings in bundles on their heads or in racks on their backs. Here and there a peddler or cobbler pulled a cart. Amid the general confusion rode soldiers whose shields bore the crossed lances insignia. Some greeted Leumas with solemn nods.

"They have doubled the guard," Leumas told her as they rode into a vast open space.

The clearing was larger than any Aerid had seen before. It rolled away in grassy undulations, rising steadily higher toward the center, toward the city commanding the highest point—a broad, tall hillock that must in ancient times have been green but was now covered with stone upon stone, building beside building, wall within wall until the whole mass of rock, brick and mortar soared up into towers at the north end. As the sun sank, the city, with the eastern sky dark behind it, seemed washed in gold. 'Twas only a trick of the twilight, but Aerid wondered how even the fabled home of the Sisters could possibly look more like an island of light.

They rode through a gentle gully that cut the vast clearing from north to south and passed near the massive gate toward which the road led. The outer wall, made of sleek, pale interlocked stone, was enormous, two or three times as tall as the wall around Druemarwin. Scores of archer slots decorated the upper level. Aerid realized as she glanced at the clearing which now sloped away behind them, the site gave the defenders an incredibly long, unobstructed view in all directions. She understood why Leumas had expressed such confidence; the city seemed made not by mortal hands but constructed by the Sisters themselves.

Surrounded by hundreds of wagons, animals, and refugees, they funneled through the gate and into a wide cobblestone courtyard. The noise and clatter in the confined space echoed like thunder in Aerid's ears, but Leumas steered her expertly through the crowd and up a narrow street. The crowd had thinned by the time they reached a second gate and rode through it. Here, vines grew along the pocked inner side of the wall, and the scent of flowers from window boxes sweetened the air that, below, teemed with animal smells. Tall buildings packed side to side leaned toward each other over the streets, each level jutting farther out from the level below it as though, Aerid thought, the builders had intended the houses to form an arch.

"'Tis a many-walled city," Leumas explained as he led her through a third gate and up another, narrower street. "Our ancestors, being clever, set the gates for each new wall not in a direct line from the previous ones. 'Tis a tangle, some days, to ride up to the palace or down to the outer wall, for all the turnings, but 'tis intended to fend off an enemy. Should they breach the outer wall, 'tis along these narrow streets they must fight ere they make the next gate. With that, plus the many deep wells throughout the city, Vinvinnysee may withstand any siege."

Aerid gave him the smile he seemed to expect. Even so, she wondered if the inhabitants of this bustling city understood the true nature of the man who came against them. She could tell them the little she knew, but they undoubtedly knew the size of the Tolemak army. Had they not attacked it twice? Truly, though, she would be reluctant to share anything. She had vowed to the Prince she was no spy. Keeping silent about her travels with his army seemed the best way to keep her word. Besides, she owed him her life—twice.

Leumas led her through another narrow archway, this time into a courtyard fronted by a modest inn and stables. In scant minutes, he secured a small room for her on the third floor, a stall and care for her horse, and a bowl of mutton for her dinner. "I must be reporting," he said as he stood with her in the public room, "but I shall come for you tomorrow. Will you abide here till then, Aerid?"

She smiled at the earnestness in his expression. "Aye, to be sure."

He caught her hand and touched his lips to it before she could react. "'Tis a pleasure you cannot imagine to be offering you such courtesies. Alas, but I fear that, too soon, you'll be seeing them for naught but your due." With another half bow, he left, still grinning.

Aerid sat at the table with her hand still tingling from Leumas' touch. Already he had touched her more often than any man except the one she refused to think about. And that one's touch had offered no courtesies...although he had been gentle, at first, when he still thought her a boy. Shaking such thoughts from her mind, she ate her dinner without tasting it, closed herself in the room the innkeeper showed her to, and fell immediately to sleep in her first real bed.

****

Loud voices, the rumble of cart wheels, and the clatter of hooves on stone roused Aerid later than she was accustomed to rising. Despite the unfamiliar noises and smells, she had slept like the dead and awakened eager to take in her surroundings. Her first delight was finding a full pitcher and basin. Stripping, she washed herself from head to toes for the first time since leaving Druemarwin. That done, she wrapped herself in the blanket from her bed and washed her clothes, one article at a time. Then she opened the shutters and spread her clothes to dry on the sun-warmed casement. Sitting on a stool with her back to the sun, she combed fingers through her hair while it dried.

Leaning against the window ledge, she looked down on a gray cobblestone street still shadowed by the overhanging buildings. Houses of every size, construction, and color lined the street in both directions, and people of various shapes and styles of dress bustled along it.

Aerid drank in the sights, sounds and smells of this vast population—more people than she had ever imagined could be found in one place—and all of them of her kind, too. Her kind had built this place, laying more stone upon stone than she would have thought the world contained. Her kind were clever, too, conceiving ways to deter enemies for generations. Her kind, whom the Tolemak and D'nalians distrusted and reviled as "word-weavers," looked industrious, prosperous, and sophisticated, so much so she suspected envy lay at the heart of the animosity. If so, she could understand some of its origins because as she looked at the bustling city dwellers and their fine clothing, she wondered how she, with her poor and worn D'nalian boy's garb, would be accepted by them. If Leumas could be taken as an example, however, she trusted she would have no difficulty.

An hour later, dressed in a freshly washed tunic cinched at the waist with the belt that held her healer's knife, Aerid fastened around her hair a kerchief cut from the material that had bound her breasts. After such a long confinement, her breasts ached with new freedom beneath her undertunic and her whole upper body felt naked. Though she still wore boy's garb, no man would now mistake her for a boy with her hair loosely contained in the way of Adanak women and her face scrubbed free of the redroot. *Sisters! How good it felt to finally be a woman again!*

When she came downstairs, her transformation startled the innkeeper, a round man with no neck and a bald pate who introduced himself as Foderor, but he quickly accepted her offer to trade healing services for room and board. He had milking goats that were not producing. His young wife was with child and sickly, and the serving maids were always complaining of one illness or another. "Besides," he added in an offhand way, "if 'tis good you be, 'tis like you'll draw some custom from folk hereabout."

Aerid understood. Each person she drew to the inn might buy food, drink, or lodging. Smiling at his shrewdness, she shook hands with Foderor to settle the arrangement and then went about examining her first patients.

When Leumas called upon her late that afternoon, Aerid was dressed in a flowing, dark skirt given her by Mairim, the innkeeper's wife, and a loose-sleeved white blouse with a square-cut neckline proffered by one of the serving maids. It was laced about the torso by a soft leather vest that Foderor—at the direction of his wife—dug out of a stack of items confiscated from clients who failed to pay their tab. She still wore the boots she had traveled in, and the undertunic, but she twirled once or twice before Leumas for the sheer pleasure of feeling feminine again.

The look on Leumas' face brought a flush to her cheeks. "Truly, I did think you fair, but not so fair as this. 'Tis a feast you be for my eyes, Aerid." He kissed the backs of both her hands before tucking her arm around his. "Come, 'tis time to properly show you my city."

They walked upward, staying on the side of the street to avoid the gutter in the middle. Two streets up, Leumas led her by the hand through a narrow, tunnel-like passage between buildings. Dark and damp, its coolness gave momentary relief from the heat of the day, but its smell recalled too vividly another dark, narrow place, and Aerid was glad to emerge into a courtyard of fruit trees and gardens.

The courtyard was backed by yet another wall, but this one had a small iron door set into the base of it. The door stood open although Aerid could see where freshly greased bolts stood ready to be shot into the stone. Inside, the passage was too cramped for a horse but just large enough for two men abreast to pass through. Cut into the stone on the other side was a crumbling staircase they climbed to reach the wall's rampart.

From the summit, the city descended in waves—red, yellow, brown, and gray roofs of tile and thatch, swelling and ebbing as if intent on crashing into the placid expanse below. Only the last, outer wall stood like a solitary dike to contain them.

Aerid shook her hair into the wind and gripped the sun-warmed stone. Aged mortar broke into granules under her fingertips. They were standing, Leumas told her, on the original wall. All that lay above were the ancient palace and gardens of Prince Adan, government buildings, and the mansions of the Masters of Vinvinnysee.

"'Tis a city of merchants," Leumas explained as he leaned against the wall at her side. "Every five years, a new Senior Master is elected from among the forty-seven who rule the city. 'Tis he who lives in the palace and signs the proclamations, but 'tis the group as a whole that wields the power. Only Master of the Guard Gaelwynn seems capable of defying them."

"Need he do so?"

Leumas shrugged. "Sometimes, mayhap. They be merchants, not soldiers." Turning, he pointed out the gate through which they had entered the city. "The city has four gates and four sectors. That one, the west one, 'tis my troop's to guard. There be three other troops, one per gate, but Master Gaelwynn keeps personal charge of mine."

Hearing the pride in his voice, Aerid said, "'Tis a fine gate, and a brave wall."

"The *mortraeders* will spend themselves against it. Had we such a city with such a wall in the Northern Wars, 'twould have been their undoing. Instead, our Masters brokered a 'peace,' if such it may be called, and the *mortraeders* departed with strength enough to regroup. Now, under their upstart bastard prince, they do come at us again." Leumas crumbled a bit of wall and brushed it from his palm. "'Tis grateful we are to the Sisters that Master Gaelwynn anticipated their coming."

A memory of Druemarwin ringed by countless warriors with painted faces who, at the drop of a lance, clamored for blood, filled Aerid's mind. She shivered.

"Be you cold?" With gentle fingers, Leumas cupped her elbows, turning her to face him.

"A little," she said, not untruthfully, for the breeze was strong, but she did not meet his eyes, looking instead out over the city. "I do but wish there were no war."

Out of the corner of her eye, she saw him smile that gentle, indulgent smile she had seen yesterday, and his hands skimmed her upper arms, their touch setting off more shivers. "As do I, Aerid, but the *mortraeders* have brought it to us. We must fight to defend what is ours.

The Tolemak understand naught else."

Where had she heard those sentiments before? Spoken by another young man with greenish eyes, one who took his duty seriously, and died for it. She shivered again, a violent shake. Stepping behind her, Leumas pulled her back against his chest and wrapped his arms around her.

Instantly, Aerid stiffened. His body heat shocked her with its warm solidity of muscle and flesh, and she flushed at the sensuous warmth enveloping her in a circle just loose enough she understood she could push out of it if she chose. He was not so tall as the Prince—no one, to her mind, could be—and his heart beat against a lower part of her shoulder blade. His hips fit neatly behind hers, and his breath tickled the hairs at her forehead. His man-smell was different, too—freshly washed and shaved with a hint of fragrant oil. Altogether a pleasant, even enticing scent, but not the raw, elemental smell of a man who has just been fighting for his life—and hers.

She stepped forward, and Leumas let his arms fall away. "Too close?" he said, when Aerid faced him. He looked solemn, not exactly contrite, but concerned.

"Too soon," she said, rubbing her arms.

His hands flexed as if he wanted to wrap them around her again, but he kept them at his sides. "Aerid, if there be another in your heart..."

Shaking her head, she looked out over the city. "Only a friend, very much like you, who is but a few weeks dead." How could she tell Leumas about the other, the man who had taken her first kiss, who had so thoroughly stamped upon her his taste, his touch that any man who dared to come after must forever be compared to him? That man cared naught for her—not in the way of the heart—yet he had shed blood for her, and she had risked the same for him. Wishing she had an answer, Aerid sighed.

Leumas had been contemplating his feet, but he looked up at the sound. "Forgive me, Aerid, for being so forward, and 'tis sorry I be for the loss of your friend, but I do mean to court you, if you'll be granting me permission. 'Tis not my nature to be letting someone as fine as you leave without declaring myself. 'Tis too short, this life, to be wasting it with hesitation."

The rolling tones of old, deep-throated bells drifted toward them on the wind, and their toll echoed the throb of Aerid's blood in her ears. She had known this man scarce a day, and his ways were so unlike the stiff D'nalian propriety she had grown up with, yet she found his candor refreshing and his attention flattering. Was this heart-racing thrill at his boldness what it meant to be Adanak and among her own? If so, she wished to sample more of it, for at least as long as she remained in the city.

Smiling, she reached out her hand to Leumas. "'Tis honored I would be to keep company with you, Leumas, but I must be warning you, 'tis northward I be yet bound."

He grinned as he grasped her hand and pressed his lips to the back of it. "Then 'twill be my special challenge to convince you to make Vinvinnysee your new home."

CHAPTER FOURTEEN

"The granaries of Adanak." Prince Arn lifted his hand, letting grain flow like streams of gold between his fingers. "They'll be hard-pressed to endure without this."

Naed sat on a stool in the Prince's tent and watched him sift more grain from the huge basket. 'Twas one of thousands contained in the storehouses of Eidvondin and Otlesend that Naed had ordered men to count, along with captured wagons and bundles of wool and casks of wine. Capturing the storehouses was a tremendous coup, but Naed could not share the elation. Wishing for his bed and the oblivion of sleep, he yawned.

Prince Arn glanced up at the sound. "You did well today. Yarl and Borth have seen with their own eyes why I chose you."

"I am gratified, m'lord."

"Gratified," the Prince echoed, his tone faintly mocking, "but not satisfied."

"Is there a difference, m'lord?" He knew very well there was, and that the difference was critical to the melancholy oppressing him, but he did not want to admit as much.

For days after the Prince put him in charge of the assault on Otlesend, Naed had walked about wire-tight, his nerves trying even Banir's steadiness. He understood the need to attack the storage compounds simultaneously, but he knew full well he had coordinated nothing larger than Druemarwin's defenses. When he suggested Borth might be better for the task, the Prince dismissed his concerns with a few words tossed over his shoulder as they rode: "Trust your instincts. And trust the men to follow your orders." Finally, Naed had, but only after studying the lay of the town's defenses and questioning Banir about Borth and Yarl's abilities.

"Victory is to be savored." The Prince poured a goblet of Adanak wine and inhaled the bouquet. "Defeat is to be learned from and left behind. Why do you look as though you've lost?"

Naed raised his head, a mistake, he realized, as the hawk's stare he had learned to be wary of these last weeks trapped him. If ever a man had the All-seeing Eye, the Prince did, using it to somehow divine what a man might think, feel, desire or even fear. Wrenching his gaze free, Naed studied his hands, pressed flat on his thighs. He had washed, but fancied he could detect blood still under the fingernails.

The combat seemed a blur. Morys, with great excitement, told everyone how Naed led the charge at the storehouses and smote three Adanak before he and Grodar could catch up. Banir, whose leg was not yet limber enough for combat, reprimanded them for leaving their officer vulnerable. Later, while Naed washed and changed, Banir discovered arrow dents in Naed's shield, a rip in his tunic, and a gash above the elbow on his sword arm, all of which Naed could not remember taking. The news compounded his melancholy, confirming once again he had fought not like a man, a proper D'nalian, but like a mindless beast.

"Did you shed blood today?"

Naed started out of his reverie. "Aye, m'lord, you know I did."

"Did it wash off?" The Prince was looking full at him now, long fingers splayed under the bowl of the goblet.

"Aye, but—"

"Then let it go, into the ground with the water." He sipped, then set down the goblet. "But you don't, do you? After the blood's cooled on your blade, your good D'nalian conscience insists you think about what you've done. Trust me, my young friend, your enemies have no such conscience. Any of those you struck down this day would have killed you and thought no more of your blood than that of a squashed insect. You're not a man to them; you're an enemy. Remember that."

"Aye, m'lord, I do, but—"

"You see this?" The Prince traced a finger down the scar on his cheek. "I thought to spare an enemy once. He left me a permanent reminder of my folly."

Naed imagined the horror of the injury, how close the

Prince had come to losing his head, but the scar was clearly old. "Begging your pardon, m'lord, but I came against you once. You spared me."

"Aye, but not for pity. Pity is a dead man's mercy; those that receive it often wish they had suffered honorable death, and those that give it, sooner or later die at the hands of their mistake. Heed me on this, and you'll live to see your future."

When Naed nodded, the Prince's face, all hard planes, softened. Reaching out, he cuffed Naed's shoulder the way a man might cuff his son or younger brother. "Besides, 'twas precisely for your good D'nalian conscience that I spared you. When properly applied, it keeps you on the right side of your honor. And your honor, my friend, is what makes your future of value to me."

The Prince's gesture, so unexpected and so un-D'nalian, startled and warmed Naed. He had no idea how to react. He only knew his heart ached in that moment.

The Prince turned away and poured another goblet of wine. "Join me, will you? 'Tis time I was telling you more of my plans."

Naed accepted the goblet the Prince handed him and sipped. The wine slid smoothly down his throat, warming as it descended. The taste awakened his tongue, filling his mouth with the most exquisite flavor. Even Druemarwin's best wine could not compare to this. "Splendid."

"The wine?" The Prince refilled his own cup. "Aye, but 'tis not why I've come to take Vinvinnysee, though others—even those among my own—may think otherwise."

Standing beside the basket, he stirred the grain. "Truly, eight of every 10 men in my army thinks of naught but food, shelter, and a woman to warm his bed. These eight—good men, all—fight for the gold victory brings because gold will secure them more food—and wine—better shelter and fairer women. 'Tis common among men, this seeking of gold. Your own compatriot—Yormoc, is it?—would trade his eyes for coins."

Naed chose to sip his wine rather than agree. 'Twas bad enough Yormoc was an embarrassment to his kind, but worse that a Tolemak should point it out. "What of power, m'lord? Do not men fight for power?"

"Ah, but gold *is* power. And power is gold. 'Tis the having that matters, having more than the next man—more gold, more land, more soldiers with which to wage war in order to gain more. Do you see?"

He did see, but the wine had spread its magic to his extremities, relaxing them down to the toes inside his boots, and the same glow was creeping into his brain. "You mentioned 10, m'lord. What of the other two?"

"The ninth man has no desire for gold. In truth, he would give away what gold he has if the doing so would bring him what he seeks—the glory of having his name known. Having his name known will not only secure him food, shelter, and his choice of women, but also assure him of a place in men's memories."

"You have glory, m'lord." Naed lifted his cup in a toast. "Men already tell tales of you."

The Prince watched Naed drink without joining him. "So they do." He scooped a handful of grain and turned his attention to the seeds flowing between his fingers. "'Tis a seductive thing, glory, and many a good man feels the pull of it." He let another handful drizzle out, making Naed wonder if he found the cascading wheat equally seductive, until the Prince caught him in a direct gaze. "Krenin believes you fight for glory. I think perhaps he's right—to some degree—and 'tis why your good D'nalian conscience pricks at you as it does today."

Naed flushed. He wanted to set the goblet down, but he had nowhere to put it. Instead, he rose from the stool. "M'lord, I—the Adanak do but defend what is theirs. 'Tis only their right. You cannot deny that I—we—come to take it from them."

"So *we* do, but not for gain. And, truly, not for glory—although, you must admit, 'tis some pleasure to be had in the adulation that comes from success."

Naed's flush spread to his throat and ears. He could blame some of it on the wine, but the gray gaze locked on his had undoubtedly seen the truth in his heart.

"You and I, we enjoy the glory, make no mistake. And we enjoy the fight itself. Your good D'nalian conscience would have you deny that, but I've seen you in battle. You would rather fight than stand aside, rather dare Death than wait for Him. But, if truth be told, 'tis neither gold nor glory that drives us." He touched his goblet to Naed's. "You and I—we fight for visions. For the future. For the Kingdom that once was and will be again."

Naed sank to his stool with a thump that splashed wine on his hand. Ignoring the wet trickle down his wrist, he wondered if the Prince had said what his ears reported. He knew the legend as well as any child schooled in D'nalee, how King Ekard had fathered three sons and died without naming a successor. Tolem should have had the throne as eldest, but the youngest, Adan, stole the crown, killing Tolem's young son in the process. D'nal, the hero prince who founded D'nalee, tried to mediate between the clever Adan, who claimed the child's death was an accident, and the enraged Tolem, who swore revenge, but the effort came to naught. D'nal refused to take sides in the ensuing civil war. Even though Tolem slaughtered enough men to avenge his son's death a hundred times over, the idea of the first blood—an innocent's blood—on Adan's hands had always repelled Naed.

"You—" he breathed, searching the Prince's face, "you would be king?"

There was no mockery in those gray eyes. No hint of doubt. Not even the demurral Naed would have recognized as false modesty. Instead, they blazed with clarity and a certitude that drew Naed in and held him. "Aye, Tolem restored to the throne that should have been his. My blood is true, Naed. I am Tolem's lineal heir." He gripped Naed's shoulder. "And you—your honor is true to D'nal's. We will remake the Kingdom, you and I, the way it should be—Tolem to lead and D'nal at his side. Brothers, once again."

The hand on his shoulder imparted an energy, a force that flowed through Naed, filling his body until he vibrated with it. He saw the future—one land, no enemy, no blood to be shed—and himself beside the Prince at the helm. "M'lord, you gift me with too great an honor!"

Chuckling, the Prince squeezed Naed's shoulder. "'Tis a promise, my friend, not yet a gift. 'Twill be no Kingdom restored unless you and I make it so. Are you with me?"

Naed clasped the Prince's outstretched hand. "Aye, m'lord, to the Demon's Doorstep—and beyond, if need be!"

Prince Arn laughed. "Not quite that far, I hope."

****

Near the first turn of the watch, Arn sat beside the basket and sifted grain between his fingers. The sound, so like a gentle rain, soothed him, despite the ache in his ribs several cups of wine had failed to dull. They were healing well, but he cursed them anyway for forcing him to hold Darkstar back when Illien and Nemmon led the charge on Eidvondin. The stallion had worked himself into a lather fighting the tight rein, as eager as Arn to return to action, but, though it galled, Arn knew Naed and the others could handle capturing the storehouses. He would be ready for Vinvinnysee, and that was as it should be.

A creak from his bed made Arn look toward it. Naed had turned in his sleep and pushed the blanket Arn had laid over him down to his waist. Arn smiled. The D'nalian had drunk barely two cups of excellent Eidvondian wine before being overcome and, at Arn's suggestion, lying down on his cot. He would summon Naed's second to fetch him to his own bed later, but for now, Arn had no need of a bed. This injury-enforced rest made him long for the all-senses-alive exertion of battle that left a man so depleted he slept like a stone.

He picked up his cup and swirled the wine to keep from thinking how he envied Naed, but the gesture failed to work. Setting the cup down without drinking, he ran his finger along the scar on his cheek. It had been a part of him for so long, he often forgot it was there—until a stranger looked at him with shock. Or revulsion.

Like the revulsion his bride-to-be displayed every time he caught her eye, a curled-lip look of disgust and horror time so far failed to mitigate. If anything, the togetherness their betrothal enforced upon Erodasi seemed to increase her loathing. He ought to have claimed her body before he left Val-Feyridge. If he had, she might now be breeding his heir.

Ordinarily, he enjoyed the spirited pursuit of a woman who defied him and denied him, employing tooth, nail and sometimes dagger to keep him at bay until the moment when her surrender and his victory carried them both to the heights of pleasure. Such a woman, while reviling him with her words and acts, showed him desire with her eyes. Erodasi showed him nothing, and he could not bring himself to touch her. Sooner or later, he would have to, if he wanted to secure the Tolem Stone. Perhaps after he had the Crown, the prospect of being queen would make her more amenable.

He doubted it.

Looking at Naed again, he envied his youth, his uncomplicated earnestness, his unmarred face, and his entirely inappropriate love for a woman who was not only Adanak but lowborn too. For the nephew of a lord, the D'nalian took huge risks, but he wondered if the young man truly understood the risks. After all, Naed's uncle acknowledged and accepted his nephew, even entrusted him with his will. Arn's uncle had massacred Arn's family and tried for years—even unto his dying moment—to kill his bastard nephew.

Arn stared into his wine. The D'nalian had a family, a home; Arn had an army, and a burned-out shell he would never rebuild—not as long as the bones of everyone he had ever loved rested in the ash. His fingers tightened on the goblet's stem. The D'nalian came by his virtue so honestly, Arn almost choked on it. At Naed's age, he had long stopped counting his kills. He had earned a name for himself, too—Master of Albon, his father's home—and a reputation as a swordsman so fearless even the naturally fearless Tolemak remarked on it. And why not? He had nothing more to lose, except his life, and what value was that if he could not spend it wreaking vengeance on those who had destroyed or denied him what was rightfully his?

Looking at his hand in the basket, Arn noticed bits of kernel and husk dusting his fingers where he must have ground seeds together. So much chaff, he thought, flicking the residue into the air and watching it sparkle in the lamplight. He had gained much in his life, but 'twas all so much chaff when laid in the scale with someone like Naed. Arn tossed down the remainder of his wine, almost choking on it. Maybe it was anger that closed his throat. Or envy.

Well, he had won something of value the D'nalian had not dared to achieve. He had tasted the Adanak woman and knew Naed had left her untouched. She had reacted like an innocent to his kiss—if he dared to call the assault he had forced upon her mouth a "kiss."

Arn cringed. He had been unspeakably crude, treating her like a woman who knew what a man wanted when it should have been clear to him from the start she knew nothing of the kind. If she had not been an Adanak—and in that damned D'nalian marsh with green hands—he would have seen her for what she was instead of the witch or whore he had expected to see.

Scowling, he looked once more at the sleeping young man. That Naed dared was key to his value, but the young man apparently had not dared enough with the woman. Arn sucked in a breath. Despite the wine's excellent bouquet, the earthy scent of grain dust in the air, the reek of a hard-used tent, the smell of wood smoke and lamp oil, he fancied he could still detect elements of her scent. Cup after cup of wine could not mask the memory of her taste. It came upon him at odd times, full and potent, like the memory of a particularly vivid dream. Except 'twas no dream.

She was gone now. Too far away, he hoped, for he or Naed to encounter her again. Neither of them needed the complication of a small, thin, brown-skinned, common-blooded, Adanak healer with the wit and fire to challenge their every word and action, no matter how her eyes radiated the lush blue of summer or her skin the honey-cream of a banquet. If either of them found her, Arn knew in his gut he would take sword and claim her—no matter who opposed him. Such action was not logical, not rational—not even practical and most assuredly not right—but he would have her, and Demon damn the consequences!

****

The Lancers, Leumas promised, would soon clear the roads. In the meantime refugees streamed into the city, filling every available inn, stable, and even the narrow alleys that ran down from one level of the city to another. Each afternoon Aerid ministered to the needs of those who found their way to Foderor's inn. His wife Mairim, though thick with her first child, insisted on helping now Aerid's herbs enabled her to leave her bed.

Leumas visited her daily, twice if the timing of his

watch permitted. Often Avika joined him. Sometimes Avika walked with Aerid and Leumas, but more often, after they had supped together, he would stay at the inn and talk with the townsmen around the great trestle table.

Aerid sat on the inn's stone steps, still warm in the fading light, and watched Avika smile his white-toothed grin at something the serving maid whispered in his ear. He had come alone this eve, Avika told her, because Leumas had bade him do so after receiving orders to escort Master Gaelwynn to a council at the palace. Would she see Leumas yet this night, she asked, and Avika could only shrug. Aerid sighed and stared down the evening-darkened streets.

These city folk had been kind to her, but she had come to depend upon Leumas. Without him by her side, the city lost its perfume, its energy, even its color and became, as on this velvet night, merely a maze of blank stone passageways. Where did they lead? Aerid had always planned to go north, but during these weeks of enforced immobility, that goal remained as distant and as dim as the stars winking through the haze over the old tower. The image shook her. She rose, driving it from her mind with the action of her limbs.

A passing cart had snipped a flower from a window box and it lay, a splash of red, on the gray cobblestones. Aerid stooped and picked it up. She sniffed the delicate fragrance that still clung to it, then stroked her fingertip across each vivid petal. All too soon, the edges would curl and the bloom would be no more than a withered memory.

'Twas a melancholy thought, and she pushed it from her mind. The night was warm, sweet with multifarious scents, and Leumas was coming. With a quiver of excitement, she recognized his figure emerge from the passage beside the tinker's shop. "Look," she said, twirling the flower's bit of stem between her fingers as he approached, "'tis beautiful, aye?"

Leumas' gaze did not touch the bloom; rather, it fixed on her face. A somber gaze, it looked so long and deep she sought shelter from it under her lashes. He broke the look long enough to glance at the inn's patrons before grasping her arm and turning her so his body blocked what he

Helen C. Johannes

carried from their view. "Take this," he said, pushing a round, tightly wrapped bundle into her hands, dislodging the flower.

"Leumas, what—?"

"Speak not, Aerid, but listen. 'Tis bread—good, hard bread that will keep. Hide it where only you may find it. Let no one know you possess this bread."

She searched his face, noticing his mouth, always curving upward at one corner, did not do so. Stomach knotting, she hugged the solid bundle to her breast. "What has happened?"

Taking her arm, he steered her up the steps. Finding the landing occupied, he hurried her all the way up to her room and closed the door. The shutters stood open and torchlight from the street glinted in his eyes as he took the bread from her and set it on her bed. He had never entered her room before and, though he was not a large man, his body seemed to fill the room, making it seem cramped. Craving light—and air—she walked to the window and leaned against the sill. On the street below, a peddler's cart rolled over the flower, flattening it. Shaken, Aerid turned away and fingered the birthstone at her throat.

Leumas followed her to the window, not touching her, but his gaze remained fixed on her face as though he might memorize the details of it. "The storehouses at Otlesend and Eidvondin were taken two days ago. Tomorrow, all grain shall be tightly rationed. Promise me you will keep this loaf against the day the bread should run out."

He had not said those words. Yet the chill settling around her heart told her she had heard all too clearly. "'Tis true, then, what the whispers say? We are besieged? Trapped?"

"Besieged, yes, but—oh Aerid, I did not seek to frighten you." Leumas hesitated, then pulled her into an embrace. "Besieged we may be, sweetness, but never trapped. The city is too well-fortified. The *mortraeders* may deprive us of bread, but they will spend themselves against our walls ere we suffer one pang of true want. Besides, there be yet the Lancers. Master Gaelwynn means to send them out this very night."

His hands traveled across her back, warm and soothing, and his shoulder under her cheek felt solid, strong, and true. Aerid relaxed, savoring the comfort of arms that promised, by their very tenderness, to protect her. Not since early childhood had she experienced such an embrace, one that demanded nothing but offered so much. The Prince had embraced her, true, but only to throw her onto his horse or push her face down in marshy grass while a lance tore into his back—a lance aimed at her!

Aerid shuddered, and Leumas stepped closer so his body touched hers from head to knee. Lips brushing her temple, he murmured, "Fear not, sweetness, the city will not fall. 'Tis ever true—the Lancers strike terror into the hearts of the *mortraeders*. You will see. They will chase the demon prince and his beast-like followers from our lands."

Remembering the slow, deliberate swing of a lance and a glimpse of malevolent eyes targeting her through slits in a helm, she clenched fingers in Leumas' tunic.

With an indrawn breath, he tightened his embrace.

His heart throbbed under her hand, but her mind suppressed the signal. Instead, it fixed on a horrible thought: How could the Lancers prevail against a man who, on foot and armed with only a sword, could turn aside their weaponry? The Lancers had killed Naed, but unless the blow to her head had conjured her memories of that night, had not the Prince faced down a Lancer alone and his men killed or captured several of these "invincible" warriors?

Pushing back, she sought Leumas' eyes. "If the city be taken—speak not! Hear me! If the city be taken, you must not stay to surrender. You must come with me to the mountains, you and Avika. They will not follow us there." Her hands fisted in the cloth of his sleeves. "Promise me that you will come!"

His brows bunched. "Aerid, sweetness, 'tis but your fear that speaks. All will be well. That I promise you. Do you not trust me?"

She did—with her life—but he could not know what she knew about the force gathering about the city. Nor, she saw, could she convince him of the truth. He was a man and, like Naed, he would do what honor demanded. Still, she made one more attempt. "Mayhap, as you say, 'tis naught to fear, but promise me you will not sacrifice yourself foolishly."

Leumas smiled—a warm, vibrant smile that took her breath away. He unfastened her fingers from his sleeve and spread them. "For your sake, Aerid, I would do anything." Raising her hand, he pressed his lips to her palm. His face hovered inches from hers, lids lowered over eyes that seemed not green but pools of darkness, gaze fastened on her mouth.

Sisters! Aerid thought. He meant to kiss her. Unnerved, she pushed at his chest, but his arm behind her back tensed, resisted.

"'Tis but a kiss I desire, sweetness. Will you deny me something so small?"

Hardly small, Aerid thought, remembering a knee-weakening maelstrom of lips, teeth, tongue, and hands. Part of her wanted to test his kiss against the other, to see if it would drive away the imprint of the first. Another part remembered only Krenin's appearance had broken what had clearly gone out of control. In the shadows behind her was a bed, and that would hardly speak up on her behalf—or Leumas'.

"You should not be here." She braced her arms against his chest and lowered her head. "'Tis unseemly."

He blinked, seeming to take in the room for the first time. His gaze found the bed and lingered. Under her hand, his heart beat in heavy, ragged thuds. "Aye," he said, turning to her with eyes that hid none of his desire. He skated a hand up her arm and trailed the backs of his fingers down her cheek. "'Tis true, and I would not for all my life may be worth have you compromised in the eyes of these good people."

A tiny shudder rippled through her body. She tore her eyes from the green fire in his. "I—it grows late."

"Indeed, it does," he said, his voice thick with reluctance. "Come, I will see you back downstairs."

CHAPTER FIFTEEN

Arn opened his eyes to find rain spitting from a gray sky. The cool drizzle had stirred him as it plastered his hair to his forehead and ran in rivulets down his cheeks. His side ached. His head throbbed. He wondered where he was, what had happened.

Overhead, trees intertwined their branches, the leaves glistening. A shudder ran through the boughs. Huge drops plopped down on his face. He sat up and dashed the water from his eyes.

"So, 'tis to yourself you've come at last, eh, *mortraeder*?"

Arn froze. His sword hilt lay at the edge of his vision. The enemy seemed somewhere close behind him. He spun, and his hand was on his sword before his heart beat again.

A foot pressed the blade to the earth, a heavy, mail-clad foot. White teeth flashed in a copper-skinned face. "Be still, Tolemak, and your sword shall be yours again." The Adanak adjusted his grip upon his own sword, the point of which rested on the ground between his feet.

Arn's gaze took in the formidable armor of the man who sat on the log before him—the armor and the shield leaning at the man's side, a shield bearing the insignia of crossed lances.

The day's events came back to Arn in a rush. He remembered the news of the Lancers' approach. And how Naed galloped off with Illien and his men to lure them into a trap. It was ridiculously easy to contain the Lancers once they rode into the prepared clearing. Naed's men scattered, and the Lancers, dividing to pursue them, rode directly into ropes that twanged up chest high across all the exits.

On foot, the Lancers, who were deadly mounted, found their armor a mortal hindrance. Those who remained mounted were set upon by three and four horsemen, one to lure the lance, the others to knock it away. Deprived of his main weapon, the Lancer had to rely on his sword—to no great advantage. Only a handful escaped the carnage. Only a handful...

Arn looked again into the dark eyes returning his gaze. They were watchful, but he detected none of the malice he ought to have seen in Adanak eyes. Particularly these Adanak eyes. Instead, the man seemed content to sit—as long as Arn made no attempt to free his sword. Relinquishing the hilt, Arn eased back onto his knees.

The Lancer smiled, but his foot remained atop Arn's blade. "Rest awhile, *mortraeder*. You have wearied my horse."

"Only your horse?"

The Lancer laughed. He wiped away dark hair which, curling with the drizzle, clung to a fresh scratch over his brow. "More than my horse, then, *mortraeder*. 'Tis a heavy sword you be wielding." He gestured to his shield. "'Twill require a smith to be removing these dents."

Arn glanced at his own shield, lying upside down in the grass. He wondered if the man knew whom he held so congenially at bay in this wood closed round with the stillness of gently falling rain. And Arn wondered, too, how he could have ridden so far in pursuit of this escaping Lancer neither Naed nor Illien nor any other of his men had yet found him. He raised his hand to the knot on the back of his head. How long had he been unconscious? The leaden sky gave him no indication of the hour. More drops, stirred by the breeze, pelted him. He shivered and knew it had not been mere minutes he had lain at the mercy of the man who watched him with dark, intelligent eyes.

"Why didn't you kill me?" Arn searched the brown face with a small half-moon scar standing white upon the chin.

The Lancer gestured to an exposed tree root and a stone nestled in the grass Arn's body had flattened. "It does hardly seem just to kill a man whom tree and stone contrived to render unconscious."

A queer sensation prickled through the pit of Arn's stomach. He stared at the root over which he had tripped. He had drawn first blood, he remembered now, a glancing blow to the Lancer's head, but the man had driven him backward with blows the like of which a smith would deliver. Arn had held his own, but barely. What if—

"Indeed," the Lancer said, raising his sword and brushing soil from the point, "it did seem most unfair to press advantage o'er a man whose blade has provided me with the greatest challenge since the Northern Wars." He rose. "Pity you be Tolemak."

Arn stood. His limbs were leaden and his head throbbed with their motion, but he forced himself to retort, "Pity you are not."

The Lancer laughed. He whistled for his horse. Obediently, the animal raised its head and trotted over. The Adanak caught the reins, adjusted his saddle, and looked again at Arn. He removed his foot from Arn's blade. "Live, *mortraeder*, and fight again."

Arn held his gaze. "Perhaps I would not have been so generous."

The dark eyes glinted. "I think not, else I should have killed you." He swung aboard his bay stallion and raised his sword in salute. "Till we meet again."

"Sisters willing, may it be under less hostile circumstances."

"As you say." The Lancer inclined his head, reined his horse about and heeled it.

In seconds man and animal disappeared into the haze blurring the edge of the clearing. All sound vanished with them, save the whisper of leaves. For one uncertain moment, Arn wondered if he had dreamed the encounter. He turned, half-expecting to see himself lying in the grass. Instead, his mud-stained sword lay at his feet, and his shield, upside down, had collected a small puddle of rainwater. He reached for them, reassuring himself with their cold solidity. He moved two steps to the log—and breathed deeply. There, to the right, was the print of a heavily burdened horse.

It had been no dream, but 'twere perhaps better had it been so. He stripped water from his sword and sheathed it. Giving his shield another shake, he whistled for Darkstar.

The black stallion trotted through the trees. Its nostrils flared and it pawed the ground near the log. Arn stroked Darkstar's neck, calming the horse with low words. Still, it tossed its head and danced sideways until he mounted and rode a few strides into the trees. He sat there for a moment, looking back at the gray-green grass, a small, flat stone, and a rapidly dampening log.

****

The Crownkeeper stood at the Vinvinnysee tower window and surveyed the rain-washed jumble of stone and tile spread out below. He had tried to remain calm while climbing the 136 steps, but the news of an assassin had so eaten at his innards he had crumpled the message in his fist before making the final landing. Would that his old bones could crumple the bones of those who had conceived such a treacherous act. The Masters he served were fools, plain and simple, so schooled in their merchant sensibilities they had long lost any conception of honor, courage, duty, except as they might employ the words to influence their subjects.

Opening his fist, he looked at the wadded paper. Were he in a forgiving mood, he might suppose they had tried what they in their merchant wisdom thought best, but 'twas just such wrong-headed notions that had brought the Crown to where it lay—a dim and nearly forgotten relic of a Kingdom that had collapsed when honor had been betrayed, duty compromised, and courage forsaken. Murder begot murder. Would they never learn? Trembling, he ripped the message to shreds and tossed them into the rain. But doing so gave him no satisfaction. The future he had glimpsed but weeks ago seemed clouded now, danger pressing darkly upon it.

****

Arn found Naed at the edge of the clearing. The young man sat his horse and directed men who tossed armor onto a pile under trees. Weapons lay glinting dully in another heap. "We have won, m'lord," Naed said, his face shining with more than the drizzle that had washed it. "We have broken their backs. The Lancers are no more."

Arn surveyed the bodies strewn about the clearing. Despite the drizzle, the salt-sweet smell of blood hung heavy in the air. He had gloried in the scent often, knowing it as the odor of victory. Now it repelled him.

"Carry on," he said, and turned away.

A line of horses laden with bodies blocked his path. Arn waited while the Tolemak dead were taken to the far side of the clearing, to graves newly-taken captives had begun to dig. The Adanak dead were hauled from horses and dumped on the ground near him. Men bent over the bodies and stripped them of weapons, armor, valuables, even clothing.

An Albon archer sat on the ground pulling on an Adanak officer's boots. "Mine be worn through, m'lord," he said when he noticed Arn's gaze upon him. Flushing under his Prince's continued stare, he stood and hurried to help his companions unload the next body.

"This one's still warm," said one of the men.

"Demon be damned! He's bled like a stuck pig!"

"'Twill wash, if you'd have the armor."

"'Twas the saddle I wanted. *Pfaugh*, these bastards stink!"

They flung the body onto the ground. Blood from an arrow in the neck had run up the side of the head and matted dark hair curling over a scratch on the forehead. A half-moon scar divided the flow of blood across the chin.

A foot soldier from Val-Feyridge bent to unbuckle the Lancer's sword belt.

"Don't touch him!" Arn leaped from his horse and hurled the soldier away. The dead man's dark eyes were open, fixed on some distant point only the vanished soul could see. Bending, Arn snapped the arrow shank from the Lancer's neck. He stared at the feathered end then broke it upon itself until splintered bits remained in his trembling hands.

Fragments trailing from his fingers, Arn saw his men standing in a half circle staring at him. Even Naed wore an expression of consternation. How could he tell them that this...Adanak had spared his life? How could he tell them what this—this puny arrow had taken? How could he tell them when he himself barely knew?

"Bury him untouched," he said in a ragged voice. "And bring me his sword when you've finished." He hurtled past Naed without waiting for a response and leaped aboard Darkstar. At the touch of his heels, the horse carried him out of the clearing and into the silence of the forest.

****

Banir heaved the Lancer's helm from his head and wiped his sleeve across his lip. "'Tis like a baker's oven inside one of these."

"We should have made the bastards roast in the sun, then," Grodar said, rubbing his bandaged elbow. "'Twould have saved us the trouble of smashing 'em."

Morys held out a dagger with a jeweled hilt. "What's this like to be worth in trade?"

Naed turned away from the fire as Grodar and Banir bent over Morys's dagger. Gripping the sheathed sword he had taken from the dead Lancer, he walked across the pine needle-strewn strip of earth between his and the Prince's tent. The tent had been dark since the clouds parted at sunset. Ordinarily, the Prince's lamp would burn until well past midnight, his shadow large against the tent walls as he pored over charts and made plans.

Naed glanced once more at the three Tolemaks who sat around the fire before his tent and haggled over the value of a captured dagger. They had buried the Lancer's body as directed, asking none of the questions that must have been in their hearts. Mayhap they understood the Prince's strange outburst since they, too, were Tolemak. Naed dismissed the idea. More like they accepted their lack of understanding because he was their Prince.

Taking a deep breath, Naed stepped into the shadow of the entry flap. "M'lord?"

"You have the sword?"

Naed flushed. He knew the Prince was within; hearing the man's voice should not have startled him. Still, as his eyes adjusted to the darkness, he wondered if he had roused the Prince from sleep, so thick had his voice sounded. "Aye, m'lord."

"Put it on the table."

With the light from the men's fires, he could just make out the table and the Prince's silhouette next to it. Naed approached and laid the weapon on the wood. He stood for a moment, rocking on his heels and wondering if he ought to speak, then wondering what he ought to say. Finally, he stepped backward. "By your leave, my lord, I—"

190

"He saw me as a man. What's more, he made me see him so." Naed heard the faint scrape of metal on wood and the whisper of the blade exiting the scabbard. "Can you understand that? Can you understand that he made me see him—as a man?"

"I-I think so, m'lord." Was that the answer the Prince sought? The Prince had done so for him. Still, the Prince spoke of an Adanak—and a Lancer besides.

"I've seen thousands of men die. Killed hundreds with my own hands. Adanak, Tolemak, D'nalian—what did it matter? They were all enemies." The sword glinted as he laid it across his knees. "But this man..."

Like a shadow, the Prince's hand traversed the length of the blade. "Only one other man has ever so completely held my life in his hands. 'Twas my first battle. I had scavenged a sword from a dead man. My enemy's blade was at my throat, but he held back. I think he pitied me."

"What did you do, m'lord?"

"I killed him. He was a fool."

A chill whispered along Naed's neck. "This Lancer was no fool?"

"Not for pity. But the Sisters have made him their fool—to give life and have it taken so ignobly away!"

The sword chinked into the soil at the Prince's feet. Naed resisted the impulse to snatch it safely away. "The Sisters determine when we must die. 'Tis naught we may do to alter it."

"That's where you're wrong. That's where you're all wrong! We may alter it as much as we dare." The Prince rose. "Too many men cling to what little they have, telling themselves they're content when, in truth, they're afraid—afraid to take their destiny by the throat and shake it till it gives them what they want!" Wrenching the sword from the earth, he slammed it into the scabbard. "This man had no such fears, and I'll be damned if I'll let his death signify nothing!" He swept to the tent flap and loomed in the entryway. "Send a messenger to Krenin. Tell him to advance on the city. Let them see us and know that they're trapped."

Naed found that the muscles he had tensed still moved, but weakly. "As you wish, m'lord, but how will that—"

"We'll win, my friend. We'll win, and then no more will die."

CHAPTER SIXTEEN

She visited him again, as she often did in those dim moments between sleeping and waking. When she came, she touched him—fingers fluttering over his skin as gently as they had ministered to his shoulder or radiating fire like the flushed cheek held captive against his—

Arn wrenched his thoughts free. It was enough she haunted his dreams; he would not permit her to invade his conscious hours. He had waited too long for this day. Fixing his eyes on a gap in the thinning trees, he heeled his stallion and rode toward it.

Krenin sat his horse before a vast clearing, but Arn rode past him into grass so deep it brushed Darkstar's belly. He drew rein at the rim of a gully that cut a marshy swath from the forest's edge to the gate of the city huddling on a rise behind it. His gaze traveled over the city's long, sleek outer wall, colored cream in the mid-morning light, touched the banners fluttering above the gate towers, then rose over rooftops to the inner walls, and over each of those to the palace standing washed in sunlight on the height. He would sleep there. Not tonight, but soon.

His stallion danced sideways, champing at the tight rein. Arn wheeled him around.

Krenin sat with his hands crossed over his saddle pommel. "Vinvinnysee," he said, "sealed tighter than a barrel pasted with pitch."

Arn rode forward and laid his hand on Krenin's shoulder. "Well done, my friend."

"'Twill be the Demon's own trick to get in. They have water, and the gates are solid Athellyn oak."

"Water isn't enough." Arn cast one more glance at the city. "And even Athellyn oak surrenders to the ax." Turning, he signaled Naed to join them. He watched Krenin's gaze flash over the D'nalian, and Naed's, noncommittal, meet the glare. "Are the wagons ready?"

"Aye, m'lord."

"See they're delivered, one to each gate."

"Wagons?" Krenin said, frowning.

"Filled with the Lancers' armor," Naed said. "'Twill be scattered before the gates."

Krenin looked from Naed to Arn. He grinned. "Well, that should thin the bastards' blood. How long before we let it flow?"

Arn looked once more at the silent, stainless wall. He touched the hilt of a sheathed sword hanging from his saddle horn. The Adanak characters adorning it drew his fingertips into their indentations. He stroked across them, wondering again what name they signified, then pulled his hand away. "Soon," he said, and wheeled Darkstar about.

****

The crack of Leumas' hand on the table made Aerid flinch. "Why do they not come?" he demanded. "Seven days have they ringed us thus and made no move, no sign."

"Save for the scattering of the Lancer's armor," muttered one of the men at the other end of the trestle table.

Leumas swung to him. "'Twas a foul act, fit for beasts, to be scattering such blood-stained pieces and sitting about them like vultures!"

"Who may read the thoughts of a *mortraeder*?" Avika said, licking the last bit of stew from his spoon. He grinned. "Such as what may pass for thought among them, that is."

The men at the other end of the table laughed, but it was a half-hearted laugh, Aerid noted, not like the belly-shaking laughs Avika had drawn a scant week before. Nor did the men look long at each other.

Just as she had done on the previous six nights, she used the diversion to surreptitiously ladle half of her stew ration into Leumas' bowl. "Eat," she said, pushing the bowl toward him, "or you shall be having no strength to watch tonight."

"Strength to watch what? Shadows in the dark?" His gaze roved the room, the green eyes murky, the flesh beneath the sockets shadowed. "They do ride about at night, whispering and taunting. We shoot a flamed arrow to see, and they are gone. Dispersed. Vanished like ghosts. At day, they do sit afar off, ringing us like the wolf pack rings a sickened beast." He clenched his fist. "Would that they would come for us like men!"

What could she say? That she wished the Tolemak would grant his request when, with all her heart, she wished they had never reached the city? But wishing would not turn them aside, and wishing would not hold them at bay, although each hour they hesitated gave her one more hour with Leumas to sit with their arms nearly touching, to watch the liquid mutability of his eyes, to forget, in the warmth of his nearness, the man whose touch still troubled her dreams.

The common room suddenly seemed too close, too hot. Slipping free of the table, Aerid hurried through the kitchen and out into the small courtyard behind the inn. The air was cooler there, and evening shadows soothed her flushed face. She paced among Mairim's vegetables, plucking a weed here, snapping off a dead leaf there. Leumas was with her every day, as solid and real a presence as the vegetables, the garden, the stone courtyard. His constant attention made clear his devotion. He would wed her; she was sure of it—if she would but give him her kiss. He had not pressed her since that night in her room, but she could see the longing in his eyes each time he bade her goodnight.

With a groan, she sank onto the stone bench and pressed her apron to her cheeks as if to contain the turmoil burning across them. What did she owe the Prince? He had taken her kiss and wiped himself clean of her—but that was the first kiss. 'Twas the second that had undone her—and him—had it not been for Krenin. Even then he insisted he owed her naught. Doubtless, he could now scarce recall her name or place her features. If he should find her among the people of Vinvinnysee, he would not know her. Why, then, did the certainty of his presence bring a spiral of heat to her most womanly place?

Because she knew with all her heart he *would* know her. Had he not recognized her from the very first, from that brief glimpse in the dark wood of Druemarwin?

Indeed, he *would* know her—and Aerid feared with all her soul what she might then do.

She heard the scuffle of gravel and Leumas' voice, tender and close. "Aerid? Forgive me. I did not wish to distress—"

"Oh, Leumas!" Rising, she turned blindly into him, pressing her face to his throat, clinging with arms wrapped around his body. She drank in the scent of him, the hint of fragrant oil, the warm man-smell of a body that had worked in the sun but was now at rest. 'Twas nothing elemental about his scent, but everything pleasing. Why did it not seem enough? Her breath hitched with a sob, and her lips brushed the crisp hairs edging his collarbone.

Under her cheek, his pulse jolted, then raced. His hands rose to her hair, touching it, stroking it, then thrusting into it. "Aerid, sweetness!" rushed warm across her ear. His lips grazed her forehead, caressing it with whispered endearments.

She trembled, knowing if she raised her head now, he would see her gesture as consent, see in the upturning of her face the offer he so desired. Would his touch, his taste be enough to hold her memories at bay—even to wipe them out? Fingers locked in his tunic, she closed her eyes and leaned away from his throat. "Leumas...?"

His fingertips touched her lips first, and she sensed the tremor that shook him, but she kept her eyes closed, waiting. His sighed, "Sweetness," warmed her face before he fit his mouth to hers. She leaned into him, accepting his gentle coaxing, letting him know by the parting of her lips he could take more. Pulling her against the length of his body, he did.

Moments later, when he raised his head, Aerid was quivering. The quaking had begun in her stomach and radiated outward until her whole being shook with it.

"Aerid, sweetness," Leumas soothed as his thumbs brushed tears from her cheeks. "We will be wed, I do swear it. When the city is saved, I shall bear you to your home, the bride of a Vinvinnysee Free Man."

Aerid's heart contracted. His face swam before her eyes like something from a dream, now close and real, now distant and fanciful, now tender and green-eyed, now dark and...gray. She gripped his arms. "Wh-why must we wait?"

Leumas laughed gently, but his eyes glowed. "Because I would celebrate our wedding, and now is not the day or hour for such revelry." He nuzzled her throat. "Come, let us go in, or I shall taste more of your delights and forswear myself."

Mayhap you should, Aerid thought as he turned her toward the inn. If he would but kiss her again, and bend over her under the fragrant honeysuckle, the stars might this time leave their orbits as they had once before under a star-drenched sky weeks, and worlds, ago.

****

"Hand me my cloak."

Naed lifted the scarlet cloth from the pommel of his saddle and passed it to the Prince, who flung it around his shoulders and fastened the clasp at his neck.

Krenin, sitting his horse to his left, growled, "Would that you'd let me hail them. Or even send *him!*" He jerked his head in Naed's direction. "He's your Second."

Naed's fingers tightened on his reins. It gave him no pleasure to agree with the man. "True, m'lord. You should not risk yourself so. Either of us may rightly deliver your terms."

Taking the white-flagged lance from Banir, who stood at his stirrup, the Prince said, "Stay behind the gully's edge, and have the archers fit arrows to strings, but keep their bows down." He held out his free hand. "Now, the sword."

If Naed had learned aught in the weeks he had served as the Prince's closest companion, foremost was the man could not be dissuaded once he had set a course. With an inward sigh, Naed passed over the Lancer's weapon. The Prince laid the scabbard across his horse's withers and rode forward. Naed let him ride thirty feet ahead, then signaled his men to follow the Prince.

Krenin urged his mount next to Naed's. "What in the name of the Four Winds does he want with that tin-head's weapon?"

The sneer with which Krenin had greeted him continued to curl the Tolemak's mouth. Naed told himself he did not care what Krenin thought. What mattered was

197

the Prince had made no move to alter their current positions. Krenin's displeasure had been obvious, but if he had voiced it to the Prince, he had done so in private. Naed nudged his mount into a trot as the Prince picked up the pace. "'Twas a Lancer's blade."

"I can see that! What does he want with it?"

"'Twould be better if you sought such answers from the Prince himself."

"Don't you know? Are there things he doesn't tell you, Second?"

"I am privy to this, but 'tis unsure I am that I could find the words to make a matter of ideas clear to such a one as you."

"You bloated swamp toad! The Sisters may have smiled on you thus far, but your thread will run out. And when it does—" Krenin leaned over and jabbed a finger in the center of Naed's chest armor. "—'tis I who'll be there to make the cut clean and final!" Veering his mount, he spurred it to the other side of the Prince's escort.

Naed took up his shield and fastened the strap of his helm. Naught had changed, he thought with a hot rush of irritation, naught at all.

****

Arn paused at the lip of the gully and surveyed the walls. They seemed bare, devoid of movement, as still as the stones of which they had been constructed. Yet he knew at least twenty archers should have measured the distance to his chest and drawn their bows accordingly. He rode into the gully, through the streamlet that filled it, and up the bank to the flat, bare ground before the gate.

Driving the butt of the lance into the earth, he called, "Hail within!"

A face appeared between two closely placed stones. It was a thin face, almost skeletal, topped with iron-gray hair that fluttered in the morning breeze. "Speak your terms, *mortraeder*."

"Gladly, but only to the man who may tell me the name of he who wielded this weapon." Arn lifted the Lancer's sheathed sword from his saddle pommel and held it upright. Despite the distance, he could see the man's eyes close longer than a mere blink would allow.

"Have you no pity that you would blaspheme the

dead?"

"'Tis no blasphemy to ask a man's name. Or have you no honor that you would deny to know him?" Heeling Darkstar, Arn rode directly to the foot of the wall. "Tell me the name inscribed here, or fetch me a man who can! I'll speak to no other."

The man studied him for several heartbeats. "The name inscribed thereon is Sevig. How came you by his sword?"

Arn returned the Adanak's scrutiny. His face was all edges, lined and leathered with the passage of perhaps sixty years. The nose was sharp, beak-like, and his eyes, despite the distance, watched Arn as those of a hawk might. Arn lowered the Lancer's sword. "Was he your friend?"

"I did number him so."

"Then I will speak with you, friend of Sevig." Darkstar danced about, and Arn tightened the reins. "Your name?"

"Gaelwynn, Master of the Guard." He braced a hand on the wall's edge. "What would you say to me, and to the Masters of Vinvinnysee through me?"

"Surrender, and I will do you no harm."

"And if we do not?"

"I have men, food, water, and time. Your granaries are under my control, and your Lancers..." He stretched his arm toward the armor littering the opposite bank of the gully. "There lie your Lancers, Master Gaelwynn. Sevig covered himself with honor. The others merely died." He wheeled his horse again. "Surrender and spare yourselves. Or fight and die."

"Vinvinnysee has withstood others before you, *mortraeder*. She will do so again."

"As you wish." Arn wrenched the lance from the earth. "I wish you health, Guard Master Gaelwynn, for fortune is already mine." Reining his horse around, he trotted back through the gully, past the scattered armor, and into the ranks of his escort.

****

"So, now we have seen the celebrated Prince of Val-Feyridge," Avika said as he approached where Leumas sat with Aerid on the inn's sun-warmed steps.

To make room for Avika on the stoop, Aerid tucked her skirt under her legs. Leaning against Leumas, she laced her fingers tightly into his. The actions gave her time to master her nerves after the jangle mention of the Prince had sent through them. "You have seen him?"

"He spoke with Master Gaelwynn today, but we heard none of their conversation."

"They say he bears a Lancer's blade, that he employs it to execute captives," Leumas said.

"I did see the blade." Avika reclined against the wall. "'Tis a splendid piece of work."

"'Tis said he be a giant among men." Leumas folded his hand over Aerid's. "But to see him today, dwarfed by our gate—why, he be no more than a man. Certainly naught to be feared."

"Would that I were a horseman yet. I should like to engage him."

"I as well. Sword for sword, we are the better. Look, they hesitate to engage us. Why—"

"Oh, aye, he may be no more than a *man*," Aerid interjected, heat rising in her cheeks, "yet he is to be feared. You do forget, I have seen them fight."

For a moment Leumas and Avika stared at her, and she thought she had spoken too forcefully, but she could not hold her tongue while they so blithely underestimated the man who came against them. Then Leumas smiled and patted her hand. "You have seen them with the eyes of a woman, my love, not those of a warrior. There is—"

She would have argued, but a sudden cacophony of bells filled the air. Leumas and Avika sprang to their feet. "The west gate!" Avika said.

"Run ahead! I shall follow your heel." While Avika sprinted off, Leumas swept Aerid to her feet. His gaze took in her face, touching every detail as though he would commit it to memory. Then he bent, kissed her quickly, and was gone.

Aerid leaned against the door frame while other men poured out of the inn, some with clothes still rumpled from sleep, others with wives trailing after them begging for one last kiss, afraid to leave off looking lest the looked-for husband not return. Aerid watched them all, but she knew only two things—her lips still felt the pressure of

Leumas', and her heart had become a great, leaden weight in her chest. She turned mechanically and went inside.

CHAPTER SEVENTEEN

Naed studied Prince Arn's profile. Flames licking up behind the city's west gate cast the Prince's red-and-blue-painted face now in darkness, now in a flickering, preternatural light. The shadows accentuated the hollows of his face, making it mask-like, carven, like an image Naed had seen perched on the eave of an inn south of Ort. The image had been neither man nor bird nor beast but winged and clawed and faced with such a frightful visage Naed had ridden on rather than sleep under its auspices. He had forgotten that image—until now when the impulse to ride on possessed him with a suddenness that made his knees grip his mount's sides and his hand pull the horse's head around.

The confused animal responded with a snort and a stamp of hooves.

Naed brought the horse to a halt facing away from the Prince. 'Twas foolishness to let such fancy rule. He had wit and reason, and both told him no demons lurked in this darkness, only men—the men of Tolemak who sought to conquer the Adanak of Vinvinnysee.

Keeping his flushed face averted, Naed scanned the sky, looking first at how the roiling smoke obscured the palace on the height, then westward for the ridge of thunderclouds he remembered seeing at dusk. A flicker of lightning told him the ridge had advanced and thickened. "Mayhap, it will rain," he said, pointing in the direction of the flash.

"Let it rain," muttered Krenin. "If it puts out the fires, we'll start them again."

"But not at this gate," the Prince said with a glance at the advancing storm.

Seeing the Prince's face was his own again, Naed chided himself for the relief he felt.

"When the storm ends," the Prince said, "bring out the battle towers Borth's men built and set them against the north and east walls. Bring them as close as you can under cover of darkness. When dawn breaks, mount an attack with catapult and arrows while Krenin, you take Gorm and Illien and worry the south wall. Let them think you intend to scale the gate tower."

"With pleasure."

Naed looked away from the gleam in Krenin's eyes. "What of the west wall, m'lord?"

"We'll let them think our attention is fixed elsewhere. With attacks on three sides, they'll be hard put to keep the west wall fully manned. When the time is right, we'll use that gully—" He pointed to the blackness slashing the darkened clearing. "—to our advantage."

"How long ere the time is right?"

"They've been without supplies for over three weeks. Their bread must be gone by now."

Krenin grinned. "With that multitude, they'll be eating the dogs soon." He drew his sword and fingered the blade. "I wonder how long they'll last on rat stew."

Naed's stomach churned. His horse danced sideways at a grumble of thunder. "They have their women and children with them. Will you not offer them the chance to surrender?"

"He already did," Krenin growled. "They chose to eat rat."

Suppressing a retort, Naed turned instead to the Prince. "When they have experienced our might, mayhap they will change their minds. Will you not offer them the opportunity?"

"If there be behind those walls men like he who wielded this sword—" The Prince indicated the Lancer's weapon suspended from his saddle pommel. "—they will fight until there is no hope."

"Then I pray there are few such men."

"On the contrary, pray there are many, for they're the only ones worth winning." Reaching down, the Prince snapped heads from the tall grass touching his stirrup. "The rest—" He crushed the seed between his thumb and fingers. "—are merely chaff."

The powdered hulls drifted across the fire-lit city behind the Prince's silhouette, and disappeared. One part of Naed agreed with the man to whom he had bound his fortune. Another part thrust into his vision the graven image he had avoided in Ort. Now it looked, leered, and laughed at him. Shuddering, he jerked his gaze toward Krenin.

The Tolemak watched the city, his painted face distorted by the distant, writhing light.

Naed sensed the web of light touching his hands, his body, his face. He wheeled his horse away from it, then felt the sting of chagrin. There was no demon here. Only a Tolemak. *But when*, a small voice niggled at him, *has a Tolemak become less than a demon?* Naed set his teeth together. "By your leave, m'lord, I shall see to the battle towers."

"By all means," the Prince said, "carry on."

****

Predawn rain steamed on the streets of Vinvinnysee. Runoff collected in the center trough of the cobblestones. Aerid watched while, at each corner, grimy streams converged and sped out of sight toward grates Leumas had told her lined the outer wall.

She pushed tendrils of damp hair from her forehead and stifled a yawn. The rain had been a blessing, coming as it had in time to smother the fires Tolemak arrows had set. Indeed, there seemed little to burn in a city of plaster, stone, and slate, but enemy arrows had found a cart loaded with bedding straw, a wooden scaffold, even a catapult frame. With the help of the rain, though, the men had quickly smothered the flames.

Mayhap, Aerid thought, the rain had even helped them fend off the attack. Regardless, it had been after midnight when the wounded ceased to arrive at the Golden Horse. And it had been after the third hour when Leumas, sooty-faced and haggard, had been released from duty and promised to wait for her by the pillar in the corner. There he sat, and there he slept until the bells, the wild, frantic bells, summoned all able men to the walls again at dawn.

It was the north gate, Aerid heard as she tended her last charges.

"No," other men said, "'tis the east wall."

"They be storming the south gate!" frantic messengers shouted as they rushed by the inn.

204

Be thankful, Aerid silently told them as she watched two men carry yet another shrouded body from the inn. *Be thankful the Sisters have thus far spared you.*

****

Dropping his reins beside a battle tower, Arn grasped a rough-hewn timber and cross-beam. He swung his legs out of the saddle and found a foothold on the tower's crudely laced ladder. Shifting his grip to the rungs above, he climbed quickly, passing the first and second levels to the topmost.

A flaming arrow thudded into the upright near the ladder. A soldier threw water on it. "Good work," Arn said.

The man grinned. He lowered his empty bucket on a rope and pulled up a filled one.

With two quick strides, Arn crouched beside a gray-whiskered man kneeling beside twenty shielded archers. Bowstrings twanged in unison, and a hail of arrows converged on the city wall opposite. Arn watched two find their marks.

"Can't we get closer?"

Borth yanked an arrow from the top of the barricade. He gestured to the feathering. "They shoot ours back at us already. Their own they save for better opportunities."

"How long before we can move in?"

"Two days, perhaps." He nodded toward the gate tower. "'Twill take heavy battering, m'lord, but if we could tumble that, we'd be above 'em."

"And have a clear path forward." Arn surveyed his forces arrayed about the battle tower. "I'll divert a catapult from the north side. That should do."

"Aye." Borth signaled to the archers, who let arrows fly again.

Moments later, Arn's feet touched ground in the shade of the tower, and he reached for his stallion's reins. A shadow flashed past the edge of his vision. There was a *whump!*—too close. Darkstar shied, but Arn held fast to the reins. Around him, men under the battle tower rose from their crouches and looked at what had stirred the nearby dust. Arn shoved between two of them. On the ground scant feet away lay a spilled water bucket—and the man who still held it. Through his neck was an arrow bristling with Tolemak feathers.

Suddenly cold, Arn turned away. Beside him, an under-officer seized the bucket, handed it to another man, and ordered him up the ladder.

"Demon curse you nine times over, you bloody bastards!" another man shouted, shaking his fists at the wall.

A third man yanked an Adanak arrow from the battle tower's leg. "Here's one of your own back at you!" he shouted, kneeling to fit it to his bowstring.

Arn grabbed the arrow's shaft. "Flame it." Handing the arrow back to the startled man, he turned to the under-officer. "Tell Borth to collect Adanak arrows, flame them, and send them back. Whatever they fling at us, send back in flames."

The men looked at Arn. "Aye, m'lord," the under-officer said, "that'll teach 'em to strike at us with our own. You!" he shouted at the man nearest the ladder. "Tell the Master. The rest of you, fetch oil and rags."

While soldiers hurried off, Arn looked once more at the fortified wall. It would come down. If not today, the day after. It would come down, and then the killing would be over.

****

The constant bombardment with flame and stone had driven all but soldiers out of the streets nearest the outer wall. Within the second wall, refugees packed the squares and slept in the streets. Aerid watched them from the stoop of the Golden Horse whenever Mairim ordered her outside for a breath of air.

Before he went to the wall to defend his city, Foderor agreed to let his wife convert the inn to a hospital, and the trestle tables at which men had eaten only days before, ran with their blood as Aerid and others removed arrows, bathed burns, and set bones. The rooms upstairs held the bedridden wounded. Aerid and the others took meals in the kitchen, and she shared her room with three other women who slept in shifts.

When Leumas came after darkfall, she filled his bowl with his portion of stew or soup and added to it half of her own. Then she huddled next to him while he ate. If he noticed the smaller amount in her bowl, Aerid said she must have eaten more quickly than he. Weary as he was, he mumbled agreement, ate the rest, and laid his head on her shoulder.

Aerid never felt hungry. She ate only when Mairim insisted, and then only enough to satisfy the woman—not much older than herself—who watched over her. Indeed, if she felt anything at all during these endless days of heat and smoke, 'twas a leaden weariness, the kind that hung about her heart and limited her smiles to a fleeting curve of lips. Except for when she sat close beside Leumas.

After they had eaten, Leumas would hold her while she wiped the soot from his face. They would talk for a while—about anything but the present. Mairim would grant her an hour, perhaps more, to sit with him thus. Only when the feverish required bathing did she touch Aerid on the shoulder. Then Leumas would rise and, taking a blanket, go to the inner court where Avika, snoring softly, slept where the vegetables had lately grown.

Now Aerid leaned against the door frame of the Golden Horse and watched men bring another cartload of wounded through the crowded streets. Women fluttered around the cart, looking for, yet hoping not to find, a familiar face. But one face, much too familiar, detached itself from those about the cart and walked directly toward Aerid.

"Avika!" she said, pushing away from the door with a tremor in her stomach.

"'Tis naught but a scratch," he said, nodding sheepishly toward the hand he clutched to his shoulder, "but Master Gaelwynn insisted it be bound."

"Well that he should. Such a thing could fester." Aerid led him inside, moved his bloody fingers, and opened his tunic. The arrow had sliced back a section of flesh.

Avika winced as she cleaned it. When she turned away to rinse the cloth, he touched her arm. "Fear not, Leumas be safe."

She hesitated, then darted a glance at his face. "How may you be certain?"

"'Tis the east gate tower that crumbles. If the

mortraeders breach anywhere, 'twill be there. But, rest assured, we shall resist them."

****

"We've pounded that cursed gate for five days," Krenin muttered, peering through slits in the battle tower's barricade, "and still it won't fall."

"We'll bring up the ram." Prince Arn strode toward the ladder at the back of the second platform. "'Tis time to force the gate." He grabbed a rung and clambered down.

"The west one?" Naed hoisted his shield and prepared to follow. Climbing the ladder with the shield banging against his elbow had been awkward, and he did not relish descending in like manner, but the intermittent thud of arrows against the barricade convinced him the action was prudent. He set his shield, swung out, and found a rung with his foot.

"The south," said the Prince as he reached the ground and looked up. "Let's delude them a little long—"

Prince Arn was spinning—spinning and falling!

That it was an arrow that spun the Prince registered later, only after Naed kicked free of the rungs, dropped 10 feet, and flung himself and his shield over the Prince's prone form. And only after Krenin thundered down the ladder, grabbed their tunics, and, cursing, dragged them both behind the horses. It was only then, too, Naed noticed the second arrow, the one wedged in his shield, stuck fast in the dent he had tried to remove weeks ago.

But he noticed none of that until the Prince sat up, shook off their hands, and jerked the first arrow from his side.

"Are you not hurt?" Naed sputtered.

The Prince snapped the arrow in half and flung the pieces away. "Cursed thing only winded me." He sprang to his feet and brushed dust from his tunic. "Some idiot up there is boasting to the Sisters over his good fortune. I'll have to show myself and steal his glory."

Naed, kneeling, stared at him. "But the arrow..."

Krenin, whose face had not regained its color despite the grin now fixed on it, stood and tapped the Prince's chest. "Albon mail over leather and plate. 'Tis none stronger."

While the Prince mounted and turned his stallion,

Naed rose. Finding himself in the animal's path, he did not step aside but seized the reins. "'Tis you who are fortunate! You tempt the Sisters too much! Albon mail or no, you who are Prince—"

"Aye! And I am he because I've dared the Sisters to become so! Who are you to tell me to do otherwise?" Pulling the stallion into a rear, the Prince broke Naed's grip. "Your orders are to deliver the ram to the south gate. Do so, or I'll find a Second who will!" With a slash of the reins, he spurred his horse past Naed and galloped across the battlefield.

Naed's face burned. He had presumed too much, but the words were out of his mouth before he could think the better of them. Besides, they were true. Scowling, he watched the Prince draw rein beside a catapult and urge the men on. When they did not move quickly enough, he leaped down and loaded stones with them.

"Be about your duties, Second, or 'tis sure he'll know where to find a replacement. He's been daring the Sisters since before you were weaned, lowlander. Don't think a pup like you can change that."

Naed glared at the finger Krenin jabbed at his chest. When the Tolemak lowered it, Naed said, "'Twould be remiss of me not to try," and strode past him.

"Why? What concern have you for whoever buys the use of that metal whore you wear strapped to your side, 'Free Swordsman'?"

Knuckles white on the reins he had untied, Naed drew in breath and let it out before he said, "Do you doubt me so because 'twas I who shielded the Prince first today?"

"You insolent puff of swamp gas! I would have been there before you if you hadn't blocked the ladder!"

"Therein lies your answer. 'Twould have mattered naught to me who covered the Prince, only that he was safe." Mounting his horse, he rode out into the afternoon sunshine.

****

Arn heaved another rock into the catapult, then stepped clear and ordered it cut loose. The missiles hurtled into the east gate turret. A section of the wall near the structure broke off and tumbled onto the rubble

209

pile below. The men cheered.

Calculating the damage, Arn guessed another such strike or two and they could gain the parapet by climbing the rubble. "More stones!" he called. "Bring that tower down!"

With another shout, men scrambled to load the catapult.

Arn bent to pick up his stallion's reins. The action made his side ache. Frowning, he ran fingers over his tunic. His ribs were healed—or nearly so. *What the Demon—?*

The tear he located made him spit out an oath, but not at the arrow. What was done was done; he never concerned himself with what might have been. 'Twas Naed's reaction that irked. The D'nalian was only obeying his heart, but—*Demon be damned!*—if only Naed—and Krenin too—would understand... could somehow sense what burned in his gut and drove him at the wall like a man possessed.

His gaze fastened on the Lancer's sword hanging from his saddle. "Are you the Demon, Sevig of Vinvinnysee?" he murmured as he wrapped fingers around the scabbard. The ornate indentations bit into his palm, the pain sharp, satisfying, more real than the ache in his side.

"M'lord?"

Arn spun. Naed's man Banir sat his horse a respectful distance away. "I'm to tell you the ram is at the south gate and to ask for further orders, m'lord."

The D'nalian's dependability pleased Arn, but having Naed's finger so close to the uncertainties of his own pulse was unnerving. He wondered if he had made a mistake in bringing the young man into his confidence, but he shook off the thought. 'Twas better to have a man like Naed close. Much, much better.

Arn surveyed the fighting about the east gate. "Tell Naed to bring the other ram to the gully just after dark. We'll take the west gate at dawn while Krenin storms the rubble pile here."

****

Palms damp, Naed gripped his sword and shield. He could smell the men crowded about him, the mingled odors of paint, sweat, horse. Here and there in the sultry darkness he discerned the glint of an eye or tooth, but he heard nothing save the occasional suck of the gully bottom surrendering its grip on a boot. From the black void that was the wall, snatches of a sentry's song drifted to him on the heavy air.

The eastern rim of the sky showed a barely perceptible lightening. Naed searched for the Prince. He would be somewhere ahead, near the hand-picked men who shouldered the ram. It would be his order that would send them charging the gate, Naed's men shielding the ram-bearers while they splintered the Athellyn oak. Naed licked his lips.

A tremor rippled through the men gathered in the gully. Naed's fingers tightened on his sword. Beside him, Banir shifted his stance, and the spark of Banir's eyes met his gaze. Naed swallowed. The bray of a trumpet broke the stillness. The Prince's shouted, "On, men of Tolemak!" echoed it. With a roar, the men surged ahead.

Naed's sword seemed suddenly light, his shield weightless. His body vibrated with the thunder of his heartbeat. "Onward!" he shouted, springing to the rim of the gully.

****

'Twas not the shouting that made Aerid and the women in the Golden Horse Inn raise their heads and look at each other. Nor was it the bells that made the man whose fevered face she bathed push her hands away and try to rise. Nor was it the running feet in the darkness outside the open door that made Mairim twist her hands in her apron. No, 'twas another sound, a heavy, booming sound more felt than heard, a sound too deep for thunder—and too constant.

She looked at the innkeeper's wife. Mairim's whitened lips confirmed it was the gate she heard—the west gate—breaking.

"Sisters be with us." Mairim smoothed a hand over her abdomen as if soothing her unborn child.

The cobbler's daughter let out a wail.

Mairim's stern, "Our men require our strength, not our womanly weaknesses," cut it short. The cobbler's wife, her own face pale, put her arms around her daughter, but

211

neither spoke. "Go and prepare more bandages," Mairim said to the weaver's wife and daughters. "The others, take some food. Shortly, we shall be having no thought to spare for aught else but our men." Picking up a bowl, she ladled stew into it.

Aerid accepted the bowl Mairim handed her but only pretended to eat. Her stomach would not accept the food, so tight and hard had it become. She wrapped fingers around her birthstone. If ever the Sisters heeded a plea, she willed they did so now.

****

Naed crouched behind a pile of stone. His eyes stung with powdered mortar. Dust filled his nose and burned his throat. He longed for a draught of water, but he had drunk what little his flask contained before noon. He scowled. If the Adanaks had not toppled this tower across his men's path, he would not now have need of another drink.

Banir crept to his side. Arrows chinked against the stone above their heads. "Master Illien's gained the parapet and the Prince be halfway to the second wall."

Naed's scowl deepened. "And we have secured but a meager square." He surveyed the street through rapidly thinning dust. "Tell Grodar to take thirty archers to the left. When I signal, they will loose arrows. We shall charge under their protection."

Banir nodded and started to move off.

"Wait." Naed grabbed his sleeve. "Have you word of Krenin?"

"He's taken the gate turret. The east gate be breached."

Naed looked over the broken tower at the Adanaks gathering to defend the street. Their faces were grimy, their limbs wet with sweat. Blood streaked their tunics and stained their swords. They were hollow-eyed men and they were tired. "Then we shall meet Krenin," he said, shoving the Tolemak's jeering image out of his mind, "more than halfway."

****

The ram plunged through a pile of burning furniture. Flaming chairs careened into stone buildings and shattered. Sparks shot to the eaves of tiled roofs. The shower of light flashed across Arn's face and sputtered out.

Arn dashed sweat from his eyes. His tunic clung to his thighs, and his throat burned with each breath. His sword arm had gone numb at dusk, and he ceased to feel his fingers soon after. Only the blade striking home still sang to him, and he moved on, driven by the scent permeating the smoke-thickened darkness. He had smelled it at Bede when blood soaked the snow and Orek turned on the high ground to charge, and at Val-Feyridge, when the stones ran red and Yinnad faced him on the turret stairs. Now his men had broken the barricade the retreating Adanaks had thrown down, and the second, inner wall of Vinvinnysee lay ahead.

Arn's lips pulled back from his teeth and he laughed. With a slash of his sword, he cleared a smoldering table leg from his path. "Men of Val-Feyridge!" he cried hoarsely to the soldiers at his heel. "On to victory!"

Like a flood loosed from a broken dam, hundreds of men coursed through the narrow street, their cries reverberating from the stones.

Arn let their dark fury rush around him till the tramp of their feet and the rattle of their weapons resonated in every fiber of his body, until his blood pulsed with their power, until the savage energy of their charge surged into him and, with a feral cry, he flung himself to their fore and raced headlong up the narrow, twisting street.

****

By midnight the Golden Horse overflowed with wounded. They filled the beds, the common room floor, and even the staircase steps. Women with whimpering children huddled in the garden while soldiers rushed through the street outside the open door.

Aerid paused while binding a man's leg and looked. In the dark, they were all shadows—floating, flitting, vanishing like the smoke that drifted in and competed with the stench of blood.

Her braid clung to her neck in the humidity. She pulled it away, then finished fastening the man's bandage. 'Twas well she had other things to think of than the too-close ring of metal on metal and the memory of

213

Leumas standing beside the old wall, the breeze lifting his sand-brown hair, his eyes aflame for his city.

Aerid swallowed. The man she tended had two heads, and she shook herself to rid him of the extra appendage. 'Twas only weariness, she told herself, and rose to fetch more bandages.

A man leaned against the outer door frame. He stood strangely bent to one side as if his elbow pained him. For a moment, Aerid thought her eyes conspired to make him appear so unnaturally tilted, but then he moved, and she saw the stain under his indrawn elbow. She started toward him, arm outstretched, before he raised his head.

Leumas pushed away from the door frame and walked slowly toward her, maintaining his peculiarly bent position. When he halted, he put out his hand and clutched the edge of the table. "Avika," he said, "is not coming." Then he bent as if to kneel, but he went on bending until he sprawled on the floor.

A shriek escaped Aerid. Flinging herself down, she cradled his head in her lap, begging, pleading, praying for the pulse she found nowhere. His eyes were open, but the green she stared into had lost its luster. From the corner of the crooked mouth ran a trickle of blood.

Aerid sat like one turned to stone. Her heart had been wrenched from her breast and her body had not fully realized its loss. Leumas was dead and with him had died all her hopes. She stared at nothing and heard nothing and felt nothing but the cold weight in her lap that no longer signified a man.

****

How long she sat thus, she did not know. She only knew, when she came to herself, the common room was in pandemonium and Mairim clutched at her shoulders pleading, "Aerid, come! Hurry! We must flee!"

Like a dreamer disturbed, Aerid looked at the woman hovering over her, then at the inn's door, beyond which she could see the rush of retreating soldiers.

Mairim shook her again. "Hurry!" Gripping Aerid, Mairim dragged her to her feet.

Aerid stumbled against the woman who locked arms with her. Leumas lay on the floor, unprotected, but 'twas naught she could do for him now. She let Mairim guide

214

her to the door.

Outside, the street ran with a torrent of panicked women and children. Soldiers fought the tide, trying to go to the aid of their comrades. Horses reared, donkeys brayed, an ox bolted from its master and plunged across the square. The dragging cart careened into the crowd. Terror-stricken refugees surged away from the maddened animal. They rushed the steps of the Golden Horse and swept Mairim and Aerid against the door. Mairim stumbled, and her hold broke. Aerid reached for her, but the hysterical crowd surrounded the woman and sped on.

"Aerid!" Mairim cried, her hand still outstretched.

Aerid started after her, then stopped. What lay on the hill for her but further terror and certain captivity?

She turned her gaze slowly to the north.

Beyond the smoke, the wall, the forest's edge lay the mountains. Her home.

Seizing a cloak from the wall, she waited until the press of refugees had passed, then she glided into the street and walked away from them.

Helen C. Johannes

Chapter Eighteen

Aerid walked steadily, keeping to the shadows. Men fled past her, white faces in the darkness. Some shouted, "Get back, woman!" but she did not heed them. Nor did she heed the heavy sound throbbing through the narrow street. Over and over it boomed, the beat steady, inexorable among random clangs, shouts, groans, and the snap and hiss of flames.

She turned into a street glowing red. The gate at the end heaved, and sparks shot into the air. Thin, black specters retreated from the shower. The gate heaved again, oak squealing against rusted iron bands. They seemed to hold, but then with a shriek the wood splintered.

A swirling mass of other-worldly figures poured through the breach, flames at their backs, sword-fire in their hands. The defenders broke and ran, sweeping Aerid up in their midst. They rushed the narrow mouth of the street. Aerid, near the outer edge, found herself sheared off and catapulted aside. Her back slammed into the wall of a house. Speckled with purple, the eerie red sky danced before her eyes and she slumped, dazed.

Moments later, her eyes focused on flames leaping and flickering behind the shattered gate. 'Twas something strange about them—there were no men outlined by their glow. Bracing a hand on the wall, she rose slowly. The gate square was empty. Only crumpled shadows and discarded weapons littered the cobblestones. Gathering her skirts, Aerid ran toward the broken gate and darted through it.

****

Arn's sword clove upward, under the Adanak's sword arm and into the unprotected armpit. The man crumpled around the blade. Arn stepped back to pull his blade free, but it would not give. Face wet with sweat, he jerked again. The body lurched towards him. Arn braced his foot

216

on the fallen man's shoulder.

"Die, *mortraeder!*" shrilled in Arn's ears. He whirled, colliding shields with a man flying at him from the palace wall. Staggered, Arn dropped to one knee while the Adanak rolled clear. Seeing the man spring up, weapon in hand, Arn abandoned his own sword and groped for the dead man's weapon. He had it half raised when Naed materialized out of the darkness and slew the man. Vexed, Arn drew up short. He would have had his attacker.

Naed looked up from the fallen Adanak. His lips were peeled back from his teeth, and his eyes, sunk in the hollows of a blackened face, gleamed red. "Are you unharmed, m'lord?"

Arn's irritation vanished. The youth was as weary as he, if not more so. "Well done." He bent and jerked his sword free of the bone in which it had wedged. "Where's Krenin?"

"Two streets yonder. We have the Adanak between us, but nigh on a dozen city Masters have taken to horse and broken past us. 'Tis said some are disguised in women's garb."

"Is Guard Master Gaelwynn among them?"

"Mayhap, m'lord. The message named no names."

"Send a man to fetch my horse." Arn cleaned his blade on a dead man's tunic. "Summon Gorm and his horsemen to the west gate. I'll meet them there."

"You, m'lord? What of the palace?"

Arn read Naed's confusion in the drawn together sooty brows and laughed, delighted as much with the legibility of the youth's face as with his honest D'nalian spirit. He squeezed Naed's shoulder. "You take the palace. Consider it my gift."

"In gratitude for this?" He gestured to the dead man. "'Tis no more than my duty."

"For your loyalty, my friend, which has gone far beyond your duty."

Color rose under the grime coating the young man's face. "M'lord, you honor me."

"Prove yourself worthy, then. Bring me alive every Master of Vinvinnysee left in the city while I make sure not a single one escapes."

"At once, m'lord!"

Arn watched him hurdle bodies and, sword held high, disappear into the mêlée beleaguering the palace entrance. A moment later, the mass organized and rushed the gate. At the cacophony of battle cries, Arn's blood roared in his ears and he stirred two steps forward, but he checked himself. Let the D'nalian have his moment of glory. 'Twould bind the young man more securely to his side. Signaling two men to follow him, he sprinted toward the city's gate, intent on closing off the last avenue of escape before he lost the most important man in the city.

****

Stealthily, Aerid made her way toward the outer wall. Once, she ducked behind a caved-in door as enemy soldiers ran up the street. Horsemen clattered down now and again, but they were so intent on picking a path through the rubble she slipped along the shadows unnoticed.

Finally, she found herself across the square from the wall. Torches lit the open gate as strings of horses laden with bodies were led through it. Broken beams, once undergirding the parapet, and crumbled stone littered the street. With a little luck, she could dart from one to the other and slip into the blackness under what remained of the parapet. From there, she could join the line of horses, keeping the animals between herself and the guards clustered on the left side of the gate. Gulping in a breath, Aerid stooped and scurried across the square.

When she stopped to breathe again, her back was pressed to the cold stone wall, and the shadows that had looked so black from the other side of the street scarcely seemed to conceal her. The Tolemaks whose glances swept the parapet and its feet, however, raised no alarm. Her knees quivering, Aerid sagged against the wall. The torches had taken on two flames, and she needed a moment to reduce their number.

A horseman approached, leading a string of seven laden horses. As they passed through the gate, Aerid slipped from the shadows and laid her hand on the mane of the sixth animal. The horse snorted, but the tight lead kept it from turning its head. She murmured softly and patted its neck. Her feet barely touched the cobblestones

218

as she tiptoed alongside, matching her steps to its strides, her movements tight, jerky.

In scant seconds, the glow of torches diminished and the dark expanse of the plain stretched before her. The rider turned his charges toward the south. Aerid let them slide past, then she bent low and dashed toward the north, toward the gully and its black promise of shelter.

A horse nickered.

"What's that?" demanded a voice.

"Where?" said another.

An arrow ripped through her cloak, pitching her into the gully she sought. A second later, she thrashed out of its muddy stream, threw herself face down on the grassy bank and listened.

"Must've been an animal," she heard a voice, now distant and retreating, say. Another voice, equally far off, murmured assent.

Aerid let air fill her lungs again. She rolled over and eased her legs out of the water. When her heartbeat had slowed, she sat up and wrung out her skirts and cloak. A breeze dipped into the hollow and slithered up her legs, making her shiver.

Struggling to her feet, she cast a glance at the eastern sky. It had been past midnight when Leumas died... A pain knifed through Aerid's breast. She swayed but did not let herself fall. For Leumas' sake she must continue. She lifted one foot and moved it forward. The grass, slick with dew, made her footing precarious. For Leumas' sake she must reach the forest before dawn spoiled her escape.

The chill soon robbed her feet of feeling, and she fell repeatedly to her knees. Each time she would rest a breath or two, then rise and push on. So intent was she on her progress, she did not hear the hoof beats of a dozen or so horses until they topped the bank of the gully a hundred feet ahead. Throwing herself down, she huddled against the grass while the horsemen spurred their mounts through the water and up the other side.

No sooner had she raised her head when another group burst over the edge behind her. Etched against the star-dotted sky, the riders' cloaks billowing like gigantic wings, they hurtled at her like panting, pounding demons of the night.

Then the flight was past, gone as quickly as it had come, and Aerid was alone. Wet and shaking, stomach heaving and gall bittering her lips, but alone. And alive.

Minutes, mayhap hours, later Aerid noticed a pine sapling snag her cloak. She wrenched the fabric free and staggered into another one, snapping it under her heel. She swayed to a halt. In the dimness, she could make out scattered, spindly shapes of more young trees, and behind them, taller ones taking shape amid the darkness rimming the gully. With a little sob, she clambered up the bank to the dry forest floor and collapsed.

When she regained sufficient strength to sit up, she noticed the sky overhead remained dark, but gray edged the distant horizon. 'Twas time to move on, to penetrate the forest, to find a thicket where she could hide and rest. Clutching a nearby tree trunk, she pulled herself to her feet. 'Twould not be difficult to go on from there. It only required handing herself from one tree to another, and covering the few steps in between.

A break in the trees brought her to a halt, teetering on the edge. In the clearing, a horse huffed and stamped. Two horses. Wraithlike, a shadow materialized in the gloom and glided toward the trees where she cowered. Something glinted from its side.

Aerid tried to swallow, but her throat refused to work. Staggering against a tree, she gripped the ridges of bark so hard a chunk broke off in her hand. It made only a little pop. But in the predawn stillness, it echoed like the crack of thunder.

The shadow paused. The metallic gleam rose.

She had been seen. *No! Not now!* Whirling, she ran headlong into the trees.

"Stop!"

Blood roaring in her ears, Aerid scrambled over deadfall. It grabbed at her cloak. She yanked it free, fell forward, clambered up, and ran on. Seconds later, the man crashed through the broken branches. His sputtered curse, too close, raised the hair on her neck.

Covering her face, she bolted through bushes. They snatched at her skirts, clawed at her cloak, and tore the hood from her head, but she plunged on. The rush of his breath impelled her, the sound gaining on and surrounding and dominating the ragged sound of her own. Aerid's throat burned. Blood pounded behind her eyes. The bushes blurred, then parted. She broke out of them, stumbled, and fell to her knees. With a little whimper, she tried to rise.

Something slammed into her back, and she sprawled face down, pine needles stabbing her chin, cheek. He straddled her, knees pinning her by her cloak, his arm—his weapon?—so heavy across her shoulders she could barely breathe. A hand probed her arms, her ribs, her hips. A rough hand. A violent hand. An enemy's hand. Aerid quivered. She sank her teeth into her lip and bit back a sob.

She closed her eyes, but cruel fingers digging into her shoulder forced them open again. With a quick shift of his weight, he jerked her onto her back. She saw the glint of his sword and flung her arm up against it. "Please! I pray you—!"

"Don't play the woman with me! I know who you are!" Breath beating at her face, he wrestled her arm away from it. "Now, tell me where the others—"

Aerid stared at the face looming over hers. Her lungs drew in no air.

The Prince's face had gone stark white. The scar stood out, a jagged ridge along his cheek. The sword in his outstretched arm shook.

His grip punished Aerid's wrist. His shock hammered at her heart. The sword, too close, taunted her, mocked her, told her she was a fool for ever thinking, for ever hoping, for ever imagining he could look upon her as anything other than an enemy. She thrashed in his grip. "You have your sword! Why do you not kill me as once you did say you would!"

His face contorted. "You little fool!" Flinging her arm away, the Prince surged to his feet. He hacked a wrist-thick branch from the tree to her right. "Is *that* what you want me to do to you? Or is it *this!* Or *this!* Or even *this!*"

Aerid stared while his sword flashed, and branches, twigs, leaves swirled around him like debris in a whirlwind. Then he slammed the blade into its scabbard and, turning his back to her, stood with fists clenched at his sides. "Go! Leave! Get out of my sight!"

The words slapped at Aerid's cheeks. They stabbed at her heart. She sat up, realized she had been cowering, and flushed. Shame made the blood beat at her temples. She ripped a handful of moss from the forest floor, barely noticing the earthy scent over the pungent odor of split pine reeking in her nostrils. Wrapping the shreds of her damp cloak about her body like so much dignity, she struggled to her feet.

The effort proved too much. The trees tottered and her legs turned to water. She managed a weak "Oh!" before the world went dark.

The first sensation to return told Aerid the scratchiness abrading her cheek was cloth over something solid but...warm. Fingers, hot to her skin, tugged at whatever constricted her throat. It gave, and a leaden weight fell from her neck and shoulders. She sucked in a deep breath. The fingertips stilled, pooling heat at her collarbone before sliding beneath her hair. They and the palm connected to them lifted her head, moving her shoulders from something damp and cold to something sinewy, warm, and alive. She turned toward it, burying her nose in fabric, inhaling the scent suffusing the weave despite the pervasive odor of pine sap and the smells of horse, leather—even blood. 'Twas a man-smell that had burned itself deep into the roots of her memory, the raw, elemental scent of the one man in whose arms she could feel absolutely safe. Drawing another breath, she opened her eyes.

At her sigh, the Prince's eyes, sparks in the shadow of his face, fastened on hers. Their expression, like the touch of his fingers, was surprisingly gentle. Even a little uncertain, Aerid thought, as her bemused mind struggled to collect itself. Dark branches crisscrossed above his head, a few still-bright stars sparkling between them. His fingers cradled her nape, their touch light yet, somehow, charged. Her body stirred, remembering a touch, a moment, a need so overwhelming her hand rose of its own accord and gently touched the whitened ridge on his cheek.

His arm under her shoulders tightened. A look as of pain flashed through his eyes, but he only said, "You must be cold."

Aerid sighed and nestled into his warmth. "No. No longer."

She felt his response as a rumble under her cheek. With a slight shift of his weight, he removed the remainder of her cloak. "How did you become so wet?"

"I fell." There was more, but fog had stretched its mist over thoughts, phrases, even words before her lips could form them. Still, there was something she had to do, some...place she had to go. She struggled to sit up. "North...must...go nor—"

"No." He cradled her in his arms and rose. "Not this time."

The timbre of his voice stirred her eyelids. In the graying light she saw the outline of his jaw, the set of his mouth, and a strange, smoldering fire in his eyes.

"This time," he said, his voice rough, "you're coming with me."

She ought to argue, but his words turned her will to water and drained it away. A warm languor permeated Aerid's limbs, and she let her body relax into the shelter of his.

****

Arn stared at the pale face nestled against his chest and the small fist twisted into his tunic. His arms trembled, but not with their burden. He wanted to crush her in his embrace, to bind her to him with promises, threats, chains—whatever required to keep close this woman he had never expected to see again, this woman who haunted his dreams and bewitched his soul. This woman who touched his face—and smiled.

His heart beat heavily against her shoulder. What did it matter that she were Adanak and he Tolemak? What did it matter that the man of her kind who had brought him to this wood lay on his back in yonder clearing, his life blood pooling at the foot of a tree? Or that others might now be escaping? What did any of that matter when she was in his arms now and nothing and no one could take her from him.

"Sisters be damned!" he spat out. "I make my own fate!" Wrapping her in his own cloak, he bore her to his horse and mounted.

CHAPTER NINETEEN

Arn, Prince of Val-Feyridge, leader of the Tolemak, conqueror of Druemarwin, Heir to Tolem, halted his stallion before the city gate that had been closed to him the day before. Against the pink and gold eastern sky, a new banner—his—fluttered over the palace at the city's height. He smiled. Adjusting the cloak wrapped around the woman in his arms, he touched his heels to his horse. The animal picked its way through the shattered gate.

As Darkstar climbed toward the palace, shafts of first sunlight pierced the haze hanging about the city. Golden light shot between buildings, burnishing broken stone, slanting across soot-streaked faces, and falling on a Vinvinnysee banner crumpled near the palace entrance. In the courtyard, men moved as shadows, some guarding groups of huddled figures, others collecting weapons, and still others clearing away bodies.

Arn noted the activity with satisfaction. He had been wise indeed in his choice of Naed. If anything, the Second's position suited the D'nalian penchant for order and propriety. No doubt the eager young man was somewhere in the city, seeing to what needed to be done. Smiling, he urged his horse toward four figures standing on the palace steps.

"Your lodgings, my prince," Krenin said with an expansive gesture. He stood like a hunter with his foot on the top step, the conquered palace under his boot. "Master Sima here—" He indicated a man who stood with downcast head between two guards. "—hopes you'll find his—shall I say—*recent* home suitable."

Arn surveyed the elegant stone facade. "Well done." He shifted in his saddle. "Here, help me a moment."

Krenin's gaze jerked to the cloak-draped form Arn lowered into his arms. "What's this?"

Dismounting, Arn tossed his reins to one of the guards. "Now, give her back." Aerid stirred as Arn once

224

more settled her in his arms. Her fingers opened, then curled again into his tunic as she snuggled into his shoulder. He would have spoken to Krenin, but her movements so constricted his throat, no words could pass. Forcing a swallow, he strode up the palace steps.

Krenin caught up to him at the gilded door. "Where are you going?"

"To find a room."

"A-a room? But the city—"

"You and Naed have it well in hand. I should think you can manage it for a few hours more." Shouldering past Krenin, he entered a narrow hall and kicked the door shut.

For a moment, Arn leaned against the door. He hoped Krenin would not be fool enough to follow him. He would have to explain then. Gazing at her hand lying curved against his chest, he doubted he could find words to explain why the city whose capture had obsessed him for months should matter so little to him now the deed was done. He pushed slowly away from the door. 'Twas not that it did not matter, but that something—no— someone else took precedence. With a deep breath, he turned toward the interior.

****

The fire he had kindled snapped and popped while Arn drew the draperies on three sides of the bed he had pushed into the circle of its warmth. Only after the last curtain had been adjusted to his satisfaction, did he walk to the open side of the bed and let his eyes look their fill at the woman who slept in the center of it.

Her washed face seemed nearly as pale as the white garment the serving woman had dressed her in, but a little color had returned to her lips. The flickering light played on the river of her hair where it rippled over the pillow. Arn longed to thread his fingers through the dark, curling length, to feel it cascade over his skin. It would be as soft as thistledown drifting on the wind and fragrant with the scent of her, the scent that—

He squeezed his eyes shut, turned away, and rubbed his hands over his face. Two days' growth of beard rasped against his palms. He looked at his hands, at the fire, then at the woman. He would wash and change. Then he would wait, here at her side, while she slept.

****

The ornate room in which the deposed Masters of Vinvinnysee conducted city business stifled Naed. Tapestries encroached on elaborately carved, high-backed chairs standing at attention beneath them. Near his head, ancient shields hung, their metal rusted, their paint flaking. They leaned away from the wall as if looking down on him, a non-pedigreed interloper. Moving out from their shadows, he asked, "Is the perimeter of the city secure?"

"Aye," Gorm said, scratching under the neck of his tunic. "And we've accounted for them that tried to flee. Four of their escort dead and all nine Masters taken. Of course—" He grinned. "—the two that be mine will be of no use till they come round."

Blocking Naed's path to the double windows opposite was a massive desk constructed of Athellyn oak. It sat upon a raised platform and dominated half of the room. He walked around it, deliberately trailing his fingers across the polished surface. "'Tis good."

A sallow reflection caught his eye. Staring back from the golden surface was a somber face with lines about the mouth and shadows under the eyes—new lines and dark shadows. Naed pushed away from the desk. 'Twas only lack of sleep that made his face look so aged—lack of sleep and the soot he had not yet scrubbed from his skin.

Surveying the room once more, Naed could not picture Prince Arn within its walls. A man of the Prince's height needed no platform for his desk. Indeed, the man rarely sat but upon a horse. A table would more nearly suit his needs—a table in the center of a large chamber with many windows to let in light and air, sharp with pine smoke and—

"What would you have me set my men about now?"

Naed jolted out of his reverie. 'Twas only weariness that made him recall the wood of Adanak and standing there side-by-side with the Prince. Walking to a window, he opened the shutter and let mid-morning sunlight pour into the room. "The Prince returned with you, aye?"

Gorm's spurs chinked on the stone threshold. "Afore us. At dawn, so I'm told."

Shading his eyes, Naed scanned the inner court one floor below. Wounded prisoners were quartered there, and women moved among them tending to their injuries. His gaze skipped across their heads, searching the perimeter. Where could the Prince be that no one had seen him in hours? The city was secure. Decisions had to be made about the disposition of captured goods, rest for the soldiers, food for the prisoners and the city folk—about such a multitude of things Naed leaned on the window frame and closed his eyes against them.

After a moment, he roused himself. "Take half of your men and relieve Illien's company on the wall. Quarter the others near the outer wall. Remind all officers of the Prince's orders: No harm shall come to the city folk, nor shall there be any spoils-taking."

"As you wish." With a nod, the big man left.

Sighing, Naed grasped the shutter latch. 'Twould not do to linger in the sun while the Prince worked elsewhere in the city. The man had entrusted him with the conquest of the palace. He must prove himself worthy of that trust.

A movement in the crowd set his heart pounding against his ribs. His gaze arrowed to a womanly form whose dark, curling hair spilled over slender shoulders. The woman turned—and he saw a stranger's face. Flushing, Naed closed the shutter and latched it. He was a fool to think Aerid would be here. She was safely in the north by now. Soon, though, when the city was properly disposed of, he would find her and—

"Oh, 'tis only you."

Krenin had already strode to the window and flung open a shutter before Naed collected himself enough to ask, "Have you seen the Prince?"

"Why?" Krenin leaned over the sill and gestured to the prisoners below. "Can't you handle that, Second?"

"My skill is sufficient, but I have not spoken to the Prince since before dawn and 'tis much about the governance of this city that must be decided."

Krenin snapped the shutter tight. "We're to manage it."

The words did not at first register in Naed's mind. They were mere sounds uttered in a rough, Tolemak accent by a man who would not look at him, but who

227

turned and strode toward the door. "We? But why are we—"

"Yes, we! You and I! Or aren't those words simple enough for your lowland brain?"

"More than adequate," Naed retorted, but his mind focused on how, after an instant of angry contact, Krenin's gaze dodged about the room. "Where's the Prince? What has—"

"Nothing's happened to him! He's well! He's fine!" Hurling himself back across the room, Krenin threw open the window again and stared out. "He's just a fool."

Something was clearly wrong, and the thought chilled Naed. "If you will not direct me to the Prince, I shall find him myself."

"Take your chances, then. He's with a woman."

"A-a woman? You cannot mean a-a whore!"

"Why not? Or are you people too close to your gold to pay a woman to spread her legs?"

The news shocked Naed, considering their orders, yet the Prince was Tolemak. Why would he not claim a woman as his prize of victory? Why should he not force her to open for him as he had forced her city—? Naed shoved the image out of his mind. 'Twas a Tolemak thought, and he would not be contaminated by it. "Why should it matter if—"

"It matters because—!" Krenin slammed the shutter. "Is there nothing but fog between your ears? He's never put a woman first. Not even his bride-to-be."

"Then...you do not approve of his behavior?"

They locked eyes until Krenin blanched. "You think you're so bloody smart, a D'nalian in a Tolemak Second's clothing! But 'tis sure you don't know a bloody thing! How could you, with that watered milk you call blood! Demon's Blood, I ought to gut myself for even thinking—!" Flinging up his hands, Krenin stormed out of the chamber.

Naed unclenched each fist and ran his hands over his face. Why should the Prince's taking a woman matter? Was that not the Tolemak way in victory? Why should it matter the Prince had shown himself truly Tolemak? *Because*, his conscience whispered, *you are forgetting who and what he is. And who and what you ought to be.*

****

Aerid surfaced slowly, through layers of golden haze. Warmth surrounded her, coaxing her to stay wrapped in its cocoon. She succumbed for a while, slipping in and out of a dream of cascading gold, milk-white stone, and banked embers until her eyes fixed and she knew the embers were real, and the warmth touching her face emanated from them. Her gaze traveled upward. Milk-white stone framed a fireplace containing the embers. Overhead, the cascade of gold formed curtains drawn around three sides of the bed in which she lay.

The last vestiges of sleep fled her eyes. She struggled to raise her arms, fighting coverlets that slid from her with strange, whispered ease. Her arms were encased in white, a soft white that clung yet draped. She stared at it, not recognizing the fabric but knowing its value must be measured in gold not copper. Swallowing, she pushed up onto her elbows—and froze.

The Prince sat on a low stool beside the bed, his arms folded upon the coverlet barely a foot from her thigh, his face buried in the tunic sleeves. One hand, long-fingered and calloused, lay almost touching her hip.

After the first flutter of her heart, Aerid realized he was asleep. With a shallow breath, she eased back against the head of the bed and rested there. She took in the averted head with the fringe of black hair hanging over the sleeve. 'Twas the position of a weary man, and her heart lurched. He had rescued her, brought her here to this warmth, this comfort. Seeing him asleep and vulnerable, she realized how the effort had cost him.

Without conscious thought, her hand stretched toward his sleeve, intent on the thick, wild hair that overlay it. Her fingers touched, withdrew, and, when he did not stir, touched again. The dense hairs yielded to her fingertips, gliding softly between them. When he still did not stir, Aerid threaded her fingers deeper, savoring the tickle on the webs of her hand.

On a third pass, her fingertips found fabric. Her heart thumped. Underneath the cloth, his blood coursed, warm and vital. She thought to pull away, but a strange heat rushed into her fingers at the contact. It spread up her arm, across her face, and through her chest until she could not breathe but stared at the Prince, certain he no longer slept.

The Prince raised his head. His mouth curved at one corner, and his eyes were pure gray with no trace of sleep in them.

A flush swept Aerid's cheeks. She drew back her hand, but his outstretched fingers closed around her wrist. Her pulse hammered against his grip. His thumb stroked over the beat with a deliberation that made her giddy. When she thought she could no longer bear to look at him, his gaze released hers and focused on her captive hand. Turning it palm up, he opened her fingers with his thumb and pressed his lips to the soft, inner flesh.

The canopy whirled above Aerid's head. Weakened by the whisper of his breath across her palm, her arms shook, and she sank into the pillows. His lips traveled to the inside of her wrist, their touch light, feathery. She closed her eyes and lay still, surrendering to the sensations rippling through her body.

The bed shifted. When her lids lifted, the Prince was leaning across her. In the glimmer cast by the embers and the dying sun, his eyes glowed with a soft twilight that drew her into them. His body heat surrounded her, warming her more thoroughly than any fire. When his hand released her wrist and, rising to her forehead, gently brushed away a strand of hair, she sighed.

The fingers lingered, then drifted downward until the tips touched the pulse throbbing under her ear. Aerid held her breath as his eyes darkened to black pools. Delicately as a feather, his thumb traced the shape of her lips. He smelled of shaving soap and clean clothing, but the faint saltiness imparted by his touch filled her memory with moonlight and molten blood and the taste—*oh, the taste!*—of his mouth on hers.

Aerid's lips parted, but no breath passed them. Her toes curled and uncurled under the bedding. Of its own volition, her hand reached up and found the arm he had braced beside her shoulder. At the stroke of her fingers across his wrist, the Prince shuddered, a long, quivering shudder that left his blood pounding under her hand.

The raw power of it, and of the muscles and tendons stretched taut under her fingers, ignited a response deep in Aerid's abdomen, a pulsating, tingling response that overwhelmed her with its force. She sucked in air, wanting, wishing he would bend and claim her mouth, confirming her memory of that night under a star-drenched sky weeks—and worlds—ago.

His thumb trembled on her lips. She willed it to drift to her chin, to begin its downward journey to the base of her throat and beyond. *Sisters!* She had never felt this wanton, never desired the touch of a man's hands on her body as much as she desired—needed—this man's touch. Eyes closed, she heard the ragged intake of his breath. His thumb traced an unsteady line across the fine bones of her shoulder. It lingered at the hollow of her throat, circled her birthstone, then—

The bed shook. A swirl of air chilled her skin. Aerid opened her eyes.

The Prince stood several feet away, his face harsh in the dimming light. His hands gripped the white stone mantle and he stared into the embers beneath it. Her gaze ran over the rigid line of his shoulders, wondering why—

He turned, and his face was blank. Only a muscle twitched under the scar. "You must be hungry. I'll see you're sent something to eat." He strode to the door.

Aerid rose to her elbows. His voice told her he was leaving. The set of his shoulders confirmed it. Bewildered, she twisted fingers into the coverlet. "Y-you'll be returning, aye?"

The Prince did not look at her but stood with his hand on the latch. "Later," he said, his voice rough. "Eat now and rest." Opening the door, he stepped out and was gone.

The room was suddenly silent, large and impersonal. Even the golden glow had faded with the sun's last rays. Aerid sank back onto the pillows, light-headed and weak. Her healer's art told her she needed food—aye—and rest, but... Why had he waited at the side of her bed for her to awaken? Why had he touched her so...? Let her offer herself so...and then...left?

Closing her eyes, Aerid could still taste his skin on the inner flesh of her lip. Her wrist tingled with the stroke of his thumb. Her palm bore the sensation of his kiss. She sighed and cupped her fingers around it.

Vaguely, she remembered another kiss planted there. Or was it a dream, she thought, as the velvet edges of sleep closed around her. It had been so long ago when she lived. So long ago when she struggled. So long ago when she loved Leumas...

Was it only yesterday he had died? A flush seared the length of her body. The man she had thought to wed was dead but a day, and here she had offered herself like a common harlot to the one who had brought about his death as surely as if he had himself wielded the sword. Tears squeezed out from under her lashes. They converged on her cheekbones and wet a path down her face. Her mouth broke and she sobbed, great heaving sobs without sound.

****

Arn stood in the darkening passage and leaned against the wall. He breathed slowly, letting his flesh absorb the stone's coolness, his blood learn from its steady solidity. He had put two halls between himself and the softly glowing room. He had set a man to guard the door and another to fetch hot food and a serving woman.

Yet he could not erase from his mind the image of full, parted lips, of vulnerable, fragrant throat, of rounded breasts draped in clinging white. Their peaks had stood out, dark under the flimsy material. His hands ached to cover them, stroke over them, strip them bare so that—

A bead of moisture trickled down beside his ear. Had he stayed a moment longer, Arn knew he would have taken her. It would not have mattered she was weak and trusted him for protection. It would have made no difference if she cried out and begged him to stop. He would have been driven, consumed by the desire to surround himself with her, to lose himself in her, to possess her. He trembled, startled by the power of his need. There was no hurry. She was safely within his grasp. He had time to see to the city, to his army, and—later—to her.

In his absence, she would sleep, eat, gain strength. When he had tended to all that required his attention, she would still be there, waiting. Arn pushed away from the wall with a satisfied smile. Vinvinnysee was already his. Soon, the slender young woman whose face and touch had haunted him for weeks would belong to him, too.

CHAPTER TWENTY

In his new quarters, Naed studied the wine in his cup. 'Twas good wine, but he was no longer thirsty. Nor was he hungry after consuming so much roasted rabbit his stomach strained against his belt. Pushing away from the table, he leaned back in his chair.

Banir slept in an armchair, chin so deep in his chest only the tip of his nose showed under the shag of black hair. Now and then his breath came in snorts and he twitched.

Opposite, Morys lay with gangly arms surrounding his cup, his cheek pressed to the tabletop. His tunic sleeve fluttered with his snores.

Naed yawned. 'Twas near dark, but he still had the Masters' account books to locate and the treasury of Vinvinnysee to count and record. He tugged at a chain beneath his tunic collar. A large key slithered from under his chest armor and dangled from finely-wrought links. He had set a strong guard around the treasury, but he would not rest comfortably until he had tabulated its contents. Rising, he returned the key to its nest between his undertunic and breastplate.

"You've done well, my friend."

Naed's gaze shot to the door. The Prince filled it, then stepped inside. He looked refreshed, Naed thought, then berated himself for envy. "Thank you, m'lord." He leaned over partly to shake Banir awake, partly to cover the flush heating his cheeks.

"Let them sleep." The Prince walked to the table and surveyed the remains of their dinner. Selecting a haunch of rabbit, he chewed on it as he continued toward the window.

"M'lord, I will send for more—"

"Later." He opened the window and stood looking out.

Naed rocked on his heels, uncertain whether to speak or wait. This was a man he had shared much with over

234

the last weeks, a man who had yielded him more and more responsibility, a man who trusted him. There should be no awkward silences between them. Naed slanted a glance at the Prince. He still looked out the window, but his face betrayed no discomfort. If aught, he appeared satisfied.

"The city is secure, I trust?"

"Aye, m'lord."

"Streets clear of rubble?"

"Two main ones. Another three passable."

"Finish the task tomorrow. Use prisoners who'll swear to go unarmed. Promise them a return to their homes if they swear so."

"Is that wise, m'lord?"

"We have no need for slaves. They only require feeding. Men with the promise of freedom will work for themselves." The Prince tossed the stripped bone onto the platter in the center of the table. "We may control this city, my friend, but 'tis they who will rebuild it." Picking up another haunch, he peeled a piece of flesh from it. "When the streets are clear, go out and oversee delivery of the captured grain. Tell Krenin to set his men about repairing the wall. Have Gorm patrol the surrounding territory. I don't want to be surprised while we're vulnerable."

Naed's brows quirked. Caution was always wise, but after such a victory as theirs, whom should they protect themselves against? "Do you fear the other Adanak lords?"

Prince Arn shrugged. "Not necessarily." He took another bite of rabbit. "But if I were they, I'd take my enemy now—" He gestured to the partially consumed feast. "—while they were fat with victory and asleep."

Another flush swept up Naed's throat.

"'Tis a mistake you'll make but once, my friend." The Prince walked around the table to clasp Naed's shoulder. "Don't misunderstand me. You've done well and I'm pleased."

A different kind of warmth ran through Naed's veins. *Why should it matter that he is Tolemak when it matters naught to him that I am not?*

"Take some rest and I'll see you in the morning."

Naed watched him pour wine into a cup and drink, then reached for his own cup. The movement made the key under his chest armor shift. "What of the Masters' treasury?"

"Later. Tell me where you've quartered the city's officers."

"The inner court, m'lord."

"Have you yet the Lancer's sword?"

Naed fumbled beside his chair where Banir had deposited his personal goods. Pushing aside his saddle, he tilted his shield back and found the sword underneath.

Prince Arn accepted the weapon Naed proffered. Grasping the hilt, he slid the blade halfway out of the sheath. The candlelit glint of sword sparked in each of his eyes.

Wondering where his thoughts traveled and what he saw in the polished surface, Naed was about to speak when the Prince shoved the blade into the scabbard.

"Take some rest," he said again, and left.

The Prince had appeared. He had given his orders. He had even dispensed a measure of praise. Naed groped for his chair and sat in it. What more could he have asked of the man?

He reached for his wine cup and stared into it. In red liquid miniature, his face looked back, haggard and weary. He drained the cup, set it down, and ran his hands over his face. Something still niggled at him, but he could not focus on it. The Prince's appearance had relieved some of the burden on his shoulders and he longed for naught but sleep. With an order to Grodar at the door, he rose, blew out the candles, and walked to the bed by the mantle. Pulling off only his boots, he lay down like a dead man and slept.

****

In the inner court, most of the wounded slept under the light of torches. Arn scanned their faces from the perimeter. He completed one circuit, then stood, wondering if he had overlooked any among the knots of men still awake and sitting on stone benches. The escapees had been caught. The man he sought must be here. *Or dead*, reason suggested, but Arn ignored it, wading into the ranks of the Adanak wounded.

"Hail, Prince of Val-Feyridge, Conqueror of Vinvinnysee."

The softly spoken words brought Arn to a halt. He turned, searching the shadow of a small tree for the glint of eyes. One figure among several reclining against the roots moved. It was a thin man with a face made even hollower by the torchlight.

Arn smiled. "Master Gaelwynn, I've been looking for you."

****

Arn lit two lamps in the elegantly furnished study. While he slid one into the center of the table, Gaelwynn settled himself in the cushioned chair Arn had pushed up to it. "Your arm," Arn said, indicating cloth binding the man's arm to his chest. "Broken?"

Gaelwynn looked up, and Arn noticed the Adanak's eyes were mismatched, one blue and one brown. A frisson of excitement tingled along Arn's nerves. He had heard of but one man with eyes like that.

"Out of joint, my lord," Gaelwynn was saying. "The deed of your young Second, so I am told, although I was certain 'twas a D'nalian."

"One and the same." Arn turned to the sideboard, located a jug of wine, poured two cups and set one before Gaelwynn. "I prize men of quality, regardless of their origin."

"I have fought beside D'nalians also, my lord." He gestured to the cup. "They do lie between us and may join either side."

Arn smiled. "Indeed they may." He walked to Gaelwynn's side of the table and perched on the corner of it. "But how often do they rise above soldier in your army?"

"Rarely, I must concede. An Adanak does not kindly accept orders from one not his own."

"Neither does a Tolemak."

The mismatched eyes searched first Arn's face, then traveled to the cup now at an oblique angle from both men. "Your Second is but one stranger in your ranks. Have you others?"

Arn leaned forward. "I could, soon."

"You compliment me, my lord."

"I would have had Sevig, had he lived. But you say you were his friend. If he numbered you so, you must be worthy."

The profiled blue eye darkened and a hint of emotion traveled like cloud shadow across the weathered copper face. "Worthy of what, my lord?"

The words revealed nothing. Neither did the voice. Still, Arn's blood quickened like that of a hound catching a scent. "Of sharing a vision, Master Gaelwynn, a vision of the future."

"The future be yours. I have been defeated."

"Have you? Your army, aye. But you? Have *you* been defeated?"

The mismatched eyes glittered, then looked away. "I have been captured."

"Hardly one and the same. The defeated man lies down and waits for death, like your Master Sima who knows his power is forever gone and he is as naked as the poorest man in his dungeon. The captured man, however, has given up nothing of himself. He will wait, watch, and seize freedom again, however it may come to him. *However*," he said, pushing the cup toward the man, "it may come to him, Master Gaelwynn."

Unblinking, Gaelwynn's gaze tracked the cup, fixing on where it stopped for heartbeat after heartbeat until the mismatched eyes closed and the man sighed. "Be you the Demon, my lord, that you do weave words with an eloquence uncommon among your kind?"

Arn unclasped a belt at his waist and laid a sheathed sword on the table. "If I am, 'tis Sevig's doing. He lives on in this sword." With a deliberate motion, he turned the hilt toward Gaelwynn. An inlaid stone caught lampfire and danced its reflection across the polished wood. "I would give it to you, in his honor, if you would accept the place I envisioned for him."

Gaelwynn's hand gripped the chair arm as though manacled there, forbidden to rise. Still, the leathery fingers flexed. 'Twas always a risk to offer an enemy a weapon, but Arn's gut told him the Adanak understood the import of his gesture.

"What cost, my lord," Gaelwynn said quietly, "would I undertake to obtain my freedom?"

"Small cost, if you care for unity." Undertunic clinging to his back, Arn stood. "When King Ekard died, Tolem should have had the rule. Adan should have been at his side, not at his throat. With D'nal, they should have been three, together, in one land. D'nal is with me already. Take my hand as Adan and end this bitterness that separates us."

Gaelwynn studied his offered hand. "Hatred does run deep between your kind and mine."

"It can be overcome. I have always admired men of courage and skill, but—let me be frank—a month ago I would not have dreamed of offering a cup of wine to an Adanak. Sevig and—" *A woman,* he started to say, but bit it back. She was an Adanak, true, but however she may have altered his perceptions, she was nonetheless only a woman. "Men of your kind have invaded my homeland, killed my companions, slashed my face, and fought me with hate in their eyes. Only Sevig saw me differently. He gave me my life when he had nothing to gain from it—and everything to lose."

Chest tight, he strode to the wall and faced a tapestry, a scene of Ekard's coronation lavishly wrought in gold and scarlet thread. Arn saw through it to an expanse of grayness broken only by a copper-skinned face with a half-moon scar upon the chin. A graying, dead face. "How many Sevigs are there among your people? Many? Or was there but one?"

"We will not be slaves, my lord, exchanging the yoke of one master for that of another, however gently he may fasten it about our necks."

Arn turned. "'Tis a shrewd man you are, Master Gaelwynn, and I'll speak plainly. I mean to unite these three lands. If you join me, Vinvinnysee will be yours to govern as you please. All I require is your allegiance and your assistance in converting other Adanak lords. My demands for gold are small, half—at the most—of your city Masters', for I have other ample sources of income. Your city will be rebuilt and refortified. Already, I've ordered grain to be delivered. In a few days, your people's hunger will be but a memory."

Arn watched Gaelwynn's face, knowing behind the impassive exterior, a thousand thoughts raced. He saw no hatred in the mismatched eyes, only a skepticism born of years of command. That skepticism, if he guessed right, was now busily sifting, assessing, deciding.

"You do promise much, my lord, but, to speak as plainly as you, we both do know 'twas not merely to secure an ally that you came to take this city."

The old warrior's eyes gleamed with a keener intelligence than they had previously revealed. Noting it, Arn leaned on the table, the earlier frisson of possibility now a blood rush of certainty. He had intended to gain the man's allegiance before broaching the subject, but as long as the Adanak had the audacity to bring it up...

"My Second will find the Crown wherever you have hidden it."

Gaelwynn inclined his head ever so slightly. "'Tis very like he shall."

"'Twould be better if you offered it up."

"So it would seem, my lord, but I must be certain your blood be true. Have you proof?"

Arn straightened and tugged his grandfather's necklace from under his tunic. "I do, but if you are truly the Crownkeeper, Gaelwynn, you should know you need no more proof but to look at me. 'Tis the Mark of Tolem to be as I am."

"Aye, but 'tis long years I have waited to see you, my lord. Since ere you were born. The Crown be a treasure to be given to but one man—he who would remake the Kingdom."

****

Crownkeeper Gaelwynn climbed the 136 steps, mindful of the man who followed. He had expected the claimant to bound ahead, so eager to lay his hands on his prize he would outstrip the light cast by the single torch on the twisting, narrow steps. But the Tolemak climbed in steady silence, his dark head—whenever the Crownkeeper chanced to glance at him—fixed on the uneven stone wedges circling upward.

At the top, the Prince held the torch while the Crownkeeper pulled the key from under his tunic and fitted it to the lock. Before opening the chamber door, he took back the torch and studied the man who waited to enter. Once again, the Crownkeeper forced himself to breathe. The resemblance was so uncanny, he could have sworn 'twas Tolem himself who stood at his side, yet looks alone were but partial proof. Taken together with the letter this bastard had produced, the claim was substantial, but not conclusive. There was but one true test.

He pushed open the door, and the torch illumined the chamber, bare but for the pedestal in the center, the cushion upon it, and the Crown.

The man at his side sucked in breath. The Crownkeeper entered, but the man did not follow. Framed in the blackness of the tower stairwell, he stared at the Crown glittering in the torchlight. "It's blue," he said. "The Kingdom Stone is blue."

"Aye, did you not know?"

The Tolemak took a step into the chamber. "I don't know what I expected, but 'twas not this." He advanced another step, gaze locked on filigreed daggers and gleaming gold. "My grandfather's tale said the Crown was mangled before it disappeared. Have you restored it?"

The Crownkeeper looked fondly at the icon he had sheltered for so many years. "'Tis not my task." Raising his gaze, he fixed it on the man whose height filled the chamber. "'Tis *your* task. Will you be having it, my lord?"

Approaching slowly, the Prince stopped within reach of the golden circlet. Torchlight sparking on the inlaid stones cast prisms of light on his garments, on the hand he raised toward the gaping prongs where the princely stones had once resided. "Tolem, D'nal, Adan," he named each vacant setting as he touched it. "Generations have shed blood for what this once was. Because of what this once signified. And this—this is what remains of it." Lifting his head, he looked full at the Crownkeeper. "Can I remake the Kingdom without them?"

"Without what, my lord? The stones or the people?"

"The missing stones. The Kingdom *is* the people. Why do you think I offered you Sevig's sword?"

The Crownkeeper schooled his face to show none of the excitement racing through his veins. "You have the Tolem Stone, have you not?"

"I know how to get it." Brows lowered, the Prince touched the empty Tolem setting. "Are the stones vital?

What if I have those at my side who represent the people?"

"'Tis the Sisters alone who may answer that."

As the Prince's fingers hovered over the Kingdom Stone, the Crownkeeper watched some inner struggle play out in his shadowed eyes. "They know I'm an unbeliever. They'll have their way with me, 'tis sure, but I'll take my chances. I always have." He turned. "Accept my hand, Gaelwynn, and the Kingdom you and I envision will come to pass—with or without the stones."

The Crownkeeper clasped the hand held toward him, shaking it once, firmly. "You have cut yourself, my lord," he said, noting a smear of red on his palm as he drew it back.

The Prince glanced at the tiny cut oozing scarlet on his fingertip. "'Tis nothing."

'Tis everything, the Crownkeeper thought while his heart hammered at his ribs. "Will you be putting it on, my lord?"

The dark head on which he thought the Crown would sit as splendidly as it did upon its cushion shook once from side to side. "'Tis neither the time nor the place. And the Kingdom is yet but a dream, no more fully formed than its symbol."

The Crownkeeper locked eyes with the true Heir of Tolem. He had never thought to see this moment—so many generations of his kind had waited for it—and his heart yearned to open to the promise of the future manifested in this man, but 'twas not yet time. He had obligations, and the Will of the Sisters must unfold according to Their wishes. He could do naught to interfere. He could only, if possible, guide.

"'Tis a dark road you travel, my lord. There be much danger in what you seek to do. But, if 'tis your intent to be offering it still, 'twould be my honor to accept my friend Sevig's sword and serve at your side."

With a smile lighting his scarred face, the Prince unclasped the Lancer's sword from his belt and fastened it to the Crownkeeper's. "Lock up this treasury, Gaelwynn. As I recall, there are two cups of some fine Eidvondian wine waiting below for us to seal our accord."

The Crownkeeper stroked the hilt of the sword at his

side and remembered the friend who had once wielded it. So much bloodshed, so many dead over so many years— all to come to this moment. Yet 'twas not finished. Turning his hand, he noted the rusty streak still marring his palm. *Let us see if, by his blood, he is worthy.* The words, uttered months ago in this very chamber, came to him like echoes of a distant past. *He is,* he thought, *but 'twill take more blood.*

Raising his head, he said, "Aye, my lord, but I pray that, after we do so, you will do me the honor of telling me all that you do know of my friend Sevig."

****

Aerid sat up. The room was dark, but moonlight streamed through the balcony window. She had slept fitfully, exhausted by her tears, the food the serving woman had set before her lying like a lump in her stomach. Hugging her knees, she rested her cheek on her arm and stared at the table beside the bed. The tray was gone, evidence the woman had returned to remove it just as she herself had often returned to Lord Dranoel's chamber to remove the remains of his meal while he dozed in the chair before the fire. Her gaze shifted to the ashes still glowing on the grate. The woman had added wood when she returned, just as she had so often done for Dranoel.

She did not belong in this enormous room and huge bed wearing this whisper-soft gown. And certainly not waited on by a woman of her own kind, a woman who feared to raise her eyes but who looked at her with sidelong glances full of curiosity.

Suddenly, the room seemed hot and stifling. Aerid flung back the covers and slid her feet over the edge of the bed. She expected cold stone, but her soles sank into fur. The silkiness of it sent shock waves through her body. She closed her eyes, swayed, and opened them again when she realized she was no longer weak enough to fall. True, her muscles quivered and her head felt light, but food and rest had restored a measure of her strength.

Aerid turned toward the moon-washed windowsill. Its light had drawn her out of sleep. It drew her still, toward its clarity, its black-white sharpness. She moved as one in a dream, slowly, unsteadily, one step on the fur,

243

the next on the cold, harsh stone.

The moonlight, when she stood in its circle, did not warm her. Nor did she expect it to. Instead, she opened her hand to it, letting the stark whiteness see what lay within—and what did not. Leumas had loved her. And Leumas was dead. 'Twas no mystery in that. Nor, she thought as she forced down the lump in her throat, was there any doubt the Prince cared for her. Three times he had saved her life, though he was, by all rights, her enemy. Twice before, he had sent her away. Would he do so again?

A tremor shook her body. Hot and breathless, Aerid leaned against the window sill. She did not want to leave. Deep in the core of her being, she yearned to stay with the man whose touch set her senses ablaze.

Shame washed over her. The Prince was a cruel warrior whose cold-hearted conquests destroyed her people's lives. Had she not seen ample proof? He was responsible for Leumas' death, and Avika's. Her moon-whitened hands gripped the stone sill. How could she love Leumas and care so for his enemy, his murderer? 'Twas not right, not just...yet, her heart replied, he was also responsible for her life. He had tenderly taken her up, sheltered her from her own kind, and touched her—not only with his hands and lips, but in some other, deeper way she could neither explain nor forget. When he touched her, it did not matter that he was Tolemak and she Adanak, that he was warrior and she healer, or even that he was Prince and she naught but a servant. All that mattered in that moment of contact was he was man and she woman.

Face flushed, Aerid pulled open the window and let the night breeze cool her skin. She knew why he had brought her here, to this room, this bed. He meant to lie with her, and there would be no promises, naught but the coming together of two bodies that yearned beyond reason for each other. Leumas would have wed her, but though she loved him, she had not yearned for him the way she yearned for this Tolemak prince who would not, could not wed her.

Mairim would no doubt think her foolish to throw away her virtue, but what had she loved in her life that she yet kept? Parents? Old Gam? Dranoel? Leumas? Even Naed was dead.

She had lost far too much to lose this chance. Especially now when it had come once more back to her.

CHAPTER TWENTY-ONE

By Arn's reckoning it was after midnight when he saw Gaelwynn comfortably installed in a room befitting his new status. He left a message for Naed and another for Krenin, then strolled through the darkened palace halls toward the central courtyard, well satisfied. He had seen to all that required his attention and—*Sisters and the Demon!*—even seen the Crown!

Stopping, he braced a hand on the wall while his heart galloped. For the last hour, he had suppressed the thrill racing along his nerves to focus on the delicate dance of negotiation. Now that he had won Gaelwynn, he could allow the import of what he had seen in that tower room flood through him. Demon be damned but he had never expected to see it this soon! Perhaps not at all. Even though he had assured Krenin the Crown was real, Arn understood he had never really *known*, had trusted but never quite *believed* the Crown on which he had pinned so much of his hopes truly existed. Now he had seen it—and it had taken his breath away. The Kingdom Stone, that astonishingly vivid—and *living*—blue, the gold, the daggers, everything but the princely stones. By the Demon, the Kingdom was truly within his grasp!

If these halls and walls did not contain him now, he thought he might soar away. He had known the pleasure of victory far more often than most men, but only the capture of his rightful home at Albon and then Val-Feyridge roused any exhilaration similar to the music singing in his veins at this moment. Against all odds, he had captured the city supposed to be impregnable; he had found the icon said to be lost. And waiting for him was the woman he desired above all others. If the rapture he anticipated in her arms in any measure equaled that intoxicating him at this moment, he would know the Three Sisters were mere superstition because the heaven They promised lay here and now in the room toward which he strode.

Stepping into that darkened room, Arn closed the door softly. She had eaten, the sentry assured him. Well and good. He would look at her first—merely look—until he mastered the fever surging through his blood. He had time, and he wanted to savor this.

It was dark within the shelter of the bed curtains. Embers in the grate cast a feeble glow no farther than the hearth's edge. Arn bent to add a log, then decided the chamber was warm enough. Straightening, he reached for the curtain to open the bed to the moonlight—and froze.

Across the room, she stood in the rectangle of light pouring through the balcony window. One hand gripped the stone sill, but she had turned toward him like a doe in the forest. The simple garment clinging to her body shimmered like an aura around her, reflecting the moon-white stone at her throat, and her eyes were twin stars in the shadow of her face.

She's a witch, Arn thought as he sucked in a shallow breath. *A spirit conjured to bewitch and bewilder*. The real Aerid, the flesh and blood woman he had held and touched lay yet in the bed. If he could tear his eyes from this vision, he would see...

She turned toward the window, placed both hands on the sill, and, darting one more look at him, lowered her head.

Arn's breath returned. His limbs were his own again, and he released the curtain. Still, he stood and stared at her. There was no woman in the bed. He knew that now without looking. Warm flesh filled the gown that still dazzled his eyes. The hair the moonlight rippled through like streams of silver was the hair he longed to touch, to tangle around his fingers.

Warmth invaded his body and he swallowed. She was his. Her eyes had told him so hours earlier when he touched his fingers to her lips. He had only to approach, to lay his hands upon her to claim all her look had offered. Why then did he tremble so? She was, after all, only a woman. And he wanted her.

Crossing the room, he entered the moonlight, not stopping until he stood directly behind her, a mere cushion of darkness separating his body from hers. A flutter of her eyelids acknowledged his presence. His heart thumped. Raising his hands, he enclosed her upper arms. The tendons of her throat flexed against her necklace. Her body burned his palms through the fabric and Arn knew, fiercely and with satisfaction, she was indeed flesh and blood—and woman.

Skating a hand over the gown-covered shoulder, he crossed the boundary of fabric and fanned his fingers along her throat above the moon-in-miniature stone nested between the fine bones there. Her head tilted and he heard the soft intake of her breath. The scent of her hair, her skin suffused the air around him. He breathed deeply, greedily, until scent alone did not satisfy and he turned his face into her hair. She quivered, and the pulse under his fingertips leaped.

Like a man drugged, he pressed his lips to her hair, her ear, the naked slope of her shoulder. Tremors rippled through her body. Her breath came in shallow whispers, the quick rise and fall drawing his eyes to the moonlight and shadows outlining her breasts. His hand followed the direction of his gaze and his palm curved around one soft mound.

She shuddered. Her thrown-back head grazed his shoulder. Her hair swept his face, the tendrils as light as thistledown, as sensuous as silk.

Enraptured, Arn pulled her against the length of his body. His hand splayed over her abdomen, pushing her hips into the hardness of his. His other hand rushed from breast to breast, kneading, stroking, finding with forefinger and thumb the tips that firmed and swelled until she moaned and arched against him, her hands no longer stiff and motionless but frantic and digging into the bones of his wrists.

His blood raced at her touch. Releasing her abruptly, he seized at his tunic, jerking it over his head. He tugged at the fastenings of his chest armor and flung it to the floor. His under-tunic flew into the shadows and his sword and knife dropped with a clatter as he stepped forward, his mind focused on one thought—her hands on his body, her skin pressed to his.

She stood half turned away, head bowed, moonlight silvering the line of her shoulder. He wanted to seize her, to spin her about, to thrust her body against his and taste the mouth he had dreamed of for weeks, but he fought down the urge. He had time, and he wanted her to know pleasure in his arms, the pleasure he alone could give her.

One hand at her waist, he raised the other to her shoulder. He stroked his fingers to her throat and chin, then trailed them back along the curve of her shoulder and slipped them under the fabric clinging there. She trembled and he knew she understood his intent. His hand on her waist tightened as the other pushed the sleeve off her shoulder. The fabric whispered down her arm and, while his eyes burned and his blood throbbed with slow, heavy beats, gently fell away.

For several seconds, he could not draw breath. Then his hand fit itself under the swell of a moon-glazed breast and closed around it. He swallowed and, breathing again while his blood roared in his ears, opened the circle of his thumb and first finger to expose the peak and its darkened rim. Bending, he touched his tongue to it. Shudders rippled through her body. He took the nub between his lips and nibbled at it. Her hands gripped his shoulders and he heard her moan. When she would have pushed him away, he opened his mouth and suckled her breast until her fingers raked his hair and dug into his scalp.

Only then did he sweep her into his arms and, with savage triumph, bear her to the bed. Pausing scarcely long enough to strip off his boots and breeches, he stretched out beside her and thrust his fingers into her hair. Turning her face with gentle fingers, he leaned across the naked heat of her breast, shuddered, and touched his mouth to hers. Her lips were warm, soft, and—he frowned—salty?

Nonplussed, Arn raised his head. In the moonlight, droplets glistened on her lashes. He shifted his thumb and intersected a damp trail to her ear. Did she yet fear him? He stroked tenderly along her cheek. "I won't hurt you. You should know that by now."

Her eyes slitted open. "Aye," she said, but her voice was faint, husky.

Rising to his elbows, he searched her face. Her lips were parted, the lower lip full, moist, tempting.

Helen C. Johannes

Swallowing, he shifted his gaze to her naked breast. On the copper-cream skin, the nipple stood out taut and dusky, evidence of her arousal. Why then the tears? "Do you—?" he said as a sudden fear rushed cold through his veins. "Do you—" he cupped his hand around her breast. "—want me...as I want you?"

Desire swept like pain across her face. "Aye," she whispered.

Relieved, Arn levered over her and framed her face with his hands. He kissed the corner of each eye, the ridge of each cheek, the corners of her mouth. "Then let me teach you how 'tis done between a man and a woman who want each other."

"And—and after? What will you be wanting of me after that?"

The words were faint, forced out. He lifted his head and looked into eyes large, dark, and deep enough to drown him in the liquid pooling in their lids.

Writhing beneath him, she dashed a hand over her cheeks. "Forgive me, I—I know 'tis naught we may be to each other—"

"What?" Arn said, conscious he trembled again. Did she wish to leave? She could not—not when he wanted her more than he had wanted anything or anyone in his life. He yanked the gown from her other breast, causing her to suck in air when he caught the nipple between thumb and forefinger. "Is this all you think I want from you?" he growled.

From under her lashes, dark, glistening blue eyes studied him. "Be there more?"

"Demon be damned, woman, have you learned nothing of me?" Gripping her shoulders, he pressed her into the bed. "I mean to make you mine, Aerid. I won't let you go. Not tomorrow. Not the next day. Not so long as there is breath in my body."

Before his eyes, Aerid's features blurred into a vision of pale hair, white skin, and eyes like bits of ice. Erodasi's mouth sneered, her face looked at him with revulsion. Sweat broke out on his body. Why the Demon had he ever betrothed himself to such as Erodasi? Pushing up, he swung his legs over the edge of the bed and sat gripping the sides, knowing full well why he had done so. She was

250

key to legitimacy, to the Tolem Stone. If he had not seen the Crown earlier this night, he would not now be recalling her and her link to it. By the Demon, he wished he could find another way to—

"M'lord?"

The tentative stroke of Aerid's fingers on his arm brought him back to the present; the uncertainty in her voice, in her choice of address cut him like a knife. "Arn," he said, inhaling deeply, knowing there would be no going back from this moment. "'Tis my name."

Turning his head, he saw chagrin in the smile flitting across her face and knew she remembered as well as he the night he had taken her across the river. "Arn," she said shyly.

His name, formed by her lips, shivered through him. It compelled him to release his grip on the bed frame and turn toward her. Aerid had pushed herself up from the bed, her breasts naked and beautiful, the gown bunched about her hips. Eyes liquid and dark, she reached out and ever so gently traced the scar on his cheek. "'Twould be my desire..." She licked her lips, blushed becomingly, but held his gaze. "'Twould be my desire to be learning—with you, Arn—how 'tis done between a man and a woman who do want each other."

Catching her hand, he pressed his lips to the palm, drinking of her taste the way a man near death drinks of the well that will save his life. *Erodasi be damned!* This small, dark-haired, copper-skinned woman of Adanak offered what he craved, what he so desperately needed, and never until now knew he lacked. "Come here, then," he said in a voice rough with emotion, "and kiss me. 'Tis how to begin."

She laid her free hand over his heart, spreading her fingers experimentally in the hair dusting his chest. "Like this?" she murmured, tilting her face up and touching her lips to his.

He meant to restrain himself, to take her gently through the night, but when she slid her arms around his neck and her breasts flattened against his chest, her mouth opened and her tongue touched his lips so sweetly, so tentatively, he groaned, "Sisters and the Demon, aye!" and, hauling her against his body, bore her down to the bed.

****

Naed had ridden at Dranoel's heels for hours. Indeed, with the denseness of the fog, he could have been forever following that broad back with the helm that seemed to grow directly out of it. Then, suddenly, the fog thinned and daylight glowed golden all around them. In the distance, Druemarwin's gate beckoned. Naed stood in his stirrups, and they rode through it.

In the courtyard Aerid waited, her eyes bluer than he remembered, tiny purple bellflowers in her hair. She balanced a water jug on her hip. When he dismounted, she gave him the jug, but her eyes looked beyond him, beyond at...men! Men who leaped from the battlements and beat him with clubs! There were hundreds of them, swarming, shouting. He lashed out with his sword, this way and that. Someone seized his shoulder. He tried to strike away the hand, but it shook him and shook him and—

"What does it take to wake you lowlanders?" Krenin leaned over him, a scowl on his face. "Do you sleep with moss in your ears?"

Sunlight peeked through the shutter slats—morning sunlight by the slant of it. Naed remembered the room, the meal, the Prince... Jerking away from Krenin's hand, he sat up and ran his hands over his face. The stubble they encountered irritated him more than awakening to Krenin's jostling. 'Twas true he had not had the time to groom himself properly the last two days, but he would make the time now and let the Tolemak wait. "Banir," he said as he rose from the bed, "bring water."

"Here," the dark-haired Tolemak said, gesturing to a steaming bowl, cloth, and shaving soap lying on the table.

Banir's anticipation of his needs dissipated much of Naed's irritation. "Good man."

Krenin grunted. "Grow a beard, lowlander, and look like a man."

"Some of your people may cover their faces with hair, but mine do not." Wetting the cloth, he began to scrub his face. "What did you want of me?"

Krenin paced to the window. "Send your men out." When the door closed behind them, he burst out, "This is lunacy what he's done now! Did you put the idea into his head?"

Naed watched the man stride in and out of the sunshine filtering through the shutters. "Speak plainly or I shall have no answer for you."

"Plainly! Let your moss-stuffed ears hear this, then! Arn's given a sword to an Adanak! And promised him control of the city if he swears allegiance to us."

Naed knew with a prickling of his scalp precisely what sword the Prince had given. And he understood why the Prince had given it, although the timing of the gesture eluded him. They had scarcely secured the city; 'twould have been prudent to wait a day or two before handing back some of its control. However, the Prince was shrewd and—

"Did you put the idea into him? He was here last night. Your man at the door told me—"

"Indeed, he was here yester eve." Naed scowled. Krenin had not understood about the Lancer's sword before. He could not possibly understand now when the weapon was again in the hands of an Adanak. "We spoke of several things, but he told me naught of awarding the sword to an Adanak. Do you know the name of the man?"

"Master of the Guard...Gaelwynn or some such word-weaver's name. I could have sworn you had something to do with this."

"Is there aught else?"

Krenin slammed his fist on the table. "First a woman, now an Adanak! What are you going to do?"

Naed waited for the water in the bowl to calm before he soaked the cloth again. "'Tis naught for me to do but my duty." He scrubbed his neck. "I am assigned to clear the streets and deliver the captured grain to the city. You are ordered to repair the wall. I suggest you be about it, or the Prince may find another more eager to perform the task."

Red blotches broke out on Krenin's cheeks. "Don't think I won't remember this."

A D'nalian should not return insult with insult, but the exhilaration speeding through Naed's veins was like a potion numbing him to all else but the pleasure of the moment.

Until Krenin departed, and Naed felt empty, disgusted, and dirty. 'Twas too easy to become one of them. But he would resist. He had to—for Aerid's sake.

CHAPTER TWENTY-TWO

Arn woke to the rat-a-tat-tat of knocking. He opened heavy eyelids to sunlight streaming into the room. Aerid lay curved into his body, one small breast cradled in his palm. Rising a little, he gazed at the sweep of dark lashes on her cheekbone, at the curve of lips whose delicate touch he remembered on his skin, at the seductive line of her naked shoulder. Her scent filled his nostrils, warm and musky. Closing his eyes to savor it, he lay back and stroked her breast.

The knocking sounded again, more insistent.

He had told the guards he was not to be disturbed; it would have to be important for his orders to be disregarded. With a grunt, he rolled to the edge of the bed and groped for the knife he always kept within reach. *Not there.* He sat up and saw it lying in the middle of the floor. His sword lay equally out of reach beside the heap of his chest armor.

Scowling at his lapse of caution, he pulled on his breeches, finding beside his foot his grandfather's necklace, the irreplaceable proof of his birthright. Flushing, he picked it up and put it on. He had been bewitched last night, and it discomfited him to realize how completely. That discomfiture flamed into irritation when he opened the door and Krenin pushed over the threshold.

Krenin's gaze flashed over his face, shifted to the clothing scattered on the floor, to the bed and, finally, to the back of the woman sleeping there.

Arn blocked the doorway, irked Krenin should have even glimpsed the body that was his alone. "This better be important."

Krenin folded his arms. "I've seen what I came to see."

Arn's fingers dug into the doorframe. "Get out!"

"Was she worth it? Did she twist you inside out and

leave you begging for more? Did you ride her high and hard until—"

"Get out!"

"We came so far—all the way from Val-Feyridge—Albon, even! From a damned riverbank Demon knows how many years ago! We drove ourselves to get across D'nalee and Adanak and into this Sisters-forsaken hilltop heap of stone! All for what? Just so the great bloody fool Heir to Tolem could throw himself between the legs of some Adanak whore?"

"Get out!"

"*I* have whores! *You* don't. *I* spill my seed in any willing womb! *You* keep that ice cold cock of yours inside your breeches! Who is she? *What* is she? One of the Demon's own Nine that she's bewitched you so? Why this one? Why not any of a thousand others you could have had since I've—"

"Arn?"

Both men flinched. Arn turned, clearing his throat, reining in the fury purpling his vision, keeping it from his voice. "I'm here. Go back to sleep."

She smiled and pulled the blanket up under her chin.

His breath caught at the tenderness radiating from her face. Every fiber in his body yearned to go to her, but they were not alone. He swung to Krenin. "Get out—now!"

Krenin gaped as if thunderstruck. "She—that's the woman—"

"Who saved your life. 'Tis good of you to remember her, considering when last you saw her, you thought she was a boy." He shoved Krenin over the threshold into the vestibule and followed him there. He hoped Aerid had not seen Krenin. The thought of her suffering fear, embarrassment, discomfiture of any kind because she had given herself to him made the blood beat behind Arn's eyes. "Perhaps, if I tell you her name is Aerid and she's from Druemarwin, you'll be even better able to place her! Now, get out! And take the rest of your questions with you!" Turning, he shut the door behind him and threw the bolt.

Aerid sighed and rolled onto her back. "Arn?"

He crossed the room, catching the hand she stretched toward him and pressing a kiss to it. "Rest easy," he said, his voice a rasp as he tried to soften it. "I'm not leaving."

Pulling off his breeches, Arn slid under the blanket and gathered her into his arms. She came to him easily, snuggling into his shoulder. Her willingness assured him she had heard nothing of Krenin's rant. He inhaled the fragrance of her hair while her hand drifted down his chest. After a tentative pause, it coasted over the arch of his ribs and down to his abdomen.

His body stirred in instant response. He had possessed her, but his need had not abated. If anything, he wanted her the more for having lain with her. He caught her hand, brought it to his lips and kissed each fingertip. Then, pressing her palm to his chest, he rose to his elbow and flung back the blanket, intent on looking at all of her.

She glanced at him from under her lashes, then devoted her attention to a scar on his shoulder. "'Twas Krenin, aye?" she said, tracing the whitened ridge with a fingertip.

So, she had heard—damn the man! "I'll speak to him later." He laid his palm on her stomach and splayed his fingers toward the juncture of her thighs. This morning, he thought with a quickening of his blood, he would teach her the pleasures his lips and tongue could bring. He bent toward her breast, intent on nibbling what tempted him.

Aerid's forearm, braced against his shoulder, halted his progress. "Do you—" she said, her gaze hesitating, shy, "do you...regret me?"

His heart swelled. He lifted his hand from her stomach and threaded his fingers through her hair. "Because of Krenin? Don't be foolish. I'll see he understands."

Her arm yielded. He leaned closer while her fingers fidgeted along his collarbone. "Do you—?" she murmured, a flush coloring her cheeks. "Do I...please you?"

Arn chuckled. "Vastly." Shifting his leg over hers, he nudged her knees apart. The heat of her inner thighs, as they enveloped his, made him suck in a breath. When he could speak again, he asked, "Have I pleased you?"

Aerid's hands danced along his upper arms. She lay with her face averted, shy, vulnerable. Lovely, he thought, bending to brush his lips over her cheek.

Helen C. Johannes

"The second time...aye," she murmured, darting a glance at his face.

Arn stilled, remembering how she had stiffened at his first possession. She had not cried out, but he had seen the tracks of tears on her cheek when he roused himself after, and her lower lip still bore a bruise from her teeth. He closed his eyes with a groan. "I didn't mean to hurt—"

Her hands touched his cheeks, the thumb tips stilling his lips. "'Twas not unknown to me what a woman must endure to be possessed by a man," she said when he opened his eyes again.

She smiled and his heart banged against his ribs. She had to feel it, for his whole body shook with its beats. "Sisters, woman! How I love you!" Claiming her mouth, he devoured her response, knowing by the faint, breathless vibrations deep in her throat, she was completely and entirely his.

****

Aerid lay with eyes closed, listening to birds chatter outside the balcony window. When they had awakened again, Arn had sent for food. She sighed, remembering the pleasure of watching him dress, of seeing at last all the planes and angles of the body she had begun to know by touch and scent and—

A delicious shudder curled through her abdomen. She stroked a hand down her stomach and across her thigh. Her muscles ached, muscles she had not known she possessed, but the ache was pleasant. 'Twas as if she had feasted and now cared not a whit if she moved ever again. Except, she thought with a smile, to open her arms to Arn when he returned in the evening.

She sighed and, winding a lock of hair around her finger, remembered how he had located her gown and coaxed her into it. Then he had swept her into his arms and carried her like a pampered child to the cushioned chair beside the table and tucked a fur around her legs.

After the serving woman had delivered their dinner and left, he insisted she eat everything he placed before her. She had stared, astonished at the abundance of food. 'Twas true she had gone without for much of her stay in the city, but the servings of quail, rabbit, and vegetables

258

shamed even the standards of Dranoel's private table. Reluctant to displease, she ate as much as her stomach would hold. Before long, she was forced to shake her head to his entreaties and, hands restless in her lap, murmur, "Forgive me, but 'tis more to eat than I be accustomed."

Arn sat silent across from her, but when she darted a look at him, he smiled and set a goblet before her. "Drink as much as you like. I'll finish the rest."

Aerid smiled, remembering the warmth of the wine in her veins and the pleasure of sitting across a table from him, his knee pressed to hers. He was everything she had ever hoped he would be, and more. She had many times witnessed his courage and his strength. Lately, his passion had played her into this state where she lay now, mindless and content. But she knew 'twas his tenderness that had captured her heart. She sighed, wondering how she could ever have thought him cruel and cold-hearted.

The door opened with a quiet slip of the latch. Aerid sat up, expecting Arn, but it was a woman who entered and gently closed the door behind her.

The woman turned, saw Aerid, and quickly curtsied. "Forgive me, my lady, I do but come to clear away. If it should please you that I come later, do but say, and I shall obey."

The young woman, whose servant's cap bulged with tight brown curls, had earlier trembled as she set out the crockery, and her face, with respectfully lowered eyes, had been white as a spring lily. Aerid had sat ill-at-ease in her presence, wishing she could calm the woman's fears about her Tolemak master, yet uncomfortable with the idea of being waited upon.

"Please," she said, sitting up fully, "clear what you will. You'll not be disturbing me."

The woman curtsied again. "Thank you, my lady." She bustled about the table, collecting crockery and goblets and wiping her hands on the apron fronting her full-skirted gown.

And it was a gown, Aerid noticed as a flush that had formed with the woman's first curtsy swept up her throat, a gown nearly as fine as that worn by ladies of lesser lords in D'nalee. *Here, such finery is worn by servants—and I am served by one so dressed!*

259

"You must not be addressing me so," she said, swinging her legs to the floor. "Indeed, I be no more than you. Less, if truth be known, for I have never served in so fine a place as this."

A goblet clunked to the table. The woman blanched, then ducked her gaze and fumbled for the goblet. "My lady, I—"

"You must not be addressing me so." Belting the white robe about her waist, she walked bare-footed to the table. While the woman hurriedly loaded her tray, Aerid laid a hand on her arm. "'Tis a woman such as you that I be."

The woman froze. Aerid saw the flutter of her lashes, but the woman did not look at her. "Not such as I," she murmured. "'Tis not I who be keeping company with a prince."

The words dripped into Aerid's consciousness like successive lead weights, each one small and unimportant, but piled upon the others becoming such an accumulated burden it forced her to release the woman's arm and sink into the nearest chair. Was she so changed she was no longer who she had been scarce days ago? She looked at the sleek robe encasing her arm, the fur on the floor and the gilded chair leg beside her bare foot. Her clothes had changed. Her lodging had changed. Indeed, if what the woman said were true, her very life had changed. *But within, I be ever as I was, common-born and a servant.*

She heard the woman pick up the tray and asked, "Wait. What may I call you?"

"Estra, my lady."

Aerid sighed. "'Tis not fit that you should address me so."

The crockery rattled. "How shall I be addressing you then?"

"Do as you will. But, I pray, do not be calling me that which be not true."

A look of consternation grooved Estra's forehead under the profusion of curls. Suddenly, she brightened. "Might I be calling you 'mistress' then?"

With a sigh of surrender, Aerid nodded. "Aye, if 'twould please you."

Estra smiled. "I'll be bearing these to the kitchen,

260

mistress, and then fetching you slippers. 'Tis too cold to be walking these floors without them, and you scarce out of bed after such a chill." Curtsying, she bustled to the door.

Aerid rubbed her bare feet together. She would appreciate slippers. Now she was out of bed, she could dress and... "My clothes—what has become of my clothes?"

"Muddy, mistress, and torn, too. I could do naught..."

"Then I have naught to wear but this." She plucked at her robe.

"Oh no, mistress. I'll be fetching you many fine clothes. Shoes and scents, and combs for your hair. Oh, aye, mistress, 'tis most pleased I'll be to dress you."

"Wait." Aerid hesitated to damp the woman's enthusiasm, but she could not bear the thought of being dressed as royally as Estra suggested. "Bring me but one dress, I pray you. A simple garment. And the slippers, too. No more."

****

Under the noon sun, Arn rode Darkstar down from the palace to the west gate. Across the courtyard, Krenin stood beside a rubble heap and directed sweating Adanak prisoners to carry stones from it up ladders to men of Albon who set the stones into holes broken by the catapults. The Albon men secured the patch with mortar mixed outside the wall and hauled up in buckets.

In another part of the courtyard, Arn spotted Gaelwynn. The Adanak stood with his right arm bound and useless but the sword Arn had given him strapped to his side. Vinvinnysee men worked under his supervision to restore the gate to its hinges. No Tolemaks guarded the group, but Arn saw that his men on the wall watched them. So, too, did the Adanak prisoners who labored to clear the square. So, too, did Krenin.

When Arn urged his horse into the courtyard, Krenin left his crew under Yarl's direction and strode to intercept him. Arn reined to a halt. Usually, Krenin's face was open to him, but the man who approached him now wore only a grim, set expression.

Krenin stopped beside Arn's stirrup. Unbuckling his sword, he presented the sheathed weapon hilt first. "If you don't trust me, then I'm not fit to serve in your army."

Arn stared first at the sword, then at the stony face

of the man offering it. He had expected an argument, hot words, shouting. "What do you mean, I don't trust you?"

"You never told me she was your spy. I knew we had the man at Druemarwin, but you never told me about her. If I had known—"

Ah, Arn thought, *leave it to Krenin to focus on the woman.* "She's not anyone's spy."

"Not a spy? Then—"

What words could explain what he hardly understood himself? Why did it have to be this woman? Why her, indeed? He waved Krenin's sword away.

"She *is* a witch. She's bewitched you."

Why else would he be so consumed by his need for Aerid that even this briefly out of her presence he was haunted by her face as he had seen it last—eyes half-closed with the passion of his kiss, lips parted and moist. Mastering the image, and his body's response to it, Arn told himself Krenin would understand enchantment. It would be too much to ask his friend to understand how Aerid's touch on his face made him feel for the first time whole and complete, how her eyes looked at him as if she saw all that he was, saw it without fear or revulsion, and embraced it as she embraced him...

"Play the fool for a woman if you want to." Krenin squashed a fly on his sleeve and flicked the remains away. "If you're so besotted with this one, 'tis a pity you didn't find her before you decided you needed a wife."

Arn stared at Krenin, wondering if he had heard correctly. "She's an Adanak."

"Any woman's better than Erodasi of Roines! Tolem Stone or not, she's Rolnar's spawn! 'Twere me, I'd not be linking myself to my worst enemy!" Before Arn could reply, Krenin thrust his sheathed sword in Gaelwynn's direction. "What about him? Was he your spy? I know *he* didn't save my life!"

The tension slid from Arn's shoulders. This was the Krenin he knew—and understood. "No," he said, relishing the response he was about to provoke, "he's the Crownkeeper."

Krenin gaped as though thunderstruck. "Demon's Blood! It's real then, aye? You've seen it? Where is it?"

"It's safe. And he," Arn said, nodding toward

Gaelwynn, "has the only key. That's why I've given him a sword and a command. He's pledged his loyalty, and I trust him. The city folk hold him in high regard. They'll follow him to our side."

"Sisters willing, you mean." While the familiar scowl returned to score even deeper furrows across his brow, Krenin folded his arms. "A D'nalian Second! An Adanak woman! A Vinvinnysee Guardsman! Who in the name of the Demon will you recruit next—Yinnad's ghost?" He strapped on his sword. "Someone had better watch your back."

Arn smiled. He leaned down and laid a hand on Krenin's shoulder. "'Tis what I rely on you for, old friend."

****

"You did bid me bring but one dress, mistress," Estra said. "Does it not please you?"

Aerid stared at the gown draped across the bed. The sky blue fabric glowed as vividly as if the sun hazing the balcony window lit the gown from within. Delicately wrought lace dripped from the cuffs and edged a bodice far less modest than that to which she was accustomed. Still, she could not take her eyes from the gown. She reached toward it, saw the work-roughened skin of her hands, and laced her fingers together. "I cannot wear this. My hands—they would tear it."

"'Tis sturdier made than that, mistress." Estra swept the gown into her arms. "Do but pull on the shift, and I'll be seeing to the gown."

"I cannot—I dare not wear such finery!"

"'Tis the Prince you be dressing for, mistress. He will expect to see you thus arrayed when he returns this eve, or he shall be taking me to task for it, and 'tis certain I'll not be wishing his wrath upon me."

"He has seen me dressed as a boy. 'Tis sure he cares naught how I do cover myself."

Aerid thought the maid would faint, so quickly did the color drain from her face. "While he may have seen you dressed...less than pleasingly and said naught, 'tis a prince he be, and such as he, 'tis sure, desire seeing their women dressed in such manner as to display their beauty."

Aerid plucked at the undergarment lying on the back

of the chair, dropping it when the material snagged on her fingertips. "I do fear I have no such beauty."

Estra sighed. "To be in the protection of a Prince is to be beautiful." Laying down the gown, she picked up the shift. With expert hands, she bunched the material and slipped the exposed openings over Aerid's head and arms, dressing her as one might dress a child. "He has chosen you, mistress, from all others. It does follow, then, that 'tis beautiful you be."

"In his eyes." Aerid stood awkwardly while Estra observed the undergarment's fit.

"Aye, and 'tis his eyes which alone do matter. 'Tis prudent to please them, do you not agree?"

"I would prefer a plainer gown."

Estra lifted the gown over Aerid's head. "Do but wear this and see what he does say."

CHAPTER TWENTY-THREE

Naed brushed a pair of gnats from the ledger page. The Eidvondin grain clerk's script was hard enough to read without the interference of insects. Or of heat. The oak tree's shade still surrounded the table and chair he had brought from the granary, but mid-afternoon sun burned between motionless leaves and flecked the ledger lying open under his hands. Wishing for a breeze, he watched three heavily laden wagons emerge from the trees lining the Alaris road.

"Grodar," he told the man lounging against the roots of the oak, "tally their load. Keep them aside till I have entered it. Theirs is new grain, and I would send the stored grain first."

"Master Borth could use the wagons," Banir said from his seat on the grass. He ran his thumb along the knife blade he had been sharpening. "There be two bins empty. 'Twould be easy enough to fill them afresh."

"See to it, Grodar. And fetch me the count." When the Tolemak mounted, Naed turned his attention to a wagon groaning through deep ruts on the Eidvondin road.

Morys rode past the struggling oxen and drew rein under the oak. "Forty-three baskets of oats and twenty-one of rye," he announced as the wagon lurched onto the Vinvinnysee road.

With a careful stroke of the quill, Naed deducted forty-three baskets of oats. He blew gently on the ink to dry it, then turned the page. Finding the column for rye, he reduced the total by twenty-one. "Tell Borth to load no more rye. Oats and wheat in the next wagons."

"Aye, sir." Morys turned his horse and cantered back along the road to Eidvondin.

Naed plucked a gnat from the half-dry ink and flicked the struggling insect away.

Beside him Banir yawned, then pushed himself to his feet. "The Prince," he said, nodding toward riders who reined their horses aside to let the grain wagon pass.

The Prince rode into the oak's shade and halted his horse. He surveyed the traffic at the crossroads, then turned to Naed and smiled. "The first wagons are halfway to the city. You're moving them much faster than I expected."

"Master Borth and his men load them quickly, m'lord."

"Under your direction, of course." While Naed flushed, he asked, "What new task have you set yourself to?"

"The tally, m'lord."

"Ah, yes. D'nalians and numbers. Your talents continue to please me, my friend." Swinging out of the saddle, the Prince addressed Banir, "Take my men and keep count while my Second and I talk." While Banir mounted and rode up the road with his escort, Naed offered the Prince the chair, but he walked to the tree's trunk and hooked an arm over the lowest branch. "You've no doubt heard about Guard Master Gaelwynn."

Now he knew why the Prince had come from the city to see him. And it had naught to do with grain. He bent to flick a dragonfly from the quill. "Aye, m'lord."

"And?"

Krenin must have spoken to the Prince already. Naed wondered what the Tolemak had said, although he could guess the shape of it.

"You know I gave him the Lancer's sword."

"Aye, m'lord."

"Still no comment?"

Picking up the quill, Naed stroked the feather. What was there to say? The deed had been done. However, if the man insisted... "I thought it rather soon."

"Perhaps." Prince Arn pushed away from the tree. He withdrew the quill from the young man's fingers. "But if we're to build a new unity, 'tis necessary to make changes now, before the old ways have a chance to return." He tossed the quill on the table.

"Do you trust him, m'lord?"

"As much as I trust you." The Prince smiled and his eyes were warm. "I want you to work with him. You know my mind. You know my goals. You even know ciphers.

With you as steward of the realm, they'll not dare cheat us of our share of the trade."

"Steward?"

"I'll give you men and the authority to support yourself and them with a portion of the gold you collect. You'll protect the traders—with Gaelwynn's help, of course—until the rest of Adanak comes under our control—a year or two, I should think."

Naed's mind reeled. He would have command. He would have gold. He could find Aerid, wed her, and give her the protection of his position. And she could yet live among her own people. His heart hammered against his ribs. "M'lord, this is an honor!"

Prince Arn smiled. "Continue to serve me well, and I'll continue to reward you. Can you work with Gaelwynn?"

"Gladly, my lord!"

"Give me your hand on it, then."

****

Aerid walked carefully, easing herself around the room's furniture lest the gown catch on an edge and tear. The lace seemed as fragile as frost-weave and she hesitated to let it even brush against her hands. How did women who wore such finery live, she wondered as she cautiously wiggled her toes in brocaded slippers. Afraid to sit, she wandered again out on the balcony and stood staring at the courtyard below.

The scene had not changed despite countless viewings. The half-dry pond wore rings of white shading into green. A lily blossom floated amid several pads. Thirsty trees and withered flowers lined stone paths where no one walked. Bushes with yellowing leaves sheltered benches no one occupied. A small, quiet, forgotten garden, Aerid thought—until the image of another garden invaded her vision, a garden shrouded in night and the perfume of honeysuckle.

Aerid squeezed her eyes shut, remembering the tiny courtyard behind the Golden Horse. Leumas had kissed her there and vowed to wed her. Later, he and Avika slept there, on the ground where the vegetables had grown, while the wounded took the rooms and filled the steps and lined the walls and bled on the tables and...died.

Tears trickled down Aerid's cheek. They slipped into the corner of her mouth and ran along her lower lip, salting it. Raising her hand, she wiped the back of it across her cheek. Something scratched her skin. She drew back, stared at her hand, and saw lace.

How long she stared, she did not know, but with each moment the beat of her blood intensified until her heart shook her chest wall and throbbed so against her throat she could barely breathe. *Here do I stand, dressed in lace and fine slippers with food and wine to spare while others have naught.* Closing her eyes, Aerid let shame burn across her face.

The sound of the door latch brought her spinning about.

Estra bustled into the chamber. "Some refreshment, mistress," she said, setting a pitcher and cup on the table.

Aerid's fingers powdered the balcony mortar. "Estra, tell me—how goes it in the city? Be there many ill and wounded?"

Wiping her hands on her apron, the maid stood as if considering her reply, then bent and smoothed wrinkles from the tablecloth. "Mistress, 'tis naught to concern you."

"My healer's oath does make it my concern. Now, I pray you, tell me true—how goes it in the city?"

The woman's glance flicked over her. "There-there be many ill and wounded, mistress. Guard Master Gaelwynn does all he can to see to their care, but..."

"Do the Tolemak healers assist him?"

"Now and then, 'tis like, but they do have their own to tend."

Aerid returned to the balcony and surveyed the limited view. Since the city had fallen, she had seen no more of it than this room, this courtyard, these few palace roofs. 'Twas peaceful here, and luxurious. She had known passion here in the arms of the man who spoke words of love to her. But the peace was only an illusion, and the luxury a prize of war. Only the passion was real, she thought as she clung to the balcony stone. Yet she knew with a contracting heart 'twas no certainty even in love unless it could survive beyond these walls—outside, where she was an Adanak healer and Arn a Tolemak prince.

Particles of stone bit into Aerid's palm, their sting a portent of what lay outside. For a moment, she hesitated. 'Twould be so easy to stay, to forget her calling and ignore what she could not see for a few more hours, a few more days—to keep the world at bay as long as possible. But 'twas already too late; she knew, and she could not turn back.

In the confusion of her escape attempt, she had left her pouch behind. It should still be at the Golden Horse— if the inn yet stood. "I must be leaving the palace for a while. Will you aid me?"

"You cannot—the Prince—Mistress, what of the Prince?"

"I shall be returning before he arrives this eve." Crossing to the door, Aerid opened it a crack. Two armed Tolemaks, backs to her, knelt to a game of dremel beads. She eased the door closed. "Know you their orders? Will they be letting me pass?"

Estra wrung her hands. "Mistress, I beg you. Tis certain they will not."

"But they will be letting you." Aerid swept around Estra, considering first the bed curtains, then rejecting them for a blue woolen blanket draped over the foot. "This will do as a cloak," she said, arranging it over her head and shoulders.

"Mistress..."

"Distract the guards. Drop this." She scooped from the table the tray Estra had brought and placed it in the woman's hands. "While they do assist you, I shall be slipping out to wait for you in the next corridor." She pushed the maid toward the door. "Then you may be showing me the way to the palace gate."

"Mistress, no..."

"I am a healer," Aerid said, her voice firm. "I must serve."

****

'Twas surprisingly easy to leave the palace. Even though she passed under the very noses of the Tolemak guards, none appeared interested in a solitary female. Still, to be safe, Aerid fell into step behind a pair of women and three children.

The buxom woman scowled at the meager sack she

269

carried. "A measure each—hardly enough for hearth cakes."

"Master Gaelwynn says 'twill be more tomorrow after the wagons come."

"Gaelwynn! 'Tis he who kissed the *mortraeder*'s sword!"

"To be saving us all." The second woman picked up the smallest child of the three clinging to her skirt. "My husband comes home tonight because he follows Gaelwynn. Aye, and yours would, too, if he would so swear."

"Cowards!" The buxom woman spat on the cobblestones. "He would rather die."

The second woman stopped so abruptly Aerid almost collided with her. A tear ran down the woman's face, but she did not wipe it away. "Too many already have." Clasping the hand of her oldest child, she straightened her shoulders and crossed to the other side of the street.

The buxom woman eyed Aerid—and the lace peeking from under her cloak—before her eyes narrowed. Muttering, "Palace trollop!" she spat toward Aerid's feet.

Face hot, Aerid backed away. She clutched the make-shift cloak more tightly around her gown and wished she had thought to switch clothes with Estra before rushing into the city. Still—she glanced at the palace roofs now streets away—she had come this far. Gathering her skirts, she ran after the woman with children. "Wait! Know you the Golden Horse? Stands it still?"

The woman halted. Her gaze ran the length of Aerid's garments.

Lest she be spat at again, Aerid backed away. "I be no trollop, but 'tis glad I would be of an answer."

"You cannot be going by the square." The woman looked up the street, saw the buxom woman still watched them, and continued in a lowered voice, "There be soldiers there. 'Twill be safer to pass by the cobbler's shop."

"My thanks." Aerid turned to leave, but the woman caught at her cloak.

"Guard Master Gaelwynn," she whispered, "what he does be for the best, aye?"

How could she answer when she only dimly understood what the man had done? Still, if he supported

Arn... "Aye," she said with all the confidence as she could muster. "All will be well." If it was not, she vowed to do what she could to make it so.

Alone moments later, she realized much was already well within the city. Far less rubble cluttered the main street than she expected. Carts of broken stone followed loads of mortar as crews of soldiers patched house after house. Here and there, a shop stood open. But here and there, too, prisoners labored and red stained the stones. Aerid shivered, knowing while the color would fade, the mark would linger as long as men remembered who had died there and why.

When she stepped from the passage beside the cobbler's shop and saw the Golden Horse, she paused while her heartbeat settled. The inn's door was unhinged and fire had scorched the stones below the left window, but its sign still swayed gently above the cobblestones. That it was still being used to treat the wounded, she knew by the smells invading her nostrils as she climbed the stoop.

First were the pungent odors of healing herbs. Underlying this was the lingering scent of blood. Finally, 'twas a subtler smell, one perceived rather than sniffed, but one Aerid knew all too well. It emanated from stoop-shouldered men with vacant eyes and women who sat in corners and stared at naught—all waiting for a death that had not claimed them outright. For a death, Aerid thought with a rush of anger, that was unnecessary and would flee if they only would fight it.

She knelt beside the nearest man, a soldier with a chest wound. "Have you a wife?" she asked, tucking the lace safely inside her sleeves before she examined his wound.

His listless nod suggested he had not noted her garments. "Children?" Another nod. "In two days they may bear you home and tend to you there."

His gaze shot to her face. "To die!" he wheezed.

Aerid stood. "To live, if you do so desire."

"What be there to live for? The Tolemak do hold the city."

"Then live among them," she said, removing the make-shift cloak from her shoulders and folding it. "Or do

271

you fear to try?"

Dots of color appeared on the man's cheeks, but he said nothing.

Aerid turned before the sight of her trembling hands could undo the effect of her words.

"A true healer," said a stranger's voice, "does heal with words as well as touch."

At the long table in the common room sat a gray-haired man, right arm bound to his chest. He was so thin as to be naught but bone and sinew, but his expression, on a hawk-beaked face, was gentle. Aerid approached him. "Require you aid?"

He smiled. "I have been seen to, *maidelyn*, but there be many others who would benefit from your words—and your touch." Before Aerid was aware of it, he had taken her hand in his free one and bowed over it. "Gaelwynn, at your service."

She flushed. "'Tis Aerid I be."

"Of Master Sima's court?"

She flushed again, realizing he had noted her gown. "I—no. These be borrowed." She freed her hand and cast about the room for Mairim. 'Twas too much to explain now and to this stranger when she had come only for her pouch and to be of service.

Voices sounded from the kitchen. Mairim emerged, bearing an armful of binding cloths. Seeing Aerid, she dropped the cloths on the table and opened her arms. Aerid rushed into her embrace. "I did think you dead, or lost," Mairim said after a moment.

"I was," Aerid murmured, thinking of the firelit gate, the spectral warriors, the terror of the gully, "but no longer." Arn had found her and she was his now.

Mairim held her at arm's length. "These clothes...how came you by them?"

"I—later." Aerid stepped free of the gentle hands. "Have you yet my pouch? 'Tis much to be done and I would be about it now that I may."

****

By late afternoon Aerid stretched tired back muscles. She looked out the window at shadows advancing toward the stoop and sighed.

"We have a little flour." Mairim offered a hearth

cake. "Tomorrow 'twill be more."

Aerid's first inclination was to refuse. Mairim and the child growing within her needed the nourishment, but Mairim's expression implored her to accept. "So I have heard," she said, dividing the cake and handing half back. "Foderor, be he well?"

Mairim looked at the portion, then brought it to her lips. "Aye. Master Gaelwynn did come to tell me the Tolemak be releasing him on the morrow. 'Tis a need for the services of an alehouse now there be so many soldiers within the gates." She smiled. There were dusky circles under her eyes, Aerid noted, and on her hands tiny blue and red veins crisscrossed under parchment-thin skin. But her eyes were still bright, and they looked into Aerid. "Where have you been these several days?"

Aerid focused her gaze on the hearth cake in her hands. "I-I have been well cared for." She broke off a piece of cake, ate it, but tasted nothing.

Dusting the sill, Mairim sat on its sun-warmed surface. "Guard Master Gaelwynn tells us the *mortraeders* may not be taking our women. There be grumbling, he says, but they obey their masters." She plucked crumbs from her apron and ate them. "'Tis talk the Prince has a woman, and that he does keep her at the palace."

The hearth cake broke between Aerid's fingers. "What else do they say?"

"That she be no stranger to him and—" gentle fingers closed over her hand "—he did rescue her."

Aerid's shoulders shook. Her chin dropped to her chest and her eyes burned shut. "I did care for Leumas. Truly, I did." Her fingers dug into Mairim's. "I would have wed him, followed him happily wherever he would go if only…"

"If only 'twere not another."

"Months ago," she said, and let the story, so long pent inside of her, pour out.

Mairim listened without a word. When Aerid finished, the innkeeper's wife sat smoothing her hands across her swollen womb.

"I—he being Tolemak does distress you."

"'Tis cause enough for concern, aye. However—"

"He does not see me as Adanak. He sees me as a woman. And I do see him as a man."

Mairim smiled and patted her abdomen. "Indeed, and I understand thereby lies a great attraction."

Aerid flushed.

Mairim sighed, and the humor vanished from her face. "No, 'tis his being a prince that does concern me."

"Such difference matters naught to him. He has said—"

Raising her hand, Mairim tucked a wayward lock of hair behind Aerid's ear. "He has said many things because 'tis new you be to him. Later, however..."

Aerid's stomach balled into a knot. These were not new fears, but it hurt to hear them voiced by another. She laced her fingers together. "He has risked much for me already. He will not play me false."

"Mayhap he has a wife. Men, such as they be, oft tell us not all that they should."

A wife. The words stung like knives flung at her heart, yet Aerid knew she should have expected them. He was a Prince. A man of power and position. Daughters of noblemen would vie to be wife of such a man. Mayhap one of them had succeeded.

Would it matter if one had? Would she love him any less? She had not dreamed of marriage, only passion and the ecstasy his touch promised. Leumas had loved her, but Leumas was dead, taken before her love for him could ripen—if it could ever have become what she felt for the man who had so often risked his life for her. Arn was here, now. He offered love, tenderness, satisfaction of the need that had ached so long in both of them. What did it matter if he could not wed her? She had already chosen to lie with him. It did not matter if he would stay with her a month, a week, or even a day. She would have him, now, before she lost him forever. And she would treasure these moments in her heart.

"Leumas died. I will not be losing love again. For as long as love shall last, I shall live with the man I do love."

Mairim sighed. Leaning forward, she touched Aerid's cheek with a dry, cool hand. "Do what you must, but know you be ever welcome here."

Aerid closed her eyes. Bending forward, she rested

her forehead on Mairim's shoulder. The innkeeper's wife stroked gently over her hair as they sat together in the open window, warmed by the lowering sun.

****

His men were lighting the torches along the corridors when Arn returned to the hilltop palace. He had enjoyed the freedom of the forest and the meadows after the confined spaces of Vinvinnysee, but the return trip seemed interminable. In the gathering dusk, he rode faster than he should have, outdistancing all but the fleetest of his escort.

Once away from the bustle of the courtyard, Arn forced himself to listen to the restored knell of the bells. Aerid had been waiting all day. She could wait a moment longer while he mastered himself. It would not do to burst into the chamber, seize her, and bear her to bed, though he had thought of nothing else for hours. Even now, when he closed his eyes, he could feel the heat of her thighs surrounding his, smell the fragrance of her skin, taste—

With a groan, Arn flung himself into the corridor. *She's bewitched me, but Demon take me if I care!*

CHAPTER TWENTY-FOUR

"Where is she?" Arn bellowed. "By the Demon, you'll tell me more this time than 'in the city!' That I can guess for myself!"

Tears flooded down the Adanak maid's cheeks. "M-m'lord, she did say no more. Only that she was a healer and-and must serve."

A healer. The fear, the panic that had leaped screaming at Arn moments ago from the silence of an empty room, retreated. Aerid had not fled from him. He would find her and bring her back. And when he did, he would see she never left him again.

He opened his hand and the sobbing maid collapsed into a heap at his feet. "Keep her here," he said to the white-faced soldiers standing stiffly at either side of the door. "I'll deal with the two of you later."

****

"'Tis late. I must be returning." Aerid tied a string around the neck of a cloth pouch, then slipped the bundle into her bag.

Mairim handed her three more such pouches. "I fear I have used much of your store."

Aerid packed the pouches around a long, narrow root sack. "I shall ask the Tolemak healers for more." Closing the leather bag, she slipped the strap over her shoulder. The familiar presence of the bag on her hip and the gathering dusk made her think of the forest around Druemarwin and collecting herbs there in the spring. Had it been mere months earlier? She touched Mairim's hand. "I shall return as soon as I may."

"And I shall be glad of it."

****

Arn flung open the door to Gaelwynn's chamber. "Show me where your healers practice in the city."

Gaelwynn laid aside the parchment he had been studying. "My lord, of course."

"Now!"

Despite his useless arm, Gaelwynn caught up to Arn at the top of the courtyard steps. "My lord, if I may be so bold, be it a woman you seek?"

Arn's hand went for Gaelwynn's collar, but he forced it to halt midway to its target. "I won't ask how you know that, but I expect you to tell me why you're asking."

The mismatched eyes seemed to take Arn's measure, but there was no scorn in the judgment rendered. "If she be modest, slender, dark of hair, and gifted in the healing arts, 'twas my pleasure to be meeting her this afternoon."

"Where?"

"Not far." Gaelwynn gestured toward the horses waiting for them in the courtyard. "Allow me to show you the way."

****

Stepping out of the passageway, Aerid turned onto the main street. On the hill, she could see the palace walls rose-tinged in the diminishing light. She stood, torn between what lay behind and what lay ahead. It did not seem right to leave the service of the ill for the pleasure she knew awaited in Arn's arms.

She sighed. The motion rubbed a bodice seam across her nipple. The tingle radiating through her breast brought the memory of Arn's teeth and tongue teasing, tasting, and... Aerid closed her eyes and let desire wash over her. 'Twas not only that she was needed by others, but also she herself had needs. Turning, she set her gaze on the palace and hurried toward it.

Around the next corner, a cluster of mounted men filled the narrow street. Intent on her progress, she veered toward the nearest stoop to slip behind them as they passed. A sudden shout jerked her feet to a stop. 'Twas an order, certainly, but not a word. More of a roar, it sucked the strength from her legs. She turned, knees shaking.

A horse skidded to a halt, hooves striking sparks at her feet while a man sprang from the animal's back. Hands clamped about her arms, hands like iron manacles. In the evening dimness, the planes of Arn's face were like granite walls, his eyes black caves. She could not see his gaze, but she felt it sear her from head to foot. Trembling, she managed, "I-I was on my way back."

"Indeed," he said, too softly. With a sweep of his arms, he lifted her upon his horse.

Aerid clutched at the stallion's mane, but Arn was behind her in an instant, his arm banded about her waist. He wheeled the stallion, and Aerid caught a glimpse of a sling and a thin, leathery face.

"My thanks," Arn said, his voice as tight as the rein he held on his stallion.

Guard Master Gaelwynn met Aerid's gaze briefly, then, with a bittersweet smile, he inclined his head. "Your servant."

The stallion sprang forward at the release of its head. Aerid fell against Arn's chest. His arm righted her, but her fingers still dug into his sleeve. The buildings flew by, a blur of muted color and shadow. She had ridden this fast once before, held like this in a saddle at night. They had been in flight then. 'Twas not now the same. There were no enemy soldiers, it was not midnight, and there was no need for escape—or was there?

Aerid caught one last glimpse of the city before the palace walls blocked it from view. An image of the garden below her balcony flashed by. Then it, too, was gone as the stallion sat back on its haunches. One moment Arn held her securely in the saddle; the next he was striding up the palace steps carrying her in his arms. Soldiers fell back deferentially, but Aerid felt every man's gaze touch her. She flushed, loosening her hold on Arn's neck. "I can walk."

With no break in stride, he shouldered open the door at the top of the steps. "Perhaps you can," he said, kicking the door shut behind them.

"I was returning when we did meet," she said as a guard shoved open the door to their chamber, then closed it quickly behind them.

"So you said." Arn set her on her feet in the room.

"Estra be not to blame. I did intend to return afore you."

"So she said."

She risked a look at him. In the candlelight, his face looked rough-chiseled, as if from some ancient, adamantine stone. "She did beg me not to go."

"A clever maid." Arn stepped closer.

Aerid swayed as a wave of heat crashed into her. It swept around her, closing behind her so she was contained within it. She could breathe, but not deeply, and her heart hammered against her ribs. Arn stood only a breath away, his eyes pinpoints of candlelight under a black slash of brow. A shiver ran up her spine as she realized this power, this force holding her helpless in its invisible grip emanated from him, from the emotions raging within him under the stony exterior. She shivered again as his hand circled her throat, the tremor in his touch telling her how fragile the shell of his control was.

"More clever than you." He tilted her head, forcing her to look into his eyes. "Why did you do it?"

She swallowed, and his fingers flexed with the movement. "I was—I was needed."

"Needed!" Arn choked. "*I* need you!" His free hand seized the make-shift cloak and ripped it from her shoulders. He flung off her healer's pouch, then hauled her against his body. "Demon take me," he groaned as he thrust his hand into her hair, "but I need you!" His mouth came down on hers, his tongue invading her mouth, seeking, thrusting, possessing every corner, every soft fold until, robbed of breath, she thought he would devour her soul.

Colors danced behind Aerid's eyes. His arm was like an iron band around her ribs, crushing her against his chest armor. He had shoved up her skirts and his fingers dug into her flesh, searching, demanding, taking, hurting—

Trapped against his mouth, her whimper was no more than a bubble of sound.

Arn froze, his fingers still gripping her flesh. When she shuddered, he released her lips, but his breath rushed hot over her face. "Aerid..."

Eyes closed, she gulped in air. His arm about her back trembled. At the sensation, she flushed, suddenly hot, uncomfortable, not at all sure why. "Please, I—"

"Aerid...!" It was a groan this time, ripped from his throat. "Aerid, I—forgive me!" Dropping to his knees, he flung his arms around her hips.

Aerid staggered, unbalanced by his embrace. She

should have been able to breathe now her upper body was free, but somehow she could draw in little air. That this man should kneel, and before her, was unnerving enough. To have his arms fastened around her hips and his face buried in her skirts was more than she could bear. She touched his shoulder. "Arn, please..."

His shudder shook them both. "I don't want to hurt you—by the Demon, you know I don't!—but when you weren't here, I—"

She threaded fingers into his hair, seeking to soothe, to comfort, understanding her actions—though she could scarce believe it possible—had frightened him. "I should have returned sooner. I shall not stay so long tomor—"

He rose, and his fingers dug into her shoulders. "You won't go again."

Was it possible? Had he denied her? Aye, he was angry she had gone without leaving word. Being late in returning hurt him further, but he could not mean to keep her from her duties. "My skills be needed."

Cupping her cheek in his palm, Arn gazed at her, his eyes the indistinct gray of dusk. "*I* need you." He trailed his fingers down her throat, along the lace of her collar and into the exposed hollow between her breasts. "I want you, here, with me."

Aerid quivered as he slipped two fingers under the lace collar. She closed her eyes, waiting, while they drifted toward the nipple already aching for their touch. "I am a healer. I must—I must serve."

His fingers spread, then descended, one on each side of her breast. Slowly, they closed. The moment of contact sent a jolt through her loins. She would have fallen, but for his hand spread on the small of her back. "You serve me. Isn't that enough?"

Her heart throbbed. Her fingers dug into his arms. Sensations rippled through her stomach, coiling and uncoiling, wreaking havoc with her reason. "Arn..."

He pushed her arms behind her back, imprisoning her wrists in one hand. With the other, he pulled the gown from her shoulders. Dress and shift slithered to her hips. His indrawn breath was a hiss, his shudder an echo of hers. "Tell me," he said as his thumb and finger grasped a nipple and tugged gently at it, "that you're mine."

Aerid's knees shook. She writhed in his arms. "Arn..."

His grip tightened. "Tell me," he said, fingers teasing the other nipple, then splaying on her abdomen. "Say," he breathed against her throat, "that you belong to me." His hand slid under the gown and over the mound at the juncture of her thighs.

Her legs turned to water. "I-I love you," Aerid panted, feverish with the desire jolting through her at each stroke of his fingers. She arched against him, struggling to free her arms.

"Say it again," he rasped, first lifting her, then pressing her down, down into blankets, a bed, her legs pinned apart, her body at the mercy of the exquisite torture his fingers performed.

"I...love you."

Arn's breath rushed across her breasts. "Tell me...that you *belong*...to me." He stretched across her, slick, naked somehow, hot between her thighs.

"I-I belong to you."

He lifted her hips. "Completely."

Aerid quivered, feeling the heat of his nearness, the pressure, knowing with the slightest move, he could fill her, driving deep to satisfy the need forcing her to stretch toward him. "Completely," she panted. "I belong to you...completely."

With an exultant sound, he swooped.

****

Aerid hugged her knees and surveyed the man sprawled on the bed opposite her armchair. Candlelight accentuated the hollow of his back, the length of his thigh, the musculature of his shoulders. He breathed deeply, regularly, his thrust-out arm embracing half the bedding. Under tousled black hair, his forehead was smooth, the creases she had always seen there and about his mouth absent in the relaxation of sleep.

She straightened the hem of her shift and settled deeper into the chair, resisting the urge to lie beside Arn and stroke away any remaining lines. If he should touch her, she would be lost again. Her hand drifted to the healer's pouch at her side, but its substance was too diminished to offer any comfort. Somehow she would have

Helen C. Johannes

to find a way to replenish it.

Heaving a sigh, she stared at the dark terrace windows. When Arn was with her, naught mattered but his touch, his kiss, the warmth of his leg pressed to hers under the table. When he was gone... Aerid sighed again. How could she make him understand she was not accustomed to idleness, that such fine surroundings—

She froze, aware by some means that he no longer slept. She closed her eyes, unnerved by his propensity for coming instantly and silently alert, then turned her head.

He lay propped up by an elbow, unconcerned by his nakedness.

Desire burned through the pit of her stomach, igniting tiny pulsations of fire where his fingers had stroked. She quivered, then pulled her gaze from his body and fixed it on his face.

His brows were a level slash, the eyes beneath glowering at the pouch under her hand. "You said you belonged to me."

"Aye. Completely."

He sat up. "Then why—"

"Because I cannot be complete without it." She hugged the pouch to her chest. "Do I ask you to go without your sword, your knife?"

"Don't be foolish—"

"'Tis a warrior you be. I do not like fighting. The blood you do shed, I staunch. The wounds you do cause, I bind up. Yet, do I ask you to cease fighting, to lay aside your arms, to become...less than whole...for my sake?"

He watched her, his expression dark, a crease deepening between his brows. "What are you saying?"

Aerid's heart raced against the pouch. "You be Arn, warrior Prince of Tolemak, and the man I do love. Should you cease to be Tolemak, or a warrior, you would no longer be...the man I do love."

He rose. She quivered as the wall of heat emanating from his body assaulted her. "Continue."

She opened her arm in a gesture of supplication. "'Tis Aerid I be, *maidelyn* of Adanak, servant, and...healer. Aye, and yours completely—healer and all."

Grasping her shoulders, he pulled her upright, fingers digging into her bones as though probing their strength. He towered over her, expression forbidding, weight of his gaze pressing down on her. She willed her legs to stiffen, to resist the power, the invisible force of his will. One part of her yearned to surrender, to collapse at his feet and be taken up into arms that would restore her with caresses, but another part knew she could not. Not this time.

"Aerid!" he groaned, catching her close. "'Tis dangerous."

A thrill raced through her body. She pressed her lips to his throat. "Then, grant me an escort."

Groaning again, he carried her to the bed. "I want you here, waiting, when I come."

"Gladly." She gave him a delighted smile as he tugged the shift over her head and flung it away. "I shall not overstay again."

Lacing his fingers into hers, Arn pressed her arms down on either side of her head. "I don't like it," he growled, stretching himself over her. "Where I am, you should be."

"Come with me, then," she said, victory making her bold.

Arn shook his head. "When I'm here, I want you like this—serving me." Thrusting her legs apart, he arched upward between them.

She sucked in breath. Another move and he would be inside her—and she could do naught to resist. With half-closed eyes, she watched him in the candlelight. She had won, but at his price. "'Tis a jealous man you be," she breathed.

He leaned over her, cheeks drawn and tight, eyes hooded. "Remember that, *witch*."

Aerid smiled, but his mouth captured her lips.

****

Arn stood in the shadows watching the Golden Horse. From the alley, he could see partway into the open window, enough to see Aerid was well and the men he assigned to her took their duties seriously. Enough to see she was right—her healing skills were needed. The furrow in his brow deepened. He could not deny practicing the healing arts pleased her greatly—and he was loath to deny her any pleasure—but, by the Demon, this request...

Helen C. Johannes

"'Tis an asset she will be to you," Gaelwynn said from the dimness behind him. "She will be winning you many allies."

Arn grunted. He had kissed her goodbye in the morning, but, unwilling to let her out of the protective range of his sword, had followed her. He scanned the street again, squinting against the sunshine.

"No one will be harming her, my lord."

"You have more faith than I in your fellow man." Arn's gaze swept the inn once more and found nothing amiss. Still, it was with great reluctance he turned away. Even though he knew it was her healer's heart that had won his love, it galled him to share even that innocent a part of her with other men.

He snatched his reins from the man who held them and mounted Darkstar. At the action, a memory flashed into his mind, a memory of how Aerid had opened for him the night before, taking him into her so deeply he knew she embraced his very soul. Arn closed his eyes as liquid fire blazed along his veins. She was his, wholly and completely, but he was not fool enough to deny her corresponding claim on him. Nor did he doubt, as he turned Darkstar down the narrow alley and away from the inn, that he would kill, personally and with his bare hands, anyone who dared to come between him and the woman he loved.

****

In Val-Feyridge fortress Erodasi paced. Outside her chamber, Val-Feyridge was abuzz with the news of Arn's victory at Vinvinnysee, but she did not share the inhabitants' excitement. Summer was half gone. Her betrothed would be returning soon, as full of himself as when he went away. And when he did, he would force her to the marriage bed. She clutched her stomach, enduring another wave of nausea. 'Twas the thought of him touching her that made her ill.

The door opened. Dlaniger slipped inside and threw the bolt behind him.

"How did you get in? You know you're not to come here."

"How you greet me, my love." Flinging his cloak onto a chair, he stretched out his hand and grasped her chin.

"'Tis no one to see me. They are all drunk toasting their master's victory. A victory, my love, that could be his last were you to provide me with the letter I requested."

"My father will never see a D'nalian."

He stepped closer. Erodasi searched his face as her mind recorded the deliberation with which his fingers entwined themselves in the hair at the nape of her neck. A wave of nausea swept up her throat, and she closed her eyes against it.

"Sweet, my love, have you been ill these past days?"

"'Tis—'tis only when I think of him—"

Dlaniger's fingers tightened on her hair. "Shh, my sweet, and open your pretty little mind to what you and I have done these past weeks. Many times I have spilled my seed inside your womb. Mayhap it grows there now."

A shiver ran down Erodasi's back. She gripped Dlaniger's belt. "No—"

"'Twould not be so ill a thing, love. You may be betrothed, but you are not yet wed."

"What are you saying?"

His hands skated down her arms. "Provide me with the letter to your father, love, and all will be well."

"He'll kill you."

"Your father or your betrothed?"

"Either. Both."

He laughed. "Mayhap your betrothed, but not your father. He and I have much to offer each other." With his hands, he propelled her toward the bed. "You are mine, are you not, sweet? 'Tis time, then, you stood with me against your husband-to-be."

Erodasi heard all his words, but her mind fastened on the last. If the Prince found her with child, he would be within his rights to kill her. So would her father. She licked her lips. "You'll have to kill him."

Dlaniger pushed her down on the bed and unbuckled his sword. "Sweet, you read my mind." He reached into a pouch at his waist and withdrew two velvet cords.

Erodasi recognized them. It was a game they played on the straw bed in the goat-herder's cottage. "If anyone comes in—"

"I'll kill them, love, just as I shall your betrothed." Drawing his dagger, he slit her gown from neckline to thighs.

Erodasi stared, blood thundering in her ears while he pushed her gown apart and trailed fingers across her breast, over her abdomen, and down to the crinkly hair at the apex of her thighs. This was not the gentle, solicitous lover she was accustomed to. This man smiled at her with a predator's eyes. The knife in his hand glinted in the lamplight.

"Write me the letter, sweet, and I'll employ my blade where 'twill do us both good."

She licked her lips again. He frightened her. He thrilled her. She reached down, took hold of his wrist and pushed his hand against her womanly mound. "What will you do for me if I agree?" She spread her legs, offering his hand access, willing him with her eyes to thrust his fingers inside her.

He complied, sending shock waves through her. "Anything you desire, my sweet."

"Then kill him—" she panted, "for me."

****

Naed paused in the palace corridor and brushed more Adanak dust from his clothes. He was weary, but 'twas a pleasant sensation. Even Krenin's surliness at the west gate had not spoiled his good humor. 'Twas the Prince whose response mattered, and the Prince would surely be pleased he had personally escorted the last of the supply wagons into Vinvinnysee at dusk.

Stifling a yawn, he approached the guarded door at the end of the hall. The muffled sound of a woman's voice, and a sprinkle of laughter, brought him sharply alert. Krenin had told him the Prince had taken a woman, but he had chosen not to believe the tale—then. Now, as he raised his knuckles and knocked, he wondered what kind of woman the Prince would take to his bed—and what kind of woman would laugh with the man who so used her. He hoped, when he heard the latch slide back, the harlot had the decency to hide herself from his view.

"Naed!"

Summer-sky blue eyes locked with his, the profusion of dark hair that swirled about the face in his dreams, curling now about the same but astonished face in the doorway. "Aerid?"

She flung her arms about him. "Oh, Naed! 'Tis alive you be!"

Her hair brushed his face, the familiar scent of tiny purple bellflowers filling his nostrils. He inhaled, and his arms stole around her. Her warmth raced through him and he knew, as he savored the curve of her spine, the indentation of her waist under his palms, she was not a dream. "Of course, I am alive," he murmured into her curls. "Why should you believe otherwise?"

She leaned back in his arms. "I did see you pinned by a Lancer."

Dimly, he recalled some such incident, but unshed tears shone on her lashes, and their sparkle entranced him. "I...he pinned my tunic. A scrape..."

She hugged him again, fiercely, and his capacity for thought evaporated. All that remained was sensation and longing. Aerid was here. She was in his arms.

"Arn, why did you not tell me Naed was alive?"

Naed tried to cling to her, to pull her back as she twisted out of his embrace, but the singular other presence in the room had somehow stolen his limbs' ability to move.

"I forgot you still believed him dead." The Prince stood unsmiling in the center of the chamber, his eyes the gray of ash over smoldering coals. They stared at Naed, into him and through him until Naed's thoughts clarified and he knew why this man and this woman were in this room—together.

A pulse pounded at Naed's temple. His jaw tightened. He tried to breathe, but his chest armor had somehow shrunk around his ribs. Sweat trickled between his shoulder blades. "I would speak with you, m'lord. Alone."

Out of the corner of his eye, Naed saw Aerid's brow pucker as she looked from one man to the other. She clung to his sleeve but a wall had sprung up between them. He imagined her in a tower, as distant from him as Druemarwin, and as irretrievable. With a deliberate step backward, he pulled his tunic from her grasp and strode out.

In the corridor, around the corner from the candlelit doorway, he leaned against the stone and panted. He sought dimness, coolness, escape, but these walls radiated heat. They echoed with the beat of his heart. With footsteps.

Naed swung on the man who followed him. "You—you arrogant, grasping Tolemak bastard! You take for yourself whatever comes within your reach!"

"You had ample opportunities to win her at Druemarwin. Aerid is mine now."

"As your mistress, you—you—adulterer!" His fists clenched.

"What could you have offered her that I cannot? Captain of the Guard's quarters in some rat-infested fortress on D'nalee's frontier? A straw bed and stone floors, new shoes twice a year, a goose when your master deems it appropriate! What could you possibly have offered her that I can't surpass?"

Each of the words, the taunts, struck like separate, stinging blows. They were all true, but they were not enough. Not nearly enough. "What could I have offered her? Why, I would have *wed* her!"

Color drained from the Prince's face, leaving the scar a stark white cord.

Scenting blood, Naed strove to wound again, to cut deeper this time, to slice straight to the heart, but the Prince recovered before he could.

"Oh, aye, you may have wed her—if you'd dared to ask when you had the chance! And 'tis like she'd have agreed—then. But trust me, she'd soon weary of that pedestal your fine D'nalian prudishness would put her on, and 'twould be to me she'd turn—just as she has now. 'Tis a *man* she wants—one who knows how to bed a woman. Aye, a *woman! I* know how to make her come—what she likes, what she wants—"

Blood gushed into Naed's face. His breathing roared in the narrow passage. At the fringe of his vision, his sword sprang into his hands. He stepped forward, raising it to strike the man who could utter such lewdness, such obscenity, such gross and abominable slander!

That man back-stepped, hands flexed at his sides—empty hands. No scabbard hung at his hip, no knife sheath. "Aye," the Prince acknowledged his vulnerability, "'tis your chance. Your *only* chance."

Naed trembled. He had only to roll his shoulder,

unbend his elbow, and let his wrist guide the weapon home—a series of small motions, all so natural the effort required no thought. Sweat streamed down his temples. The blood throbbing in his ears screamed at him to swing, to *strike now!* It would be so easy...

CHAPTER TWENTY-FIVE

Jaw clenched, Arn stared down an empty corridor and castigated himself. Oh, aye, he had managed *that* moment with finesse and skill. Why had he not anticipated Naed's return and met him elsewhere? He could have guessed the young man would react badly, and he should have planned for it—would have planned for it—but he knew very well why he had not.

Silently, he cursed himself for letting one part of his life command altogether too much of his attention. Now he would have to deal with the mess his blindness had failed to avert, the mess he could have minimized if he had not resorted in kind to Naed's insults. Demon-be-damned, but he should have known better than to rub the D'nalian's nose in it—however much he may have relished flaunting his claim to Aerid and destroying Naed's hopes.

But Arn knew why he had relished that too, remembering Aerid's look of delight when she came face-to-face with the man she thought dead. By the Demon, if he and Naed had both been armed, this might now have been settled—and in a much different way! Seething again, Arn looked down the dark corridor and wondered if *that* way might not have been better.

****

Aerid stared at the open chamber door, at the darkness beyond the candlelight puddled on the floor. Naed had disappeared into that darkness, and Arn after him.

Naed was alive. She had felt him as flesh and blood in her arms. He had spoken. The red-brown hair, shaggier than she remembered it, hung as ever over his brows. He looked fit, strong, astonished, delighted, and then...

She hugged her arms. Something Arn had said? She had said? One moment she held Naed's sleeve in her grasp; the next moment a mountain jutted up between them and she could no more reach him than she could reach the peaks of Adanak.

Voices sounded in the corridor. Angry voices. The hair on the back of Aerid's neck prickled. She rushed forward, saw the attention of the guards fixed on the corner to the left, and ran headlong toward it. "Arn!" she called. "Naed!"

Arn's shadow, looming across the passageway, brought her to a halt. "He's gone." He stepped between her and the darkness beyond. "Leave him."

"But—"

His fingers clamped around her arm. Aerid froze, sensing danger in the grip. She raised her gaze, noting how the cords of his throat strained at the skin covering them. He walked her to their chamber, closed the door behind them, and turned her to face him. "Just what is he to you that you would run after him?"

A shiver ran along Aerid's spine. Arn's power surrounded her, pressed in on her, pinned her to the square of stone before him. Somehow, her future, their love—everything—depended on her response. She licked her lips, wanting to reassure him but wondering what it was he feared. "A friend—a friend who has risked his life for me."

Arn's fingers flexed on her arm. "Nothing more?"

What more could there be? Unless... Her mind flashed to the night Arn had discovered her identity. Did she dream it, or had he called Naed her *lover*? 'Twas much that was yet muddled in her mind about the night of the Lancers' attack, but this memory came back with crystalline clarity. *Sisters Three!* How could he yet be so mistaken?

Touching the birthstone at her throat, Aerid gathered her courage. Arn's gaze, with all the power of his will behind it, ignited frissons along her nerves, but she lifted her chin and met his eyes without flinching. "I think there be much *you* should be telling me ere I be answering a question that, to my way of thinking, has been answered many times in this room—in this bed—and much to your satisfaction."

A dull flush darkened Arn's skin, making the scar stand out white and knotted. He enclosed her arms with both hands, but the pressure of his grip eased.

Aerid watched him, waiting while he reined in his fury and considered her words. Now she had seen beneath that fearsome exterior, she wondered how she could have thought him cold and calculating, a heartless warrior. She had seen him naked, had glimpsed his soul and begun to know the passions that compelled him—the supreme self-confidence that, while propelling him fearlessly into battle, drove him to browbeat, cajole, outwit or blatantly manipulate anyone within the range of his power. Had he not unleashed the considerable force of his persuasion on her? She had resisted, but barely, and only because he understood he could not deny her healer's calling and keep her love. Aerid wondered how Naed had fared, suspecting 'twas not well.

"When did you come to know Naed yet lived?"

Opening his fingers, he skated his hands up and down her arms. "The next day. I told him you were safely gone." He glanced down, met her eyes. "I thought you were—then."

She remembered his rage at discovering her identity, and for reasons she could not yet understand, his frustration at having to personally take her across the river to freedom. He had wanted her then, just as she had wanted him, but both of them had turned away from that need. She reached out and closed her hands at his waist, finding the tunic damp under her fingers. "Tell me, and tell me true, did you truly forget I thought Naed dead?"

"Aye." He wrapped a lock of her hair around his finger. "But I can't say, if I had remembered, I would have told you. My mind was occupied with other, more pressing thoughts. As well you know."

A smile ghosted across his lips, the movement so fleeting Aerid might have imagined it but for the jolt of awareness raising the fine hairs on her body. He had only to look at her and her body played like an instrument in the hands of its master. Still, she resisted his seductive power. "When 'tis to me you come, you bring naught of your army's business, yet 'twas to this chamber Naed came. What has passed between you and Naed that he would come to see you here?"

Shadows flickered in his eyes. "Naed made himself a hero; I made him my Second. 'Tis sure the bloody fool's done everything I asked of him—and better than I anticipated!"

This was news. Naed...in a position of authority among those who typically shunned D'nalians? 'Twas more than she could absorb just now, especially when, under her palms, Arn's torso had gone rigid. She made tiny circling motions with her thumbs, trying to soothe his tension. "And...now? You did quarrel?"

He fingered her hair, rubbing a curl between his thumb and fingers as if testing its texture, studying it as if it held secrets he was loath to reveal. Finally, he inhaled deeply and, pulling her a step closer, trailed his knuckles along her cheek. "Aerid, tell me and tell me true, if—if you had known he was alive, would you still be here...with me...now?"

Aerid shivered, hearing the need, the fear he tried to keep from his voice. She had seen it yester eve when he had snatched her from a Vinvinnysee street, terrified he had lost her. "Aye," she said, stepping hip-to-hip, letting him know by the pressure of her body against his, the caress of her arms sliding up to grip his shoulders, that she understood what he asked. "'Tis naught could change what is between us, what has been between us since Druemarwin. I love you."

A look of pain swept across Arn's features. "I haven't lied to you and I swear I won't but...Naed worships you, even if you didn't realize it, and I've made you a whore in his eyes."

Motionless, she absorbed his words. They had fallen on her like icy water, but the shock was not entirely unexpected. Had not Mairim implied as much? Had not she herself spent hours considering her choices? Unblinking, Aerid searched his face, the stricken eyes that nonetheless met hers, willing to accept whatever recriminations she might hurl at him.

She was not sure Naed felt as Arn thought he did. He was D'nalian, after all, and a lord's nephew. However kind and generous, Naed nonetheless harbored the prejudices of his kind. He could not possibly consider her, an Adanak and a servant, as worthy of aught more than friendship. But she did agree Naed might now consider her a pariah, both for having lost her virtue and for having done so with a man clearly her enemy. Nevertheless, if she had the opportunity, she would try to make him understand why she had made the choices she had, just as she would do now for the man who stood before her.

Sighing, she leaned into Arn, nestling her cheek over his heart. "Though 'tis most persuasive you may be, 'twas my free choice to lie with you, knowing the consequences. I have no regrets, my love."

"Aerid!" he groaned, crushing her in his embrace. "I don't deserve you. Demon knows, I don't, but I love you!" Seizing her hands, he pressed a kiss to each palm, then scooped her into his arms. "We'll eat first," he said, his voice ragged.

She slanted a look at him from under her lashes. Arn needed her now. Later, she could satisfy her concerns about Naed. "'Twould not distress me to wait a little, for food."

He closed his eyes, and his heart banged against her side. "Sisters, woman!"

****

Naed did not know when he began to run. Perhaps down that last dim corridor where echoing voices pursued him. He lost them, but now his chest ached and he could not draw breath.

A vision of Aerid in the Prince's arms flew at him from a darkened doorway. He swerved, but it sped after him, blurring, shifting, metamorphosing into a scene he had stumbled upon in the stable at Druemarwin— Yormoc, half-naked, riding the kitchen maid Elthred. Naed jerked to a halt as the vision cut in front of him, filled the corridor, and altered once more. This time it was the Prince who rode, pumping and driving, and Aerid who lay beneath him, face contorted, grunting and moaning like an animal.

Horrified, Naed blundered into the wall. The stone bit into his palms, but he barely felt it. He wanted to vomit, to turn himself inside out, to reach into his soul and rip out the vision that tormented him even behind clenched-shut eyes. Gasping for air, he ran. He would run until he outdistanced it. Run and run and—

He collided with something, bounced onto his back,

294

saw a shower of stars. Before his vision cleared, hands seized his collar. They jerked him to his feet, shook him. "You half-brained idiot! Haven't you sense enough to watch where you're going?"

Shoving out of the hold, Naed hunched, panting, while Krenin's face floated into focus.

"I might have known only a D'nalian could be so clumsy and stupid!"

Naed's heart pounded in his throat, in his ears, behind his eyes. The passage narrowed, darkened, until the man before him stood bathed in an eerie reddish light. "I have had enough," he breathed, "of Tolemak sneers!"

"Then perhaps you should conduct yourself more like a man and less like a—"

Naed's fist cracked into Krenin's jaw. Before the Tolemak could recover his balance, Naed leaped. They crashed to the floor, grappling and grunting. Hands dragged them apart, many hands. As if from a distance, Naed recognized Banir's voice shouting and Banir's arms pushing him into the wall, holding him there.

Against the opposite wall, Krenin shook free of his men's restraint. Blood ran from his mouth. "You sneaking piece of lowland trash! I'll teach you to jump a Tolemak!" Throwing off sword, knife, and chest armor, he commanded, "Release him! We'll see if he wants to continue this on a more even footing."

"With pleasure!" Shoving out of Banir's grip, Naed flung off his weapons and armor and launched himself at Krenin. They wrestled, boots scraping stone, pushing, shoving, twisting, grimacing faces close until Naed jammed his knee behind Krenin's.

The Tolemak slammed to the floor. A look of fury contorting his features, Krenin rolled to his knees and lunged at Naed, barreling into his legs before he could twist away. Naed's elbow hit the floor first, exploding white streaks of pain through his arm, his shoulder, behind his eyes. When he tried to rise, Krenin scrambled atop his back and snaked an arm around his neck. "No one gets the best of me! Least of all, a D'nalian!"

Fighting for breath, for time, for survival, Naed bucked and twisted until Krenin slipped on the stone and Naed could drive his good elbow into the man's ribs.

Again and again he punched until, as colors danced about his eyes, the hold loosened. Gulping in a breath, Naed broke free and staggered to his feet.

In dimness flecked with green and yellow, he watched Krenin struggle to stand, one hand clutched to his side. The Tolemak's eyes smoldered. Pushing away from the wall, Krenin advanced. They circled, boots shuffling on the stone like drunken dancers, until Krenin's fist snapped Naed's head back.

"There!" the Tolemak growled. "Now, we're even."

When Naed's knuckles came away smeared red, the corridor closed in. Hissing, "You Tolemak son-of-a-whore!" he lunged.

They crashed to the stone, Naed's fingers slipping, then finding a hold on Krenin's throat. Krenin rocked back and forth, tearing at his hands. Snarling, Naed levered up and drove his thumbs into the Tolemak's windpipe. The frantic man's blows shuddered through his body, but Naed clenched his eyes shut and hung on. With his bare hands he would kill his tormentor. With his bare hands he would kill the man he hated. With his bare hands he would kill the Prince—

"Naed! Leave off! 'Tis enough!" Banir grabbed his arms, shoved him against the wall and held him there, but Naed did not see him. He saw only Krenin lying on his side in the middle of the passageway, retching and gasping.

Spasms twitched through Naed's hands. His fists clenched and unclenched. Gasping for breath, he raked his fingers across the stone at his back. *I have nearly killed a man, and for what?* But the monster of his rage loomed yet over him, grinning and feeding, beastlike, on the hate still surging through him, the primitive, mindless, animalistic loathing he felt for the man who was not there, gasping on the floor, but who should have been!

With a shudder, Naed closed his eyes. *Sisters, I have become no better than they!*

CHAPTER TWENTY-SIX

Arn lay staring into the bed's canopy. A black void, it
showed him nothing of itself but played for him every
thought, every image, every memory of the previous
hours. He had been a fool to doubt Aerid. If he had not
been so blind, so jealous, so terrified of losing her, he
would have seen that. Her eyes told him everything, her
eyes and her body when he made love to her. Shifting his
hand, he stroked it over the arm draped across his chest.
Aerid stirred at the contact. With a sigh, she snuggled
into his side and hugged him to her.

Arn closed his eyes, waiting until he could breathe
again, until the ache in his throat passed. Days ago, he
had sought her love the way he sought everything else in
his life—by assailing her with his power, his energy, his
force of will. He laid siege to her while she was trapped in
this room, this bed. He assailed her with tenderness,
anger, strength, passion. When she surrendered, she gave
him her body, her heart, her love. Aerid was his, and now,
as he drew a labored breath, he wondered why.

True, he was a prince. He had thrown that in the
D'nalian's face, boasting how he could give her fine
clothing, a palace, jewels—anything she could ever need
or want. Anything, that is, but his name.

He forced down the emotion welling in him, forced
his body to lie still, his eyes to stare at the canopy. He had
endured the stigma of illegitimacy and survived, but it
had nearly killed him. It had stolen away his mother, his
grandfather, his home, everything. It had left him
brutalized, hunted, alone, trusting no one but Krenin,
loving no one until this woman beside him.

Arn forced his fingers to unclench from Aerid's arm.
When he had control of them again, he stroked gently
over her skin, smoothing away any indentations. He
marveled at her softness, her fragility, her innocence.
Aerid had given herself to him, but how could she know

the truth, the enormity of what she had done? He knew, and he should not have taken her.

Naed's face appeared on the canopy, looking as Arn had seen it pressed to Aerid's hair. He had read the wonder, the ardor, the adoration in the youth's unguarded expression and hated him for it. Arn sucked in a breath. The sound was more of a hiccup than a groan, but it had escaped his control. He forced his lips together, forcing the sound back inside, holding it beating against his teeth. Gathering Aerid into his arms, he rocked with her, his cheek buried in her hair. Taking her was wrong, but how could he have acted otherwise when he needed her so?

Rolling atop her, he woke her with rough, hungry caresses.

"Arn?" she murmured as her arms encircled him, sensed the tension in him. "What...?"

His mouth captured hers, swallowing her words, her question, her concerns, kissing her until she arched against him, as desperate as he to be one.

****

Naed sat hunched in his bed. His elbow ached and he cradled it against his body. The poultice Banir hours ago had laid on it to ease the swelling reeked, but this pain, this discomfort was no more than he deserved as a D'nalian who had lost himself.

Silent as a cat, Banir rose from his bed. He knelt by the fire, ladled a bit of paste out of a pot nested in the coals, and spread the material on a square of cloth. Crossing the room, he laid the fresh poultice on the blanket beside Naed's knee.

Naed glowered at him. "I do not require further care."

Banir untied the cloths securing the spent poultice. When he encountered Naed's fingers, he unfastened them from the injured joint with motions equally sure and patient.

With a frustrated exhalation, Naed leaned back against the wall. "Why do you stay? I have nearly killed one of your kind."

When the elbow was exposed, Banir peered at it in the faint light. He ran gentle fingers over the swelling, then laid on the fresh poultice. "You let him push you too far. 'Twould have been better if you'd fought him a month ago."

"How could I have done so? He is the Prince's man."

"So be you."

Naed closed his eyes as Banir returned to his bed. "No. No longer."

"'Twill be no trouble from the Prince for this. The bastard deserved the thrashing."

"'Twas not Krenin I wished to kill." There, he had said it. Perhaps now the stalwart, stubborn Tolemak would realize he followed a fool. Naed rocked his head against the wall, grinding his skull into it. If only Banir would leave him alone, he could double over, ball his fists into his eye sockets, and let misery claim him.

"You think too much. It eats at you. Steals your sleep."

"Indeed! And how might you understand this when you yourself sleep like the dead?"

When the silence lengthened, Naed decided his retort had scored. In a few moments, the Tolemak would surely be snoring. Somehow the victory gave Naed no pleasure.

"'Twas not ever so." Banir rose on an elbow. "I was not always a soldier." He studied his palm before closing it into a fist. "I killed a man."

He had lived beside this man for weeks, trusted him, depended on him, enjoyed his silences. Now Naed realized how little he knew the man who rested in the bed opposite. "With your bare hands?"

"Aye." Banir stared into the coals. "'Twas over a woman."

How much had the quiet man with the dark, watchful eyes read in his face? Or was it merely a guess, one that hit uncomfortably close to the mark? "Did you wed her?"

"She wed another. Made a cuckold of him."

Naed's face burned. This was indeed a lesson, as he had suspected, but Banir was wrong. "Not all women are so faithless."

The Tolemak shrugged. "You be sworn to the Prince. He'll not let you go."

"He surely shall! I drew on the man! I—he was unarmed—do you understand? I could have killed him!"

The words hung in the silence like an echo that

would not end. He had nearly killed the Prince, the man who, outside of Dranoel, meant more to him than—

He sat upright, stiff as the stone behind him. Prince Arn was a Tolemak, a barbarian, and a bastard! Like his kind, he was true to no one but himself. Naed knew he had been a fool to trust the Prince, to allow him to weave his web with words and favors until now Naed was so entangled he could not breathe. Throwing off the blanket, he gulped in air.

"Aye, but he'll not let you go," Banir repeated, his voice as sure and patient as his hands had been. "Any other man would have taken the chance and tried to kill him."

"Mayhap I will yet do so." But he knew very well why he had not: the Prince had been unarmed. Whatever other breaches of D'nalian honor he may have committed, he could not bring himself to strike an unarmed man. If only he had thought then to do what he had done with Krenin—throw off his weapons and take the Prince man-to-man—but he had been a fool, so lost in his outrage, his shock, he had thought of nothing but flight.

Banir shrugged and lay down. "Sleep. Thinking makes the night too long. And the morning brings what it will." In moments, Naed heard his familiar, soft snoring.

Banir was wrong about Aerid, about him, about the Prince. But he was right about the night and thinking. Lying down, Naed stared at the faint outlines of the beams overhead and dared sleep to come.

****

Sensing something amiss, Aerid rolled over in bed, seeking Arn. She found instead the depression where his body had lain. Opening her eyes, she saw him standing beside the bed and shrugging into his tunic. "Arn? 'Tis not yet dawn, aye?"

"I couldn't sleep." Face unreadable in the dark, he laid her shift on the bed. "Get dressed. 'Tis time I showed you why I came to Vinvinnysee."

Clinging to his hand moments later, Aerid followed him through the still palace to rouse from his chamber a man she recognized as Guard Master Gaelwynn. Arn had given him a measure of command, she remembered from her visits to the Golden Horse. Nodding at her deferentially, the Adanak led them deep into the palace to a dark tower where the steps wound endlessly upward. Arn's hand at the small of her back braced her while she held her skirts and climbed until, when she stepped onto a landing, her body continued to turn.

"Steady," Arn murmured, catching her arms. "We're here." Meshing his fingers with hers, he took the torch from Gaelwynn who, after giving both of them what Aerid thought was an assessing glance, fitted a key to a large lock. Opening the door, he stepped away from it. Arn led her through and set the torch in a holder along the wall.

****

The Crownkeeper watched from the tower landing as the Prince led his woman into the chamber. This predawn visitation had not caught him unaware. If the Prince desired secrecy surrounding the Crown's existence, 'twas best served by such timing.

He had expected the woman, too. She looked even younger than when he had first observed her at the Golden Horse, but her eyes were as mesmerizing as he remembered. No wonder the Prince had remarked on the blue of the Kingdom Stone, though the Crownkeeper doubted the Prince had consciously noted the connection.

She had smiled a tentative, apologetic smile when her lord roused him from his chamber. Alongside the height and hard planes of the Tolemak, she seemed a will-o'-the-wisp, slender and easily bent, but she looked at the Prince without fear, and he handled her with a gentleness that bespoke more regard than a man of his power need show a woman of her origins.

She seemed more accustomed to the clothing of her new state, but though her coloring and features marked her as Adanak, she yet looked as exotic, as out of place, as uncommon as when he had first marked her. The Crownkeeper decided it had as much to do with the stone about her throat as with her calling as a healer and the history his inquiries had pieced together. He doubted anyone without his knowledge had recognized the Sisters' Tear for what it was. 'Twas too rare.

An audible gasp roused the Crownkeeper from his meditations. 'Twas the magic of the torchlight, he thought, smiling inwardly as the explosion of sparks—

hundreds of them in green, gold, red, blue, even purple—flashing from the Crown captivated the Prince's woman. Stepping to the threshold, he watched while she gazed, wide-eyed, at the gem-studded circlet sitting on a cushion-topped pedestal in the center of the room.

"The Crown of Tolem," the Prince was saying as he placed his hands on her shoulders. "Have you heard of it?"

"'Tis a legend..."

"'Twas stolen by Adan, generations ago, when he broke the Kingdom. Though he had the audacity to steal it, he must have feared to wear it. Instead of returning it, the coward hid it—apparently here—and it passed into legend. A scant few—" he nodded at the Crownkeeper. "—know of its existence. Far fewer know of its whereabouts. Now you are one of them."

As she turned to look at her lord, the Crownkeeper watched an expression of wonder steal over her face. Though she lacked a fine upbringing, her eyes confirmed she possessed more than enough intelligence to grasp the significance of the Prince's gesture. Pleased, the Crownkeeper nodded to himself. The Prince could hardly have chosen more fortuitously.

"'Tis a king's crown, aye?" she was saying.

The Prince nodded. "Adan has no direct heirs. Nor does D'nal. I can trace my heritage from prince to prince in a direct line to Tolem." He took her hand. "Aerid, I have come here to make the Kingdom whole, but this is all I have to work with, a desecrated crown."

The Crownkeeper watched as she moved a tentative step toward the circlet gleaming in the torchlight, seeing this time—he thought—beyond her first impression of shining gold, fabulous gems, to signs of damage. "'Tis but a few stones missing. Can you not find others?"

"Perhaps. And no." When she looked at the Prince, he sighed and touched the empty settings. "Stones might be found to fit, but those missing are the princely stones, the ones the Sisters are said to have ripped out to punish the royal brothers. Although I am Heir to Tolem by right of blood and gender, the Tolem Stone is not in my possession. D'nal's stone is thought to exist, but its whereabouts are unknown. Adan's stone seems to have been lost or destroyed. Gaelwynn, does your lore even suggest what kind it was?"

"There be some indications, my lord. Naught of substance." The Prince's question had startled him, so intent had he been on watching the woman. She stood facing the Crown, brow puckered, the fingers of one hand linked with her lord's, the other barely touching the tasseled corner of the burgundy cushion.

"So, you did come to conquer Adanak," she was saying, "to make war in order to make the land whole?"

"I wouldn't choose those words, but 'tis the gist of it."

"To my way of thinking, 'tis a foolish business what men may do to keep alive a wrong for so long countless folk have died for it, aye, the innocent and the guilty. 'Tis true, Adan stole what was not his and did lie to keep it. D'nal, 'tis said, did naught because he feared to choose a side. And Tolem, 'tis he who began a war that did pit brother against brother. 'Tis clear to me what you must do if your aim be to make the land whole: Let Adan return what was stolen, let D'nal choose again, and let Tolem make peace. 'Twould be of more value than replacing stones."

The Crownkeeper shot a glance at the Prince to confirm he, too, gaped at the woman who stood looking at them with tilted head and a question in her eyes.

"'Tis not so simple," the Prince said, tugging on her hand.

She resisted, looking from him to the Crownkeeper. "Why not? Master Gaelwynn does possess the key to this place. Does he not also possess the power to act as Adan and return the Crown?"

Suppressing a smile, the Crownkeeper laid a hand over his heart and inclined his head. "Indeed, I do. And I have."

"And you as Tolem have made peace?"

"Here in Vinvinnysee, but there are others who may not so readily accept my overtures. And, after yester eve, 'tis like your D'nalian friend may wish to alter his previous choices."

"Oh." A look passed between the Prince and his woman.

The Crownkeeper fingered the key at his chest. In his experience truth was often childishly simple; 'twas a pity the Demon had his way with it before humans could respond.

****

Aerid followed Arn in silence back to their chamber after taking leave of Master Gaelwynn. The glowing, sparkling circlet of gold and gemstones still danced in her mind's eye even as she sat in front of the cold fire while Arn lit candles on the mantle.

"You understand now, aye?" he said, kneeling beside her chair and taking her hands in his.

She studied the sharp edges and beard shadow of the face she had come to love. Once she had feared the white skin, the ugly scar, the forbidding brows of this man who knelt at her feet, holding her hands with the long fingers and calloused palms she had once associated with weapons and war. He had terrified her then, not so very long ago. She had spent these past days learning how much she loved him.

If 'twere possible, within this last hour, she had come to love him more. He had entered her life as a warrior, a conqueror, and she had loved him despite it as much as because of it. Now she had seen his vision, Aerid felt herself unworthy, ashamed she had not guessed, had not suspected, had not even dreamed he could be capable of so much.

Blinking back tears, she focused on the interlocked white and copper of their fingers in her lap. "'Tis a worthy aim—to bring peace. Why must such a deed be so difficult?"

He raised her hands and kissed them. "As I recall, 'twas a rather impudent *lad* filling a water skin who once told me 'twas because 'men be naught but fools and savages'."

Flushing at the memory of her indiscretion, she glanced up. Arn's smile, and the tenderness radiating from his eyes, captured her gaze. She allowed him to raise her from the chair so he could sit in it and draw her down on his lap. "'Tis a remarkable memory you have," Aerid said, fidgeting with his tunic laces.

"It serves me well enough." His fingertips on her chin raised her gaze to his. "Every word you said to me, every look you gave me played over and over in my mind on that endless march to Vinvinnysee. Did you think of me, too, when we were apart?"

"Aye. Think and dream." He smiled, and her breath caught, but Aerid ducked her head again, afraid to ask the questions the tower visit had spawned in her mind, yet knowing her heart could not endure without answers, even if the answers would break it.

"What—what must you do now? With the Crown?"

She sensed the change in him, felt against her shoulder the long rise and fall of a heavy sigh. "'Tis but one thing to do: Bring the Crown secretly back to Tolemak, then produce it when 'tis likely to convince the greatest number of people that I can, indeed, remake the Kingdom, and 'tis to their advantage to help me—or let me—do so."

"That does mean...you will be leaving Vinvinnysee soon."

"*We* will be leaving." Arn grasped her chin with fingers that, though gentle, insisted she face him. "Don't for a moment think I intend to leave you behind, Aerid. I'll not be parted from you. You are the woman I've chosen to share my bed, my life." He paused, and she glimpsed the uncertainty, the need she had come to know lurked behind his willful exterior. "You—you *are* willing to come with me—to leave this place—aye?"

Aerid smiled with all her heart. Even though Mairim would likely remind her he had said naught about wedding her, his words were no less a vow. They told her—if showing her the secret of the Crown were not enough—all she needed to know about her place in his heart. "Aye. 'Tis my desire to go with you, my love, wherever you may be taking me."

Later, when birdsong heralded the beginnings of dawn, Aerid stroked Arn's hair while he slept. She felt deliciously light and whole, knowing she had found her place at last. Though she may yet have kin in the mountains of Adanak, she no longer needed to find them to know herself. The Sisters had given her a special boon, this man and his dream.

****

Cradling an earthenware jug, Krenin rocked on his heels in the corridor. The D'nalian's chamber lay half a hall away. Two of his guard had left. The other would likely remain behind when the lowlander quit his chamber. He would have to pass this way.

Krenin shifted the jug to his left arm, but a protest from his ribs forced him to adjust the jug's position. "Bastard!" he muttered, wincing as the utterance jerked the scab on his lip. He scowled, but his lip resented that as well. Growling, he yanked at his tunic collar. Nothing fit right this morning thanks to that D'nalian!

A door opened and closed. Krenin stepped into the center of the corridor, sucked in breath, and waited.

"What do you want?"

Noting the D'nalian's scabbed lip, purpled cheek, and the telltale bulge of a bandage under his tunic sleeve, Krenin felt a surge of satisfaction. At least he had done some damage for all the pummeling he had received. Pity he had not returned a few measures more. "Here." Krenin thrust out the jug. "If you ache half as much as I, you need this."

"What is it?"

"Some of Adanak's best wine." When the D'nalian made no attempt to reach for the jug, Krenin shoved it at him. "Go ahead, take it. 'Tis only wine."

"Why do you offer this to me?"

"Because, you lowland tripe, you nearly broke my neck!"

"I do not understand."

Krenin closed his eyes, inhaled. 'Twas difficult enough without the D'nalian ass acting thick-brained as well! "Then I'll make it plain enough for your ears. I still don't like you, but 'tis sure you could have killed me and—" With a frustrated snarl, he clunked the jug on the floor between them. "Curse you! I'm trying to apologize! Take the wine and let's be done with it!"

"Done with it?" The young man laughed, but it was not a sound of pleasure. "Oh, this is wondrous. Wondrous, indeed!"

As quickly as it began, the laughter vanished. "Keep your wine and your apology. It comes too late, for I intend this morn to be quit of all of you, to take what is mine and leave."

Krenin gaped. "You're an idiot! A fog-brained idiot!"

"You are entitled to your opinion." Sidestepping the jug, he strode away.

One part of Krenin wanted to charge after the D'nalian, to seize him about the collar and thrash him for his insolence. Another part recalled the fingers digging into his windpipe, the look on the face that had blurred above him. He had seen that look again, just now, in the chipped stone of the D'nalian's face.

Cold sweat beaded on Krenin's forehead. He remembered that look, years ago, on another, much younger face. He closed his eyes and banged his fist into his forehead. *Now*, he understood about the D'nalian! If Arn lost the youth, if he broke away and turned against them—

Spinning, Krenin kicked the jug. It thunked into the wall and shattered, the sound small balm to his frustration. *Demon's Blood!* They could not lose the D'nalian! While red liquid rushed under his boots, Krenin reassured himself Arn would not let it happen.

****

"As you've no doubt guessed," Arn said, entering Gaelwynn's chamber without knocking, "I need to bring the Crown to Tolemak. I'd like your thoughts on how best to do it."

The Adanak looked up from his wash basin. "Indeed, I did think you might, my lord," he said, wiping his hands on a cloth.

Arn crossed to the window, opened it, and looked out on the courtyard below. He had left Aerid sleeping, a look of such peace on her face he had been loath to wake her. In truth, he had never seen her happier, and he wanted nothing more than to keep the concerns that had gnawed at him since first light from disturbing her. He had come to a number of decisions as he dressed, and he saw no reason to delay implementing them.

"I'll be leaving shortly. Krenin will remain as my steward. At the first snow, he'll return to Val-Feyridge. Master Illien will continue as steward in his place. Can you work with them?"

"My lord, I shall do my utmost to be agreeable, but I was given to understand the D'nalian—"

"I've altered my plans."

"Ah."

The single syllable grated on Arn's nerves, saying nothing while implying all too much. Gripping the stone sill with more force than necessary, he turned. "Now about the Crown—"

"Forgive me, my lord, but 'tis yet some matter of importance I must ask of you." The Adanak folded the cloth in his hands and carefully laid it beside the basin.

Arn scowled. Days ago in this palace on the hill he had been happier than ever before in his life. He had conquered a people, captured a city, regained the thought-to-be-lost Crown, and won the heart of the woman he loved. Now he could hardly wait to be free of this pestilence-ridden place. The walls had ears, and a thousand tongues repeated whatever they heard. Arn powdered a chunk of mortar between his fingers. And people like Gaelwynn saw far too much.

"If you're concerned about the woman Aerid—" Naming her before another man felt strange on Arn's tongue, pulled at something in his chest, but the sensation was not disagreeable. "—she's going with me. When I take something—someone—as mine, I keep faith. Your spies should have told you that, Gaelwynn."

The man inclined his head. "Indeed, they have, and I do not doubt your faithfulness, my lord. However, unless my spies, as you call them, have been wrong, there be another obligation you have made regarding the Tolem Stone. Does she know of this?"

"No. And you'll not be telling her." Somehow, he would bring Aerid to Val-Feyridge. Even if he had to offer Albon and its lands to Erodasi in settlement of their marriage contract, he would do it to obtain the Tolem Stone and the freedom to do what his father had been too weak or too afraid to do—live openly with the woman he loved.

"'Tis not my desire to be interfering, my lord. 'Tis only that—well, 'tis my understanding your grandfather did tell you much of the lore of the Kingdom and the Crown, aye?"

"You understand a great many things that should be obvious, Crownkeeper. Perhaps you could better expend your energy understanding something more productive."

"Naught, to my mind, could be more productive for the man who would be king than understanding King Ekard's mistake." The mismatched eyes bored into him.

Arn guessed the look would have daunted most men. 'Twas difficult, however, to daunt a man who knew how the stare worked. "You mean when he thought he could rule his life as he ruled his kingdom? I haven't forgotten the lesson. Nor have I forgotten that death and jealousy ensued. You may be Crownkeeper, Gaelwynn, but you are not Tolemak, nor do you know Rolnar of Roines."

Gaelwynn bowed slightly but did not alter his penetrating look. "I have some knowledge of that name, my lord, and of your history. If I have offended you, forgive me. 'Tis my intent—and my solemn desire—only to be of service to you and to the Crown. Since I, too, desire to see the Kingdom restored, will you be accepting some well-intentioned advice?"

"No." Arn strode to the door. "When I want advice, I'll ask for it."

Around the corner, he bounced a fist off the wall, punishing the stone. Damn the Adanak and his honeyed words! Demon take Naed and his D'nalian self-righteousness! What only yesterday seemed so promising—a kingdom, a unity, a future without war—now seemed as likely to collapse as a stack of twigs in the wind. He would hold it together. He had to, whether the D'nalian stayed or not. Pausing before the chamber he had chosen for his office, Arn tugged at his tunic laces, loosening them. He was fully dressed this time, with chest armor, sword and knife, and ready for whatever the D'nalian chose to do or say.

As he entered, his gaze flashed through the room, imprinting on his mind every detail of the scene. The first told him the weapon in the hands of the young man standing on the other side of the table was sheathed. The second noted the battered condition of the knuckles gripping the scabbard. The third recorded scabs and bruises he had not seen yester eve on the D'nalian's face. Masking his surprise, Arn lifted his hand from his sword hilt as smoothly as if it had been a continuation of his final stride. "To what do I owe the pleasure of your visit?"

"I have come," Naed said, placing the sheathed sword

on the table between them, "to resign from your service."

Arn searched the young man's eyes for a flicker of pain, discomfiture, anything but detected none. Nor did Naed offer explanation for the obvious marks of a brawl upon his face. Instead, Naed watched him, stiff, stubborn, proud. Ignorant as the youth was of his own power, Arn could not risk letting Naed go. He drummed his fingers on the wood.

Krenin was right; I should have killed him at Druemarwin. But that would have altered everything. Without Naed, there would have been no Aerid in disguise for him to rescue at the river... to rescue and fall in love with. And that, Arn thought with a twist of lips, would have simplified everything. Were it not for Aerid, he would not be deciding whether to accept the resignation of a man who no longer trusted him or to *kill* that man solely because he was a rival...to kill him out of jealousy and envy...

Nor have I forgotten that death and jealousy ensued.

Arn froze, shocked, while the words he had uttered mere moments ago rang like alarm bells in his mind. He saw clearly what Gaelwynn had done—perhaps even why—but he would be damned if he would be grateful! Cursing himself for playing into the old word-weaver's hands, he seized the sword and shoved it with such force across the table only Naed's reflexive grab stopped it from flying off the edge.

"Put it on! Your sword belongs to me. You swore as much at Druemarwin and again at the Adanak border, or does your honor mean so little, you've conveniently forgotten that?"

"I have fulfilled my every obligation. I owe you naught!"

"You're my Second. You owe me the courtesy of carrying out your duties until I find a suitable replacement."

"Krenin will be more than pleased—"

"Krenin will be my new steward to Adanak. Aye, the post I once offered you."

Naed's knuckles whitened on the scabbard, but he said nothing.

"Krenin will be occupied until snowfall. I intend to

depart for Val-Feyridge long before that. Perhaps as soon as a week." There was a certain pleasure in holding the youth at bay like this, and Arn sought more of it. "You'll accompany me, of course. You'll fulfill every Second's task—and any others I see fit to assign you—until we reach Druemarwin."

At the fortress' name, color rose on the young man's face.

"I found you at Druemarwin, and I'll return you there, Free Swordsman. If you're fortunate, your former master may be willing to take you back into his employ. If not, well..." He spread his hands.

The cords in Naed's neck strained against his skin. "I trusted in your honor, Prince of Val-Feyridge! But you have none! Everything I was, I foolishly allowed you to steal from me. But you will not steal my honor!"

Arn blocked his rush to the door. "Hear me and hear me well! I *took* nothing from you, nothing you didn't willingly give."

"Tell yourself that—" Naed swept Arn with a scathing look "—if it pricks your conscience less to do so!" Pushing bodily past, he stormed out of the chamber.

The pleasure Arn had sought moments ago now leaked like acid into his gut. He flung a chair at the wall, but its splintering did nothing to abate his rage. Slamming his fists on the table, he stared at his image in the dark wood. Where his eyes should have been, the grain swirled into a knot. In the center, in the glossy core, a miniature face detached from the droplet of resin and settled into focus. He saw beneath him Aerid's face as she had lain in his arms that first night before he had taken her, before he had made her irrevocably his. Dropping his head, he whispered, "I took nothing that was not...willingly...given."

****

"Val-Feyridge means to be king!"

In Tolemak, Rolnar of Roines surveyed the short man who had leaped to his feet and slapped the tabletop. "Oh? And have you only now reached that conclusion, Lede?"

"Don't tell me you've known his intentions all along and done nothing about it! Or is it because he's to be your son-in-law that you've sat on the fence?"

Rolnar smoothed the gold embroidery adorning his tunic. "In case you've forgotten, 'twas I who first moved against Arn when he took Val-Feyridge from Prince Yinnad."

"Aye, first to signal a retreat!"

Rolnar's brows bristled. He rose slowly, until his barrel-chested bulk imposed on the table's edge. "I seem to recall 'twas *your* back leading us away from Val-Feyridge."

The Lord of Lede flushed and sat down.

"As to his intentions—" Rolnar surveyed the Tolemak lords assembled around his war table "—once he crossed into D'nalee this spring, any fool could have guessed what he had in mind."

"If that's the case," Edad of Koth said, a smirk on his squirrel-like jowls, "why didn't you call us into assembly earlier?"

Rolnar sighed. "Because, my dear Edad, why should we risk our forces against his strength when the Adanak can do so for us?"

"Do what?" muttered Lede. "He's won Vinvinnysee and a chunk of Adanak with it."

"Not without cost. While I didn't expect him to succeed in this venture, 'tis sure he's been weakened by it. And he'll have to leave a portion of his army behind to secure his Adanak holdings." Rolnar fingered the ruby-studded medallion dangling from his neck. Decades ago his late father-in-law Prince Yinnad had set the Tolem Stone into the medallion's center, where it gleamed now, so deep a red as to be nearly black. "As to calling you together, I've only now been able to pry you two from each other's throats." He glared at Edad and Ladnar of Ormo.

"His men hunt my deer!" Ladnar charged.

"And his men trespass on my land!"

"Be silent, both of you!"

Edad shot Rolnar a sullen look. Ladnar glowered at both of them.

"And," Rolnar continued, shifting his glare to another section of the table, "'twas only now I've been able to get Lede, Belac, and you, Nor, out of that stretch of sandbar you three have been arguing over for two years."

"The island is strategic!" Lede snarled, fingering the

312

jeweled knife hilt at his belt.

"It'll soon be strategic to 'King' Arn if we don't come together against him." Rolnar glowered at Lede until the small man placed both hands, empty, on the tabletop. "Or is it your preference to live under his boot?"

"I'll live under no man's boot!"

A rumble arose as the other lords echoed Lede's sentiments.

Rolnar of Roines smiled. What a pack of fools. One had only to throw a tempting piece of meat before them and the whole lot snapped and snarled to have at it. Hold the wrath of the Demon before them and they quickly joined ranks to fight off the threat. What tastier meat was there to offer than Val-Feyridge and what more convincing threat than Prince Arn? No, it took no great skill to direct this lot.

The challenge lay not in controlling this pack of wolves, but in mastering Prince Arn. He had underestimated his future son-in-law once, but only because the bastard was still a stranger then. Rolnar stroked his thumb over his signet ring. He would not make the same mistake again.

A hush settled over the room. Lord Belac leaned his lanky frame across the table. "'Tis sure you wouldn't have called us into session if you had no plan. What is it and how much time do we have?"

Rolnar frowned at Belac's directness, but he said only, "Quite right, Belac." Savoring the attention the announcement produced, he resumed his seat with a show of deliberation. "Since the Prince has no doubt provided for the defense of Val-Feyridge itself, a strike there would prove fruitless. We must mass against him here, on this side of the Arbez River."

"And meet his army in the open?" Edad exclaimed.

Rolnar rolled his eyes. "Aye! But don't forget, 'tis fresh we'll be and he'll have marched all the way from Adanak with an army that's been fighting since spring."

"We'll have to move quickly," Belac said, stroking his beard, "before his allies in the west can divine our plans."

"Rumors about a strike at Val-Feyridge should keep them contained until it's too late." Rolnar stretched his legs under the table and added with studied nonchalance,

"Besides, if the Sisters are with us, the Prince won't return to Tolemak alive."

For a moment, no one spoke.

Ladnar coughed. "We'll send skirmishing parties, of course."

Rolnar made a castle of his fingers. "No, we don't want to give ourselves away."

"Why, what then?" said Edad, scowling.

"Assassins!" breathed Lede. He slapped the tabletop. "Why didn't I think of that?"

"Because you've had your mind on Belac and Nor, and you're not capable of entertaining more than one thought at a time," Rolnar said.

"Watch your tongue or you'll find a knife in your own back!"

"Save your knife for Val-Feyridge." Rising, Rolnar studied the assembled faces. Lede would be the first to go after the Prince had been dispatched. Belac next. But not just yet. He needed them both. "Two months, my lords. Possibly only six weeks. I suggest you return home at once and assemble your forces."

Rolnar hastened through the protocol of leave-taking and made his way to his study. Opening the door, his eyes narrowed. A flush swept up from his collar through his beard. Why his daughter had taken up with a piece of lowland trash such as the man who lounged at his very own desk, escaped him. Oh, this Dlaniger had bloodlines, and his unblemished features were the kind women found pleasing, but he was D'nalian. *D'nalian!* And this D'nalian made not the least effort to rise at his entrance!

"Take your feet off my desk!"

"You did instruct me to make myself comfortable."

"Even I don't put my feet on my desk." Rounding the desk, Rolnar disdained the chair the younger man reluctantly vacated. He reached for the wine jug on the sideboard with the intent of pouring himself a much-needed bit of refreshment when he noticed his "guest" had significantly depleted its store. With tightened lips, he emptied the remaining wine into his cup and turned.

"My guests have left. The men and horses you asked for are assembling in the courtyard. You'll leave at once. That is, if you're capable of riding." He gestured to the jug.

"My lord, I am capable of many things, a fact of which I believe I have made you aware."

The ice-cold eyes both fascinated and repulsed Rolnar. In his youth he had willingly—even eagerly—carried out Yinnad's purges, but the killing had always been an expedient means to ensure his own rise to power. He would never have *sold* his skills like this Dlaniger. "Kill Prince Arn and I'll see you receive the reward you'll so richly deserve."

"No, my lord," Dlaniger amended, with a smile that was no more than a polite movement of lips. "Not the reward you believe I deserve, but the recompense I have requested."

"You D'nalian snake!" Rolnar slammed his fist on the desk with such violence his cup leaped and spilled its contents. Wine ran unheeded like a river of blood over the earth-brown wood. "Your insolence will yet tempt me to murder!"

"Refrain yourself, my lord. 'Twill not serve your purpose to kill the man who has bred you an alternate heir to Tolem."

Rolnar trembled. His fists clenched, itching for the throat of the smiling man opposite, but he kept his tone civil. "I have agreed to let you have Erodasi, but as to Val-Feyridge, you must realize there are the other lords to consider."

Dlaniger removed his cloak from the chair and draped it over his shoulders, his movements confident, graceful. "I am certain you shall see that my claim prevails." With a perfunctory bow, he added, "Farewell, my lord."

Rolnar glared at the door that closed. Silently, he cursed Erodasi for her stupid, empty head. "Don't overestimate yourself," he growled at the departed young man. "You don't have any allies." Satisfied with this insight, he called for a servant to wipe away the spilled wine.

****

"Demon's Blood, I wish I were going with you tomorrow," Krenin grumbled, catching Arn at the bottom of the palace steps.

315

"It won't be long and we'll be together again."

"You need me now."

Arn gripped his friend's shoulders. "I need you here. I'm relying on you to leave Illien in a position of strength. And I trust you—only you—to deliver the Crown safely and secretly."

Krenin scowled. "Naed's a fool."

"He's made his choice." Releasing Krenin, he surveyed the courtyard, its stones dark with gently falling drizzle. Naed had appeared only when his presence was required. Otherwise, he quietly and meticulously went about his duties. And he made no move to speak to Aerid. Arn sucked in a lungful of damp air. That thought, rather than pleasing him, left him disquieted.

"He's still a fool," Krenin muttered, shrugging deeper into his cloak. "You're risking your life if you're depending on his loyalty."

"I'm depending on his honor. Something very dear to a D'nalian."

Krenin snorted.

Arn looked at the man beside him, at the thick, lowered brows, the volatile eyes, the stubborn chin. For more than half his life, Krenin had stood at his shoulder, guarding his flank, tending his wounds, providing food, shelter, companionship...

Forcing a smile, Arn punched Krenin's shoulder. "You always worry too much."

Krenin returned a half-hearted poke to Arn's chest. "Somebody has to. You never have."

Arn watched Krenin's figure dissolve into the grayness under the palace gate.

A vague feeling of unease shivered down his back, but he shook it off. This was not the first time they would be parted.

Nor would it be the last.

Turning, he strode up the palace steps.

316

PART IV: TOLEMAK
CHAPTER TWENTY-SEVEN

The army marched quickly through forests burnished with gold. They ate fat deer, squirrel and rabbit, and crossed rivers made low by late summer's heat. Dressed in boy's garb, Aerid rode at the Prince's side, her hair flowing over her cloak. Each day, Naed was forced to watch her from his place at the rear of their party. When they camped, he watched her air blankets, cook, or tend the fire. He sat by his own fire and snapped bits of tinder between his fingers while his companions fetched water, polished weapons, mended, cooked, or dozed.

When the Prince guided her into their tent at night, his hand intimate on her hip or hidden under the hair at the nape of her neck, Naed rose, flung the broken twigs into the fire and strode away, returning only when the fires had died to embers.

This night he abandoned his companions earlier than usual because the Prince dared to kiss Aerid while they could yet be seen under the tent flap. Now, while more stars emerged from the pockets of the night sky, he stood on the bank of a dry streambed and kicked pebbles along it until his boot found a fist-sized stone. Picking it up, he tested its fit in his palm, then flung it towards the trees. It cracked against a branch, ripped through leaves, and clattered to the ground.

"Naed?"

'Twas only one syllable of sound, but he knew the voice.

Aerid emerged from the trees, a slight, cloak-draped figure smaller than he remembered, and glided toward him. "Will you speak with me?"

She held out her hands to him, and he grasped them between thumb and fingertips, afraid if he pressed into the flesh, his fingers would pass through it as through an illusion.

317

"You do not know," she said, smiling, "how it pleased me to discover you alive."

Nor do you know, he thought as her warmth seeped into his fingertips, *how it pleases me*—He stiffened. "Where is the Prince?"

"He has gone with Master Gorm to see the river we cross tomorrow." She searched his face. "What has come between us, Naed? You were ever my dearest—"

"*He* has come between us! By the Sisters, if I had known what would befall you, I would never have allowed you to masquerade as my manservant!"

"Naught has befallen me."

At the stubbornness in her voice, he groaned. "He has made you his mistress. He has taken what is beautiful..." Loosing one hand, he raised it until the fingers hovered, trembling, over her cheek. "...wonderful and...innocent and..."

She watched him, eyes large, dark, and...frightened?

Naed seized her arms. "Come away with me, Aerid! I will fetch the horses. We will go—we will go to the mountains of Adanak! We can be wed there. Or before, if you like." His heart hammered in his ears. She smelled of wood violets and dark honey, and he trembled with the need to hold her, surround her, touch her.

"Naed..."

A liquid pearl, reflecting starlight from the inner corner of her eye, stole all movement from his limbs. He watched, fascinated, while it dangled from her lashes. "Have no fear," he whispered. "I shall see we are not followed."

"Naed..."

He watched as the droplet slid down her cheek and splashed on his hand.

Disentangling her fingers from his, she drew a shaky breath. "Naed, you have ever been my friend. My dearest, closest friend. But I do not—I cannot wed you."

"It matters not that he has dishonored you! I love you, Aerid. I would have you as my wife." *There.* They were said—words he should have spoken months ago, words he had longed for months to speak.

Aerid's sigh told him as clearly as the hand she placed on his chest that something was wrong. "'Tis dear

318

you be, Naed, as only a friend can be, but I do not love you, not in the way you desire. And Arn has not disgraced me. 'Twas my free choice to lie with him because I love him." She smoothed his tunic, then stepped back. "'Twill be no other for me."

He stared as she drew the cloak around her shoulders. She was within reach and yet he could not move, speak, or do aught but watch, astonished, while a chasm yawned between them. He teetered on the precipice and took one last, desperate chance. "He is betrothed. Did he make that known to you? He will wed upon his return to Tolemak."

Her lashes dropped and she seemed to study the ground between them. "'Tis not entirely unexpected news, but 'tis of no account. Much has passed in my life since I thought you dead. 'Tis my intent to take what happiness I may while I may yet have it, for too quickly may it be snatched away." Raising her head, she looked him full in the face. "For as long as I may be having Arn, 'tis sure I shall be living at his side. 'Tis he I love. Do you understand?"

He did, far too clearly. Every time she had smiled at him, it had been out of friendship. Every time she had touched his hand, it had been out of kindness. Every time she had placed her trust in him, it had been out of sincere regard. Not once—not once!—had her face, her hand, or her heart spoken of love. His own foolish fantasies had deluded him. His own hopes and dreams had played him false. He drew a shuddering breath. "Aerid, I—forgive me. I have been a fool."

"'Tis naught to forgive."

Aerid's voice sounded distant, but her hand on his shoulder was warm, solid, and real. There was comfort in the gesture, but it was the comfort offered by a friend or even a sister. He swallowed and his eyes burned.

"Now I do but better understand all that has transpired between you and Arn and me." She sighed.

He longed to bring her hand to his lips, but the time for that kind of gesture had passed. Instead, he gently unfastened her fingers from his sleeve. "Come, I will see you back to camp."

She walked beside him in silence until they reached

319

the outermost ring of sleeping soldiers. "Stay," she said. "I shall find my way from here." And then she was gone, gliding across the camp like an apparition.

Like a dream, he thought. Only the ache in his heart was not dream-induced, and it would not vanish into the night with the shards of his fantasies. No, he would see her every day, and know each time what a fool he had been.

****

Aerid slept fitfully while she waited for Arn, but he did not return to their tent until dawn, and all the next day he repeatedly rode ahead to join the advance party or to check on Gorm's scouts. Some news from the previous evening preoccupied him, and now was not the time to tell him she had spoken to Naed, especially since Arn had been right about Naed's feelings for her. Looking back at all the times Naed had been in her company, she saw now what she should have seen then, but the possibility had not entered her mind a D'nalian—especially one as upright as Naed—might so overstep his people's propriety to risk a relationship with such as her. Still, scant weeks ago she had thought the relationship she and Arn shared 'twas not only impossible but inconceivable.

Sighing, she swatted at the gnats buzzing about her face. The river they crossed brought them into D'nalee and now, at twilight, wisps of fog rose from the lowland meadows. Deer flitted like ghosts along the edge of the forest. Blackbird songs thrummed beneath the noises of hooves, wagon wheels, leather harness, and men's voices. Aerid stretched saddle-sore muscles and yawned. She would speak with Arn tonight. Glancing ahead, she watched him gesture toward the bearded Gorm, who rode beside him. That she had spoken with Naed would not please him, but she would make him understand why.

Something whizzed past Aerid and landed with a thud that made her go clammy inside. Spinning, she knew what she would see even before she beheld Naed clutching a feathered shaft protruding from his thigh. She wheeled her horse toward him, but the air hissed with more arrows. One thunked into her saddle, startling her mount, jerking the reins from her hands. Around her horses squealed, men screamed, officers shouted commands. She

320

clutched a fistful of mane and tried to turn her mount to follow the men scattering into the trees, but the white-eyed animal bolted with a bunch of riderless horses.

Through the whipping mane, Aerid glimpsed a rider racing toward her. "The reins!" she shouted, thinking the man meant to stop her runaway, but he only spurred alongside and, with a yell of "I have her!" snatched her from her horse. Heaving her onto his hip, he reined not toward but *away* from the army.

She heard Naed cry her name, saw him, face ghastly in the twilight, galloping toward her with drawn sword. He had snapped off the arrow's shaft, but blood ran glistening down his leg.

"Take him!" shouted the man she realized meant to carry her off.

His companion wheeled into her sight, shield up, sword aloft. Naed's weapon smashed into it. Over the mêlée, over her own panting breath, Aerid heard the sickeningly familiar rend of cloth, saw as in a living nightmare the image of Naed falling before a lance, of Arn flinching under another lance's point. "No!" she gasped, bucking in her captor's grip, kicking, clawing at anything within reach. She could not, would not let them be hurt again!

Her heels pounded the horse's ribs, the man's shins, making the animal swerve, the man curse. When he tried to heave her like a sack over the horse's withers, Aerid caught one of the reins and yanked it down. The horse stumbled, throwing the man onto its neck. Aerid plunged to the ground and rolled.

As if in a dream, she watched clods from the horse's hooves arc past her face. They were yellow hooves, and the clods contained bits of dry, broken grass. They passed out of view and the marsh grass, brown and ragged, rotated before her eyes. Her shoulder bounced, then her hip, and then she was airborne again, weightless, while her hand dove for a nest of stones, and Naed, his face contorted into a demon's mask, swept past her.

For a second, there was nothing. Then the blackness vanished and Aerid tasted marsh grass in her mouth. Her palm burned when she leaned on it, but she pushed herself up, thinking, *Naed! Where is Naed?*

Her frantic gaze found his horse, saddle askew, and her would-be captor, sword in hand, reining his mount in a tight circle around something—someone?—stirring in the grass. With a little gasp, Aerid threw herself into a run while hoof beats sounded behind her, gaining. She would reach Naed this time. She had to reach him. She could not let him die!

****

Panting, Arn let the sword slip from his numbed fingers. The man into whose body he had plunged it, yawned up at him, mouth frozen in a soundless scream. He had driven it deep, through armor, and now Arn felt nothing but an overwhelming urge to retch.

He backed a step and turned, ignoring the dead man's horse lurching to its feet beside him, and his own stallion that stood, blowing, a few feet away, and even his shield, ignoring everything but the precious but oh-so-white face that rose from a clump of grass.

When Aerid was in his arms, Arn could breathe again. Her shoulders heaved and her face ground against his throat as if she would squeeze into his skin. He closed his eyes, locking her in his embrace while the rising breeze licked up his back, cooling the soaked undertunic and lifting from there a scent not sweat or blood but something equally familiar. He shuddered. Before, it emanated from other men. This time, however...

"Naed," Aerid said. "I must see to Naed."

She turned, and his arms released her as though there was no strength in them. Like a statue, Arn stood while she knelt beside the young man. Blood, oozing between the fingers he pressed to his thigh, soaked the grass under his leg. Arn watched as Aerid touched Naed's knee, watched as the young man's eyes closed and his mouth struggled to smile, watched as Aerid's teeth caught her lower lip and her hand, ever so lightly, brushed hair from Naed's forehead. Arn trembled. He forced his gaze up and into the distance, saw horsemen approaching, and compelled his legs to walk toward them.

"M'lord," Gorm said, reining to a halt, "I see we've come too late."

"Fetch a litter. Naed is wounded." Legs still quivering, Arn laid a hand on Gorm's mount while the

Tolemak dispatched a man to the wagons. "What of our attackers?"

"Gone as quickly as they came." Gorm gestured to a body slung over a horse. "This one's Adanak by his dress." He held out an arrow. "The feathering speaks of northern Adanak, but 'tis clumsily done. See?"

"Made in a hurry?"

Gorm shrugged. He signaled two of his men. "Search the dead man. And fetch the Prince's sword and shield."

"My thanks," Arn said, glad he did not have to return to the body in the grass, although why he should not wish to nagged at him. He had pried swords out of bone, and he had broken them free of armor. Now and then he had struck with such force he punctured breastplate. Each time he had freed his sword, stepped over the body and gone on. Not since his childhood had he struck with such blind, raging fury as he had this eve.

He cast a furtive glance at Aerid, to assure himself she was indeed well, then shook off the thought that made sweat prickle again between his shoulder blades. Now was not the time for it. "Our losses?"

"Three dead, a handful wounded. 'Twas a small party by their tracks."

Plucking the arrow from Gorm's hand, Arn rolled the shaft between his finger and thumb. "Why would northern Adanaks send a party to raid us now, after we crossed into D'nalee?"

"'Tis sure the dead won't tell us."

"Direct the men to set up camp. 'Tis nearly dark and 'tis unlike they'll try again so soon, but double the guard any—"

"M'lord!" A soldier stood over the man in the grass. "This man bears a Tolemak sword!"

****

"So, this is what your master provides me with!" Dlaniger surveyed the faces surrounding him in the darkness. "Where is the vaunted Tolemak taste for battle? Where is the fabled Tolemak discipline? Or are you naught but a collection of misfits your master foists on me under the pretense of offering assistance?"

The under-officer cleared his throat. "We did what we were told, sir, but the woman's horse broke away from us and—"

"So you have said." Dlaniger tugged on his gloves. "However, you could have employed what little intelligence you possess to anticipate just such an occurrence and act accordingly."

The under-officer dropped his gaze. "Aye, sir."

"But, sir," said a short man, "we killed or wounded nigh unto 15—"

Dlaniger seized the speaker's collar. "We did not come to kill the men of Val-Feyridge," he hissed each word into the startled man's face. "We came to kill the Prince! However he, so you say, remains untouched." With a curl of his lip, he shoved the man into his companions. The line staggered, but no one fell.

"As insurance against such a possibility, I ordered you to seize his woman—a mere woman, mind you!—but you incompetents could not accomplish even that small task!" Grasping his horse's reins, he swung into the saddle. "We shall have another opportunity at Druemarwin. There, I shall personally see to the Prince's demise." Hauling his horse about, he heeled it.

The men sprang out of his way as he rode off. "D'nalian bastard!" murmured one.

"'Twould be a pleasure to test my knife on him!" said another.

"Mount up," said the under-officer. "We have our orders."

"Aye," grumbled a third, "can't touch the overgrown snit till he's done the deed."

"So, let's see that he does," said the under-officer. "The sooner the better, lads."

With a rumble of assent, they hurried to their mounts and rode after Dlaniger.

****

The oil lamp Arn held provided needed light while Aerid fastened the last bandage on Naed's thigh, but the heat it gave off made moisture bead on her upper lip. She washed her hands in the basin Banir held. "'Twill be fever. The fighting...and falling..." Pressing damp palms to her cheeks, she used the coolness to steady herself. "'Tis much damage to the muscle and the bone. He may— belike he may be lame."

Beside her, Banir swallowed. She followed his glance to the pallet where Naed dozed under the influence of a sleeping draught. He would be waking soon, and he would be thirsty. "He must be watched. I shall stay with him tonight."

Arn hung the lamp on the tent pole. "His man can watch him. He can send for you if there's any change."

Aerid knew by his voice he would brook no argument. Sighing, she rose from Naed's side. The tent dipped. Colorful explosions dotted her vision. She watched Arn's face turn upside down, then vanish into a velvet darkness.

When sensation returned, she was enclosed in familiar, strong arms. Warm fingers brushed her throat and a pulsating beat throbbed under her shoulder as they had done once before... somewhere.

"Aerid?"

She peered at Arn's features as they settled into focus. Strange, she thought, but he has lost his color. "Be you ill, love?" she murmured.

He bit off an exasperated sound. "Not me. You. You fainted."

"Oh." She glanced at her surroundings and realized he had carried her outside and now held her in his lap before the fire. She breathed deeply of the cool air.

"Better?" When she nodded, he raised her face to his inspecting gaze. "'Tis sure you are, you weren't hurt...before?"

She watched his mouth struggle with the words. "A bit of dizziness. 'Twas too hot in the tent." Sighing, she lifted his hand to her cheek and leaned into it.

Arn grunted. "Eat something and then I'll put you to bed."

Her stomach churned. "No. No food. 'Tis better I sleep."

Arn studied her face again. "Aerid, tell me true..."

"'Tis Naed." She made a small gesture. "He did injure himself to rescue..."

His thumb, stroking over her lower lip, stilled its trembling. "He's young," he said roughly. "He'll mend." Rising, he carried her away from the fire and toward the tent they shared.

****

Arn lay in the dark tent, listening to a bit of music one of the sentries hummed. 'Twas a sad song, a lament from one of the old tales, and it suited Arn's mood. He nuzzled Aerid's hair, breathing in the scent of it. As long as he lived, he would never forget it. It had haunted him day and night before he found her in Vinvinnysee, and it would haunt him long after—

Another lump rose in his throat, another in a series that kept his eyes open and unblinking while Aerid slept in his arms. Forcing his lids shut, he pressed a kiss to her hair.

She stirred and snuggled against him. The movement, so guileless, so trusting, tore at his heart like a dull-bladed dagger. How could he have been so foolish as to think he could protect her? By making her his, he had made her a target. If not for Naed, he might have lost her already.

He had seen the wound in the young man's thigh, how the arrow lay in the bone and how being unhorsed had driven the shaft through surrounding muscle. He knew without being told, Naed's life hung as much in the balance as the use of his leg.

He could have lost them both. The thought startled Arn. The youth was his rival, his competitor for the woman in his arms. If he had any doubts Naed loved Aerid, the D'nalian's actions at twilight had dispelled them. If anything, Naed loved her more. The upright youth would never have taken her into his bed without vows of marriage. Why, then, should he mourn Naed's death, particularly if he had no hand in it himself?

The image of Aerid tenderly stroking Naed's forehead burned into Arn's vision. Though she insisted she regarded Naed as only a friend, her face betrayed her. Arn had come between them, he who cynically disregarded legitimacy to satisfy his physical needs! And by doing so, he had doomed them, doomed them both!

The tent seemed too hot, too small, too confining. Aerid's weight on his chest pressed into him, pinching his lungs, crushing his heart. Moving carefully, Arn eased out from under her. He restored the blankets and waited until her breathing deepened. Then, dressing quickly, he threw on his cloak and strode out into the night.

CHAPTER TWENTY-EIGHT

Naed woke slowly, conscious of a jolting, swaying sensation. Over his head, something dark lurched back and forth. He peered at it, trying to bring it into focus.

"So, 'tis to yourself you do come at last."

The familiar voice, soft and musical, chased the remaining fog from his eyes. The dark thing over his head coalesced into an unlighted oil lamp swinging from a wagon strut. Light filtered through wooden slats. "Is it...day?" he croaked.

Settling down beside him, Aerid nodded. She placed a rolled blanket under his head, then braced a cup between her knees, filling it from a water skin.

He gulped the tepid liquid she touched to his lips, greedy for the feel of it on his tongue.

"Enough. You must not be taking so much at once. 'Tis very ill you have been."

"How...long?"

"Nigh onto three days."

She gave him the cup again, but he drank only a little more. He remembered taking an arrow in the leg, and being unhorsed, and returning to camp in a litter. Banir had been near, and Aerid, and the Prince, but—

"My leg! Have I yet my leg?"

"Have no fear." Aerid thwarted his attempt to rise with a hand on his chest. "'Tis whole you be, and complete."

Naed flushed, ashamed of his fears and ashamed of how his hand shook when she offered him the cup again. "Sisters, I am as weak as a newborn calf."

"'Tis stronger you shall be this eve. And then Banir may shave you." She rubbed fingertips across his stubbled chin and smiled. "Indeed, you do look the ruffian."

Another flush started up Naed's throat, but the cart dropped into a rut, and he winced. Aerid clung to the wagon frame as the cart righted itself.

Naed noticed shadows under her eyes. "Where is Banir?" he said, conscious of how his injury must have burdened her. "Banir may tend to me."

The wagon jolted through another rut. Aerid paled. When it steadied, her lips formed a wan smile. "He does tend you at night. By day, I be as confined to this cart as you."

Naed unclenched his fingers from the bedding. "Confined?"

"Until Druemarwin."

She avoided his gaze and offered him the cup again. When he had drunk a few swallows, he murmured, "A wise decision," remembering how she had almost been carried off.

"Aye, belike 'tis so."

Something about her voice pricked at Naed, but fog had invaded his mind and he could concentrate on nothing else but an overwhelming need to close his eyes. "Safe," he mumbled. "Keep you...safe."

"Sleep," she said, and he surrendered.

****

Aerid sat with her hands in her lap and studied the D'nalian countryside through the cart flap. She would be home soon. *Home.* She sighed. The word sounded alien when she applied it to Druemarwin even though she had spent so much of her life there. Somehow, years had passed since spring and the place seemed as distant in her memory as the village of her birth.

How would Dranoel receive her now she belonged to the man who had taken his birthright? Drawing a deep breath, she blew it out. The air in the wagon stifled her and the swaying unsettled her stomach, but Arn adamantly refused to let her ride. She understood his concern. And she understood how the raid increased his preoccupation with the security of his army. Still, she wished he would lie down with her at night or wake with her in the morning instead of slipping in and out while she slept. Indeed, if she did not feel his arms about her in the dark hours after midnight, she would suspect she slept alone.

Heaving a sigh, she smoothed the hem of her tunic. It should be better at Druemarwin, she thought. *We shall be safe there.*

****

His injured leg propped with rolled bedding and his good leg braced against the flooring, Naed lifted his face to the sun. Though the cart driver smelled of garlic and spat constantly, his faults could not diminish Naed's pleasure in riding on the front seat of the cart. Only the familiarity of the road and the knowledge that around the next bend lay the gates of Druemarwin, could steal the warmth from the light dappling his knees.

Naed lowered his gaze to the switching tails of the team. The advance party had arrived hours ago. Dranoel would be waiting, perhaps on the parapet. What would he say to his uncle whose D'nalian ideals he had abandoned to willingly serve a Tolemak? It did not matter he had resigned his position. It mattered only he was returning disgraced and a cripple. Naed gripped the crutch Banir had carved for him. He had been a fool too many times to be of value to any master. And, worse, he had been ruled by his emotions too many times even to be called D'nalian. In truth, he could expect naught but to be turned out.

The road cleared the trees. Naed's blood quickened at the sight of familiar turrets dominating the green. Behind him, at the opened flap of the cart, he heard Aerid's quick inhalation. "The east parapet," she said, nodding toward it.

His gaze fastened on a bulky figure outlined by the late afternoon sun. Approaching the drawbridge, Naed noticed his uncle's attention was fixed not on them but on the man who rode through the gate ahead. And that man's appearance was not welcomed.

"A stopover, my lord," the Prince was saying when the cart rumbled to a halt in the courtyard. "I'll not trouble you long." He had dismounted and begun to pull off his gloves. "Come down. I want you to meet my Second."

Naed's face flamed. If he were not descending from the cart, and if the act did not require all of his, Aerid's and the driver's strength, he would have spoken. As it was, he jammed Banir's crutch under his armpit and, disdaining Aerid's offer of a shoulder, hobbled toward the man who mocked both him and the position he was about to be stripped of.

****

Dlaniger pressed his back into the southwest turret wall. The guard, his attention on events in the courtyard, remained leaning over the inner wall. In two strides, Dlaniger drove his knife into the man's neck.

Dlaniger's companion stepped over the body. "We'll be hard pressed to escape." He nodded toward armed men filling the courtyard and green.

Kneeling at the wall overlooking the courtyard, Dlaniger reached for one of the bows his companion had laid on the stones between them. "This is my home, or have you forgotten that?"

The other man dropped his gaze and strung an arrow. "Where should I aim, sir?"

"We shall aim for the Prince. I shall shoot first. Let your arrow fly upon the feathers of mine." He glanced behind at the sun, satisfying himself its brightness obscured their presence. "We should have time to loose three arrows each. Make them count."

The man nodded and wiped his face on his sleeve.

Gaining entrance to the fortress had not been difficult. All it required was proper dress and timing. Dlaniger smiled, pleased with his ingenuity. Soon, he would have it all, Druemarwin, Val-Feyridge, and Erodasi.

Looking left, he made out the unmistakable bulk of his father descending the parapet stairs toward the man marked for death. 'Twas fitting the Prince should die this way, at the hands of the heir to the fortress in which he sought refuge. Sighting along the arrow, Dlaniger drew the bowstring taut beside his cheek.

****

'Twas only a few steps from the wagon to where the Prince stood with his uncle near the stone well, but sweat stood out on Naed's forehead when he completed them.

The Prince, face unreadable, was holding a folded parchment and saying, "This letter, my lord, 'tis yours, I believe. 'Tis sorry I am to report it was not properly delivered."

Dranoel's gaze rushed from the Prince to Naed to the letter, his expression flashing first impatience, then

331

astonishment, then anger. "What have you done—?" He snatched the letter from the Prince's hand, his face white and mottled.

"To protect the bearer, your nephew gave his life and his sword into my hands. 'Tis admirably he has served these months as my Second, but by his own request I return him to you." The Prince folded his gloves. "'Tis out of the purest of motives Naed has asked me to release him from his sworn obligations. D'nalian honor being such as it is, I feel compelled to explain to you why he seeks to nullify the oaths he swore to me, but being Tolemak, I confess to not understanding why he should wish to give up such an advantageous position, but then 'tis like even D'nalians can be foolish where a woman is concerned."

Naed understood now. The Prince meant to leave him no scrap of dignity but to strip him of everything, here, in front of his uncle and his countrymen. Well, 'twas no more than he deserved for falling prey to the man.

"M'lord?" From behind his shoulder, he heard Aerid address Dranoel and saw the flash of her gaze before her hand circled his elbow, the touch warm, supportive.

"Child...you are alive...both of you...are alive!" Dranoel breathed, engulfing Naed and Aerid in an embrace that nearly toppled Naed and crushed their bodies together.

In the instant of contact, Naed saw the gray peppering Dranoel's hair, the lines etched about his mouth, the faded color of his eyes. He felt his uncle's hand tremble as it flexed on his arm, saw the look of wonder on Dranoel's face as he leaned back and surveyed their faces. Naed's heart ached. He had been so many times a fool these past months, but his fear of Dranoel's censure had been most foolish of all. He should have known love when it looked out at him from under those bristling brows.

"Naed, lad!" Dranoel said, and hugged him again, one to one, a bear hug that jammed his chin into Dranoel's shoulder. "Sisters be thanked for your safe return." Releasing Naed, he touched Aerid gently on the cheek. "Sisters be thanked for both of you. But I still do not understand," he said, swinging toward the Prince, "how they come to be in your—"

An arrow thudded into Prince Arn's chest, flinging

him to the ground. Dranoel, still turning, sprawled atop the Prince, a feathered shaft quivering from his back.

With a choked "Arn!" Aerid lunged for the Prince.

"No!" Naed threw himself into her, knocking her down. Two more arrows chinked into the flagstones as he rolled with her under the cart. Through the wheel spokes, he saw soldiers pulling the Prince and Dranoel to cover behind the well.

She shoved at his chest. "What—let me—!"

"Be still! 'Tis not safe." Naed captured the arm she had worked free, but she cried out. He jerked away and stared at blood streaking his palm, staining his tunic, soaking Aerid's sleeve.

****

"You—you—imbecile!" Dlaniger flung his companion to the floor and seized his throat. "You have shot my father!"

"I—he moved!"

"You...have...murdered...him!" For each bitten-out word, Dlaniger slammed the man's head into the stone.

"Please!" The man pawed at Dlaniger's hands. "They—they're coming!"

The sound of shouts and boots scuffling, many boots, penetrated Dlaniger's brain. He glanced towards the turret steps. "So they are. How fortunate for you, or this would not be so quick!" Drawing his knife, he slit the man's throat.

He rocked to his knees, cleaned his blade on the man's tunic, and stood. Glancing at the courtyard, he saw the Prince struggle to his feet amid a crowd of his soldiers. Dlaniger's nostrils flared. "Your cat's lives will not save you next time, Prince of Val-Feyridge!" The sounds of pursuit almost upon him, he vaulted the turret wall and slipped into a side passage below.

****

Arn leaned against the stone well and grasped the arrow shaft with both hands. Gritting his teeth, he yanked it free. Warmth trickled down his belly, but the mail, leather and plate armor under his tunic had absorbed most of the arrow's impact.

"Adanak." He snapped the arrow in two. "Another hastily made fake." A soldier handed him a cloth and he

333

shoved it under his armor. 'Twas a small wound, the depth of a fingertip, and he could tell by the ache it had nicked a rib. "What of Dranoel?"

"Dead, m'lord." Gorm nodded toward the body slumped against the well.

"I want them found! Dead or alive, I want these murderers found!"

Gorm inspected the stain spreading on Arn's tunic. "'Tis best I fetch a healer, m'lord."

"These raiders are Tolemak. I know they are. But whose?"

Gorm made him sit on the well rim and tugged loose the lacings of his armor. "Roines?"

Who else, Arn thought, but his soon-to-be father-in-law? Who else stood to gain as much from his death? While Gorm removed his tunic and armor, Arn's gaze roved past Gorm's huge shoulder, over the cleared courtyard, and came to rest on a rough-hewn crutch lying in the dust.

Terror—the pure, absolute panic he had endured but once before in his life when he was twelve and Rolnar's men had tried to drown him—that panic induced by knowing, though his hands could grab at it, though he could see the surface glinting with sunlight scant inches away, the air his lungs craved was bubbling out of his mouth while arms held him, thrashing, in cold, rushing water that sucked him down into it—*that* terror propelled Arn, shaking, to his feet. Stumbling past Gorm, he saw arrows imbedded in the earth, a spatter of blood on the dust, Naed hunched behind the cart and the driver kneeling at his side, cradling between them a slender form with a pale face.

"They struck her!" Naed shouted. "The bastards struck her!"

Arn quivered, the roar of his blood drowning out the beat of his heart, the throb of his pulse, the sounds of the courtyard, Naed's voice, everything. Dropping to his knees, he gathered Aerid in his arms and clutched her to his chest.

****

A smoldering log split, shooting out sparks. The sudden flare of light chased shadows into the recesses of the beamed ceiling and illuminated the bed nearby. Seeing Aerid still slept, Arn leaned back in the huge, carved chair. For hours he had sat thus, watching and waiting.

She had resisted the healer's drug, but Arn had insisted. Now he watched her toss, made restless by pain and the dreams he knew all too well accompanied such an injury. He could not sleep, nor had he slept much in the nights previous. Each time he closed his eyes, he saw the blood-stained riders, heard his mother's death shriek, smelled the burning—

Aerid stirred, murmuring something he could not catch. Arn straightened in his chair, but she fell silent and he heard her breathing deepen.

He closed his eyes, longing to go to her, to cradle her in his arms and comfort her, but he dared not. To touch her now would turn his resolution to water. His fingers dug into the rough-carved wooden arms. To touch her now would be to condemn her to death as surely as if he wielded the knife himself.

Arn forced his fingers to unclench, willed his heart to beat more evenly, ordered his eyes to open and focus on the figure in the bed. He would do what he had to do.

****

Naed stood in the doorway of Dranoel's chamber and leaned on his crutch. Every candle in the room had been lit. They were half burned now, as befitted the hours after midnight.

When the Prince disappeared with Aerid, Naed had looked at the faces of the people he had once served among. Their master was dead, and they did not know what to do. When no one stepped forward, he gave the orders himself, directing Ekwul to prepare the lord for burial. Now he approached the body and gazed at his uncle, at the shuttered face and folded hands and wished they were not frozen forever in the sleep of death. All too briefly he had known his uncle's love. All too quickly it had been taken from him. Ordering his eyes to open and remain clear, he touched Dranoel's hands. Then he turned and hobbled out of the room.

****

Aerid heard someone stir the fire. Her arm ached,

her tongue seemed stuck to the roof of her mouth, and she had no clear idea where she was. She forced open her eyes. "A-Arn?"

"Ekwul."

Twisting her head, she saw the somber face of her master's personal servant. He had aged since she had last seen him. His hair had whitened and lines scored his jowls. He wore his best clothes, Aerid noticed as her memory returned with a rush. "Your master is dead," she said, leaning back on the pillows.

Ekwul set a cup and a hunk of bread on the table beside her bed. "Eat. Master Naed will be to see you soon. He would have you come to—to—" He dashed a sleeve under his nose.

"To bury the master," Aerid finished for him.

Ekwul nodded. He threw another log on the fire and left.

Aerid stared at the bed's canopy. Where was Arn? Had she dreamed he sat in the chair opposite? That he watched her in the night and brooded? She closed her eyes, fighting their burn. Something was wrong, terribly wrong, but she would not cry. No, she vowed as liquid oozed from under her lashes, these tears were for Dranoel.

****

Naed laid a hand on the latch to Dranoel's study. The man to whom it once belonged lay under clods of D'nalian earth, Druemarwin rock heaped over his resting place. He had personally seen the proper ritual respectfully carried out. Now 'twas done. Finished.

He pulled the latch and pushed the door open. "You wished to see me, m'lord?"

Prince Arn turned from contemplating the slate-gray sky. "My compliments." He gestured to the fur-trimmed cloak Naed removed. "You wear elegance well."

"'Tis not mine. Master Borth graciously lent it to me."

"However you came by it, I'm pleased to see you'll cut a satisfactory figure in the role to which you'll shortly ascend."

Frowning, Naed draped the cloak over a chair. They had spoken so little of late he had forgotten how the man played with words, how he used them to keep his opponents off balance and vulnerable. This time, Naed decided as he brushed beaded moisture from the fur, he would resist the Prince's manipulations. "Speak plainly. Tell me what you will and be done with it."

"I recall you bear your master's will. Have you opened it?"

In the days and months—a lifetime, it seemed—since Naed had left this room bearing the cylinder around his neck, he had forgotten it dangled there. Reaching into his tunic, he withdrew the container and broke the seal. The contents spilled onto the table illumed by thin light from a rain-spotted window. There was a tightly rolled parchment and something small wrapped in cloth. Naed smoothed open the parchment first, conscious the Prince watched, until what he read made him drop with a thump into his uncle's fur-lined chair.

Prince Arn plucked the parchment from his limp fingers and read the message out loud. "'If 'tis you reading this now, Naed, know that however much your mother may deny it, you are my son, conceived when your mother came to tend her sister in her last illness. 'Tis ashamed I am to have broken my marriage vows and caused her to break hers, but know you, son, that I have loved your mother all these years, even before I wed her sister. You are my son and my heir to all I hold. Dlaniger receives naught. He has forsworn all that is D'nalian and thereby surrenders all rights to his inheritance.'"

The Prince looked at Naed over the parchment. "'Tis more. Did you read all of it?"

Shaking his head, Naed raised a hand and let it fall back to the chair arm. "I—why did he never tell me?"

"'Tis like he tried. He gave you his will. Did you never wonder why?"

"Did you?"

"Aye, more than once. 'Twas in my mind when first I saw you together."

Naed held his head in his hands. Would his world never stop tilting? Now his father was not his father, and his mother forsworn, and his uncle...*his father*?

"Had your uncle—your father—not done so, 'twas my intent to make you lord and master of Druemarwin anyway. You've proven yourself more than fit for the role."

"'Tis not yours to give."

"Unless I'm mistaken, my men still hold this place." The Prince returned his glare. "While I don't wish to interfere with the rules of inheritance, 'twould be my responsibility to appoint a steward for Druemarwin until the heir should appear. Happily, he's here." He tossed down the parchment. "Dranoel has left you something else. If 'tis as I suspect, the cloth that wraps it bears some message too."

Sweat soaked Naed's undertunic and every muscle in his body shook with the light-headedness still gripping him, but he found the energy to resent the Prince's manner. "Why do you not read that too?"

"Understand me—I'm sorely tempted, but 'tis not mine. 'Twas left to you."

Snorting, Naed picked up the bundle and unwrapped it. A gemstone fell out. Polished and faceted, it lay like dark honey on the tabletop.

Naed looked up at the Prince's indrawn breath, but the man said, "The cloth, read it."

Dranoel's tight script had bled into the cloth, but Naed could make out the words: "Let he who finds this care for it as I have. 'Tis the D'nal Stone, treasure of D'nalee." He read the message twice, not trusting his eyes, but the truth of it leaked slowly into his brain. His uncle—his father—keeper of a legendary treasure? 'Twas more than his already confounded mind could comprehend—except for one thing.

Deliberately, Naed placed his hands on either side of the stone and looked at the Prince. "You have Vinvinnysee to crown yourself with. This you would have too, would you not?"

"Aye, I'll admit it, but I'll not have what's not freely given." Prince Arn backed a step and flexed his fingers. "I've not lied to you, Naed. 'Tis still my desire to unite our lands, to have you at my side as D'nal with Tolem, but as you've chosen otherwise, I'll remake the Kingdom with what I have. Keep the stone, and let the secret of its existence remain ours alone."

"'Tis generous of you, m'lord, and I do not doubt your sincerity, but I have learned too well that what you give comes always at a price. What is it to be this time?"

The Prince had the grace to look discomfited. "You have Druemarwin. Keep Banir and any of your personal guard who wish to stay. When I leave tomorrow, I'll take all but a small number of my men with me. The remaining contingent will return to Val-Feyridge with Krenin after the first snow. After that, defense of Druemarwin will lie entirely in your hands. Defense and control."

I shall be free, Naed thought. "You will make no further claims upon my allegiance?"

"None whatsoever."

Naed stared at the desk that would now be his, at the ornate cup he could call his own. 'Twas more than he had dreamed possible, a title, a fortress, a future—and freedom from the Prince—but he could muster no joy, only an odd, hollow ache in his chest. Feeling suddenly burdened, he leaned on his elbows. "Why? Surely you would rather see me dead."

The Prince's mouth twitched. Some emotion darkened his eyes. He walked to the desk and grazed his knuckles along the surface. Outside, the rain that had threatened during the burial broke from the sky and poured in rivers down the window, its shadows streaking the Prince's face. "You asked me to speak plainly, so hear me. I'm leaving tomorrow, but without Aerid." His knuckles whitened on the desktop. "You once wanted to wed her. Now you are Master of Druemarwin, 'tis my wish you do so."

Thunderstruck, Naed drew breath. "She—'tis you she has chosen and well do I know it!"

"And well do my enemies know it, too! She was almost killed yesterday! They have already tried to kidnap her! When we leave this place, it should be clear even to you they'll try again! I won't have her hurt again because of me!"

"You should have considered that before you took her to your bed! Aye, mayhap then your conscience would not now trouble you!"

Lunging across the desk, Prince Arn seized Naed's tunic. "I ought to kill you!"

"Naught would please me more than for you to try."

For the space of heartbeats, neither spoke or moved.

The air between them crackled as if the storm outside had directed all its energy into the small room. Finally, the Prince shoved away. "For Aerid's sake...for Aerid's sake—!" With a last, savage look, he ripped open the door and plunged into the corridor.

Naed trembled as the door banged to. For the first time, he had faced down the Prince and won. Prying his fingers from the edge of the desk, he wondered why he felt no elation.

Because he had not won at all. *For Aerid's sake*, he had escaped with his life. *For Aerid's sake*, he would do what honor required—fulfill the obligation the Prince had so callously dumped in his lap! Rising, he seized his crutch, but it caught on the chair leg and he crashed to the floor.

Naed lay on his stomach, rain shadows streaking the stone around him. His leg throbbed, his chin stung where he had struck it on the floor, a scrape on the heel of his hand burned, but he did not move. He stared at the silent wall, the closed door, the empty chair by the fire. A gust of wind lashed the window, but he paid it no heed. Slowly, his fingers closed into fists. Lowering his head into the crook of his arm, he let the grief he had kept so long at bay wash over him.

****

Like the leaden sky that had prevailed during Dranoel's burial, Aerid felt burdened, unable to summon energy for anything but necessary functions. Her arm pounded, and a sense of queasiness came and went with the pain.

Dry-eyed, she had stood with a somber Naed while Dranoel had been laid to rest in the dark, D'nalian earth. Later, the folk of Druemarwin had offered tentative expressions of respect to the young man who had presided over their master's burial. Aerid had watched from the fringe while he accepted their words with a dignity beyond his years. Then he refused the cart, refused her offer of help, refused everything but the crutch and hobbled alone over the rutted road and back to the fortress. If she had never left Druemarwin, she would have wed him. And she would have been content with his kind love and gentle heart—if she had never met Arn.

She had seen Arn but once, from a distance. He stood on the ramparts watching the funeral procession, his cloak billowing in the wind, his hair tossed, his expression brooding. The uneven footing demanded her attention and, when she looked again, he had vanished into the mist swirling about the fortress walls. Now she sat before the fire in her chamber, willing its heat to drive the chill from her bones, seeking in its dancing lights a balm to raise her spirits.

A draft rushed past her feet and she knew someone had opened the door. "Here. By the fire," she said, sensing Arn's presence.

When he neither responded nor approached, she began to doubt her perceptions. Just as she twisted to see if he were really there, Arn closed the door and entered her line of vision.

Relieved, she leaned back in the chair.

Stopping before the fire, he extended his hands as if to warm them, then lowered them to his sides. "I'm leaving in the morning. Dranoel's will made Naed his heir. The new Lord of Druemarwin will look after you."

While she heard his words, Aerid saw how the skin was drawn tight over his cheekbones and the scar showed silver in the firelight. His stance, for all its apparent stillness, was as rigid as a drawn bow. Her stomach tensed. "I shall not be delaying you. My arm mends quickly and—"

"Don't, don't make this any more difficult."

She watched his eyes close, saw how he sucked in an uneven breath, and understood. These past days, since the attack that wounded Naed, her heart had sensed all along what her mind had steadfastly ignored, even as he daily pulled farther and farther from her. "'Tis true then, you will go and not be returning," she whispered as the world fell out from beneath her.

He shook his head. "I should never have taken you for my own. Demon take me, but I should never have taken you!" He leaned on the mantle, gripping it with both hands. "I have nothing—do you understand?— nothing to give you. Nothing but dishonor and—"

"It matters naught to me that you be betrothed. 'Tis enough that I have your love."

He flinched as if she had struck him. "I meant to tell you. Erodasi means nothing to me. 'Tis a contract, no more. If I could have, I would... I don't know what I would have done. I wasn't thinking that far ahead, fool that I am." He pressed his forehead into the mantle, and she fancied she could hear bone grind against stone. "Aerid, believe me, I would do anything to keep you. I love you more than I've ever loved anyone, but I can't keep you with me now my enemies know what you mean to me. They've already tried to harm you twice."

"I do not fear them."

"But I do!" Arn whispered, meeting her gaze at last. "Don't you see? One day they'll kill you and I couldn't bear that! They took everyone I loved once. I can't live through that again."

The torment etched in his features tore at her heart. She pushed up from the chair.

"Don't!" he choked, holding out a hand to ward her off. "If you touch me, I won't be able to leave. And I must...now...while I can leave you...safe."

Aerid sank back into the cushions. She hugged her bandaged arm, wishing it was Arn's body she held, his pain she comforted, but he would not permit it. He had to leave, and she understood why. Had he not shown her all of himself, his passions as well as his fears? That terror she had glimpsed in his eyes on a street in Vinvinnysee had risen up these last days and she knew it held his heart in a stranglehold.

Though he needed her now more than ever, he could not see that need, would not acknowledge it no matter how hard she tried to show him the truth.

No, she had to let him go. To cling to him now would be to destroy him.

Closing her eyes, she cleared her throat. "I will not be detaining you further."

She heard Arn move, heard the scuff of boot on stone, heard his whispered, "Aerid..." but she stoically refused to open her eyes. One look at his face and she knew she would rush to him and clutch his legs to beg him to stay one more night, one more hour, one more moment...

Aerid forced air down her burning throat, past the lump threatening to gag her, and into a chest that would not expand. She would not wound him so. She loved him too much. "Fare you well, m'lord," she whispered.

She heard Arn's ragged breathing, felt the rush of chill air on her feet.

"Goodbye," he said in an odd, tight voice, and then he was gone.

CHAPTER TWENTY-NINE

The wind tore at Arn from the north, bringing frosted nights and crystalline days. He pushed his army, urging them on, striving to cover ground, to return home. To escape. He slept little, his nights disturbed by restless dreams. Sometimes, he felt Aerid's warmth beside him; other times he breathed the scent of her hair. Each time he would wake, drenched with sweat, and find himself alone. 'Twas not new, this being alone. Had he not lived for years in this condition and suffered no ill effects?

The men did not complain of the pace. They knew each step, each league brought them closer to home, to family, to the women who waited for them. Arn refused to envy his soldiers as they plunged eagerly into the river dividing D'nalee and Tolemak.

****

Within a week, Naed burned his crutch. His game leg dragged and climbing a single flight of stairs left his undertunic drenched, but he threw himself into the administration of Druemarwin, wanting as much to forget the past as to honor the memory of Dranoel. He made Banir his Second and gave Grodar and Morys positions in the guard. At first, the people looked askance at a D'nalian lord who surrounded himself with Tolemaks, but only Ekwul openly resisted, disputing with Banir the duties that should have been his as the lord's personal servant. Lately, a truce prevailed and Naed hoped the worst had passed.

Aerid kept to herself, joining him for meals but otherwise venturing out only when her healing services were required. After dinner, she would not sit long before the fire but excused herself and went out to walk the walls. Often, from his window, he saw her silhouetted against the starred sky, a solitary, huddled figure staring westward.

Naed cursed the Prince then, until, bitter and spent,

he sat in Dranoel's chair and stared at naught.

****

"What's the news?" Rolnar demanded of the man dripping water on his tent floor.

"The last attempt wounded the Prince, m'lord."

"Wounded? How badly?"

"Not to the death, m'lord."

"Fools! Blunderers!" Rolnar's chair toppled with his upward surge. "Where's that D'nalian halfwit I gave you over to?"

"Disappeared, m'lord."

"Disappeared? Do you mean dead?"

The under-officer shrugged while a servant righted Rolnar's chair. "Master Dlaniger went into Druemarwin with one of my men. They struck the Prince, but my man was killed. We heard nothing of the D'nalian. 'Tis like he never planned to rejoin us."

"Why that lying, lowland bastard!" Rolnar sat in the chair his manservant had restored to its proper place. "Did he know your orders?"

"No, m'lord. We never gave ourselves away."

Tapping his index finger against his lips, Rolnar leaned back in the chair. The D'nalian would probably make straight for Val-Feyridge and Erodasi, but he would have the Demon's own time getting into the place with Belac surrounding it. "And the Prince's army?"

"Less than a week behind us, m'lord."

"Did you observe their strength?" At the man's nod, Rolnar rubbed his hands together. "Fetch my officers. And summon the other lords. You may inform us all together."

"Aye, m'lord."

"And for pity's sake, change your clothing! You've dripped all over my dry floor."

****

Aerid studied her forearm in the firelight. The arrow had laid back a flap of muscle, and making a fist troubled her, but the skin had healed. All that remained was the shrinking scab and pinched, pink new skin where the scar would form. She sighed, wishing the wound in her heart would mend as quickly.

She tended the ill, but when she approached Naed about returning to her other duties, he blurted, "You shall not return to servitude! Not in my fortress!" When she and others in the hall stared at him, he flushed scarlet, muttered something about discussing it later, and limped away.

At supper that evening, Naed cleared his throat and suggested if she desired to be useful, she could help him manage the household. When she agreed, he appeared so relieved he drank a second cup of wine. Now, sitting before the fire in her own small chamber and resting her hands on her stomach, Aerid wondered what promise Naed had made to Arn regarding her and how what she must soon tell him would affect that.

****

The rain that pelted the men of Val-Feyridge for two days turned to sleet. They hunched into their cloaks and their horses lowered their heads into the prevailing northwesterly winds. Arn drew rein alongside Gorm. The huge man roused himself from a trance-like state and brushed bits of ice from his beard. "Has the scout returned, m'lord?"

Arn shook his head. Ice beads fell from his hood and sprinkled his gloves. "They should have been back hours ago."

"'Tis like the weather has delayed them."

Arn squinted into the sheeting gray. "We've less than two days to the Arbez, even in this, and we haven't heard from Val-Feyridge. Lord Tylus and the others ought to have received my messages days ago."

"Shall I be sending another pigeon, m'lord?"

"Later." Arn scanned the leafless forest and narrow valley through which they marched. "Let's wait for the scout."

****

Naed shook sleet from his cloak and hung it beside the mantle. He grunted in response to Banir's nod and sat at the table while the servants quickly laid out dinner. 'Twas easy to grow accustomed to being served. Aerid, he thought as she slid into the chair next to his, would never forget where—

"Your pardon," she blurted, a stricken look on her face.

"She should not have tended the ill," he said as she

346

fled. "She is too weak yet and—"

"'Tis no illness she has." Banir speared a leg of lamb. "She's shared a man's bed. Belike 'tis the fruits of it."

"Fruits? What are—? By the Sisters!" Naed bolted up, staggering when his leg refused to comply. "The cowardly bastard Prince has begotten *another* bastard—and of *this* woman!"

"What will you do if she's truly with child?"

"Kill him!" He shoved a chair out of his path.

"Aye," Banir said, reaching for a chunk of dark bread, "'twould be wise to kill the father."

Naed glowered at the Tolemak. "I should *like* to kill him! Is that wiser?"

"Belike 'tis truer."

With a muttered oath, Naed hobbled away. What in the Name of the Sisters *could* he do?

He found Aerid lying on her bed, face pale but composed. She had been sweating, he saw as he moved a chair to the bedside. Damp tendrils of hair clung to her forehead and her eyes glistened, but not with fever brightness. Lowering himself into the chair, he placed his game leg on a stool. "You are with child, are you not?"

Aerid shifted on the pillow. "I shall not be burdening you. I shall move to the cottage in the wood. 'Twill please Gam to have company, and—"

"We shall be wed as soon as it can be arranged."

He saw the tumble of her hair, felt the touch of her fingers on his arm. "Naed..."

Pushing out of the chair, he limped to the mantle. "I shall claim the child as mine. 'Twill be no need to mention the child's true parentage."

"Naed..."

"I know you do not love me," he plunged on, pacing, "but I cannot permit you to bear this child alone. As my wife, you and the child will have a name and a title. You will have my protection."

"And you?" Aerid said, rising. "What shall you be having?"

He shrugged. "A woman to call my wife. A child to call my own."

"Another man's woman. Another man's child." She slid against the mantle to face him. "What if you should

347

fall in love?"

"I have already done so." He turned away. "I made myself the fool."

He heard her shift against the stone, saw, out of the corner of his eye, how her hands worried the folds of her skirt. "Arn did ask this of you, aye?"

"No!" But that was a lie. "I—Aerid, believe me, I would do no less if he had not!"

He turned, and she met his gaze with a melancholy smile. "Then understand, my dear friend," she said, touching his hand, "why, for both of our sakes, I will not wed you."

Naed's fingers wrapped around hers, and he savored the texture of her skin, the warmth of her nearness, the scent of her hair before he uncurled his fingers and let her hand fall away. "Then understand why, for all of our sakes, I shall nonetheless claim the child as mine."

Her gaze searched his face as if probing his resolution. "If that be your will, I shall not be disputing it." Rising on tiptoe, Aerid touched her lips to his cheek.

For months he had dreamed of her touch, her kiss. Now he could think of naught to say but, "Get you to bed," and naught to do but leave.

****

Darkness overtook Arn's army. The men dispersed among the shelter of a fir-studded forest and made camp. They coaxed reluctant fires into life and huddled about the warmth.

Arn paced. He accepted a bowl of stew from one of his guard and poked at it. Finally, he handed the half-eaten meal to Borth. "I'm going out to find the scout. Choose ten men and have them meet me at the horses." Without waiting for Borth's response, he strode off.

Halfway to the next fire, Arn froze. The huddled men dropped their cloaks and turned toward the trees, toward a rising sound that was not thunder or wind. The hair on the back of Arn's neck rose. "Your weapons!" he shouted, drawing his sword. "Take your weapons!"

Mounted men burst from the darkness. They plunged into the camp, leaping fires, trampling and slashing and screaming, "Death to Val-Feyridge!"

"Stop them!" Arn shouted. "Turn them back!" But the

invaders poured into the camp like a river through a broken dike. Arn flung himself at the nearest attackers, taking down three before a rearing horse struck him alongside the head.

"The Prince!" someone shouted.

"Kill the Prince!" another cried.

On his knees, Arn dashed blood out of his eye. He saw four riders reining their mounts about, saw the main attack rushing on behind them, and understood he faced them alone. Snatching up a discarded shield, he scrambled to his feet and retreated toward the trees, intent on using the close quarters against his attackers.

The first rider charged before he could reach cover. Deflecting the blow with his shield, he spun to meet the second's rush—and tripped over a dead man. His attacker sliced air where Arn's body had been. Seeing a flash of hooves, Arn flung himself away from the third man, but something clipped his shin. Bits of stone pelted his face. Rolling to a crouch, he tasted blood.

The fourth man spurred his mount.

Dodging the horse, Arn slashed the man's leg. "Kill him!" the man shrieked.

His three companions charged as one.

Arn backed toward the trees, but they were on him in a blur of swords and hooves. Flung to and fro with the force of their blows, his arms ached, his ears rang, his breath came hard and fast. A horse trod on his foot and he cried out, shoving against the squealing animal. A sword blow smashed his shield into his face. Another flung him to the ground. Gasping, he crawled between milling hooves and groped for his shield while blood, sweat or both stung his eyes.

If I'm to die, Arn vowed, *it won't be on my knees in the mud!* Surging upright, he sliced the girth of one man's saddle, unhorsing him. Arn spun to the next rider, but it was Gorm he saw bearing down on him, a massive hand outstretched. "Here, m'lord!"

Gorm hauled him onto the rump of his horse and galloped into the forest. "Be you hurt, m'lord?"

"Bruised." Arn looked over his shoulder, but no riders followed. "How did you find me?"

"Instinct, m'lord." The big man grinned. "Where else

should I find my Prince but where the odds be four to one?"

"My thanks," Arn said, allowing his forehead to rest a moment on the broad back.

"So, you found him," said a voice from the ridge line above.

"Aye, and in the midst of a tangle, too," Gorm said.

Arn recognized the rider as Borth and asked, "Did they rout us?"

"Aye, but we have our horses."

Through a gap in the trees, Arn made out the fires of their overrun camp. Tiny black figures rushed from one point of yellow light to another. "And they have our supplies."

"They didn't pursue us, m'lord," Borth added.

Arn slid to the ground amid a murmur of relief from men gathered nearby. "Can we regroup quickly enough to mount a counterattack?"

Gorm stroked his beard. "'Twould be a pleasure to strike fear of the Demon into 'em."

"More like a healthy respect for the mettle of Westerners." Arn ripped up a handful of moss to clean his sword. "Well, can we do it?"

"Aye, m'lord!" said several men standing to the side. "Filthy Kothmen!"

"And Roines! We saw his banner."

"Ormo and Lede, too, m'lord!"

"'Tis like the whole of eastern Tolemak be assembled against us," said Gorm.

"Borth," Arn said, "take some men and observe their composition. The rest of us will give them a couple of hours to think they've routed us before we show them otherwise."

A rumble of assent ran through the men.

Arn shoved hair from his forehead. His fingers encountered a sticky, matted mass.

"You'd best have that head looked to, m'lord," Gorm said, "while there's time."

Arn frowned. His head throbbed. "Very well," he muttered, wiping his hand on his tunic.

****

Rolnar of Roines sat his horse and surveyed the

littered remains of the camp. "Where's the Prince?"

The officer at his side avoided his gaze. "I'm told we wounded him."

"Wounded! Is that all you pack of incompetent idiots can accomplish? Wounded!" He slapped his quirt against his boot.

"We have them on the run, m'lord," the officer said with a sullen look.

Rolnar surveyed the soldiers who stood at a respectful distance from his horse. "You'll never finish them as long as they have the Prince." He unfastened his money pouch and held it up. "I'll pay a hundred pieces of gold to the man who brings me proof of the Prince's death. Do you hear? A hundred pieces of gold to the man who kills the Prince of Val-Feyridge!"

The men looked at each other. The officer licked his lips.

Rolnar smiled. A hundred pieces of gold would hardly be missed from his treasury, but to rabble such as this...

The forest roared. Horsemen exploded from the trees.

"Val-Feyridge!" Rolnar shrieked, grabbing his sword.

Two attackers rode directly at him. One struck his shield while the other slashed his sword. Lifted out of the saddle, the Lord of Roines somersaulted over the tail of his horse.

Gasping and sputtering, Rolnar heaved himself out of a mud puddle. "*Two* hundred pieces of gold!" he bellowed, shaking his fist at the vanished attackers. "I'll give two hundred pieces of gold to the man who kills the demon Prince!"

****

Krenin eased out of the saddle in Druemarwin's courtyard. He had pushed his troop hard since leaving Vinvinnysee and he looked forward to a fire and a proper bed. "Not much snow here," he said, his breath making a cloud.

"Not yet, sir," the soldier who took his reins said.

His men rapidly filed into the courtyard. "How far ahead is the Prince?"

"Less than a fortnight, sir."

"We've gained time on him, then." He stamped blood to his feet. "Where's your officer?"

"'Tis the preference of Lord Naed that he see you first, sir."

"*Lord* Naed?" Krenin surveyed the fortress with new interest. "Why don't you tell me how this all came to pass while you show me to *Lord* Naed's chamber?"

CHAPTER THIRTY

"You let them attack Arn twice?" Krenin bellowed into the lord's chamber. "Demon's Blood! What have you been doing, you lowland frog? Sticking your head in the mud?"

"You have more men than we were told to expect. I shall do what I can to quarter them."

Eyes still adjusting to the interior dimness, Krenin could not make out the expression on the face of the young man standing by the window, but the voice was as impersonal as the stone.

"My Second," Naed continued, "will assist your men in finding appropriate lodging."

A dark-eyed man Krenin recognized rose from adding a log to the fire. With a respectful nod, he left, closing the chamber door. Krenin scowled, irked to see the man had exchanged a Tolemak soldier's garb for the trappings of a D'nalian lord's second. Flinging off his cloak, he advanced to the fire, holding out both hands. "Well, *Lord* Naed—"

"Let me make myself clear. I am obliged to provide shelter for you and your men. However, once you pass Druemarwin's gate, my obligation to you—and to the Prince—ceases."

Krenin stared at the man separated from him by a desk. "Why, you lowland muck-ant! Don't tell me you've wrapped that perverted D'nalian sense of honor so tightly around your neck you've choked on it! How could you abandon Arn!"

"I did not abandon the Prince! 'Twas he who abandoned us!"

"Us?"

The D'nalian rapped knuckles on the desk and looked as if he had tasted something sour. "You shall learn of it sooner or later. Mayhap 'tis best I tell you now."

"What?" The soldier had assured him Arn was well. What could possibly be wrong?

"Aerid is here. You shall behave toward her as if she were my—"

"He left her here?"

"He feared for her safety, or did your informant neglect to tell you she was wounded in the attack that killed Lord Dranoel?"

"He didn't have much time." The D'nalian's tone irritated him, but he decided to ignore it. "Arn'll come back for her when 'tis safe."

"No, he will not. Listen and understand; 'tis ended. The...illicit relationship is over."

Krenin searched the young man's face for some weakness, some trace of uncertainty, but found none. "Arn's a fool."

"At last, something upon which we can agree."

He opened his mouth to retort, but the D'nalian uncorked a jug and poured out a cup of wine. "Lest you find my hospitality wanting, let me amend that impression with this."

"Why should I drink your wine? You wouldn't accept mine."

"That was an apology. This is a courtesy." Reaching past Krenin, he set the cup on the mantle. "Do what you will; however, you may find it helpful in banishing the chill."

Though he glowered while the D'nalian walked away, Krenin grabbed the cup and drained it. Wiping his mouth on his sleeve, he said, "What happened to your leg?"

"'Tis none of your concern."

"Defending Arn, eh? I thought as much."

"Your conclusion—as usual—is far off the mark."

"You're as committed to Arn as I am. You're just too ass-brained to admit it!" Replacing the cup on the mantle, he offered his back to the fire. "Besides, once Arn discovers Erodasi's lover, he'll be back. He might," he said, grinning at the verbal jab he was about to unleash, "if you're fortunate, even take you back."

"The Prince's betrothed has a lover?"

Disappointed his words did not produce the desired result, Krenin lifted his tunic to expose more of his backside to the fire. "Since spring. The message came just ere I left Vinvinnysee." Noting the D'nalian's perplexed look, he leaned forward and jabbed a finger at Naed's chest. "Well, lowlander, what does that news do to your perceptions?"

This time, he was rewarded with a glare. "The infidelity of the Prince's betrothed does in no way excuse his own!"

"You self-righteous prig! Erodasi of Roines is a cold-hearted, spiteful, selfish brat whose father only dealt her to Arn to keep the Tolem Stone in the family. Arn's never touched her, and 'twere my choice, he'd never have accepted anything from that viper Roines. Did you know 'twas he who murdered Arn's father and massacred his family?" Krenin had not meant to say so much, but the thick-brained lowlander had provoked him. Bending over to rub the kinks out of his calves, he muttered, "I'd beat some sense into your head if you weren't lame."

There was a knock on the door, and a woman entered. "There be broth and bread. Will you be having it here?"

"Anywhere," Krenin said, straightening his tunic, "if you promise to accompany me." Crossing the room, he captured Aerid's hand and bowed over it. He had recognized her instantly despite Arn's having kept her so sequestered in the city, a man had to dress as a dying Adanak just so he could speak to her. He had not wanted to risk another round of Arn's wrath—he had never seen Arn so furious as that morning in the palace—nor would Krenin stoop to wearing Adanak dress—not after Herset—but he had something to say and he would take his opportunity. "I've never thanked you for saving my life. 'Tis more you've given me than I deserve at your hands. Please accept my apology and my thanks."

Aerid blushed. "To my way of thinking, 'twas Arn who did rescue the both of us."

Modest, he thought, but not too shy to speak her mind. "If you hadn't fought for me—beside me—'tis sure I wouldn't have lived till then." Tucking her hand into his arm, Krenin noticed the contrast between her coppery skin and his sun-bitten fingers. With a rush of shame, he remembered more than once recoiling from her touch. He would never be an Adanak lover, but—Demon's Blood!—some people deserved better than their origins might provide. "Arn's a fool. I'll bring him back to you."

"I—perhaps 'tis best if you do not try."

Silently, he cursed Arn for the shadows under her eyes. The bloody great fool ought to see this was the woman the Sisters had chosen for him. Even that damned Crownkeeper knew it. Thinking of the Adanak sent Krenin fumbling in his tunic pocket. "'Tis for you," he said, pressing a letter into her hand before opening the chamber door. "Coming, *Lord* Naed?"

"I—no. I shall join you later."

Krenin shrugged. He turned to Aerid, smiled, and guided her into the corridor.

****

When they were gone, Naed groped for his chair and sank into it. The interview had not gone as planned. Although he resisted much of Krenin's bluster, the Tolemak still found words to provoke him. He flung a quill onto the desk and scowled at it.

Turning in his chair, Naed stared at the fire. Considering the Prince's own behavior, it would not be unlikely to expect both partners in a Tolemak marriage to be unfaithful. Therefore, why should the news the Prince's betrothed had a lover disturb him? After all, what would he do if the Prince returned? What would they all do?

****

Erodasi sprang to her feet, spilling her embroidery. "How dare you enter my chambers!" she demanded, putting a chair between herself and the hooded man who had thrown open her door and shouldered his way into the room.

"I do not *dare*." He flung wet gloves onto the ornate table at her side. "'Tis my due."

"Dlaniger!" she gasped as his cloak joined his gloves. "How did you get in?"

"Is this how you greet me, love? I who have been away far too long? Where is my kiss?" Pulling her into his arms, he stifled further words with the pressure of his mouth.

Moments later, Erodasi opened heavy-lidded eyes. Dlaniger's hair was damp, but her breasts had warmed the cheeks and lips he nested between them. "How did

356

you get past Belac?" she murmured, stroking his shoulders. "He's had the fortress surrounded for weeks."

Raising his head, Dlaniger smiled. "A challenge, I admit, my sweet, but do not forget I have men in the guard who depend on my gold. They chanced to be guarding the secret entrance and graciously let me pass."

Erodasi shivered. His mouth traveled to her shoulder and his fingers slid under her hair. "You didn't kill the Prince. I would have heard."

Dlaniger's lips stilled their delicious explorations. He leaned away from her. "No, my love, I shall have to make a third attempt." Running his gaze over her naked upper body, he murmured, "And you must assist me."

"Me?" Jerking her gown onto her shoulders, Erodasi paced into the center of the room. "He's dangerous!"

"Easy, my love," Dlaniger purred, catching her in another embrace. "If you truly desire your betrothed's death, you must be prepared to do whatever is required. I have risked much for you. Do not be petty when I ask a favor in return."

"I'm afraid!"

"I do not require much of you, love. I ask only that you lure him away from his guard and deliver him to me." He slid his hand into her bodice and cupped her breast. "If we may also divest him of his armor and weapons, so much the better."

Erodasi shivered. His thumb and forefinger caressed her nipple, sending spirals of pleasure through her abdomen. "If 'tis all..." She peeled her gown from her shoulders. "Let me touch you, love," she urged, tugging at his tunic. "It's been so long."

"Soon," Dlaniger murmured, nipping her neck. "You must also know that while your father desires your betrothed's death as much as we—" He caught her hands. "—his plans for your future do not include me."

Dizzy with the need for his touch, his caress, Erodasi tried to focus on his words. "What would he do with you, then?"

"Kill me, I suspect."

"He can't do that! I won't let him." She rubbed her hips rhythmically against his. "I need you, love."

The darkening of his eyes pleased her. "And I require

you. But you must understand this," Dlaniger insisted, holding her body at bay. "When I kill your betrothed, I shall claim your hand in marriage and possession of Val-Feyridge as my due and reward. I shall not hand it over to your father."

"What are we to do, then?" Erodasi pouted.

"We shall deny your father entrance. Hold his forces off as your betrothed did when he first took the fortress from Prince Yinnad. With no knowledge of the secret entrance, your father and his companions will soon tire of sitting in the cold and will accept what has come to pass."

"Mmm," she said, offering him her throat and all that lay below it. "You have such wonderful ideas, darling."

"And I have more," he growled, freeing her hands at last. Sweeping her into his arms, he kicked open the door to her bedchamber. "However, they require the use of your bridal bed."

"Be quick. Oh, be quick, my love!"

****

Naed swilled the wine in his cup. To his right, Aerid smiled at something Krenin said. It amazed him how she could abide the man. But then, he thought as he watched Krenin's animated face, the Tolemak became almost bearable in her presence.

A tap on his shoulder roused him, and Banir bent to his side. "A courier from Vinvinnysee, m'lord. 'Tis a message for Commander Krenin."

"Take the man to my study. Commander Krenin will hear him there."

Krenin stood. "It must be important. He can't have left much after I did." He drained his wine. "You'd better come."

"Why?"

The familiar sneer twisted the Tolemak's features. "I haven't passed your gate yet, that's why." He reached for Aerid's hand, smiled at her, and bowed. "You'll have to excuse us."

"Do not wait for us," Naed told Aerid as he pushed back his chair.

The courier, face wind-bitten, snapped to attention when they entered. "Master Illien sent me, sir. Lord Tylus' man arrived the day after you left."

"Tylus," Krenin told Naed as he closed the door, "is an ally from the Northern Wars. Arn left him in command of Val-Feyridge." He turned a chair and straddled it. "Carry on, soldier."

"Lord Tylus reports that Lord Belac threatens Val-Feyridge. His army lies hard by it and this is one of three messages sent separately to ensure at least one might reach the Prince."

"Belac!" Krenin sputtered. "What in the name of the Demon possessed him to go against Val-Feyridge?"

"'Tis more, sir. Lord Tylus suspects Belac's move is only a diversion, and he heartily warns the Prince to watch for Roines, Koth, Ormo, and other of the eastern lords. Rumors suggest they are massing an army at the Arbez River."

"The bastards!" Krenin burst from his chair and ranged the room. "The pack of yellow-livered rats! And Roines most of all—the traitor! I told Arn not to trust him!"

"What will they do?" Naed asked.

"Lie in wait until we cross the Arbez, then ambush us!" Krenin slammed both fists on the mantle. "They're fresh, too, the worm-bellied scum!"

The messenger cleared his throat.

Krenin whirled. "You're dismissed, soldier!"

"Uh...'tis more, sir. The captain of the guard at Val-Feyridge reports that Lady Erodasi's lover appears to be a fair-haired D'nalian. He has not been seen of late, but she is increasingly wary of your spies and may have found a new way to hide him."

Krenin remained where his pacing had been interrupted. "Is that all?"

The man nodded.

"Tell my officers we'll be leaving at first light." Krenin swung to Naed. "It won't stretch your hospitality to let this man rest a day or two before returning to Vinvinnysee, will it?"

"No, of course not. My man Banir will see to your needs."

When the door closed behind the soldier, Krenin strode to the darkened window and stared out.

Naed leaned against the mantle and stirred the fire,

grateful for something to occupy his body while his mind and heart sorted out reactions to the messenger's news. A piece of tinder had caught on the grate. He poked it free and watched the fire consume it. Standing back, he wondered if he was like the tinder, doomed to be consumed by forces beyond his control.

"Are you coming with me tomorrow?" Krenin said, crossing to the desk.

"I? Why should I accompany you?"

"Arn's in danger. That ought to be reason enough. What was it you said to me outside Vinvinnysee? Something about not caring which of us got to Arn first as long as he was safe?"

"That was before." Before he had discovered Aerid and Arn together! Before he knew how the Prince had used him, and her!

"Whatever you and Arn fell out over, it can't be important."

"You would not understand."

"And I don't care!" Krenin picked Naed's goblet off the desk and rotated it in his hands. "What matters is, even now, Arn would rather have you with him than against him."

"I am neither for nor against your Prince! And I shall maintain my impartiality unless he provokes me!"

"Neutral, is that it? Like your precious ancestor D'nal, who couldn't make up his mind, you'd rather stand aside and watch him die?" He banged the cup down. "Well, lowlander, just because your hand isn't on the knife, doesn't mean Arn's blood won't be on your hands! Arn needs me and I'm going! You can stay here and rot in this Sisters-forsaken swamp!" Charging through the door, he slammed it with such force, mortar crumbled from the crossbeam.

Naed watched gray powder streak the wood. His blood beat behind his eyes, and his fists itched for the face of the man striding down the corridor, but both reactions paled in the face of self-loathing so intense, he trembled with it. Spinning away, his lame leg dragged and he blundered into the desk. "By the Sisters, I owe you naught!" he shouted at the wood beneath his palms. "Do you hear me? Naught!"

****

In her chamber, Aerid sat before a banked fire and contemplated the letter lying across her knees. Although she was grateful to Master Gaelwynn for telling her Mairim had been safely delivered of a healthy girl-child, she wished he had been better informed, but she could not fault him for believing she was yet with Arn, not even when Gaelwynn's message ripped afresh the shreds of her heart.

For most of the night, Aerid had sat thus, schooling her emotions until she thought she could read the rest of the message without dropping tears on it. "My dear," he had addressed her as though she were kin, and, while she should have thought him presumptuous, she felt instead strangely comforted. "'Twas my intention to be telling you this in person, but as your lord did depart Vinvinnysee so suddenly, I must be doing so by means of this letter. Mark me, Aerid, there be no less risk in birthing a Kingdom than there be in bringing forth a child."

She could not read past that point without a hitch in her breath. Master Gaelwynn could not possibly know the truth. 'Twas only to Mairim he referred, yet she could not help wondering as she fingered the birthstone at her throat. Those curiously mismatched eyes seemed equally as penetrating as Arn's, but when she had last seen him, Gaelwynn could not possibly have known what she herself had not suspected.

Since she had used Gam's potion to suspend her monthly bleed while disguised as a boy, her cycle had not returned despite casting off that disguise in the city. Limiting her food to provide for Leumas had likely interfered further and she quite simply had given the matter of conception no thought in those days and nights Arn had shown her the delights two people who desired each other could share. Now Aerid knew by the slight swell of her abdomen and the heaviness of her breasts, the child was well established in her womb.

Steeling herself, she focused on the letter again. "Mayhap there be more danger in building a Kingdom since not all involved may welcome the change. Belike you have already encountered the assassin these foolish city Masters did engage."

361

So, that was what Arn—and Naed—had not told her regarding the two attacks. But she remembered someone saying the men were Tolemak, not Adanak. And Krenin's message—the gist of which had spread throughout the fortress like smoke from a green-wood fire—implied Arn's Tolemak rivals planned to come against him at Val-Feyridge. She wondered if they knew—or suspected—he had gained the Crown everyone thought was but a legend.

She forced her attention back to Gaelwynn's flowing script. "'Tis essential, the Crown, to your lord's efforts. But, as you did say yourself, 'tis not the stones that matter; 'tis the people. He must have Adan, whose role I do gratefully fulfill, and he must have D'nal. This D'nal must come from Druemarwin. Show this letter to the Master of Druemarwin, and he will show you why." Aerid stifled a sob. Gaelwynn could not know Dranoel was dead, killed so suddenly whatever her beloved master may have known of the Crown had surely died with him.

Wiping her cheeks, she read the final lines. "Though your lord knows or guesses much of the lore of the Crown, he may not understand the significance of each of his actions regarding it. He goes ahead into dark times, and I fear he may lose heart, especially now he and Naed of Druemarwin have become estranged. 'Tis upon you, Aerid, to see D'nal chooses aright and Tolem keeps his heart, for you wear a Sisters' Tear. Indeed, I did mark it upon our first meeting. 'Twas the Sisters who did scatter the princely stones. 'Tis for Them—through you—to collect them again and heal what was broken."

Fingering her birthstone once more, Aerid laid the letter in her lap. At her window pink barely colored the east, but despite the heavy glass, she could hear the tramp of many hooves in the courtyard and the high-pitched whine of gate gears. Shortly, Krenin and the remaining occupiers would thunder across the drawbridge and depart Druemarwin for good. That much she understood about Arn's promises to Naed.

Sighing, Aerid willed a prayer for Krenin's protection, knowing as she did so, 'twas an act she would never have considered mere months ago. Though she had been wary of the change, Krenin's new regard for her seemed genuine, and she had warmed to him. Besides, she had never doubted his devotion to Arn.

Sighing again, Aerid looked at the letter on her lap and wondered if Gaelwynn knew what he asked of her. She would risk anything for Arn—her life, even their child's—but he would not permit it. How could she be to him what he needed if he would not let her close enough? And how could she sway Naed when even this new danger to Arn had not moved him? Belike Naed had idolized the man who rewarded him with privileges and promotions beyond his dreams, but though she had gone willingly to Arn's bed, Naed seemed to blame her dishonor entirely on Arn. Stroking her birthstone, she wondered if now might be the time to challenge that notion.

****

Arn stood on a jagged outcropping and surveyed the plumes of many campfires in the valley below. Even though the cold wind bit at his cheeks and ears and tore the breath from his nostrils, he would not raise his hood against it.

"M'lord?"

He recognized Borth's voice, but did not shift his gaze from the thin ribbon shimmering in the distance. "The Arbez, can you see it?"

"Faintly, m'lord."

"We'll be across today." Turning, he leaped from rock to rock to the place where Borth stood. "Let's not keep the men waiting in the cold." He headed toward a substantial clearing amid pine and spruce, where footmen, archers, and horse soldiers stood. Their breath smoked as they huddled into their cloaks.

Mounting a fallen log, Arn surveyed the faces turned to him. Some had applied paint and shorn their hair even though, without a fire, there could be no proper Tolemak ceremony, but the sight heartened him. Many of those he knew by name, and all had served him with courage.

"Men of Val-Feyridge, Albon, Tylus, Brede, Westerners all! 'Tis cold and tired you are, and 'tis home you want to go. Well, my friends, at the edge of the horizon lies our home! In our path stands an army of Easterners intent on stopping us, on dividing our homes and families among their masters, on continuing the fragmented order under which we have chafed for so long!

Will you lay at the feet of Roines and his cohorts the weapons that took you boldly to Adanak and back? Will you allow them to destroy the newfound unity you've so valiantly fought for? Will you render worthless the blood of those who fought and died to take the city that could not be taken? Or will you rally now and drive them out of our path?" He thrust his sword into the sky. "Men of the West, will you follow me on to Val-Feyridge? To the Arbez and across?"

Metal scraped as dozens of swords rose, sunlight shooting shafts of light from each blade. "To Val-Feyridge!" the men shouted. "On to Val-Feyridge!"

Others clashed their swords against their shields. "To the Arbez and across!"

"Mount, then, and let's show them how Westerners fight!"

With a roar, the men raced into formations.

"They're sure to hear us coming," Borth shouted over the clamor.

"Let them!" Arn leaped down from the log, his cloak billowing like wings. "'Twill make them wonder. And a wondering army is easier to frighten than a confident one."

****

The afternoon after Krenin's departure, Aerid located Naed in his study. Pale and unshaven, he scowled when she set upon the desk Gaelwynn's letter, a scribbled note, and an unadorned wooden casket of the size that might contain a lady's jewels or a lord's treasury.

"What's this?"

'Twas evident he had not slept and Krenin's visit had upset him, but she could spare him no sympathy. "'Tis known to you, aye, that Arn does mean to remake the Kingdom? To bring Tolem, Adan, and D'nal together?" When he expressed no surprise, she indicated the letter. "Master Gaelwynn does say D'nal must come from Druemarwin, and your uncle did know this."

Naed flushed scarlet. "How—what—in the Name of the Sisters! How does he—?"

"'Twas in the Master's will, aye?"

Thrusting a hand into his tunic, he yanked out a wooden cylinder suspended from a leather cord and dumped the contents onto the desk. "There! How many others know what no one bothered to tell me? Did you know he was my father too?"

The misery etched on Naed's features told Aerid instantly what he meant. Reaching for a chair, she placed it before the desk and lowered herself to the hard, cold wood. This was news she had not anticipated, but it explained much. "'Twas clear to me how much he did love you—more than ever he loved Dlaniger—but no one has said aught. Why have you not told them?"

"How?" Naed groaned, burying his face in his hands. "Why?"

"Belike they will be no more surprised than I." When he peered over his fingers at her, she smiled. "'Tis clear the folk prefer you to Dlaniger. 'Twould comfort them to know you be a closer blood heir than a nephew."

After a moment, he flopped back in his chair and knuckled his eyes. "What you seek is in the bundle there. Mayhap you will know what to make of it."

She did not know precisely what she sought. A message, aye, some indication of where it might be found, but not the object itself. When the stone lay glinting like dark honey in her hand, and she could breathe again, Aerid pushed the casket across the desk. "Look within."

Naed ran fingers through his hair, dislodging yet more from its queue, before lifting the lid. "What—?" Face as white as Gaelwynn's parchment, he shoved the casket back. "Is this what I think it is?"

"The Crown of Tolem." Aerid placed the D'nal stone upon the thick burgundy cushion that held the circlet securely in place. "Arn should have told you 'twas what he sought at Vinvinnysee, but 'tis clear to me now you fell out before he could do so."

"He gave it to you?"

She shook her head and picked up the scribbled note. "'Twas Krenin's task to bring it to Arn. He has left it here, and this is how he does explain why: 'Arn will have my head for this, but if he's in danger, I can't risk letting this fall into the wrong hands. No one but Gaelwynn and Arn know I have it. Only I know that you do. I know you'll keep it safe. Arn's a fool and Naed's an ass, but I'll do my part to bring Arn back to you if you'll make that bloody fool D'nalian see how much Arn needs him.'"

The blood rushed back into Naed's face. His mouth worked as though he would spit oaths but could not find words foul enough.

"So, you will be going, aye?" 'Twas a reasonable assumption, given what she had shown him, the people's most precious icon. Given, too, that he had inherited one of its missing pieces.

Naed slammed his hand on the desk. "By the Sisters, I will *not!* If Krenin thinks he may move me by this underhanded means, he is more the fool than I took him for!"

"And Arn? You would deny to help him?"

He bolted to his feet. "Aerid, look what he has done to you!"

"Given me his child, do you mean? Aye, and more moments of happiness than ever I have felt in my life! Aye, his trust, too, and his regard." She rose, but not because Naed had risen and she should stand in the presence of a lord. She rose slowly and deliberately, meeting him eye-to-eye across the desk. She had no official title, no status beyond what his good grace and the grace of others might give her, but Aerid knew now that she needed none of their approval, their grace to know precisely who she was and what she was worth.

"'Twas not Arn's intent to be loving me. Indeed, he did put me away from him more than once—ask Krenin if you would know how we did meet in Adanak—but when we did come together again in the city—mark me—'twas my free and willing choice to lie with him. This child be as much mine as Arn's, and 'tis that you must understand."

"He hurt you," he sputtered. "He left you."

"Aye, his leaving did hurt me, but not mayhap as badly as it did you, for *you* have used me to drive a wedge between the two of you. Aye, do not be denying it! You do know as well as I, Arn would not have rewarded you if he had not believed in you. Aye, and trusted in you, too."

"Aerid—" He stormed to the window and back. "When will you understand, he has used both of us!"

"When the giving be on both sides—and from the heart—'tis not to be called *using*. And well do you know it, Naed of Druemarwin, for naught has ever been between us but free giving."

He had the grace to look sullen. "Prince Arn wanted me on his side. 'Twas why he gave me so much!"

"Aye, belike he did, but he *took* naught. If your heart does ache now, 'tis out of longing." Carefully, she took the D'nal Stone out of the casket and wrapped it once more in its protective cloth. "Keep what you would have. Tolem and Adan will do what must be done." She closed the casket and carried it, the letter, and the note out of the chamber, letting the door fall shut behind her. Outside, she stood for a moment, wondering if she had said enough or too much. She would know soon enough.

****

All day, Naed haunted the ramparts and corridors, seeking places he might be left alone to pace and brood. Finding himself at last in the cellar storage rooms, he walked the dim underground corridor, his limp more pronounced than usual. The chill had invaded his thigh, and, though it disgusted him, he longed for his chair before the fire as much as an old man might.

A rustling, shuffling sound sent him fumbling for his knife. He gripped the hilt, cursing his dulled reflexes even as he demanded, "Who comes?" and peered into the dark ale cellar.

A female shriek, then the kitchen maid Elthred, face pink and fingers clutching disarrayed clothing, rushed past him, murmuring, "Your pardon, m'lord."

He straightened, but before he could rebuke her, a man's voice said, "Why, 'tis my *Lord* Naed, 'tis," and Yormoc emerged from the shadows.

The D'nalian cohort had returned with Krenin's party, but Naed had not seen his former companion in months, not since they parted after the Lancer raid. Now Yormoc lounged against the wall with tunic unlaced and an intricately carved Adanak dagger in his belt.

"'Tis far you've come, Naed of Tumin. Hero. Prince's Second. Lodgings at the palace in Vinvinnysee. Aye, rubbing elbows with the cream of Tolemak, so far removed from the folk that bred and bore you 'twould be easy to think you'd prefer them to us. Ah, but no, 'tis back to us you've come. And all in good time to seize land and a title that properly belongs to another."

Helen C. Johannes

Everything about Yormoc that had grated on Naed in the spring returned in force. He could not believe he had once missed the man's company. "'Twas Lord Dranoel's will that I inherit. If Dlaniger would dispute it, let him come and do so."

"Aye, he will. Depend upon it. 'Tis borrowed, your time. Had he known his father would name you, 'tis sure one of his arrows would have found *you*."

A hot pain, like a phantom recurrence of the arrow strike, seared through Naed's leg and raised the hairs on his neck. Seizing Yormoc's tunic, he slammed the man against the wall. "Tell me and tell me true, what do you know of arrows and Dlaniger?"

Yormoc smiled. "'Tis fond you are of pushing people about, *Master* Naed. You'd best be prepared to use that knife at your side if 'tis aught you want of me."

Months ago, the youth Yormoc had known might have hesitated, but not now. Naed pressed his dagger to Yormoc's throat. "You underestimate me, as ever you have. 'Tis many a man I've killed since we last spoke, and many a month I've spent among the Tolemak. They care little for insolence, but respond remarkably to a knife in the throat. As, I am sure, will you. Tell me what I ask, or I'll spill your worthless blood all over *my* cellar. Depend upon it."

****

Moments later, Banir stuffed clothing and drycake into Naed's pack. "You should send me instead. 'Tis but twice you've ridden since..."

"I must go myself." Naed buckled on his sword. "'Tis my own cousin who would act as the Prince's assassin. 'Tis only right that I should act to stop him." He gripped Banir's shoulder. "I need you here. I trust you to protect Aerid and look after my interests."

"I know the way," Banir said sullenly.

"So do Grodar and Morys." He shrugged into his cloak. "Summon the courier from Vinvinnysee. I would send him back to Captain Illien with a message of my own."

"You are going." Aerid faced him at the bottom of the stairs. She had pulled back her hair while she assisted in the kitchen, yet despite steam-red cheeks, her face was

368

pale. Wisps of hair had escaped the braid and they dangled about her ears.

For a moment Naed yearned to touch the strands, to feel their softness between his fingertips, to tuck them behind her ears, but he would put aside the ache because he understood, at last, she belonged to Arn—and so did he.

Kissing her forehead, he said, "Pray, Aerid," and strode out into the cold night.

CHAPTER THIRTY-ONE

"They've broken through to the river, m'lord. We couldn't hold them any longer," the messenger panted, icicles dripping where sweat had run into his beard and frozen.

"Cowards!" Rolnar shouted. "You outnumber them! And you're fresher!"

"Begging your pardon, m'lord, but the Prince's men be seasoned warriors. We have common ruffians and thieves among our number. They lack discipline."

Rolnar whirled to the officer who had spoken. "'Tis of Vral, you are, aye?"

"Aye, m'lord. Lord Vad of Vral be my master."

"Well, my fine man of Vral, these common ruffians and thieves, as you so disdainfully name them, will serve our cause well given the proper incentive! And two hundred pieces of gold for the death of the Prince is fine incentive, indeed! Go and remind them of that!"

"Aye, m'lord."

"The rest of you, after them! They must not reach Val-Feyridge! I'll hang you by the wrists and flog you once for each man that does!"

❀❀❀❀

The horses stepped gingerly through fresh white powder. Mindful of the ice beneath, Naed resisted the urge to hurry his small party. If a horse should fall and break a leg or injure a man, they would lose precious time. For hours they had passed snow-covered evidence of fighting, each sign more recent than the last. Knowing they gained on the army made him chafe at the slow pace, but he dared not risk an accident. Not now when they were so close.

The path ahead dissolved into white-flecked grayness. Shadows he took to be trees bordered the area. Blowing on numbed fingers, he shoved them inside his cloak and under his armpit to warm them. Snowflakes clung to his eyelashes and coated his legs like a second skin.

The surrounding wood lay wrapped in stillness broken only by the occasional creak of leather or the huff of a horse clearing snow from its nostrils. Although Naed's men rode in customary silence, he fancied the quiet had somehow deepened. He strained his ears for some sound, some sign they had not crossed an unseen border into the shadow world, then shook himself. 'Twas only his imagination, a product of too many miles with too little sleep and the cold that crept unnoticed into more than fingers and toes.

A twig snapped, echoing like a small explosion. Naed drew rein, every sense alert. Behind, he heard the muffled scrapes of his men loosening their swords and raising their shields.

"Hold!" boomed between the trees. "Identify yourselves!"

Knowing the voice could have come from anywhere in the thick grayness, Naed raised his own shield. "We are D'nalians on business of our own! Who seeks to know?"

For tense seconds, he sat poised, expecting the whisper of an arrow. Sweat beaded on his upper lip and ran down his back. His injured thigh crawled.

"D'nalians," called a shadow gliding toward them, "from where?"

Naed's fingers tightened on his sword. "From Druemarwin! Now, identify yourselves, or we shall take you for thieves and brigands!"

"Thieves and brigands?" the figure on horseback chuckled. "'Twill hardly please Commander Krenin to hear that."

"Krenin?" The tension rushed from Naed's body with such force, he had to support himself with a hand on his horse's withers.

First Horseman Yarl rode to his side. "Why, Lord Naed! 'Tis sure, but I hardly expected to see you here, m'lord. Forgive me, but the beard..."

Scowling, Naed plucked at his unshaven chin. "We have ridden hard and fast and not taken time for vanities." He urged his horse forward. "Take me to Krenin."

Helen C. Johannes

****

So effectively did the snow conceal the camp, Naed found himself in the midst of it before he realized they had arrived. Soldiers, who sat or stood under shelters of lashed-together pine boughs, watched his party approach with dark, weary eyes that told the toll of their pace.

Yarl dismounted before a group of tents and shook the accumulated snow from his cloak. "Commander Krenin," he said at the entrance of one, "we have guests."

Naed eased his lame leg from the stirrup. He leaned forward, heaving his good leg over the saddle. When balanced, he relaxed his arms and dropped to the ground, taking most of his weight on his good leg. He disliked the awkward dismount, but hours in the saddle and the cold so stiffened his leg he could reach the ground no other way.

"Lord Naed!" Krenin burst out of his tent. "By the Demon, you look a sight!"

Keeping one hand on the saddle, Naed waited for his leg to recover. "'Tis the beard, I know. Yarl has already informed me it alters my appearance."

"For the better. You look more the man."

"I thank you for your kind observation. As soon as I have the opportunity, however, I shall remove it."

"'Twas a compliment, thick-head! I only meant you look more like the leader everyone says you are!"

A peculiar sensation crept up from Naed's chest and stole the use of his tongue. Dropping his gaze, he fumbled with the frozen thongs securing his pack.

"You there," Krenin barked to Grodar, "see to your lord's horse and belongings. First Horseman Yarl will make you as comfortable as we are." He grinned. "Granted, 'tisn't much we have to offer but, by the looks of you, 'tis more than you've enjoyed for days."

"Indeed," Naed said, stumbling as his horse was led away, "we have scarce stopped to eat and sleep." He glanced about for something else to lean on, but found nothing.

"You wouldn't have caught us even then, if it weren't for this cursed ice." Krenin shivered and turned toward his tent. "Come on. Let's talk where it's warmer."

Naed willed his leg to move, but it would not. "Go. I

372

shall be along shortly." Bending, he worked his hands over his thigh, seeking to rub some life into the cold, scarred flesh.

"You can't walk, can you? You stiff-necked D'nalian, you'd fall on your face in the snow before you'd ask me for help! You're as pig-headed as Arn, and just as proud!"

Forced to hop ungracefully or be dragged by Krenin's strong grip, Naed sputtered, "'Tis only the cold."

"Cold, hah! If I'd known how crippled you were, I'd never have asked you to come with me." He steered Naed into his tent and lowered him to a blanket spread on pine boughs. Pulling off Naed's cloak before he could protest, Krenin thrust it toward the man at the tent flap and barked, "Dry this! And fetch Lord Naed a bowl of that stew. A hot bowl!" Then, casting about the tent, he located a blanket and flung it around Naed's shoulders. "What in the name of the Demon possessed you to come after us?"

Naed huddled into the blanket, savoring its dry warmth. Krenin stood over him, glowering, but not, he sensed, with anger. For a crystalline moment, he stepped outside himself and understood, in this tent in a snow-covered wood in Tolemak, how Krenin regarded the Prince and why, for so long, the Tolemak had fought him for the man both of them loved.

"What has possessed me to come? 'Tis you who are right, and I who have been wrong. I am as committed to him as you are, and I truly do not care which of us reaches him first so long as he is safe. I pray you accept my apology and allow me to join you, but even if you do not, I shall tell you what I have learned of the man who stalks the Prince."

For a long time, Krenin stood, meeting his gaze. Finally, he seated himself cross-legged on the tent floor. "You're too self-righteous for most Tolemaks to abide, but 'tis sure you're too pig-headed to take in a fair fight." He thrust out his hand. "Take it. 'Tis better than wine."

Naed clasped the hand that had once been offered him solely out of loyalty to Arn. "Why is it better?" he said, voice rough.

"Because 'tis a promise. A promise between... friends."

****

Aerid stood a few feet away, a welcoming smile on her lips. As Arn reached for her, she vanished. In her place he saw a huddled figure staring into a fire, a figure whose demeanor indicated pain and suffering. Arn moaned and tossed. The image faded and Aerid returned, this time pale and quiet, her eyes hollow with grief. Arn reached to comfort her, but Naed materialized. The young man wrapped Aerid in his arms and stared at Arn, his expression dark and recriminating. Slowly, although they did not move, the figures receded. Arn ran after them, but they moved inexorably away.

Gasping for breath, Arn bolted upright. He blinked, but blackness surrounded him, a blackness so deep he could not see the hands he dragged over his drenched face. All around lay absolute quiet. For a terrifying moment, he fancied himself dead.

A sentry coughed. The ordinary, inelegant sound sent a jolt of relief through his body. 'Twas only a dream. Real danger lay scant miles away in the camps of Roines, Koth, Ormo and others.

Lying down again, Arn curled up on his side and closed his eyes. His body ached, but sleep, once startled, refused to return. He rolled to his back and focused on Val-Feyridge, on the sleek walls and bold ramparts lying only days away. Already it called to him. The nearer he approached, the more restless he became to reach it, to wrap himself in its stone arms and seek shelter from the world, or at least from the dreams, the faces haunting him.

Even in daylight, he would see Aerid or Naed in a laugh, a gesture, an expression of one of his men. Each time, it required all of his will to return his mind to the present. He expected time would dull the pain, and perhaps it had, but the hollow feeling remained unchanged. The hollow feeling had a name, and Arn knew it.

He had known it as a youth when he had been driven from his home and hunted like an animal in the forests of Albon. He had known it, but he had not acknowledged it. Then Krenin found him, and the swaggering Free Sword with the handed-down weapons banished the feeling with his offer of friendship. Now the feeling had returned, and with a vengeance, all because of Aerid. And because of Naed.

Arn swallowed down the thickening in his throat. Krenin would join him soon. He would be on the road already, likely in Tolemak now. The enemy would hardly expect him, and his troop should pass unscathed. Arn squeezed his eyes shut, knowing he missed his friend as he had never missed him before!

****

"'Tis sure you are," Krenin said as he fastened his pack behind his saddle, "that this Dlaniger is Erodasi's lover?"

"As certain as I may be of evidence given at the point of a knife." Once Yormoc's tongue had loosened, what he told of Dlaniger's activities, both past and present, left Naed so appalled, he shivered yet at the memory. "'Twould explain much," he said, thinking of Dranoel's will.

"'Tis like he's gone straight to Val-Feyridge to wait for Arn. Filthy gold-grubbing, back-stabbing D'nalian!" Reddening, he shot a glance at Naed. "No offense, aye?"

"Aye," Naed said, grinning. "The Prince is mayhap two days ahead of us?"

Krenin swung into the saddle. "They've been worrying him like a pack of wolves. We'll have to ride like the Demon is on our tails to catch him."

****

At midmorning, they sat a ridge and looked down on a ragged line of horsemen following a streambed. "The banner of Vral," Krenin muttered, "one of Roines' eastern scum!"

"They head the wrong way," Naed said. "And they have many wounded."

Krenin loosened his sword and hefted his shield. "Let's see if we can persuade them to tell us why." With a signal to his men to follow, he rode down the slope.

Naed's horse danced sideways, snorting, while riders flowed around him, but he could not unbend his arms to give the horse its head. Something held them stiff, the same thing that made sweat ooze from his chest and his heart throb in his throat. *I am afraid, afraid of arrows and swords and...death!*

Below, the enemy hurried into a protective formation while Krenin's men fanned out around them. They could do well enough without him. 'Twas no need for him to risk himself. No need at all, but Aerid's. And Arn's. Sucking in the icy, bracing air, Naed forced his arms to unbend, his heels to touch the horse's sides. The animal sprang forward with a whinny and trotted down the ridge.

"We mean harm to no one," the Vral officer was saying as Naed drew rein beside Krenin. "'Tis at the hands of both sides we have suffered losses. 'Tis our intent to return home."

"'Tis a lie!" Krenin said. "Vral's always been thick with Roines."

"Lord Vad has been badly misled and 'tis my intent to tell him so. Vral men be soldiers who fight well and with honor. We be not common thieves and ruffians who fight only in packs and for the price on a man's head. Nor will we stoop to fight alongside such rabble! You may take us prisoner if you wish, but the men of Vral have no quarrel with you or your prince."

"We shall allow you to continue in peace," Naed said before Krenin could speak, "but we would have information from you in exchange. 'Twould be a sign of good faith the Prince would remember when he considers the fate of those who oppose him." He knew it was a risk to make such a promise, but something about the Vral officer's bearing suggested he would accept.

"Who be you, a D'nalian, to speak for a Tolemak prince?"

"This D'nalian," Krenin said, shooting Naed a glare before turning the full force of his displeasure on the Vral man, "is Lord Naed of Druemarwin, the Prince's Second! 'Tis safe you may be to assume he speaks for Prince Arn."

The man's gaze darted from Naed to Krenin and back while he considered. "Well then, Roines, Lede, Ormo, and Koth have the largest forces with troops from ten or so others. They mean to join Belac tomorrow and ring Val-Feyridge so tightly 'twill be impossible for the Prince to enter. 'Tis said Belac's meeting fierce opposition from Lord Tylus at the fortress walls. Too, Roines be without the supplies he expects. If you reach the Prince ere the supplies come, 'tis like you'll have a chance to catch them unawares."

"Good," Krenin muttered. "Let's keep it that way."

The Vral man raised his chin. "'Tis my understanding that when your prince gives his word, 'tis kept. So, too, is mine!"

"You have my word," Naed said, "as a D'nalian whose honor is his life, that Prince Arn shall look kindly upon Vral when the fighting is over. Go home in peace."

The Vral man inclined his head. "May the Sisters bless you with victory."

Krenin signaled his men to open a path for the Vral troop. To Naed, he hissed, "So you think you can trust him, do you? What do you know about Tolemaks?"

"Mayhap more than you may know of D'nalians. Aye, tell me, how many months has it been that I have traveled and fought alongside the likes of you?"

Krenin returned his jibe with a glower. "Will you be wanting to give the signal to proceed, *my lord*, or may I lead my own men?"

"I have no wish to interfere with what is rightly yours."

"'Tis generous of you," Krenin muttered. Heeling his horse, he ignored Naed's grin while he shouted to his men.

****

Aerid stirred, eyes heavy with sleep that would not come. She kicked away damp, tangled bedding, and peered at faint light coloring her window. Since Naed had left, each day passed slower than the one before, and each night lasted an eternity.

She stroked a hand over her abdomen, over the swell betraying the presence of the child growing within. A sigh caught her unprepared, and her lip shook, but Aerid bit down, holding it still. 'Twas Arn's hand she yearned to place on her stomach, his strong, calloused hand with the long fingers that, when spread, would completely encompass their child, holding it, protecting it, comforting it. And comforting her.

Aerid dashed the back of her hand across her eyes. Tears would not bring him back. Nor would Krenin or Naed. No, he must come of his own choosing, impelled by his need for her and his love, or he would not stay. And to lose him twice...

Shivering, Aerid sat up and dragged a blanket around her shoulders. The fire had long since died in the grate and her breath smoked. She sat hugging her knees in the gray room and staring at the casket sitting on the mantle. *'Tis upon you, Aerid, to see D'nal chooses right and Tolem keeps his heart...* Gaelwynn's words echoed in her mind like the refrain of an endless song. She had done her part for D'nal; Naed *had* chosen. 'Twas fear for Tolem's heart that had settled like a weight around her shoulders and grew heavier with each dawn.

The suspicion Arn needed her, that she should—no—must go to him haunted her dreams, each succeeding one more vivid and threatening than those previous. Somehow, she feared, his life—and the future of the Kingdom—lay not so much in Krenin or Naed's hands, but in her own.

Aerid stared at the ash-covered grate and thought of Leumas, who loved his city enough to give his life for it, and of Mairim, who cared enough for her to let her learn about life for herself. She sucked in a breath. She loved Arn enough to let him go. Did she love him enough to go to him when he needed her regardless of the consequences, regardless of the pain? Flinging back the covers, she rose and dressed in her warmest clothes.

****

"I must undertake a journey."

Blinking, Banir rubbed his eyes. "'Tis a sorry task, this ciphering," he muttered, shoving a ledger aside to look up at Aerid. "What journey? Where?"

Even away from Naed, the dark-eyed Tolemak remained as quiet and contained as ever, and as solidly dependable. She could not lie to him. "I must go to Tolemak, to Val-Feyridge...to the Prince. To be sure, Krenin and Naed have promised to protect him, but I fear—" She spread her hands. What could she say? It all sounded so foolish.

"Aye, 'tis troubling, these dreams." He dragged his hands over his face. "But 'tis winter, and you with child, 'twould do no one good if we be captured or killed."

Aerid's heart pounded. "I know."

"There be no wagons, naught but horseback and hard

378

riding. And cold. And snow."

"Aye."

"There be few inns along the road. And nights when I'll not risk a fire."

"'Tis more than I hoped that you would come."

Banir looked away, reddening. "'Tis you I'm sworn to protect, not this cursed pile of stone!" He pushed back his chair. "Pack what you will. I'll tend to the rest."

****

Scant hours later, Aerid's mount clattered across the drawbridge and into bejeweled snow carpeting the clearing around Druemarwin. Banir rode ahead, a pack horse at his mount's heel. He had given command to the captain of the guard and, grudgingly, directed Ekwul to tend the household.

Aerid looked over her shoulder and returned Ekwul's tentative wave. Once before she had ridden out of Druemarwin accompanied by Tolemaks. This time, though, she did not hide among them in order to escape. This time, she would ride into the heart of their land and find among them the man she loved.

CHAPTER THIRTY-TWO

Arn's sword clove through armor and bone. The Roinesman fell to the rock-studded ground. Catching his breath, Arn watched the man's blood steam on the snow beneath his body. *Another down*, Arn thought, wheeling Darkstar.

Around him, metal clashed, horses plunged and screamed, men grunted, cursed, and shouted. Arn looked toward the hilltop and saw his men had closed on it. They would be over soon, over and through the trees to Val-Feyridge.

"M'lord! I've found Lord Tylus!"

Arn saw Gorm yards away, waving. "Take me to him!"

Smashing through three men who rallied to block their path, he and Gorm galloped into the trees and rode at a breakneck pace through dense pines, aspen, and spruce. Moments later, they broke into sunlight almost at the foot of the fortress Val-Feyridge.

Arn drew rein, fixing his gaze on the rocky base out of which rose sleek basalt walls. Nature had created the monolith, and man had shaped it to his purpose, carving a fortress from its eastern summit. Now like the mountain panther gracing its banner, the fortress Val-Feyridge perched on the outcrop and watched ant-like men struggle for the right to call it theirs. *But 'tis mine*, Arn thought. *And so it shall remain!* Spurring Darkstar, he galloped toward the banner of Tylus and the white-haired man fighting under it.

"Sisters be thanked, but you're a sight for sore eyes!" Tylus clashed his shield into Arn's.

Grinning, Arn tossed wayward hair from his eyes. "So, this is how I'm welcomed home, with a fight."

The stout-shouldered man with the crooked nose laughed. "And a fight it is. I've not had the men to rout Belac's bullies, but 'tis sure we've sent plenty of the bastards to their graves!"

"They'll shortly have company. Roines and his pack of wolves are just over the ridge. No doubt they mean to join Belac."

"Aye, and to keep you out of the fortress. But my men have seen you. Look!" Tylus pointed where his men rushed a troop of Belac, scattering them. "'Tis your leadership we need."

"And we need it from inside." Arn looked once more at the walls that were his by blood, both born and shed. "If I show them they've failed, that they can't keep me out no matter what they do, they'll fold. There can't be much more than the promise of Val-Feyridge keeping that pack together."

"Aye. That and a price on your head."

"How much?"

"Two hundred pieces of gold!"

"'Tis substantial."

"Bastards!" Gorm breathed, clenching a huge fist.

"Still," Arn said, "if they're fighting for gold, 'twill not overcome the shock we'll give them once I get inside. Borth's men will lure Roines and his companions here. Their added numbers should draw Belac's men from the rear lines so Gorm and I can slip through unnoticed with ten men." He clasped Tylus's hand. "Give me two hours, old friend, then look to the walls."

****

"He's returned!" Erodasi gasped, seizing Dlaniger's sleeve. "They've sighted his banner!"

Prying her fingers from his arm, Dlaniger reached for his sword and buckled it about his waist, his movements unhurried.

Erodasi watched him, her hands twisting in her skirts. "What do we do?"

"The Prince will undoubtedly seek to enter by the secret way. When he does, you shall greet him and contrive to draw him, alone, to the staircase outside the living quarters. I shall hide where you do not know and strike him as he passes."

"Somewhere I don't know? Why?"

His thumbs stroked over her face as he cupped it in his hands. "Why, my sweet? Because I would not have these lovely eyes give me away."

"Oh, Dlaniger, I'm so afraid!"

"Courage, my love. You desire to be free of him, aye?"

His eyes were cool, yet they glittered in a strange, hypnotic way. Erodasi nodded.

"Then make no mistakes and Val-Feyridge shall be ours ere this day ends." Draping a fur-trimmed cloak about her shoulders, he took her arm. "Come, we must make ready to greet your betrothed."

****

Krenin reined his mount to a sidestepping halt amid the carnage of a recent battle, bodies of men and horses littered among broken swords and cloven shields.

Naed pulled up beside him while riderless horses, breath smoking and ears pricked, stared at them. "How far to Val-Feyridge?"

"Through this wood." Krenin loosed his sword and raised his shield. "Let's take them!" he cried to the men behind him. "On to Val-Feyridge!"

"To Val-Feyridge!" the soldiers echoed, metal scraping as they drew their weapons.

Late afternoon light skittered about, flashing fire from sword to sword and shield to shield until Naed thought himself lost in the brilliance of the stars. Swept up in the rush of the charge, he drew his weapon and galloped after Krenin. Moments later, he glimpsed towering rock walls, pinnacles, and ramparts before his ranks broke upon the enemy.

A sword whooshed past Naed's nose, and he barely deflected it. Sweat pouring down his face, he backed his mount and cursed his reflexes. He caught the next blow on the edge of his shield, turning aside the blade, but not before the hand guard ripped across his cheekbone.

He heard his own voice scream as if it were the voice of another. He saw the enemy wheel and swing again, felt the blow shudder through his shoulder and down his leg until his foot gave up the stirrup and trampled snow rushed at his face. Then, somehow, his knee held and Naed righted himself. Warmth trickled between the hairs of his beard and red spattered the back of his glove, but he set himself in the stirrups and smashed his sword through the enemy's helmet.

"Your face—" Krenin demanded, drawing rein at his side.

"A lesson." Naed flexed numbed fingers. "Have you sighted the Prince?"

"Arn's already gone in the back way. Come on. He has less than an hour on us." Barking an order to Yarl to take command, Krenin galloped up the hillside and away from the battle.

Naed followed him through snow-laden underbrush, up rocky gullies, and across slanted clearings. They sped around the south face of the rock supporting the fortress Val-Feyridge. Once, they burst upon a trio of riders from Lede and, dividing without a word, killed them. Under other circumstances, Naed would have remarked on their efficiency.

Krenin halted at the edge of a small clearing. The rock itself soared out of the brush on the opposite side. In the foreground, broken rock poked up between patches of snow and clumps of yellowed grass. Dismounting, Krenin whistled. The chatter of a squirrel answered him. Nodding to Naed to follow, he led his horse across the clearing toward a man who materialized out of the brush. "We go on foot from here." Taking his shield, he ducked into the scrubby trees and disappeared.

Naed kicked free of his stirrups and dropped to the ground. A piece of loose shale rocked under his lame leg and he stumbled. Flushing, he shouldered his shield and limped into the bushes after Krenin.

Inside, he found a dark slash in the rock large enough to admit a horse. Treading carefully on broken rock, he passed through a tunnel to a room from which ran a honeycomb of holes.

Krenin bent over a torch, igniting it with a crack of flint. "Follow me."

"'Tis marvelous!" Naed breathed. "I had no idea..."

"Neither do they. So far."

Krenin led him unerringly through tunnels sometimes so narrow, the men squeezed through sideways, others so low they had to bend double. Soot blackened the lower ceilings and Naed saw where men had taken picks and widened passages. Here and there, they stumbled over broken rock. In other passages, they trod on limestone so slick Naed fell more than once. His leg ached, and before long he gritted his teeth to maintain the pace Krenin set.

At one point Krenin grabbed his tunic and dragged him bodily up a set of uneven steps.

"Mayhap you should go on alone," Naed muttered as he collected his dignity.

"Don't be a stiff-necked idiot!" Krenin jammed the torch into a crack by his feet. "We can spare a moment to rest."

A drop of something splattered on Naed's forehead. He looked up, saw another droplet glistening on the ceiling, and shifted away from it. His breath still coming fast, he bent over his thigh and massaged the warmth of his hands into it.

Moments later, Krenin stood and held out his hand. "Ready?"

Naed grabbed it and pulled himself up. "How much farther?"

"Not far, but 'tis mostly uphill. Can you make it?"

"Aye, depend upon it."

****

Arn bounded up the last, straw-littered steps and emerged in the stable. "Spread the word that I'm here," he told two of the startled guards. "And you," he said to a third, "tell the captain of the guard to meet me on the ramparts."

"Aye, m'lord!" they said, and rushed in three directions.

"The Prince! The Prince is come! He's here!" rose like a chorus while Arn waited for Gorm to lower the trap door.

"That should raise the hair on their necks, m'lord." Gorm grinned as he joined Arn in the stable doorway.

"Indeed, it should." While he surveyed the ramparts glowing in the lowering sun, Arn tugged at his chest armor. "This thing keeps choking me. The lacings must have come loose. See if you can tie them up again."

The huge man bent to Arn's side and lifted his tunic. "'Tis broken, m'lord. The lacing's torn away."

"I can't fight when it rams my throat every time I raise my arms. Here." He pulled the armor over his head

384

and handed it to the stableman's apprentice. "Tell your master to mend this at once and bring it to me on the ramparts."

"Aye, m'lord," the boy replied, face glowing. "'Twill be done at once, m'lord!"

Arn shivered as the breeze licked at his damp undertunic now the protective layer of armor had been removed. Gorm offered his cloak, but Arn shook his head, intent on drinking in the beauty of the place he loved, Val-Feyridge.

He had come up through the bowels of the rock, become one with it again. Now it sang to him and he felt renewed, revitalized, filled with energy and purpose. Val-Feyridge would not fall. Here within these impregnable walls he could turn back any challenge, defeat any opponent. Here he was whole and he should never have thought otherwise.

"To the ramparts, Gorm! We mustn't keep our enemies waiting." Striding across the courtyard, Arn made for the nearest stairs.

****

Krenin braced his shoulder on the door above and pushed it over.

Instantly, swords bristled like porcupine's quills through the opening.

"Let us pass!" Krenin barked, pushing his way through. "Where's the Prince?"

A shout rose from the fortress. It began on the westernmost wall and rushed like a tidal wave along the wood and stone parapets until it reverberated from the rocks above, deafening them with its thunder. "The Prince! The Prince! Long live the Prince!"

"He made it," Naed shouted over the tumult.

"But he's still not safe!" Shoving through the celebrating soldiers, Krenin ran across the courtyard with Naed at his heels.

****

Rolnar of Roines spun in his saddle at the uproar from the fortress. "What in the—?"

"The Prince!" Lede shrieked, face as white as the muddy, blood-soaked snow once had been. "'Tis the Prince!" He pointed toward the ramparts. "He's got in!"

"We're doomed!" Edad of Koth whimpered. "We can't hold them now!"

Rolnar's raking gaze found the figure he sought, the tall, arrogant figure who stood with open disregard for the arrows that should have been loosed at him from below. Should have been, but were not, Rolnar realized with a snarl of frustration, because all below were as stunned as his companions by the sudden appearance of this figure.

"Shoot him, you idiots!" Rolnar bellowed at the archers. "Shoot him down!"

A flock of arrows rose into the sunlight, but the figure sprang away. The missiles clattered against the walls and fell.

"All is lost!" Edad whimpered again, his squirrel cheeks sucked in.

"Don't be a fool! We still bar the gate!"

"Not for long," Lede muttered, pointing into the hollow. "Look!"

Rolnar heard the roar. Twisting in his saddle, he saw the forces of Val-Feyridge and Tylus charge into his lines, screaming like madmen and demons.

"Hold them!" Rolnar shrieked at his officers. "Hold them back! We have them outnumbered, you belly-crawling fools!" Sweat poured down Rolnar's face and stained the collar of his tunic. He could not lose. Not now, not when he held Val-Feyridge so nearly within reach.

"You may fight them any way you like, outnumbered or not," Edad mumbled, "but you will have them without me and mine."

Out of the corner of his eye, Rolnar saw Edad's horse turn and the squirrel-faced lord slink away. "You cowardly snake! No one deserts me!" Seizing his sword, he drove it through the Lord of Koth's back. Then he spun to the other lords. "Anyone else care to leave?" When no one answered, Rolnar shouted, "Now, turn them back! Do you hear me? Stop them!"

****

Erodasi hurried along the parapet below the ramparts. Soldiers paused in their efforts to supply arrows to the archers above to eye her, but she brushed past them. She could see Arn ahead with the captain of the guard and the giant Gorm, and she forced her legs to carry her toward him.

Seeing her, Arn smiled, but it was a smile as cold as the stone he leaned against. "My beautiful betrothed has come to greet me on my return. How unexpected."

It had taken all her strength to come this close to him, but she must do more, say something to lure him away from his protectors. She hugged her cloak and murmured, "I-I missed you," looking away to hide the lie.

She sensed his gaze rake her, but she kept her head down. Her lip trembled. A pass of her tongue stilled it.

"Did you, now? How unfortunate your father and his companions have chosen this moment to make an attempt on my home." He turned toward Gorm.

Erodasi's heart lurched. She had to divert him. Her future depended on it. "Please!" she begged, choking the word out. "I must speak with you."

"*Please*? Such an uncommon word from your lips, daughter of Roines."

Her gaze fled to the courtyard below. She wondered fiercely where Dlaniger had secreted himself as she whispered, "'Twill, 'twill only take a moment...privately."

For an eternity, Prince Arn stood on the fringe of her vision, saying nothing. Finally, he spoke to Gorm. "Direct the men." Reaching for her arm, he said, "Where shall we talk?"

Dancing backward, Erodasi dodged his hand. "I-I thought..." Where was it Dlaniger had told her to take him? Her frantic gaze landed on the parapet around the living quarters. Yes! That was it, the staircase, the sheltered, deserted staircase. "This way," she said, starting for the steps with jittery movements.

****

"The bitch has found him!" Krenin shouted. "They're heading for the living quarters! Arn! Wait!"

Naed dodged men Krenin bowled aside and reached the staircase Krenin had charged up. Digging his fingers into the outer wall, he dragged his leg up the steps, hopping, jumping, staggering, even falling and crawling across the first landing.

Prince Arn stood at the top, hands on his hips, the last rays of sunlight illuminating him from behind. A woman outlined in gold stood at his side. "Krenin! Naed!

387

What—?"

"Stay away from her!" Krenin bellowed.

As if in a dream, Naed saw Krenin strain toward the Prince, saw the woman jump away, saw another figure, its arm upraised, materialize from behind a chimney. A sudden flash blinded Naed and he stumbled forward. When he righted himself, two figures careened across the landing, the arm of one plunging and rearing. "No!" Naed gasped, but it was not his cry he heard.

"No!" Krenin roared again, his sword arcing out of its scabbard.

Naed saw him clear the last steps, saw him shove the woman against the wall, dislodging a newly-lit torch, saw the falling torch shoot a flare of light over Prince Arn, Prince Arn tearing at the arm locked around his neck, his face contorted, a bloody knife rearing again over his chest.

"Whoreson! Murderer!" Krenin's sword slashed down.

At the crack of bone, a woman screamed, "Dlaniger!" Energy shot into Naed's limbs. He scrambled up the last steps while Krenin hacked at the body beside the wall.

Blood splattered everywhere jerked Naed to a halt as suddenly as if he had run to the end of a tether. The Prince lay in a gleaming, glistening, spreading puddle of it. Dropping to his knees, Naed tore strips from his tunic, but—*dear Sisters!*—he hardly knew where to begin.

"Naed..." The Prince grasped his arm with a bloody hand. "Who...?"

"He's dead," Krenin panted, flinging his blood-splattered sword to the stone. "I killed the bastard!" He dropped to his knees and laid a hand on Naed's shoulder. "How is—Sisters!"

"A healer!" Naed pressed wads of cloth to the Prince's chest. "We must have a healer!"

Krenin rocked back onto his heels. "I'll see—"

An animal-like cry drowned Krenin's words. High-pitched and bestial, it raised the hair on the back of Naed's neck.

Krenin spun halfway and stopped short, a stricken look on his face. His eyes, wide and astonished, rolled toward Naed. Uttering a strangled gurgle, he toppled sideways.

Naed stared first at the knife hilt protruding from

Krenin's neck, then at the slender hand drawing back, fingers daubed in blood. Over the hands, feral eyes locked on his. Their frenzy leaped at him from orbs the blue of ice.

"I did it!" Erodasi hissed, her body crouched, fingers spread like claws. "I killed the whoreson! See? I killed him!"

"You...witch! You she-demon!" Bolting up, Naed lunged for her.

"Don't touch me!" She sprang against the wall, the hem of her cloak brushing the smoldering torch knocked down in the mêlée. With a whoosh, flames rushed up the wool and exploded through the fur collar. Before his eyes, Erodasi's hair flared about her head like an orange halo. Her face disappeared. A shrill, unearthly howl rose from the curtain of flame before the human torch rushed blindly past him and tumbled over the low outer wall.

Naed flung himself against the stone. What was left of Erodasi of Roines smoked in the courtyard below, a twisted mass of charred flesh. Retching, he hauled himself back and stumbled across the landing.

A hiss and crackle made him stop. He stared at a smoking, blackened vine and, above it, flames racing across a thatched roof. "Fire!" chorused from the courtyard below. Covering his mouth and nose with his tunic, Naed dashed through swirling smoke and across the landing.

He found the Prince with his back braced against the wall, Krenin cradled in his arms. "'Tis—'tis nothing," the Prince whispered, a hand fumbling from Krenin's hair to his cheek to his still open eyes. "You've had worse, damn you!" He rocked, and his fingers gripped the front of Krenin's tunic. "Curse you! You can't leave me now!"

Kneeling, Naed's throat burned. Krenin, for all his faults, deserved better than death at the hands of a woman, but 'twas no time to give the man his due. The smoke thickened and he knew full well 'twas not only Krenin's blood running dark red across the stones at his fingertips. "We must go."

Prince Arn twisted out of his hands. He clutched Krenin to his chest and stroked through the dead man's hair.

Overhead, the fire hissed, and a shower of sparks fell around them. In moments—seconds, perhaps—the roof supports would burn through and smoldering wooden beams would tumble onto the landing. Naed pried at the Prince's hands. "Krenin is dead! You must leave him now and come away from here!"

"I'm not...leaving...Krenin!"

Hauling the body out of the Prince's arms, Naed wrenched the Prince's fingers from Krenin's tunic. Smoke drifted over the landing. Coughing, Naed grabbed the Prince under the arms and dragged him through it to the stairs. Heaving the taller man over his shoulder, he staggered down the steps one at a time.

Sweat poured down Naed's face. His leg shook with each step. Behind him, he heard the roar of the fire and knew it raced beyond the roof of the living quarters. Below, he heard frantic cries and shouted orders; he caught glimpses of figures rushing back and forth through the smoke. His eyes stung, his throat burned, and blood seeped warmly into his clothing. Somewhere between the top of the stairs and the first landing, the Prince's struggles faded. As his hands swung limply at Naed's back, Naed prayed he was merely unconscious. If he were not... Gritting his teeth, Naed stumbled down the last steps. "Help! The Prince...!"

Hands seized Naed's burden, removed it, disappearing with it into the smoke. Other hands grabbed his arms, picked him up, and hauled him away from the burning building.

"Lord Naed!" Gorm said as he set Naed on his feet under the parapet. "How—?"

"I came with Krenin." Hands on his knees, he gulped air.

"Commander Krenin? But—"

"Dead. Up there." Straightening, he pointed to the tower whose top level raged with flames. "There—'twas an assassin—"

Blanching, Gorm spun toward a knot of men kneeling and standing around a body on the ground. "The Prince!" the giant demanded. "Is he—?"

"Alive," said a healer Naed recognized from the march on Vinvinnysee. "But barely." He pressed another bandage to the Prince's bloody tunic.

While Gorm swore graphic oaths, Naed squeezed between onlookers and knelt. In the shadows, the Prince's face stood out white and ghastly, his closed eyes sunk into their sockets. When Naed grasped his hand, it was as cold as the stone under his body. *Seconds*, Naed thought, *mere seconds and we should have arrived in time!*

"The Prince is dead!" someone shouted.

"Prince Arn is dead!" echoed another.

Naed staggered to his feet as the refrain ran along the ramparts and rushed through the courtyard. "No! He is *not* dead! Curse you all! I tell you, he is *not* dead!"

His single voice, hoarse and desperate, was lost in the roar of flames that leaped from roof to roof and transformed the courtyard into a cauldron of orange light and grotesque shadows.

"The west parapet's aflame!" The captain of the guard rushed toward them. "'Tis beyond us to stop!"

Naed stared at the inferno that was once the living quarters. "We must escape the fortress! Take everyone out!"

"How?" Gorm gaped at him as if he had gone mad. "'Tis no room for us all in the tunnel, and Roines and his rabble will slaughter us like sheep at the gate!"

"Would you prefer to roast like pigs?" He seized the captain of the guard by the sleeve. "Signal Master Borth and Lord Tylus. Tell them to cover our escape." Shoving the man in the direction of the rampart's ladder, Naed swung back to Gorm. "Send ten men out the tunnel to secure it. Then gather the people. We are going out the gate!"

****

Below the front gate, the Lord of Roines spurred his frothing horse to and fro behind his lines, alternately cursing at and exhorting his men to greater effort. A sudden flare of orange made him stand in his stirrups and drag his mount to a halt. Around him, the combatants looked up, startled. Smoke poured into the darkening sky and billowed over the west wall.

"'Tis on fire!" someone shouted.

"Demon be damned!" the Lord of Lede exclaimed, reining to a halt beside Rolnar. "What a piece of luck!" He rubbed his hands together. "We'll slaughter them now."

"The Prince is dead!" Lord Belac galloped toward them. "Did you hear the shout?"

"Dead?" Rolnar echoed as Belac's horse skidded to a stop. "Are you certain?"

"His own men say so. Didn't you hear them?"

Rolnar's mind raced to assimilate the news, the possibility. "How?"

Lede shrugged. "What does it matter how?" His eyes gleamed yellow in the orange light. "Let's finish the lot as they come out of the gate. I'll take Tylus myself."

Rolnar blinked, roused at last by Lede's eagerness and the memory of how much he mistrusted the small, rat-like man who had threatened him at Roines. Then, he needed Lede's army. Now that the Prince was dead and Val-Feyridge all but his, he no longer required this man who foolishly turned his back to watch flames leap into the night sky. Rolnar licked his lips. Pre-occupied with the fighting, neither Belac nor the others on this small hillside paid him any heed.

Rolnar raised his sword. "You'll take no one, my dear Lede, least of all me!" With a thrust like the one that killed Edad of Koth, he stabbed the Lord of Lede. The dead man slipped to the muddied snow. Rolnar pricked Lede's mount and sent it squealing.

Sheathing his sword, Rolnar told his nearest officer, "The Lord of Lede's dead. Put all of his forces under your command."

"Aye, m'lord," the man said, dragging a sleeve over his sweat-streaked face. "They've broken out of the fortress. 'Twere too many of 'em to stop, but the gate be ours." He wheeled his lathered horse. "Would you have us be after 'em, m'lord?"

Rolnar stared at the walls that had defied him for so long. "Let them go. They're nothing without the Prince. We can collect them at our leisure."

Snatching his banner from his standard bearer, Rolnar heeled his horse and, heedless of the thick smoke or the white-eyed reluctance of his mount, galloped through the newly-won gate and into the abandoned fortress. Dismounting, he ran up the nearest staircase to the ramparts. At the top, he tore down the panther banner and ripped it to shreds. Lips split in a savage grin, Rolnar drove home the staff of his own banner.

"It's mine! Val-Feyridge is mine!" With wild leaps, he cavorted across the rampart as smoldering ash drifted around him.

****

Arn fought blackness. He struggled for breath, unable to suck in air. Faces swam and lurched over him, women's faces and a man's. He recognized the man's. "What—?" he panted.

"Easy, m'lord," the healer soothed. "Don't try to talk."

Beyond the man's pasty face, Arn made out the interior of a wagon. It bumped through a rut, and pain swamped him. A thousand sparks danced behind his clenched eyelids. He forced them open again when a scent he recognized scratched at his throat. Suddenly cold, he seized the healer's tunic and strove to pull himself upright.

"M'lord, don't try—"

Arn sent the man sprawling. Clutching at the wagon frame, he hauled himself to a half-sitting position. Sweat dripped into his eyes. He blinked to clear dancing lights from his vision, then realized it was the sky that boiled with orange, yellow, and red, the sky over towering black walls. While he watched, frozen, a flare of light illuminated a banner over the rampart near the gate—the banner of Roines.

'Tis gone. All gone.

The realization hit him like a smith's hammer in the chest. Arms caught him as he toppled, laid him down, wrapped him in blankets, but he paid them no heed. He stared straight up, ears oblivious to sound, limbs stiff and cold.

****

"Something has happened." Aerid urged her mare beside Banir's mount.

The Tolemak drew rein and rubbed a gloved hand over the stubble on his chin. "'Tis the darkness. We should be stopping soon."

"We cannot be sparing the time. There be danger. 'Tis no dream."

"The horses be weary."

"Must they rest all night?"

"An hour or two." He peered at her in the dimness. "'Twill mean no fire."

Aerid nodded. "Lead on. I shall follow."

CHAPTER THIRTY-THREE

Naed limped through the low, dark halls of Albon. The Prince's old home was quiet at last. It had taken all of his patience and all of the inhabitants' ingenuity to house the refugees. Everywhere in the fortress people could be found sleeping in halls, on floors, on stair landings, in the stable, and in wagons that had come with Arn from Vinvinnysee.

Pausing at the juncture of another of the maze-like halls, Naed leaned against the wall. His leg ached so, each step required a conscious effort.

Lord Tylus had suggested they go to Albon. "'Tis near and defensible," the crook-nosed man said. Naed was certain he eyed his D'nalian clothing. He remembered the glance that passed between Gorm and Tylus, the glance that raised heat in his cheeks before the lord startled him by asking, "Be any of that blood yours, sir?"

He had looked down at stains discoloring his tunic and the sword he held at ready. They had battled out of the gate and up the hill, but 'twas all a blur. He had killed men—he must have—for the blood on his sword was still wet. "None, m'lord."

Tylus's shield clashed into his own with such force Naed nearly lost his seat. "'Tis a fine one you are! A fine one, indeed!" Grinning, Tylus wheeled his horse and, with a wild cry, plunged back into the fray.

That had been yester eve. Now, at last, all were settled, the people fed, the wounded looked to, guards set.

He had eaten, too, a meal Morys forced upon him. But eating reminded him of how little he had slept these last days, how much his body ached, how his cheek where the Kothman's sword had scraped, itched and burned. He longed for the bowl of heated water Banir would prepare before he asked for it, knowing in advance his needs.

Naed ran a hand through his hair. He would not think of heated water now, nor of a blanket to wrap himself in. He would see the Prince first and assure himself...

A lump the size of a fist bulged in Naed's throat. What would he assure himself of, that all had not been for naught? He had seen the Prince's gray face, seen the fixed gaze, heard the rasping breath. 'Twas only a matter of time, and he could not prevent it.

Bracing his forearm against the wall, he leaned his forehead on it. Dlaniger, whose plans he knew, had still struck the Prince. Val-Feyridge, which he sought to protect, had fallen. Krenin was dead. And he had been unable to prevent any of it. He had failed Dranoel, failed Aerid, failed his own people. His eyes burned. *By the Sisters, not woman's tears, too!* Pushing away from the wall, he dug the heels of his hands into his eye sockets.

"Be you Lord Naed, the D'nalian?"

He jerked around, and stumbled. The woman in the shadows reached out a hand. "You startled me," he muttered, regaining his balance and putting three quick, but careful, steps between his body and her hand. "What would you have of 'the D'nalian'?"

She advanced into the torchlight, cocking her head so a heavy brown braid fell from her shoulder and dangled alongside her hip. "'Tis true what they say; there be polished copper in your hair. Aye, and a bit of green in your eyes."

Nonplussed, Naed stared while she approached. She was young, of Aerid's years, but with none of her servant's deference.

"The color suits you. That what I can see of you under the soot." Her gaze ran over his clothing. "'Tis new garments you'll be needing, too. And this—" She reached for his chin.

Recoiling from the out-thrust hand, Naed banged his head into the wall. The jolt shook his fingers free of their automatic grip on his knife hilt. Irritated by his reflexes' inability to separate friend from foe, he demanded, "What would you have of me?"

"Why, to tend to that, of course." She pointed to his cheek. "'Tis festered, you know. My father said 'twas likely with what he'd seen of you. He sent me to look after you, knowing you'd not be looking after yourself."

The comment raised a flush on Naed's cheekbones. "Who is your father?"

She gripped his arm, cutting off escape with warm, firmly closed fingers. "Raell is my name, and my father is Lord Tylus."

Naed stared at the high Tolemak cheekbones and narrow, perfectly straight nose. "You look naught like him."

Raell laughed. "I should hope not. He's a handsome man, to be sure, but I doubt he'd make a comely woman. Come. I've a chamber prepared."

"I have no time for your ministrations, Lady Raell. I must see the Prince."

She fisted her hands on her hips. "Indeed. 'Tis stubborn you be, and proud, too. Well, 'twill do you no good to see the Prince. He's unconscious. My father's told the healers to send for you if he should awaken, but 'tis not likely for hours. There be no more you can do this night. 'Twould do you well to sleep while you may and let the folk tend to their own needs."

Overwhelmed by both the forward nature of her speech as much as the content, Naed allowed the Lady Raell to propel him along the corridor and guide him into a small, firelit chamber furnished with bed, wardrobe, table, and two chairs. When she indicated the chair beside the fire, he sat in it, but only so he could gather his thoughts for a suitable retort. Humming a tune he could not identify, Lady Raell poured some red liquid from a small pot on the hearthstones. 'Twas wine, Naed decided as he sniffed the cup she handed him, but it had been heated, and crumbled bits of some herb he could not recognize floated on the surface.

"Drink."

He watched while she laid out a square of cloth, then turned to a pot steaming over the fire. "Are you a healer?" he said as she ladled a hot cloth into a wooden bowl.

"Only of minor wounds. 'Tis a necessary skill in a household of men." She gestured to the cup. "'Twill not harm you."

Reluctantly, Naed downed the liquid. The wine warmed his throat and the fire's heat penetrated his boots. He struggled to keep his eyes open, but the lids would not rise. Nor would his hands stir from where they hung at his sides, the fingers warm and weighted with blood. Hands touched his face, unfamiliar but gentle hands. Something stung his cheek and he winced, but the pain vanished as quickly as it had come. Liquid and warmth replaced it, and he sighed.

****

The blackness receded, but as it did, the pain returned, sharp and intense with each breath Arn struggled to draw. He shifted his hand, found cloth ticking and knew he lay in a bed. He made out a room bathed in candlelight, a boxy room with a low ceiling and the blurred colors of a tapestry hanging on one wall. He frowned. This was not Val-Feyridge.

He breathed, and pain seared through his lungs.

"M'lord, do you hear me?"

A man's face swam into view. "Where...?" Arn whispered, gripping the healer's arm.

"Albon, m'lord."

"Val-Feyridge...?"

"Burned."

'Twas true. The vision of towers and ramparts consumed by flames had not been a nightmare. Val-Feyridge was gone. Krenin was gone. Aerid was gone. Everything was gone. He groaned, thrashed in the bed, flailing with arms and legs at the pain clawing at his chest, at the beast that sprang from the darkness and ripped at his flesh. Someone poured liquid down his throat. He choked on it, coughed, shoved at the cup, the hands, the arms, until the beast retreated, darkness drifted closer, and he slid into a cavern of vague, fretful dreams.

****

Naed awoke to the sound of a woman's voice, humming. Sunlight shone through a small window and illuminated a low-ceilinged, sparsely furnished room dominated by a crude stone mantle. Something that smelled like food simmered in a pot there. His stomach rumbled. Stretching, he ran a hand over his face and encountered a bandage.

"Well, and a good morning to you," Lady Raell said, smiling from the side of the bed.

Her eyes were brown, he noticed at once, the color and shape of Krenin's. And their gaze darted from his face to his body and back again. Naed glanced down, saw the bedding bunched about his waist and realized he was naked beneath it. Flushing, he snatched the blanket up to his chin. "Lady Raell, your father cannot deem it proper—"

"For me to see you so? The House of Tylus be a household of men, or didn't I say so last night? Besides," she said as she prevented his further retreat by sitting on the blanket's edge, "my father sent me to bring you fresh garments, something to eat, and the message that he waits for you in the Prince's study." Leaning across his chest, she unfastened the bandage on his cheek and examined the exposed wound.

Naed sat rigid while her body stretched over his. Her scent wafted around him, not of small purple bellflowers like that lingering around Aerid, but of delicate white lilies mingled with musk. His blood roared in his ears. He closed his eyes and tried to breathe.

"'Tis much improved," she pronounced.

When he opened his eyes, she sat at the end of the bed with folded hands and studied him. "Be all D'nalians so modest?"

"I—we do not—'tis not meet for a maid...such as you...to be alone with a man unless..." He closed his eyes, sucked in a breath. "There is much significance attached to such conduct!"

Raell said nothing for so long, Naed risked a glance in her direction. She sat much as before, hands in her lap, but her eyes sparkled and a pink flush colored her cheeks. "Then I should be making myself quite clear."

When Naed's heart beat again, Lady Raell had already danced to her feet and, giggling, swept out. Drenched with sweat, he sank into the mattress and stared at the ceiling. *I must think of the Prince. And the army, and recovering Val-Feyridge.* He had no time to think of ginger hair and eyes the color of dark honey.

****

"They be not D'nalian garments," Lord Tylus said as Naed entered the study, "but they fit you right and proper." He rose from the chair behind the desk and extended his hand.

Naed grasped it. "I thank you for your consideration, m'lord."

"They be not mine but my second son's. Raell thought you be near Toth's size."

At the mention of Lady Raell, Naed blushed. He would have turned away, but Tylus had already done so.

The Tolemak lord gestured to the crowded courtyard visible from the window. "We have much to be about, m'lord. Albon has not the supplies to keep this lot o'er winter. We may lie here to rest, but we'll starve if Roines and his wolfpack corner us here." He joined his hands behind his back and scowled at the scene below. "The bastards let us go when we broke off fighting, but 'twas not out of fear." He shook his white head. "No, m'lord, 'tis my guess Roines and his hounds think the Prince dead and us helpless without him."

"But that is untrue!"

"Is it?"

The eyes over the crooked nose were kind, but the shadows under them spoke of sadness, melancholy, defeat. Prince Arn could not be dead. He would know it. Raell would know it. She would not behave as...as maddeningly if the Prince were dead.

"The Prince lives," Tylus said. He turned to the desk and traced a finger along the wood grain. "'Twould be best if you see for yourself, m'lord. Then you'll understand why Lord Brede and I and the others have considered what we have since this dawn."

****

If anything, the man in the bed had grown grayer. Naed stood just inside the door, unable to approach the face with the sunken eye sockets and the flesh drawn like drum-skin over its bones. Prince Arn's breath rasped in the small room, echoing from the beams and whispering behind the tapestry so that Naed fancied it was the walls themselves that breathed, their stony lungs scraping against wooden ribs. Stony lungs, though, would not have yielded to a knife; they would not have let a mere blade rip holes in them, holes that now leaked an odor that slinked into Naed's nostrils and frightened him.

"You cannot die," he mouthed, mindful of the healer

who dozed in the bedside chair. "Do you hear me?" Involuntarily, he moved closer, gripping the bedpost as if it were the hand lying on the coverlet, the hand with parchment-dry skin and blue-tipped fingers. "You are Arn, Prince of Val-Feyridge, master of Albon, conqueror of Vinvinnysee, be—" His voice faltered. Naed closed his eyes and tried again. "—beloved of Aerid, and...friend...to me."

Tears trickled into his beard. They stung a path across his wounded cheek, but Naed did not wipe them away. He reached out, touched the cold fingers, and squeezed them.

****

Arn heard a distant, passionate voice, felt a hand grip his. *Aerid*? His fingers fluttered in response. But 'twas not she. Desolation swamped his soul, darker and colder than before. His body burned. He pleaded with the fire, begged it to incinerate him, to free him from torment so he could plunge into the dark, still waters of oblivion beckoning on the fringes of his dreams. Why did they cling to him? Why would they not let him go? Why must they insist on torturing him with this pain, this agony? Restless, he tossed and groaned.

****

Naed gripped the healer's tunic sleeve. "What is it? He was quiet but a moment ago!"

The man reached for a cup on the bedside table. "The drug be wearing off, m'lord."

While the healer poured drops of thick liquid down the Prince's throat, Naed's fingers tingled as they had one sun-filled day outside Vinvinnysee. The Prince had yielded him power then. Now he would with all his heart give it back, but the fingers that had just stirred in his had as abruptly withdrawn, fisting themselves into the coverlet.

Will it be ever thus? Naed blundered into the hall. He had not spoken and he had lost Aerid. He had not spoken, and he had lost Dranoel. He had not spoken, and now he had lost the Prince.

"Fool! Coward!" He slammed fists against the wall, relishing the pain, wishing he could batter his heart until it, too, bled like his knuckles, until the walls about it

401

crumbled and everything locked inside would burst out and he could feel and speak and act according to the prompts of his soul, not hesitate, stumble, and reconsider until it was too late. Until it was always too late.

****

At Banir's insistence, they stopped at a crossroads inn. "For grain for the horses," he said, giving the animals into the care of the stableboy.

Reluctantly, Aerid let him guide her to a bench near the huge fireplace filling one wall of the common room. "Stay here," he told her when she was seated, the casket she bore close by her side and their cloaks hung by the fire to dry. "I'll see to a meal."

She watched him cross the room, passing a pair of merchants dividing a chicken with fingers and knives and, on the other side, farmers hunched over ale and a game of dremel beads. Stifling a yawn, Aerid stretched. She held out her hands to the fire, then smoothed them over her abdomen. Despite their grueling pace, the child within her womb thrived. Soon, she would have to loosen her garments. Yawning again, she leaned into the corner of the bench and savored the warmth, wishing she could store it like coals in a bucket for the next days.

Banir returned with bread and cups of ale. The innkeeper followed, bearing bowls of stew. When he had gone, Banir broke the bread and gave her half. "We'll not be staying." He dredged a hunk of bread through the stew and devoured it. "Soldiers," he said, tearing off another chunk of bread. "I saw them from the kitchen. Three of Roines, two of Koth, two others likely Ormo. They be in the back, drinking ale with the innkeeper's daughters."

Banir had been careful to keep to the less traveled paths, and they had met no one thus far on their journey but an occasional farmer collecting wood or bearing a load of grain to market. Now, however, they were close to their goal and...

Aerid stared at the bread in her hands. Across from her Banir sat with the half-eaten bowl of stew in his lap, a hunk of bread in his hands, motionless but for his fingers, which twitched. Finally, he tore the bread in two with a sudden, violent jerk. "Val-Feyridge has fallen. They're celebrating their victory, the bastards!" He clenched his fists, reducing the bread still grasped in his hands to crumbs.

She had not heard those words. This was a dream, the inn an illusion, the fire a conjuring trick with no warmth to penetrate bones gone cold to the marrow. Aerid closed her eyes and touched her birthstone, seeking comfort in it. When she looked again, the scene had not changed. Only the ale mug in her hand had tilted, and liquid dribbled down its side and over her knuckles. Aerid stared at it, conscious of its warmth, its stickiness, its density, like that of blood. Her heart beat heavily. "Arn is dead...or dying. They do say that, do they not?"

"Rumors!" Banir whispered, lacing sturdy fingers into hers. "'Tis no more certain than that he's wounded and they've retreated to Albon!"

If Arn were dead, her heart would shrivel in her breast like a flower cut from a bush and left to lie on the stones below. It would wither, turn to dust and finally blow away, leaving a hollow place between her ribs instead of the ache that resided there now. No, he was not dead. "How far to this...Albon?"

"Hard by here. A day, no more." He released her hand and stared at the half-eaten stew as if it were the leavings of another man. "They say nothing of D'nalians." He ripped another piece of bread from the chunk on his knee. "Eat. Tastes like stone, but 'twill keep us till Albon."

Aerid watched Banir shovel the stew and bread into his mouth and wash it down with a swallow of ale. The dark-eyed Tolemak looked neither right nor left but at some distant point she guessed was Albon while his hands and his mouth worked, taking in the nourishment necessary to sustain his body on the remaining journey to its goal. He would not stop again. Not unless she required it.

Tearing off a piece of bread with trembling fingers, Aerid vowed she would not require it. Even if it tasted like gall, she would eat this food and follow this man as far as he wished to lead her, as far as his own love drove him, to the place they both sought.

CHAPTER THIRTY-FOUR

Naed's fists worked, clenching and unclenching the carved arms of his chair in the council room while Tylus, Brede and others talked quietly around the table. They had given him the chair of honor at Tylus's right and nodded at him as one nods to a man in mourning, but after a moment of awkward silence, they had gone about the business of partitioning the Prince's holdings, his army, and the refugees from Val-Feyridge.

'Tis as if they have buried him already, and they peck like vultures around what is left! Shoving back his chair, he stood.

Unfamiliar faces turned toward him, their gazes watchful, wondering.

Bastards! He turned to leave, but a hand on his wrist halted his progress. He swung around, furious at the restraint.

"Do not think us cold, m'lord." Tylus eased the pressure of his grip without relinquishing his hold. "Each of us here be sworn to the Prince, and sworn by more than blood or booty, else we should have left him months ago. But tell me. With your own eyes you've seen the man. Can you deny he's dying?"

In his heart, he knew the truth of Tylus's words, but he could not speak them aloud. Not yet. And certainly not with such callousness. He jerked his wrist free of Tylus's fingers.

The white-haired lord rose. "We grieve, m'lord, but we be also practical men. What we decide here must be decided and quickly if the folk are to survive."

Naed's blood sang in his ears. 'Twas a song of power that pumped blood to his muscles and to his brain, crystallizing his thoughts, flashing them against the blue sky like the tail-feathers of the wheeling hawk. Now was the time, the place to act, to stand for the Prince, to do all he should have done sooner, to make up for all he should have said, before. "And how will they survive when you divide and scatter like leaves before the wind?"

"We cannot stand against the might of Roines!" Tylus retorted. "'Tis clear we have not the men!"

"Nor the provisions," Brede said. "We'll starve here if we try to stay."

Naed looked at their reddened, earnest faces and shadowed eyes. He could yet change his mind. No one would blame him for reconsidering, for backing down. No one but himself.

"And you think that if you divide and flee to your homes, Roines will forgive you and forget you stood against him?" He coughed out a laugh. "Roines and his cohort will pluck you like apples in season, one by one, until his basket is filled with your precious heads!"

Tylus slammed his palm on the table. "We have not the men nor supplies to hold—!"

"Not the men or supplies, true! But have you yet your wits? Your hearts? Or did you leave those, too, before the gates of Val-Feyridge?"

Tylus's nostrils flared. "To my ears, that rings like an insult. However, while you be D'nalian, 'tis possible 'twas not so intended."

"Do you see before you a D'nalian?" He indicated his borrowed Tolemak clothing. "Then you see before you a lie. Do you see before you a lord? Then you see before you a lie. I am naught but a man and a warrior. Leave if you must. Take what you will, only leave me Albon and what soldiers will stay and serve under me. I mean to keep this place for the Prince's sake."

"Why, 'tis suicide! Roines will destroy you!"

"Only if I wait for him, m'lord." Turning on his heel, Naed strode out.

Raell stood against the opposite wall, her hands pressed to the stone.

Naed knew by the paleness of her face she had seen and heard everything. For one piquant, still-standing moment, he yearned to continue toward her, to touch his fingertip to the wisp of hair curling beside her ear, to breathe again her scent.

"'Twas wonderful you were," she whispered, her eyes a deep, glowing brown.

Mouth dry as cotton, Naed stepped forward.

"I'm with you!" Gorm seized Naed's hand and pumped it. "I've cracked too few of the bastards' heads to suit me, m'lord. 'Twould please me to stand with you if you'll have me."

"Aye, and me," said Borth emerging from Gorm's shadow.

"We've come this far," Yarl said, joining them. "We'd be fools to stop now."

"Then fools you be to stand alone against the might of Roines."

Naed's gaze swept the speaker from braced-apart boots to fists jammed onto hips, to scowling mouth, beaked nose, and narrowed eyes. "You be a fool, m'lord," Tylus said. "But Demon take me if I don't see the man in you! D'nalian or no, there be a look about you, and 'tis not in my nature to ignore it. But, blast and damnation, I have the folk to consider!" He pivoted, strode to the opposite wall, spun. "A week. The men of Tylus will stay a week. 'Tis all I can rightly give." With a jerk of his head to Raell, who ran to take his arm, Lord Tylus strode away.

He had won, Naed thought over the rush of blood in his ears, but what had he won?

"A week!" Gorm sputtered.

"'Tis scarce enough to secure the border," Borth said.

"'Tis all we have." Naed tore his gaze from the slender form hurrying alongside Tylus. He surveyed the Tolemak officers—his officers now—and laid a hand in turn on each man's shoulder. "We have much to be about. Let us make the most of our numbers while we have them."

****

Aerid urged her mare's nose close to the rump of the pack horse. The sky had cleared after moonset, but the riot of stars glittering above sent little light to penetrate the shadows between rock and bush, tree and stump. Only the snow-covered meadows, when they rode across them, glimmered a cold blue-white.

Twice, they had hidden in thickets—once while riders passed within a lance-length of their hiding place, another while the murmur of men's voices and the crunch of hooves drifted around them on the uncertain breeze.

They were close now. Hours ago, they had walked the horses across clearings. Now Banir pushed the animals to a trot, slowing only when the denseness of the underbrush forced him to. Aerid heeled her mare, determined to keep up.

"Back!" Banir hissed, materializing beside her, face a patch of white. "I heard something."

Aerid saw the glimmer of his drawn sword as he reined his horse in a tight circle. Stiff and still, she heard nothing but the shuffle of her mare's hooves and the crunch of crusted snow. Somewhere nearby, an owl hooted.

"Run!" Banir slapped the mare's rump.

Shadows erupted from shadows. Hands clutched at her reins, grabbed at her arms, dragged at her body until, screaming, she tumbled into chest armor, snow, and a jumble of limbs.

"Demon's Blood! A woman!"

Flint struck a torch into life. The sudden light seared Aerid's eyes as she pushed up from the snow. A forest of legs surrounded her, Tolemak legs, legs topped by tunics hemmed with red and gray. Breathless, she stared, recognizing the colors. "Take us to Albon...I beg you."

****

In the courtyard of the mud-and-stone fortress, Naed gathered Aerid into his arms, his bristled cheek chafing life into her chilled skin. He had thinned, and shadows haunted his eyes, but his embrace stole her breath.

"'Tis impossible, but you are here." Putting her away from him, he looked at Banir, who stood with a snow-packed cloth pressed to his head. "'Twas foolish, aye, more than foolish. You could have died."

"Aye, but we be here now, and are you not glad to see us?"

"More than you know!" His bear hug lifted the Tolemak off his feet. "And 'tis no more than your hard Albon head deserves than to be cracked for a fool. You swore to me—"

"To keep her safe," Banir retorted when Naed set him free. "Here she be, safe as promised."

Visibly struggling with his emotions, Naed shrugged out of his cloak and threw it around Aerid's shoulders.

"You cannot have come in better time. Let me see to food and drink and a fire to take the chill out of these hands." He rubbed hers between his.

Lines she had never seen before edged Naed's mouth. Tiny creases fanned outward from the corners of his eyes and a scab crusted his cheek. He wore Tolemak garments with D'nalian boots and sword. The short beard, red-gold in the torchlight, made him look older, no longer the youth but fully the man. She squeezed his hands. "Where be Arn? Tell me, and tell me true, how does he?"

His thumbs stroked across her knuckles while he looked long at her upturned face. "He wants to die, Aerid. But we will not let him!"

****

Raell leaned over him, lips parted, the satin flesh of her inner lip visible as she stroked the side of his face. Naed breathed in the scent of her. If he raised his hand and turned the palm outward, he knew it could contain her breast as surely as did the blue woolen gown against which the fullness of her body strained. Naed trembled. Raell leaned closer, her hand warming his thigh with a light touch, rocking gently, and sliding... ever so slowly... off the side.

Naed stared at the dish upturned on the floor and the bread crumbs scattered near it. Around him the faint gray of early morning crept between the shutter slats, showing the ash dead in the grate. *I have slept in my chair*, he realized.

A knock rattled his door. "M'lord!"

'Twas not Grodar's voice. Nor Morys'. "Who calls?" He groped for his sword.

"Borth, m'lord. Gorm's returned with a man of Vral under a white flag."

Naed buckled on his sword. The words held significance, but he could not dredge from his mind the reason. With a glance at Banir, who still slept undisturbed in the center of the big bed, Naed drew back the bolt and stepped into the corridor.

The council room was cold when Naed opened the door to it. Rubbing his arms, he wished he had thought to bring his cloak.

"Where be this man of Vral?" Tylus growled from the

corridor.

Naed's gaze shot beyond Tylus, but Raell did not materialize in her father's wake. Disappointed, he ducked his head to hide the rush of heat to his face.

"Here be your Vral man." A man rose slowly from a bench in the shadows.

Naed observed the scab marring the man's sword hand. "Good to see you again."

"You know him?" Tylus demanded.

"We met on the road."

Tylus flung himself into a chair. "Vral be in Roines' camp."

"No longer. My master has seen how Roines turns on those he no longer values."

Tylus snorted. He propped a foot on an opposing chair. "'Tis not for this grand revelation that I quit my morning table. Say what you will and be done, man of Vral."

The officer turned to Naed. "When I told Lord Vad how you kept your word and granted us safe passage, he was moved, so moved, m'lord, he ordered me to return with half my troop and offer our services. He be proud, Lord Vad, but he declares 'twas wrong to follow Roines and he would undo his mistake by offering you what remains of his might. We be not many, m'lord," he said, unbuckling his sword, "but we be yours to command."

Naed stared, nonplussed, at the sheathed sword held out to him. "You must know our position. You cannot help but know..."

"I know, but Lord Vad does not. We left afore he could receive the news." He contemplated the scabbard in his hands. "If we are to die, then why not here, together against Roines, rather than later, separately...and alone?" He offered the weapon again. "Lord Vad will thank me when 'tis done."

"If he does not, I shall."

Tylus's foot thudded to the floor. "Well and good," he said, inserting his bulk between Naed and the proffered weapon, "but what do you offer us to prove you've renounced Roines?"

Despite the man's interference, Tylus was right. 'Twould not be wise to blindly accept Vral's offer, no

409

matter how serendipitous. 'Twould not be wise...but it would be right.

Turning slowly, Naed looked from Tylus to the Vral officer, knowing each waited to see if he would prove true to the estimation each had made of him. Well, he would not disappoint either. "Forgive Lord Tylus's brusqueness, but you must understand our position. While 'tis my inclination to accept you unreservedly, 'tis in our best interests to request some proof of your master's changed intentions."

"'Twould be foolish of me to expect otherwise." The Vral man laid the sword on the table and stepped away from it. "Hear this, then. The supply wagons Roines looked for on the day we met be only now on their way to Val-Feyridge. Just afore dusk, we saw them make camp east of your boundaries."

The crack of Tylus's fist shook the table. "Do you think us fools to believe such a tale?"

"No, m'lord. I would think you fools only if you failed to believe."

"It must be true," Naed said before Tylus could retort. "Roines believes he has won. Why else should he have failed to pursue us from Val-Feyridge? Why else should he thus far neglect to attack us here? Were I he, I should have done like Prince Arn and driven my enemies into oblivion, yet he chooses not to do so. He must believe the Prince dead and us helpless without him."

"Aye," Tylus fingered the hilt of his sword, "'tis like that inflated pig bladder to sit and wait until the weather suits him!"

"Then, it stands to reason he would wait for the provisions the fighting delayed. It also stands to reason that, thinking us routed, he would order them to take the most direct road to Val-Feyridge, the one that passes within sight of our boundaries."

"'Twould be like the bastard to smear dirt in the face of a man while he's down, but—" Tylus dragged a chair out and propped a foot on the seat. Planting a forearm across his knee, he shook a crooked finger at Naed. "—'twould also be like the bastard to tempt us into a trap."

"With the provisions he knows we need." Naed placed his hands on the table and leaned forward. What better

410

tactic than to lure the weakened enemy into the open where they could be overwhelmed by superior numbers? He shook his head at the beauty of the idea. 'Twas far superior to wasting time and men starving a fortress and assaulting it. Far superior, yet...

The Vral man cleared his throat. "'Twas a large gathering of wagons. We saw men, but not in such numbers that the wagons were full of them." He laid a hand on his sword. "By my honor, m'lord, what I've said be true."

Tylus grunted. "'Tis likely you've seen what you say you have, but 'tis also likely what you saw was but what Roines would have us think it was."

"I believe you. And I accept you and your men." Before Tylus could open his mouth, Naed plucked the sword from the table and handed it hilt first to the man. "Go and quarter your men. Our store is not ample, but 'tis adequate."

The man's thin face shone. "We will serve you well, m'lord."

The instant the latch clicked behind the man, Naed spun on Tylus. "I am not a fool! Nor do I misunderstand the risks of taking on this troop of Vral, but I have taken the measure of this man, and I do not find it strange he offers his services to us now, when all odds seem against us."

He crossed the room and gripped the back of a carved chair, seeking strength in its uncompromising solidity. What he had to say next would surely damn him in Tylus's—and Raell's—eyes, but it had to be said or Tylus would never understand. He cleared his throat. "I do not find it surprising because... because I myself have once been the Prince's enemy."

The white-haired lord removed his foot from the chair. He stood as if contemplating the hardwood seat. "There be two kinds of men in Tolemak—men who hate the Prince for besting them, and men who would join the better man." Striding across the room, he offered his hand. "'Tis glad I be to join you, m'lord."

At the words, warmth rushed through Naed's body. He had won much, but 'twas not nearly enough. "I mean to capture those provisions."

"Do you, now?" With a flashing grin, Tylus bounced a fist off Naed's shoulder. "There be Tolemak in your blood, sir, 'tis a certainty! Let's be off. Nothing would please me more than to prick the pig-faced runt of Roines." Alternately bellowing a bawdy song and booming out orders, he strode away.

Naed stood in the middle of the deserted council chamber while, outside the open door, the fortress stirred into sudden life. The thought struck him crudely. Prince Arn was dying. The people faced starvation. And he was about to lead them to possible death in a trap. Why then did his blood sing? Why did his fingertips tingle and his ears hum? He looked at his hands, then at the sword strapped to his side. *Because I am a warrior and there is naught else I would rather be.*

****

Aerid bathed Arn and cleaned his wounds. Applying to each an ointment of her own making, she laid on fresh dressings and fastened them with strips of clean cloth. When she was done, she sat on the edge of the bed and allowed her hands to tremble, her stomach to churn, her throat to wrench at the enormity of the damage Dlaniger's knife had wreaked on his body. Arn should live, she told herself as salt water trickled into the corner of her mouth. Her fingertips had intimate knowledge of the scars of similar wounds he had survived. He could survive these, too—if he desired it.

Closing her eyes, she forced a swallow. How could he want to live now so much of his life was gone, his best friend, his home, his dream...

Her abdomen fluttered. Aerid covered it with her hand, thinking to still the tremor before it spread throughout her body. She had allowed herself a few moments of reaction, and they had been spent. 'Twould not do to give in to more shudders when the fire required tending, the basin had to be emptied, the—

A strange energy burned along Aerid's veins. She straightened, and her eyes opened wide. Under her hand, her abdomen fluttered again. She bent her head, concentrating on the spaces between her fingers. The fluttering continued, beating like butterfly wings deep within her body.

412

Aerid's heart beat faster. *Life!* Old Gam had told her how the quickening would feel. She herself had told other women, then delivered them months later of fat, squalling infants. She had told the women, and rejoiced with them when their wombs stirred, but she had not truly known— until now—how it felt to contain another life within the core of her own.

Her gaze flew to Arn's shuttered eyes and gray, sunken cheeks. She cradled life in her body—her life, his life, co-mingled. "You shall know your child," she whispered, and reached for his hand. Uncurling the cold fingers, she laid them across her abdomen, across the skin under which life danced, and held them there.

****

Swinging into his chamber, Naed grabbed Banir's foot. "Arise, you lazy Albon slug!"

The Tolemak rolled over and rubbed his eyes. "Be it dawn?"

"Long past." Lifting his shield, he slung it over his shoulder. "Are you fit?"

Banir sat up. His hair hung over his face and stubble darkened his chin to black in the white-skinned face. "To skewer Roinesmen? 'Twould be a pleasure."

Naed snatched up his cloak. "Fetch yourself something to eat and meet me in the stable."

****

Leaving Grodar and Morys to see to Aerid's needs, and assigning Borth command of the fortress in his absence, Naed dusted his hands of the brown bread he had broken his fast with while walking toward the courtyard and stable.

Tylus appeared in the distant hallway's juncture. Raell hurried beside him, holding his cloak and sword while her father struggled to fasten the collar of his chest armor. Red-faced and cursing, the Tolemak lord jerked the last lace tight, then punched the shoulders into place.

"Deliver me," he growled as Naed reached him, "from armor makers who know nothing of the art!" Snatching his sword from Raell's grasp, he buckled it on. "Give me my cloak, girl, and a kiss for luck."

Standing on tiptoe, Raell complied. "Mind yourself." She tucked a stray lace back upon itself. "Have you your gloves?"

"Damned meddling woman, of course I ha—" He gripped his belt and expelled a curse.

"I'll fetch them," Raell murmured.

Naed watched her, drinking in every movement of her hands, every ray of sunlight burnishing her hair to gold. He had sought a glimpse of her all morning and now she was here within the compass of his arms. Here, but not here. His joy dissipated as he realized Raell had no more than glanced in his direction, and then only from under thick lashes. Her face was pale, pinched, and she hovered like a moth about her father's bulk.

"No, you'll be two days finding 'em." Tylus rapped his knuckles against Naed's chest armor. "'Twill take me but a moment, m'lord."

Before Naed could digest his words, Tylus strode off.

Raell slunk back against the wall. Head downcast, her lashes beat on her cheekbones. "I-I wish you luck."

While she turned, something more elemental than thought told Naed he should not let her go. He wrapped his hand around her upper arm. "Raell..."

He could feel her blood coursing under his fingers, sense the warmth rising from her body, smell the scent of her emanating from the nape of her exposed neck and the wisps of hair curling there. "Raell..." he murmured, his voice heavy with enchantment.

"Don't—" She shrank away, sliding her palm along the wall behind her.

"Raell..." Her name rolled from his lips like an incantation .

She shoved at him with both hands. "Take your copper hair and charm your own woman, you lowland bastard!"

Her breasts heaved scant inches from his chest. Skin prickling, Naed dragged his gaze upward and forced it to focus on Raell's face. There, he saw her lip trembled despite the violence snarling at him from her mouth. "What...woman?"

With an inarticulate cry, Raell plunged for the corridor. His arm, braced on the wall, held. She bounced back and pushed at his chest. "You bastard! You won't add me to your string of mistresses!"

Something slid into place in Naed's fogged brain. Catching her shoulders, he held her fast. "Mistresses? Do you mean Aerid?"

"Whatever you call her! The little Adanak...whore!" She thrust her knee upwards.

It required no conscious thought to block the blow, only a reflexive movement of his hips for Naed to press her against the wall. "Aerid belongs to the Prince." He forced his mind to focus on the words rather than the intoxicating wriggle of her thighs. "She—she bears his child."

Raell stilled. Color rampaged across her cheeks and her eyes welled shut. "Let me go."

A tear forged a track to her chin. Another hung glistening on her lashes. He wanted to touch it, to brush it away, to taste the trail of it with the tip of his tongue, but he knew he should not. D'nalian honor demanded he free her arms and lean away from her. D'nalian honor demanded he ignore the heart hammering within the cage of his ribs. D'nalian honor—

"Demon take it!" Bending, he fastened his mouth to hers.

In the space of heartbeats, he glimpsed the shiver of her lashes, felt the cool softness of her lips, sensed them firm in an instant's resistance, then part with a sigh breathed into his mouth. Then there was nothing but a haze of her scent, the skin of her throat warm under his lips, her fingers wild in his hair, the small of her back curved under his palm.

The sound of a slammed door broke them apart. Panting, they stared at each other like dreamers startled awake. "I-I must go," Raell said, flushing scarlet. She brushed past him.

Again, Naed put out a hand. "Raell..."

She halted at the touch of his fingers on her sleeve, but she neither turned nor raised the lashes spread like a fan across her cheekbones.

"Do you...?" he said, impelled by the need to say something, settle something, confirm...

Her lashes fluttered. "Do you...?"

He stared at the vulnerable curve of her neck, and the word said itself, "Aye."

415

With trembling hands, Raell reached up, undid a clasp lying amid the wisps of hair at her collar, and drew a gold charm from beneath her bodice. "Take this," she said, fastening it around his neck. "'Tis my promise." Pulling his head down, she kissed him once more, quickly, and fled.

Naed cupped his palm around the charm. Still warm from her body, it seemed alive, as if it contained her essence given into his keeping.

Hearing the shuffle of boot on stone, Naed looked up. Banir leaned against the corner, a cloak draping his body to his ankles, the hood thrown back, a shield slung over his shoulder. Flushing, Naed remembered where he was bound and why. He mumbled, "I am late."

Banir shrugged. "Vral be about saddling fresh horses."

"They are coming?"

With a nod, the Tolemak stooped and retrieved a shield lying face down beside a pillar.

Naed's flush deepened. He stuffed Raell's charm inside his undertunic.

"Where a woman be concerned," the Tolemak said, his face as bland as the stone walls, "'tis no difference between men."

Heat ran the full length of Naed's body. He snatched his shield from Banir's grip. "You have the mind of your kind!"

Banir grinned broadly. "Aye, 'tis the same as yours."

Naed's fist bounced off the Tolemak's quickly raised forearm. He swung again, but Banir danced away, chuckling.

"A fortnight alone and you be all but wed."

Naed slung his shield over his shoulder with such force it clanged into the wall at his back. More heat rushed across his face. "She...she is the Lady Raell."

"A fair catch." Banir tugged on his gloves. "'Tis far you've come, Naed of Druemarwin."

Naed paused in the act of adjusting his sword belt. He looked at the dark eyes fixed on his face and knew Banir, too, saw a wood in Adanak where two men faced each other with hatred. "And far you've come, Banir of Albon." Turning in unison, they walked side-by-side

416

toward the courtyard.

****

In the windowless room, Aerid did not know how long she sat holding Arn's hand pressed to her abdomen. She only knew, when she twitched awake, that she had drifted into the twilight of near sleep. She yawned, rolled her shoulders, and tried to force her eyelids open wide. In the warm, quiet room, they resisted.

Aerid yawned again and rubbed her fingers over Arn's hand. 'Twas still stiff but not as cold. Her body must have warmed it. Perhaps, if she lay under the blanket beside him, she could warm more of his body. He slept peacefully, his breathing audible but steady. If the random spasms that jerked through his limbs before she bathed him should return, she would feel them while lying close to his side and could awaken quickly to tend him.

Besides, she told herself as she eased onto the bed, it had been so long since she had properly slept, and she must have strength to see him through whatever should follow. 'Twould be easier to call someone else to watch, but she had come too far to leave Arn's side now. Settling down with her face at his shoulder, she rested her hand on his uninjured upper arm and pressed her legs to the length of his.

A momentary shiver shook her. He was so cold, so unresponsive she could have been holding a corpse. Tears burned behind her squeezed-shut eyelids. "I love you," she whispered, twisting her fingers into the coverlet beside Arn's shoulder.

CHAPTER THIRTY-FIVE

Naed peered through shadowy trunks of birches, poplars, and scattered pines toward a faint track parting the east hillock from the one on which he stood. Twilight and steadily falling snow blurred everything into gray if he stared too long, but he dared not look away. Not now when the barely perceptible creak of a wagon wheel tickled his eardrum.

"They are coming," he mouthed to Banir, who nodded and raised his arm.

To the left, a line of archers knelt as one and fitted arrows. To the right, horsemen drew their swords while snow slid from their cloaks. Their horses stamped, then were still.

They were far too close to Roines' stronghold to satisfy Naed. Even with darkness to shelter them, even with drivers who knew the countryside, they could barely hope to outrun a troop of horse back to Albon. The darkness could work against them as well as with them, and the snow had accumulated several inches on top of the crusted previous layer.

A sick feeling clutched at Naed's stomach, and he shivered. As the damp skin of his undertunic peeled away from his chest, something slid to the left, toward his heart. He pressed Raell's charm to his skin. At the contact, warmth suffused his torso.

Banir stroked his mount's muzzle while his gaze remained fixed on the darkening road. Tylus stood with a gloved palm cradling his unsheathed blade, his heels rocking a little in the ankle-deep snow. The giant Gorm leaned against his huge horse. A bit of birch twig rotated between his lips as he chewed it. Beyond in both directions stretched lines of men who waited silently, obediently, patiently. *For a sign*, Naed thought, *from me.*

Snow mantling his shoulders pressed down on them. His hood pushed his head forward, his chin leaned toward his chest. *They depend upon me, a man who is not even one of them.*

He stared at the toes of his boots. They were D'nalian boots. Skimming them was a Tolemak cloak. The sword he held was D'nalian forged, but the gloves gripping the hilt were not. The belt was his, but the tunic was Tolemak, hemmed not with Albon colors but with the green of Tylus. Throwing the snow from his shoulders, he stared at his cloak, his sword. *'Tis our hearts that make us men of a kind. 'Tis our hearts that make us men.*

Raising his head, he looked across at Banir, whose Druemarwin tunic was visible under his Tolemak cloak, at the man of Vral, the giant Gorm, and Tylus, who stood with him as an equal. *They are men, and I am one with them.*

Infused with a sudden, glowing certainty, Naed caught Banir's eye and grinned. Banir's teeth flashed. He gestured to the road below where, like a great, creaking snake, a row of wagons labored up the gentle rise between the hillocks.

"Take them!" Naed shouted. "For Val-Feyridge! For the Prince!"

****

Arn floated through dense fog. Wisps of cloud swirled around him, parting now and then to reveal a glow ahead. The chill had gone out of his limbs and he felt curiously warm. He ached, but the pain seemed muted, subdued, somehow no longer threatening.

In time, he noticed patterns in the glow, lights and darks and flickering points of brightness. He peered at them. The haze dissipated and he realized the points were candle flames. And the patterns? Wooden beams with squares of stone visible between them.

Albon.

Memories rose one after another, circled, and settled on his chest. There was Krenin, laughing one moment, dead the next. Val-Feyridge burning, the banner gone. Erodasi...? Someone had stabbed him. He had not seen who. There was Naed reviling him, rushing to him, arguing...coughing...

He's gone. Dead. As they all are. As I should be.

Pain burned through his chest, pain so sharp and

sudden it took his breath away. *Why*, he thought as he fumbled for something to grip, crush, cling to and ride it out—*why in the name of the Demon did they bring me back!*

One hand found fabric. The other found flesh.

Arn lay still, eyes pinched shut. This was not Aerid. How could it be when he had left her miles away and weeks ago? His mind told him she could not possibly have come. His heart insisted she had.

The bed shifted. Something silky drifted across his shoulder, something silky and fragrant. His heart thudded. Hadn't the same scent haunted him for weeks outside Vinvinnysee?

Another spasm seared through his rib cage. Arn winced, and his fingers tightened.

"Peace," whispered a voice he had heard in the sensuous darkness of Vinvinnysee nights. "Rest," soothed fingertips that had caressed his face in the early mornings. "'Tis here I be," murmured a hand whose cool, gentle palm had touched his cheek and cradled his soul.

Something welled up from the deepest recesses of Arn's body, from the crevices in which he had buried his mother, his grandfather, his childhood. It pushed up under pain and lifted it. It glided into thought and scattered it. It rose into his throat, swelled into the word, "Aye," and breathed it through his lips. Then it slipped behind his eyes, squeezed between his lashes, and rolled gently down his cheeks.

It was Aerid's lips he felt as he drifted into sleep, her lips and the subtle warmth of her breath caressing his face.

****

Naed galloped wildly through the forest. Branches slapped at him. Snow powdered his face, but he spurred through blue-white darkness, laughing and whooping.

Beside him rode Banir, sword slicing snowstorms from branches. "By the Demon!" the Tolemak shouted as they wheeled their horses around a rock. "Did you see that Kothman's face? He looked like to burst!"

"So you kindly pricked him, did you?"

Laughing again, they galloped toward the last of the captured wagons.

"'Twas splendid!" Tylus boomed when they joined him. "Splendid indeed!" He slapped Naed's shoulder, dislodging a spray of white powder. "Not a man among 'em left to horse."

Naed sucked in a deep breath. The cold air sobered him. "They will be after us, even so." He gestured to the wagons visible in the shadows. "Have they changed the horses?"

"The first ones be over the hill already. This lot be near done."

"Let us be off, then. 'Twill be daybreak before—"

A horn sounded low like thunder.

Naed's gaze shot to Banir, to Tylus, to the shadows beyond. His fingers tightened on the reins.

The horn sounded again, short and guttural.

"The bloody bastards! 'Tis a trap!" Tylus drew his sword.

"Hold!" Naed seized the Tolemak lord's reins. "If 'twere a trap, they should have been on us the moment we reached the wagons. 'Tis more like a patrol sent as escort to them."

Tylus glowered from within the cowl of his cloak. "What then?"

"We shall take them, but on our terms." He turned to Gorm. "Tell Yarl to send the wagons on. Send half of your men with them."

When Gorm nodded and wheeled his horse, Naed returned his attention to Tylus. "Have your men and Gorm's form a line here. I shall take the men of Vral and circle to the left."

"And we'll squash 'em between us!" With a shout to his men, Tylus rode toward the last wagons.

Signaling to the men of Vral, Naed led them toward a ridge of snow-crusted pines. The horn sounded in his ears, closer and more insistent. Above, the half moon sailed across a tear in the clouds, its light casting the hillsides into black-white relief.

"There!" Banir pointed to a shadow that, unlike its stationary cousins, roiled and rushed between trees.

"A troop, no more." Naed drew his sword.

The Vral officer grabbed his cloak. "Look there!"

Eastward, beyond the thrust of the man's arm, Naed

saw another shadow spreading across the ridge of a hillock. It rushed outward and onward like oil spilled from a massive cauldron. It swallowed trees, filled ravines, poured over clearings. On the wind came the jangle of bits and spurs, the creak of leather, the huff of galloping horses—hundreds of galloping horses.

"Sisters Three!" breathed Banir.

"'Tis an army," whispered the Vral man.

'Tis our doom. Naed pressed Raell's charm to his chest and closed his eyes, wishing fervently he had told her, just once, that he loved her.

"Naed, look!"

A chorus of horns erupted in the distance. Some were deep-throated, vibrant horns. Others shrilled like goat-pipes, high and piercing. Naed's blood stirred at the sounds, running first hot, then cold, then hot again. Confused, he followed Banir into the light of the moon.

"Look," the Tolemak repeated, gesturing to the shadows.

"They are joining," Naed said as the larger mass rushed upon the eastward flank of the smaller.

"No, they be—they be breaking them apart. See!"

Naed stared while the horns sounded again, this time a cacophony of shrieks and moans punctuated by a sudden metallic clatter. Below, the mass tore into two, milled and surged.

"Val-Feyridge!" Banir gripped Naed's sleeve. "Those be Val-Feyridge horns!"

"Aye, and Vinvinnysee." He stared at the Tolemak. "I sent for them...from Druemarwin... and they have come."

CHAPTER THIRTY-SIX

In the Great Hall, Aerid supported Arn with his arm over her shoulder while a chair, reversed and braced against the wall at his back, discreetly took the bulk of his weight. Traversing the corridor from his chamber to the Great Hall had taken nearly all of their combined strength, but he insisted no one but she help him. Watching him as he straightened at the sound of approaching men's voices, she marveled at the willpower she had sensed in him from the first. He seemed to draw strength from the very walls, from the jangle of harness and clop of hundreds of hooves in the courtyard, from the whoops and shouts echoing down the corridor.

All within the fortress had rushed to the courtyard though dawn was yet hours away. Something was afoot, and Arn had sensed it. Aerid tightened her grip on the fistful of tunic in her right hand. The cloth was drenched with his sweat, but 'twas a healthy sweat, a sign of recovery.

He breathed—carefully—and looked down at her. "I love you."

She smiled and willed him all the love her eyes could send over the raucous clatter spilling into the opposite end of the room. He inhaled again and, squeezing her shoulder, drew himself to his full height.

Halfway across the Great Hall, the onrushing tide of men and their folk halted as one and stared. At their forefront, Naed unwrapped arms he had slung over Banir on the one side and the giant Gorm on the other. "M'lord," he said as if speaking for the group, "welcome back."

"I could say the same to you," Arn said, his voice only faintly rasping.

Passing his helm to Banir, Naed approached. He reached into his tunic and pulled out a leather thong tangled with something on a thin gold chain. Flushing, he pushed the chain back into his tunic, glancing at Aerid as he did so. But he spoke to Arn. "You offered me something I was not prepared to accept. I kept from you something you were meant to have." Removing the thong from his neck, he held out the cylinder dangling from it. "D'nal has made his choice."

Arn swallowed. Aerid knew how it pained him to breathe, but only she could detect the tremors. Very carefully, he released his grip on the chair back and laid his hand on Naed's shoulder. "Stones are but pieces of earth, my friend. 'Tis hearts that matter. In our hearts, we've been brothers from the first."

Naed clasped his hand, and the two men looked long at each other. Then Naed slipped under Arn's arm and took Arn's weight onto his shoulders. "Let me," he murmured to Aerid.

"No," Arn said. "I need you both." He looked into Naed's eyes, then hers.

The gray eyes had always been guarded, showing no more than he wished. They showed her everything now, from his heart to his soul. Aerid laid her hand gently over his heart and the bandages so near it.

"This woman," he said, addressing the assembled host, "will shortly be my wife, if she'll have me. You owe your future to her, for not only does she bear my child, but 'tis she who taught me even my enemies could have honor, even my enemies could be...friends." Pausing, he looked at a group of men who wore strangers' armor. "Gaelwynn," he said to a skeletal man at the group's head, "I have lost the Tolem Stone. Does it matter?"

The man Aerid knew as the Crownkeeper, Guard Master Gaelwynn, crossed the floor to stand before Arn. Reaching out slowly, the Adanak indicated the stone at Aerid's throat. "'Twill be other stones, my lord, but 'twill be none other than this woman for you. 'Twas the Sisters who withdrew the Crown and scattered the parts of the Kingdom. This woman bears Their Tear, the mark of Their forgiveness for he that would bring the parts together and make the land whole." The gentle, mismatched eyes looked at Aerid. "Have you yet the Crown, my dear?"

"Aye," she said, looking from Gaelwynn to Arn and seeing the question in his eyes. "Shall I be fetching it?"

"'Tis not the time to be wearing it," Arn said. "Roines has Val-Feyridge and—"

"'Tis precisely the time," Gaelwynn said, "and well do you know it, Prince of Val-Feyridge and Heir to Tolem. Was there ever a better time for hope than in the deep of winter and with the wolves at the gate?"

Over Aerid's head, Arn stared at the Adanak. "A feast," he said at last. "We'll celebrate while we may, and plan for the future."

"Not ere you take some rest," Aerid insisted, but she knew by the grin he flashed her that 'twas useless to argue. He knew his strength, and it resided here among these mingled peoples and their cause. Here, he was at home.

Home. The word sent a shiver through Aerid. Once the word had meant Druemarwin. Then it had meant a longed-for but unknown mountain village in Adanak.

For a time, she had been at home among her own kind in Vinvinnysee. Now, she had traversed the breadth of the land to a room in Albon in Tolemak where the man at her side had regained the will to live.

Where would the child they made call home? Within this wide world, she thought, and smiled.

A word about the author...

Helen C. Johannes lives in the Midwest with her husband and grown children. Growing up, she read fairy tales, Tolkien, *The Scarlet Pimpernel*, Agatha Christie, Shakespeare, and Ayn Rand, an unusual mix that undoubtedly explains why the themes, characters, and locales in her writing play out in tales of love and adventure.

A member of the Romance Writers of America, she credits the friends she has made and the critiques she's received from her chapter members for encouraging her to achieve her dream of publication.

When not working on her next writing project, she teaches English, reads all kinds of fiction, enjoys walks, and travels as often as possible.

Contact Helen at helen.c.johannes@gmail.com